A
PERIOD OF
CONFINEMENT

ALSO BY MOIRA CRONE

The Winnebago Mysteries and Other Stories

A PERIOD OF CONFINEMENT

Moira Crone

Harper & Row, Publishers, New York
Cambridge, Philadelphia, San Francisco, Washington
London, Mexico City, São Paulo, Singapore, Sydney

First PERENNIAL LIBRARY edition published 1987.

LIBRARY OF CONGRESS CATALOG NUMBER: 86-46232

ISBN: 0-06-097108-8

87 88 89 90 91 MPC 10 9 8 7 6 5 4 3 2 1

For Rodger and Anya

You do not want to see this but you do: a woman in a tight green skirt, in nylons and shoe boots, a woman who looks very tired and worn for twenty-nine, is kissing her newborn child good-bye. The room is tiny and warm and simple, the second bedroom in a narrow house in Baltimore. The woman's hair is short and clipped. She thinks she feels good about herself.

Good about herself, even though she knows I'm here. I'm a ghost. Where I am there's a faint sound of a calliope, and silly buildings in the distance, and the ocean, which breathes for me, but I don't matter. Look at her.

In the room opposite the small nursery where she stands is her husband, and when his nose is whistling breath like that, a whistle instead of a snore, you know he is asleep. He's not even dreaming about us. Perhaps the baby is, but an infant doesn't remember her dreams.

The baby won't remember the woman in the dark green skirt, either, if that woman succeeds in abandoning her. At this moment, she's descending the stairs, going down into the street. It is early in the morning. Outside, in the tiny backyard behind the house, the early October air is a kind of miracle. The Chesapeake gulls are darlings. If you go to the front of the house, you can see it is part of an orderly row of neat bleached marble stoops, a street which leads down to a warehouse, which stands next to small tugboats and ship's chandlers' businesses and harbor shops and sellers of naval brass, of ancient diver's gear. Ancient diver's gear for going down into the depths, and for coming back up, for avoiding the bends.

But this woman isn't diving, she's going on a fast walk. Without her baby. To the bank, to find a cab. To go to the train station. To get herself and her art, which she holds in a vinyl portfolio in her left hand, to New York. In her right hand she has a flight bag. She's planning to sell a chunk of herself on the market. She can piece herself out, sell parts on consignment, because she isn't whole. She's in fragments, she keeps telling herself that, telling me, telling everybody. She's a wreck. You are looking at a wreck.

But she's pretty, for a wreck. She has a small mouth with extraordinary definition, like a little bow. It curls upward. She's not wearing her glasses, so you can see her eyes. They sink down on the sides—they are sad, they sag, they are brown. Her neck is long but not exactly graceful—she's long-waisted, long-bodied, short-legged. She has sweet crescent-shaped brows, shaped the way some people like to pluck them, and skin, I don't know, it seems tawny to me, Spanish, almost. She's a woman whose Adam's apple you can sometimes see, but people do say she is pretty, I'm saying it, people say it.

She's in a Romanian-made raincoat, and she's quickening her pace. Ten days out of the childbed and she's racing along—she could collapse, I suppose, but what a will. What a will she has, this not-crazy woman. She is thinking, walking along brick streets, she's thinking, Everything I see is something I can use. The world is so particular and beautiful. She is happy. This is how her life has to be, she thinks. She thinks that this, what she's doing, is completion.

She has a long nose, and her hands are large and a little frightening. You wonder what she could do with those hands, and her grip on her bag and portfolio tightens, and she keeps moving. She is perfectly sure this is how it should be, this is the way she should leave her baby. This woman wants to let her past go. She's going, moving, racing to get away from it.

And as she walks away, the baby wakes in the nursery and is stunned by the language of the morning, by the fusion and explosion of the sunny day that dapples her wall. And the infant has fingers, she sees, there they are with her, they must be hers, she can move them, or at least see that when she hopes they move, they somehow do that. And toes, and two knees, and now hunger, and a scent which is that feeling, a scent which is identical to her hunger is one and the same with the woman going into the street, from whom she was cut away just days ago, and born. She was born coated with a substance as sweet as the contents of a fresh jar of Pond's cold cream, the way all babies come out. This baby is spectacularly new. I cannot tell you how new I mean. And now something is moving up through her body, a convulsion, a paroxysm, the arrival of a need. Where did the need come from—not knowing is as critical as its coming.

God did not make a perfect world because the place could not hold up under such a judgment, so he made it less than perfect. And thus it was separate from himself and he could love it. But imagine a world so weak and broken it cannot stand up even to mercy, much less to judgment, and you have the world where a woman can't love her child. One like this that you see but do not want to.

I've gone out of the world. And this new one in it, fresh and blithe and blended, this world-of-her-own in the crib, is screaming and vermilion now. You can hear her.

For reasons the woman in the tight green skirt is about to tell you, everything is wrong. The baby knows this too, right at the start. The infant and the world are both abandoned, and nearly one. But I can't leave her, and I can't yet leave the world.

I t isn't that I don't love people. I love everybody in this story that I have to tell you, every single one—Loretta, Lucas, Richard, Rachel, and Ruth, my baby. But the kind of love I have to give does damage, elicits disaster, fails to follow through. You'll see. You'll see.

I'll begin twelve days ago, with Lucas, who doesn't usually spend time with us at bars near the Point. He came Saturday a week ago to see if I would have it. Richard was sitting next to me, and Lucas was next to him across the table from Gina and Loretta, who was reading my cards. Lucas, who is from Connecticut, is not generally so obvious. He had a lot to ask me, and he wasn't getting a chance. I had noticed Lucas's trust in me had grown as I had grown, over the last few months, and his itch to get me alone was palpable.

My cards were mostly cups and coins, and then the Queen of Swords, a heavy. "Oh no," Gina said.

"That means female sadness," Loretta said. Because the queen was the "result" in the plot of the cards, which was miserable, she tried to make it inconsequential.

"So sadness has a sex?" Richard asked. He hates hocus-pocus.

Loretta said with aggression, "Yes", and then told him, "I've got to look it up. It is upside-down. They call that reversed." She took out a little book, *The Pictorial Guide to the Tarot.* "Probably it means joy or something," she offered.

"A bundle of, no doubt," said my husband, to keep it light.

"I know, and it's worse than normal sorrow," Gina said. "In this case, reversing what's bad only makes it worse. There are a lot of cases like that."

Gina, who lives with Loretta, used to be a boy. She was Loretta's boyfriend in high school. Loretta worked at a restaurant in Harborplace most of the nights of the week and saved her money for Gina's operation. Gina was having it Monday, thanks to the Johns Hopkins

Gender Identity Committee. Loretta denies when she's drunk that their relationship is lesbian, since Gina has only been practicing being a girl. Anyway, what everyone knows is that their thing is very tight. They have been together longer than any couple I know.

Lucas kept staring at Gina's face. She once had a heavy beard and the electrolysis has left rows of pits, badly plugged with pancake makeup. Gina was not ever very real to me: Loretta was my friend of a few years, had once been my student, and Gina was her companion. They came in a set. Loretta and I had gone through phases when she was uncomfortably interested in my life, when she stalked me, when her painting looked too much like mine, but I thought those times were over. Gina was shy around me: when the two of them sat next to each other, Gina was still *behind* Loretta, somehow.

"Oh, don't worry," Loretta said. She smiled, which brought her large eyes to cat slants. "The sorrow is definitely temporary, absolutely. It says so: 'Reversal alleviates effects.' Things will lighten up. You'll get over it. I bet it will be just postpartum or something."

Gina read the list from the text: "Malice, artifice, deceit, abandonment." She stopped. "Loretta, you said you would read her cards. You've got to tell the truth." Gina's voice was that of a child with a cough.

"It's nothing, it's going to be temporary, that's all," Loretta said, shaking her head, tossing her burnt-orange curls.

I guess Loretta knew more about us than a fortune teller should know—about me, at least. She knew that Richard didn't have a real job, that I would have to go back to full-time work the minute the baby was out. Here we were, two married people with our lives ahead of us, so to speak.

"There's plenty," Gina said. It was odd that Gina was speaking up so much. Her usual interpretation of being feminine was demure. Customarily, Loretta did the talking for both of them. Then Gina lowered her beer hard enough that it splashed, and she wet the pages of the yellow paperback. She rubbed the edge of the last card and looked at me so hard I thought I could see the erased Italian kid right under the makeup. Gina was a little scary.

"I can see it. Here it is. There's this whole plot, it has to do with family: something possesses you. You doubt everything because of certain events. Everyone wants you to be someone you just aren't. They will maim you, believe me. You are gonna have hell to pay," Gina said. "Honey, it will be so hard."

I get the feeling around Gina that she is irrelevant and she knows it, that she is pretending everything. Maybe this is because you cannot take her at face value: she's a combo, a he-she, or at least she was that night. When she threw her chin back, I could see that her rosy beige make-up stopped at the neck, in a pink-ink line, as my mother's would do. But she was attractive, you understand; people wanted to look and look at her.

"Don't be so gloomy, Gina," Loretta cut her off. "It's gonna be awful, maybe, but you will get through," Loretta said, trying to take over my attention again. She was talking too loud. "We are all going to get through, perfectly well. Well, you are just about the most wonderful real woman in Fells Point, in the world, tough—" Loretta's straight lips spread wide. "Gina and me think so, don't we, Gina."

Gina did not nod.

"You are so beautiful, and deep, Alma, really, I think you are so lovely, especially so pregnant and all," Loretta sang on.

I knew my nose was swollen. I knew my red face was a mush of edema. I knew I was carrying enough water in my cells to float a small fleet.

"Loretta," Gina said again, oddly pushy. "You are lying about the card, Loretta. All the cards." She used to get into fights when she was a boy. "You are fucking lying about the way everything will work out and be just fine, and you can't do that to us anymore."

Gina was drunk. The bar, Maria's, was the size of a living room; the small round tables were shoved up to the walls. On them were old lamps with ceramic bases decorated with bouquets of flowers. Marie Antoinette decals with gold squiggles, or pheasants flying upward toward the bulb. Loretta worked here when she wasn't down at Harborplace making real money. And this kind of night was her métier: a hot Saturday late in the season at the Point, no air conditioning.

The business about the female sadness was over. Wasn't that all over? I had an odd feeling, a kind of sickness, and felt that the fate just laid out for me was an error. It was really Gina's—she was reading it upside down, where what was reversed was meant for her, straight on. It was a confusion like the queasiness I feel when I play chess for too long and the black squares whiten in my thinking, so I decide the move for my opponent and do precisely what I do not mean to do. I was thinking of telling Gina, "I resign."

"I can't stand it and I'm not going to," Gina finished. "The hell with your daddy," she said to me.

This was wild, mention of my daddy. I had no idea what she meant by it. I took it for a general curse, although she could have been reading my mind, as I blame my father for all the weaknesses in my thinking, all my signs of feeblemindedness. Limp batch of genes that coot passed on.

Lucas had gone over to Space Invaders as soon as Gina began her harangue. I saw him sling in another quarter. I was thinking I wanted to get out of the bar. He was punching the firing button with a stiff third finger.

Loretta is a good painter, gaining. Her recent drawings look like still lifes set up by a five-year-old. She does dolls with nipples for eyes, and uses the chubby chopped-off hands she gets from garbage bins outside Anita's Doll Shop a few blocks up on our street. Dolls have always been her favorite subject. Now she looked like one, a little stiff, rubbery; she was nodding to calm Gina down.

"Yes, that's right, honey, you are right, but I think Alma knows all she needs to know, doesn't Alma know," she said, then nodding to me, to let me know I had to agree. I didn't have any idea what it was I was supposed to know all about.

"You know the baby is going to be no fun. In the start. I mean, you are turning into a mother, just like Gina is going into the hospital to become a woman. I mean, it's sea changes we're getting into, heavy." Loretta said these things, and then she mouthed the words to me, *"Gina is having the operation in two days: she is freaked."*

So I started to nod, thinking, Loretta is pulling me into her life with Gina, where there are all these strange notions I don't much believe, where I am supposed to go along with the idea that Gina is fragile, for instance. It was too subtle for Richard, beside me. He had half wanted to hear a little about our so-called future, his and mine. But there were Loretta and I, facing each other like two kewpies, nodding, I think, to keep Gina from losing it.

Something was going on I didn't get, though. It meant everything to Loretta, how I acted, that night and into the near future—you should know I didn't guess.

"You have to go home and go to bed, Alma, and quit smoking," Richard told me. Then he took the cigarette out of my mouth and yanked me up. Gina looked outraged. I didn't even come up the first try. There was just too much of my belly. I was all ballast.

"This is stupid," Richard said, "stupid, stupid, and—" Meaning to reach for me with two arms this time, he lunged a little and knocked the cards out of order and onto the floor.

Loretta got out from her corner of the table. Her fanny was soft and low and wide, her skirt black knit. "Pick them up, Kaplan," she said, in a tone she probably didn't mean to sound as fussy as it did. She lost control often, Loretta. She could be cute, a fat kitten. But she seemed to want all of us to get out of there. We were seeing too much. Her upper lip was sweaty.

Richard did yank me up on the third pull. My belly out in front of me knocked over the table and the lamp, so now things were even a little worse than they already had been at our table. The hot lamp broke and a milk-white shard fell down and scraped Gina's leg.

"Look," Gina said, detached, pointing to brownish blood bubbling up through her hose. A scab had been nicked off her knee.

"Christ," Richard said, although he is a Jew. Gina just sat there, wooden, looking at her blood, her feet in buffalo platforms. In a minute she had slid to the floor and was hiding her face in her thin bleached hairy arms, pumping tears. Richard squatted down, to try to help, but Gina said, not very convincingly, "I'm all right. I'm all right."

Richard turned to me and his eyes were sad yellow-green, like bud daffodils. "It's late," he announced. "Let's go."

"You'll be fine," Loretta told Gina. "I'm with you, I'm not going anywhere, I'm here. Everything will be taken care of. Alma's a big girl, too. We are big girls, all of us."

"Well, what if something happens to Alma?" Gina said. "We ought to tell her, see what she says."

"I will when I can," Loretta whispered. They were both being a little stagy about the secret they were keeping from me. I was too pregnant to really care. They could keep anything.

Then I was standing, and Richard said to me, "Are

you all right? Jeez, I'm sorry." He turned to Gina, to repeat himself.

Loretta looked up, snorted.

They hovered near the floor. They were unraveling there, at our feet. This was their private life. We had to go.

Then my stomach rose up hard as a rock, toughening all by itself. It hardened like Godzilla's fist. I could feel it shoving my intestines out of the way. Another time. And then another time. Lucas saw it first, and came back over. Richard touched it.

"My God," Richard said. I thought to myself, What kind of baby would want to be born into this world, this world right here, which is so wrong.

We left in two seconds, with a few loud good-byes. Richard was trying to support my arm. He was skinny, and he was all I had to depend on. Lucas was thicker around the middle. He held my other elbow and slammed the heavy door behind us.

"It is happening, I can't believe it," Richard said, as if it really weren't possible that he was a father.

When we were out on the street, the door creaked back open: "Alma, don't worry," Loretta said. "It'll be fine. Gina's fine. Be tough. It'll all turn out. I love you, Alma." She waved good-bye with the brown-red rag. Her profile is her best angle.

The streets were busy, a midnight in Baltimore in 1979, an almost-full moon. Powder clouds. Sailors, red-necks, the people who come out of Dundalk, Maryland, with shag rugs in their vans, wearing cowboy boots.

"Are you in labor right now?" Lucas asked. "How long will it take? What do you feel like?"

"Keep walking, Alma, keep walking," Richard said. He doesn't like to repeat himself.

Richard was pointing up to the hospital at the top of the hill, fourteen blocks away.

A minute later he said, "Oh, got to get the car, the car," and he left me on a corner next to an empty *City Paper* box. Lucas had me to himself. I liked having two men. I needed protection. He would ask more questions. The night sky was cloudy and red, dark lukewarm tea, slightly cooler than the bar. Lucas put his hand again on my stomach. "How does this feel?" he asked.

The contractions had receded for a minute, and I could breathe all right.

"Do they say this infant bonding thing is all with the mother? What about the father? What do they say about that?"

My belly went all the way down. I shouldn't have been alarmed. I was due, after all, but I was alarmed.

"Oh, it went down? You aren't in labor?" Lucas asked.

"I hope not yet," I said, thinking how much I had to do, nothing was ready, nothing was ready. Now I'd shrunk down to a seedless watermelon. Some sandy-haired men drove by in a black Corvette, shouting, "Mama, Mama, kiss, kiss."

"Shit," Lucas said. Then Richard was there, in his tiny white convertible.

"Well, you want to have a kid, Lucas?" Richard asked, in the car. Richard was speeding and we were all a little drunk. My husband didn't mean our kid, he meant a generic kid. He and I were passionate, more or less, about our kid.

"No," Lucas answered, putting his hands together. Up until then his hand had been on my shoulder, or my belly. It was needless for Richard to tease Lucas about having a kid—his wife, Carmen, had left him seven months ago.

But Lucas kept it up. "What's the situation if the kid doesn't nurse? From a breast, I mean. How do they act when they get the formula, do they get fat? Are they cranky? When can you feed them food?"

"She's fucking in labor, Lucas, leave her alone," Richard said, pausing, then going through a red light near the Church Home and Hospital.

"It's okay, really, darling," I said to Richard. "You know they are going to be very far apart for a while, the contractions, I mean." I liked talking to Lucas. He was more interested in this than I was.

"Can I get into the delivery room, be on the scene?" Lucas asked. He used to be a reporter. "Won't they let me in, couldn't you say I'm your brother, or something?"

Richard pulled into the emergency entrance. Lucas walked me up to the curved maternity counter. We told the nurse, a large black woman whose name tag said "Mrs. Morgan," that I was in labor. She did not rise from her chair.

The clerk next to her rang up my information on the terminal. "Did you call your doctor?" she asked.

"Taylor," I said to the clerk punching into the patient file. "T-A-Y-L-O-R."

Richard was standing behind me now, having parked the car illegally and rushed across the waiting room. He started in with me, "Look, Almy, you have to say 'Kaplan.' Otherwise there will be trouble. We agreed the kid was going to be Kaplan, right? Didn't we? Well, the records will get all messed up, I mean."

What the hospital had on me they already had under "Kaplan." I'd just forgotten. I didn't fight it. I hadn't fought with him since our argument in January, which I had lost. I kept what I thought in reserve instead.

"What makes you think you are in labor, Mrs. Taylor Kaplan?" the nurse asked, not really looking at me.

"It feels like a steel ball," I told her. "Well, look." "Come with me," she said, and in a minute I was moving down a corridor with a rail, watching her enormous silent white foam platforms copy the rhythm of walking on the linoleum. Gina and Loretta came back to me—seventeen minutes before, we had been sipping beer together, while they grew odder and odder and more maudlin. The woman beside me had said to Richard at the door that he could follow when he was done with the admitting clerk. I could hear his voice recede as he spelled my doctor's name, "F-E-L-T."

"Get on the table, honey," the nurse told me. "Put up your feet." I did. I felt romantic by this time. We were in a closet called the "prep." I was on a table on a piece of paper. I wasn't nervous around Mrs. Morgan. She got to my cervix and said it was soft.

"But you are nowhere along with your labor, honey," she said. "I can get the doctor to come out and tell you, but listen, you've been in here for about ten minutes, and well, have you had any more?"

I felt it was a failure of my attention. If I could only pay more attention, then I could go into labor and stay there. The contractions had stopped the minute I started to get into this hospital thing—what was my name, where was Lucas going to wait for the baby to come out, what would the baby's last name be. The labor had dropped off altogether.

"Now I can get Felt, or the intern on the floor," Mrs. Morgan told me, "but I don't think either one of them will say anything different. Can I ask you a question?" she asked me.

I nodded yes. I was trying to concentrate on bringing my labor back.

"Did you go to those classes here at the hospital?"

Somehow she knew how many I'd missed, I was thinking. How did she know that? I nodded yes, said, "Some."

"Well, they don't tell you the most important thing, I'm sorry," she said, pushing the stirrups back into the table, "They don't tell you that it does hurt. That's how you know. You get a feeling like being struck by lightning, most of the time, and then you are ready to go to the hospital." She put her index finger across her upper lip, then took it away. "I know I'm not supposed to scare you primiparas like this, but half that training is brain-wash."

By now I was sitting on the edge of the table, and she stood a few feet from me, her arms folded.

"Now do you want me to get the doctor, or do you want to get some rest and when you feel like you are working it right out, come back?"

"Fine," I said, high-pitched for me, in a little shock. Cramming my underpants into my purse, I stood up and maneuvered out. Richard met me at the swinging doors.

"Don't worry, you will have it," Mrs. Morgan said, behind me. "They all come out sometime."

"Alma, what's the matter?" Richard asked, ready to imagine anything, that maybe I'd had it already, that maybe it wasn't a baby after all.

"Nothing," I said. "It was nothing. It was false labor," I said, thinking how I would stay pregnant forever. But then that wasn't so, I knew that wasn't so. I have never stuck to anything.

About five-fifteen the next morning, after I had a dream-vision that my belly was the globe, I sat up in bed. I heard the leaves in the solitary ailanthus tree out the back window moving with the dawn wind. I remembered when the leaves first had enough body to make a sound. It was last April, when Rachel went into the hospice.

A house is closed at this time of the morning. Even if it is your house, it is a stranger's. The doors do not want to be opened or unlocked. The place is resting. A house doesn't want to be bothered. And Lucas, heavy Lucas with the horrible furry cough, the lawyer, was sleeping downstairs on the fold-out futon next to his chess set. I thought I might wake him and tell him what pregnancy is like. My two hands were as swollen as salamis. On the insides of my thighs, a rash so that walking was painful. I'd gained forty pounds.

My mother had written her definitive letter on the subject of her coming up to help me while I was in my "period of confinement." It was her term, left over from the time when women had plenty to hide. I saw her letter on top of some magazines in the bathroom, during one of my hundred morning pees. "It has been difficult for you, hasn't it?" she asked in her upright handwriting. But she meant, "Why can't you take this thing in your stride like everyone else?"

Because I had lost my stride, lost my bearings and my balance, and my hands were permanently numb, stunned. The name for the trouble with my hands is carpal tunnel syndrome—it developed at the time Rachel was dying, came on at almost the very hour of her death. Sometimes I felt that I was no longer myself at all, that Rachel's exit had been the beginning of the erasure of my senses, the first step in my disappearance. She was canceling me out. My fingertips were oblivious to the slick fresh varnish on the banister.

I went into the kitchen. Our house is old and small, so the idea is that we will keep it empty and gleaming. This is mostly my idea. Richard is a slob. On this Sunday morning last week, every object in the place was under threat of expulsion. There were newspapers and half-dead plants stacked in corners, there were my old clothes, which seemed impossibly small, in a pile in the dining room. I could not remember buying some of them. Richard called my recent gathering up of our shabby possessions "nesting," but I thought that if it was instinct at work I had a contrary one: our house was less comfortable since the process had started, not more so. Ordinarily, I was tolerant, but the lack of beauty and order seemed tragic to me now. I lost sleep over misplaced tattered sweaters, over lampshades with slits. All I wanted was to throw everything out, or else mend it all, make it new. But the tasks overwhelmed me and I did nothing.

Except sit down on an oak chair and pull it as near as I could to the table, and draw a sketch of a woman flat on her back with her belly a globe, the blue Atlantic up. The light grew and Chesapeake gulls sailed across the empty lot outside the kitchen window to go to the Orioles' stadium for peanuts and broken nachos. I could hear a truck pull up and the bakery a block away start the vacuum to suck flour out of its tank. Somewhat later, the drawing a bust, I got over to steal one of Lucas's cigarettes and he finally woke. It was the morning for everybody else.

I loved Lucas when his arm slapped on the futon frame. What a clean illusion dawn can be really, the hard shiny floor, the new sunlight through the blinds, his rumpled clothes on the little rug, looking as chiseled as a drapery drawing, his breathing chest. Excess love around, apparently. Richard upstairs with his odd handsome nose, dreaming about something of which I learned later. It ached to know I could not live this happy way.

"Don't do it, Almy," Lucas said when I got inside his Merits. Every day for months I had arisen from bed and faced the idea of pregnant life only because I might get a cigarette out of somebody. And I couldn't get any. I had puffs. Last night, I was afraid Lucas remembered, I'd stolen a whole one early on and waddled off to the ladies' room before Gina and Loretta sat down with the deck of French fate. The devil made me do it. You have to have a little devil, right? So things are bearable.

I lit the cigarette and handed it to Lucas, who smoked it with relish, half-closing his eyes. It takes Lucas two hours to wake up. I thought again of making coffee, then of the paper. And just as I went outside to get the *Sun*, a pang shot through my pelvis, down my leg, a charley horse with direction. The phone rang but Lucas couldn't find it behind the hills of newspapers and of clothes.

"How are you getting on, Alma?" my mother asked. The voice of a bosomy ma'am.

"I just felt something," I said.

"I thought so," she said, three hundred miles away. "I called Fred to tell him your due day, but Marva said he'd already gone up to Baltimore. To be with you and the baby? She was surprised it didn't get born yet. Did you hear from Fred?"

I said no. My father had called me only once in my Baltimore life, and that was when he was drunk and in Washington with a friend who had to see somebody at the Veteran's Administration. "Fred would never come to me," I told my mother, "unless he thought I had something for him."

"Don't be so hard on him, honey," she scolded. "Well, it could be the lucky day, huh?"

I guess the worst aspect of those days in waiting was the prospect of seeing her, my mother, keeper of the junk style, cutter of coupons, energetic, energetic. I was hoping she was finding some reason not to come. Maybe she would see something inauspicious in the date.

I said, "Yes, Momma."

"Well, I'm coming up as soon as you need me, just tell Richard to let me know as soon as . . ."

She likes to enter contests; it's her sex life, I think. How many words can you make out of the words "Real Rose Tea," for a trip to Guatemala. She wins, she goes. She has a collection of hotel keys. She goes by herself, as she no longer lives with Fred. Nobody can live with Fred. She lives alone beside the family trailer park in the twangy Piedmont Carolinas.

"Wonderful," I say.

"You want me to come, don't you?" she asked. "I have plenty to do if you have somebody else. If you don't want me to, then I won't."

Even though I couldn't bear the thought of her coming, she wouldn't have the thought of not coming. She does keep busy. She loves to drive her car, a yellow Pontiac she won in a Catholic church raffle eight years ago. She loves clothes. She combs thrift shops. Her dresses have the odd stains of age—of coffee spilled in someone else's life. She says she can't see them. She likes to go down and stake out the Goodwill. Or the K-Mart during a sale. She might come home carrying marshmallows covered with sawdust, in a plastic bag marked "Coco Mellows Neat New Treat," after six hours at the mall. The food is always old, like the clothes. I think it is this habit of hers that I like most about her, her zeal in scouting out the material world.

"I said," I repeated, "I wanted you to come. I told you months ago I wanted you to come."

"Well, then, I will if you really need me."

"Fine, Momma," I answered.

"Are you all right now?" she asked accusingly.

"I told you I just felt something a little while ago. I was in false labor last night. I went to the hospital and they sent me home."

"You worry too much about how you feel," she said. "You make pregnancy sound perfectly awful. It was the happiest time of my life. Really, the best. My labor was nothing. . . ."

"Probably nothing," I said, loading the giantess into the chair.

"Just call me when the baby comes out, and don't fret," she chided. "This phone call is costing me too much. Just call me when, all right?"

"All right," I said, propping my feet on Lucas's mattress.

"What do you mean by that?" she asked.

"By 'all right' I meant all right," I said.

"This is costing me too much," she repeated. "See you soon," she said, hanging up quickly.

When I told her good-bye, Richard the lionhearted, my new husband, walked down the stairs with so much ease I could have killed him. His feet are slender and they point slightly outward. He brought two fingers to his brow and put a thumb on his temple, which meant he was sensitive to the glare. He was very beautiful, but he was no longer as large as his wife.

In a short time, a cup of coffee was in his hand, got there by magnetism. I couldn't move: the velvet chair where I put my carcass was phenomenally deep. And I was an elephant. On the armrest was a gob of black, with a flat shiny surface, about the size of a dime, like a place where chewing gum had been removed. I wondered what it was. My mother would ask me what it was. I said, "I don't know," out loud and then realized I was with others.

"She talks in her sleep, too," Richard said to Lucas. "She says things out loud, even yells at herself, when she thinks she's alone. You figure she's possessed? Should we call in Stephen King?"

There was a laugh for everybody, and I said that I had been more or less crazy since I met Richard. That this was his fault.

What seems like a very long time ago, when I was perfectly balanced, I had a show downtown, for once. It was all my recent work, story art, self-dramatization, really, except I was the only one who knew the plot. There was a portrait of my mother, dominated by her yellow hair and her yellow Pontiac. And the green work pants (a lie—he never works) of my father represented him. In the background were seedy postcards of a carnival, half a poster of a snake lady, a reference to his imagination about women. My paintings look like patch-up jobs, but believe me, everything is connected—the Cinderella scene in the upper right corner has everything to do with the woman doing something awkward in the middle. I am pretty good, but the market in Baltimore had been only on-and-off aware of it.

I had on a burgundy voile dress, the kind of useless dressy cotton dress women in my profession wear to their own openings. Once I had a boyfriend (polo shirt) who saw me in one of these, on a date with him even, and he said, "You can't look serious in that." It was my Hindu-formal look, in contrast to my thrift-shop everyday.

And when Richard walked into the gallery, what I saw first was his coloring. And his rough curly red hair. In that light, a hard northern light, you can see everything—pores, the clarity or cloudiness of corneas, the depth of the flecks in irises. It's a light that makes people seem translucent. A Vermeer light. I thought he was my perfect opposite, somehow, my negative, except that I am white, but next to him I am not white; I'm tawny, yellow. His red wine looked almost black, and I saw he was moving close to me. He said, "Are you the painter?"

Clearly I was. There was a photo of me on the gallery brochure, if he had any doubts. And I was wearing the cotton because I couldn't afford better, and the eyegoop, a mistake. I looked like a raccoon, I saw later in the bathroom. Then he said something about all the orange in the one in the corner, the most abstract—the Steerwalls, whose gallery it was, weren't sure they wanted to show it, but this was Baltimore, hell, nobody is a perfectionist—of a bright simple orange center being eaten away by a sepia. There were scenes, figures on the canvas, but it was dominated by the color. It was a picture of my heart being mugged by its other part.

"Uh-huh," I nodded. I was trying to think of something more to say: I was a little surprised he'd come up to me, at my bidding, so to speak. This is not a love story, please don't think that is what it is. It is about something else.

He was more handsome, close up. And too young. A greenish tint around the hollows of the eyes, a finely defined bone in the nose—a bent stick holding up the cartilage, tentatively. He went in at the waist a little bit, like a European. And he sauntered off in a minute. I must have sounded dumb.

Usually after openings you go out to dinner with the possible buyers, for seafood Newburg or something. And you must be very nice. This has always been okay—the people who liked my paintings have been people who like me. And the Steerwalls are delightful, and they all talk about New York, and in my case, after dinner they offer to take me home. I hate to drive. I don't own a car. But tonight, the interested were from the deep suburbs. One pair who was ready to invest but didn't want to get to know me had already left. The paintings were all looking down at me from those high creamy walls and I wanted to sit down, rest, and hope the stragglers would leave.

This show was different—they were actually going to pay more than usual for my work, because a bald man with glasses on a public TV show in the afternoon the Sunday before said I was part of something larger—he connected me to painters with whom I had nothing in common. And therefore the attention from DC, the semi-investors, hot from their rising-in-value homes, scared of me. I was "doing better"—the more I sold my paintings for, the less I had in common with the buyers, so the money made the distance, it seemed, was the substitute it always is. A little further up the scale, if you get there, once you stop being a risk, they pay much more, and you're invited to parties, you become an exhibit. So it was this odd way I make a living—not by causing joy, but by becoming a product. Richard was still standing near the door, by the orange one I'd insisted upon hanging there. Then he turned.

There are some ugly crotches in this world, I was thinking, but he looked beautiful in his pants. For some time I had watched his pants and smoked cigarettes, while people leered at the insides of me and my past. It was a little like being at your own funeral, a thrill.

He was shy, I'll have to explain, half-timid. When I looked back it wasn't clear to him that I wanted him to sit next to me. He appeared to think I meant someone else, because he started to look behind himself, out the glass door. Then his neck got confident. He walked with nearly a lope back to the black-leather-and-chrome bench in the rear that was supporting, at five of six, me, three empty wine glasses, and my ashtray. He moved with a lot of avidity, which depressed me, almost.

"The show's going well," he said, and I saw in his fist the shadowy black-and-white photograph of my yellow momma painting. The advertisement from the gallery.

"Yeah?" I asked, then a stare.

"There are at least two people going to buy, talking themselves into it as we stand here, as I speak," he said, in a mock whisper. "And another, see, that one in the blue shawl—she's thinking about it. She's trying to talk her husband into the one with the green man."

"That's my father," I said.

"Your father goes with the carpet in her sunroom," he said, sitting down and taking out a Bugle paper. And a pouch of tobacco. His rolling was an endearing ritual. I looked closely at his fingertips, well shaped and sweet. He was not extra tall. He had veiny, muscular forearms, which I wanted to touch. When he licked the gum seal

I got a look at his tongue. He lowered his eyebrows when I looked at him so hard. Then a vein showed in his forehead—I was beside myself. "Does that bother you?" he added.

"Well, it's amazing, isn't it," I decided to say, contrary, to myself even. "That I can do this picture of my father, something completely private, nobody here will know what I mean by it, and people put a value on it, will pay me to do it?"

"You want them to have no idea what you mean by it?"

"Don't you believe in art?" I asked him.

"What if you get to the point where it doesn't matter what you do, even if it is crap, if you sign it? When it doesn't mean anything to you either?"

"Maybe that's where you want to get, sure," I said.

"That's where you want to be?" he said. "I don't think that it is. You seem earnest to me."

"No criteria, no objective criteria, just money, if money then value then art," I said.

"Give me a break," he said.

"I'm corrupt," I said.

"Actually, I like people who are corrupt," he said. "Can I have your signature?"

He started to uncrumple the program, but I took a pen I had, a Parker Big Red, out of the side pocket of my purse, grabbed his arm—I was reckless that day—and wrote ALMA T there. He jerked away a little late, I almost finished. He wanted to like this, but he couldn't immediately.

"Thanks," he said. He did mind and he didn't mind. Maybe if I licked his ears a little bit, I was thinking, watching him roll down the sleeve he'd had rolled up. "Let's talk about *your work*," he said, in the tone of an interviewer. "Where is *your work* going?"

"Somewhere deep into Balto-Wash," I said, looking at the couple he had mentioned.

"The lady is a bit of a jerk. And her husband doesn't like the painting. He has a better eye, I think. She just wants to buy something, you know, make her day, you know."

"Thanks a lot," I said.

"I mean he can see the picture is disturbing if you look at it long enough, that it is disturbing, as well as other things, that it would goad him a little if it were on the wall while he watches *The MacNeil–Lehrer Report*."

"Ted Koppel," I said. "He doesn't have time for all the back-to-you-Robins."

"And he is into wine, but she can't really tell the difference between the vintages. They both want to collect something, since their friends are into cheese, twig furniture, camping equipment, but he would rather go to France than buy your painting—" He raised his eyebrows, and had to reach around me to put out his cigarette. The eyebrow raising because he was going to *touch* me, and this couple wasn't at all what we were talking about.

He went on— "He has the heebie-jeebies," he said. "He grinds his teeth at night—money does that to people."

Then he watched the couple scoot outside. Baltimore had them disoriented. He walked one way, north, toward where he thought their car was parked, but she pulled him back by the elbow, no, that wasn't it. They were nervous people. My painting had messed them up. I felt responsible. I thought about running out and giving it to them, making it okay.

"Is this over now?" Richard said, as he watched them head south, more than likely toward their Volvo. "This show, this reception, this meet-the-artist stuff?"

Remorse. The heat and weight of me fled to my crotch. "Eat dinner with me?" I said.

He stuffed his fine upper lip into his lower teeth and

moved his chin up and down very slightly, a maybe-yes. Then he changed the subject. "Is that your self-portrait?" he asked, pointing to the orange one near the door. It was the least decorative, the most pushy in the room. Ugly, I told you. He has never been entirely kind about my paintings.

His lower lip was mild and very full. "I'm not always this way," I told him. "Actually, I'm—"

"I'm glad," he said. "I want to have dinner with you. I was planning on it, okay?"

What I felt like was having him sit right next to me on the bench in the gallery until I was calm again, until I was normal.

"Actually you are what?" he asked me, as I found we had stood up and were walking through the gallery and out the front door. I have something to say here. You could tell he had something of a heart. It showed in his forehead, in his fingertips, but his sweetness was awkward, it came up at the wrong places, and he had to control the situation, and I had to follow the rules. But I wasn't going to; I was going to kick us out of step. I did this all evening. And the evening was miserable in spots.

After I hugged Mr. Steerwall and kissed his wife and said thank you, and they said wonderful and I said I had a ride, and they said how really well it was going, we were out.

"Never mind. I like you," Richard said, meaning, Don't be an ass.

We were a little off, both of us. We were going to spend time together, I knew that. I'd be spending time sitting around, waiting for his warmth to expose itself, watching for the little flashes. He had faltered when he came back to flirt the second time. He was younger than I. All I wanted to do was to cultivate this desire. That was the extent of my ambition, then, around six-fifteen.

When I look back on it now, I don't know where it got out of hand, maybe the day I got the Modigliani book. I didn't want to be in love. In no kind of love.

It was just beginning to cool—the heat of a late June afternoon swirled around us and I could feel the edge of the air. I had an intimation that the situation was dangerous and I thought of getting out of the meal, and then I took another look at his nice round mouth.

And he was pissed! He would do something puerile, make me suffer.

"I like to eat Mexican food on Sundays," he told me. "You'll pay, I hope?" he asked. "For yourself? I'm pretty broke. My name is Richard. Kaplan. I think you are really beautiful," he added in a second.

"How old are you?" I said, and he answered twenty-four. I had taken him for twenty-six, had hoped.

In a rather purple drunk, two hours later, feeling full of sap, I was a maple, maybe. A tree—I felt very large and was beating around the edges. The kind of arousal that hurts. My blood had left my brain. I was somewhat dumb. I had two problems, as I saw it: first, I didn't want to tamp this blue-red wave down, as it was passing pleasantly through me in the middle, but I had to control it; second, I had to appear interested in what he was saying. Now he was talking about Hundertwasser in Vienna in the forties. And then expressionism in general. I hated Hundertwasser then, I don't hate him so much now. His paintings say that it is only our stringy wills that keep things from exploding, with color, with mass. While Richard talked I felt as if I were sixteen and that I was carrying the same kind of lust I could have felt then—heat in my central core, my trunk—but it was a greater burden now. I would have blushed if I had had the energy left over from the restraint. I looked into his eyes too much.

Expressionism is as ugly as it is true to me. Richard told me then about his discovery, when he was seventeen, on a senior class trip to Europe, of the second floor of the Nasjonalgalleriet in Oslo: rooms and rooms and rooms of Edvard Munch. Much worse than stills from Bergman, out of liquid, cold green. The people, rocks. I tried to tell him I am not really decorative. Regardless of how I feel about the sunrooms of buyers. I'm not a wallflower. But he seemed to want to convince me to do a more brutal, more frank kind of work, and I think he was ultimately right. When I get to New York my work will be mean and frank and fierce. I should have walked right out at that advice.

He had so much to say, though. It was in its way delightful and bright and funny. He knew plenty. He was up on Western Civ. He could read Greek. He had been in the graduate program at Hopkins, in Classics, but had left. He wanted me to do expressionism in Baltimore, the balmy northern buckle of the Sunbelt, where the people who were really selling were doing pastel patterned geometrics, which people buy by the gross in LA and Phoenix. This city is for terrapin soup and real estate developers. "I heard this guy on the radio talking about Baltimore, about colonizing it actually, turning it into a colony of DC. He said the housing stock here would last twelve hundred years. Tough, all brick, you know, row houses, solid investments, something to own, like ruins. I got the image he was thinking of it already like a ruin, something dead, to gut and do again. "The city as motif, you know," he said, "background."

It was almost nine, and my desire made it difficult to listen. I kept measuring my lips with his. Was his tongue going to be very narrow? Was he teasing me? He was wrong. I am not beautiful; I'm okay naked. But he didn't want to tell me again that I was. He wanted to talk to me about everything, and he had no idea I was tiring, and I wished he would just—

Then and again I would surface, I suppose, and tell myself, How stupid can you be. But his attention would give me the energy to carry on and would lift me off the floor occasionally, but upon lowering, I'd enter the hot trunk mode again and feel overpowered by it. It gave me courage, wanting him.

We were in his car by ten-thirty and he was taking me home, like a chum. I was desolate, but Richard seemed full of more talk. I was the old gal who will listen. Occasionally one of the edges of him would near me, and I would feel prickly at the spot of deferred contact. I felt like an old maid: the cooler the evening got, the cooler did he. He drove around my block and around the crumbling ones next to it, those not yet kissed by renovation, by the look of sandblasted brick. He was having trouble finding a place to park.

By the time he pulled up on the black glassy asphalt slab behind a dock warehouse, he had become relatively silent. I felt his hand come near my back on purpose and was glad. I was with this handsome, even pretty fair man who was being decent about walking me home. But what was I so grateful for? I was feeling enormously grateful.

He went quickly. It seemed we were sprinting down the cobblestones. I asked him what the rush was about, and he slowed but he didn't say anything. We were both talked out, finally. I told him not to knock painting or it will just go away—Peter Schjeldahl had said a few years before that painting was a doddering old lady walking down the steps and somebody had taken away her cane. Then I thought that I was the old lady. I meant to say, "Don't talk about it, it is just too sad," but instead I said, "You do it because you can do it all. It is still whole when you are done with it. It isn't half-assed. Everything else you get into—working for other people, loving somebody—has to be half-assed. There's always something about those things that you can't fix. There are faults, loose ends. But when I paint I can close the door. And try to turn something into creation again."

"You getting gnostic on me?" he asked.

I didn't know what gnostic was supposed to mean. "Is that Creation with a capital *C*?" he asked, seeing that this hurt me, so he tried to pretend he hadn't said it. One of his rounder edges was starting to show. They'd turn up, like that, all of a sudden.

"Yes," I said, "sure."

He said, "I mean, all night long, I've been really committed, you know, trying to talk to you, and you are flip, I've decided. Up until now, flip. A flip lady."

I could feel the lust weaken in me and disperse. After a while desire will make you dumb, spread through your arms and legs, and make you a ninny. Now he would have to invite himself in and carry out this particular conversation. I still had ladylike vestiges at that point. I was raised in the South. And I really didn't know whether he wanted in or out. In.

In the place where I lived, he took a short look around, asked, "Where does that lead," pointing to a white door.

"My studio," I told him, and didn't offer to show it to him. "Well," I went on, "you've known me and my work something over five hours, and you have the program notes," I said, pausing. "Can't we be dumb for a little while?"

"I'm just a guy, you know. You picked me up. I talk a lot." He was in my little place now, sitting on a daybed with a cabbage-rose-print cover. His arm was spread across the foam bolster. I put water on to boil. He was going to be a hard nut to crack, as my mother used to say.

When he took off his jacket, there they were, like those of a Pennsylvania Dutch farm boy, or a mime on TV, exactly halfway between the two. I was frightened by the fact of black suspenders. On top of his denials, they caused me to lose a little control. I turned on the radio and there were people laughing on it. I turned it off. On the couch he gave me a pile of limp kisses.

Then he dove at my breasts and I sprouted like a garden. At a little past eleven—I always know what time it is—we were still on the upper body. The head of his cock had created a little tent in his loose slacks. I wanted to just brush near it during the head-and-neck kissing, but I felt it would be a breach to do that. We were faking it, anyway. We were angry at each other. He broke off dryly, and started to talk.

"I'm not just a guy, you know. You picked me up," he said again. "I've seen you before, around. And at the Maryland Biennial. I could have planned this. I've been wanting to fuck you for about two months."

"What?" I said. This was his opening to be charming. But he wouldn't be, I knew him already.

"Because you looked like you needed one. A good steady one."

"What?" I said.

"Fuck," he said.

"Christ," I said.

"I'm not a nice guy," he said. "You had better know that. 'Cause I see you could be hurt. I mean, I seem like a nice Jewish boy, but the first time I saw you, I had this compulsion. So all night I've been trying to talk to you, open the lines, as it were, you know, engage you, entertain you, converse, have social intercourse, and you haven't really been present. But at the same time, this is where I have wanted to be for a couple of months, now, on your couch with a hard-on. You should know this."

Then we just rested a little. No point in going on. Fully clothed on my wrinkly couch, and the water had been boiling for some time. I made some drip coffee which we both drank as if it were blood broth. It was a bitch, having so hard a time getting into bed. All I really wanted was to see him naked and sit on him. But I felt hot and funny and as if I didn't really know him well enough. Not a nice guy. It was a compliment that he'd been after me, but it seemed more like a threat. Then I felt bad about not wanting to listen to him. So I made no more moves except to get a cigarette and to drink the coffee. This was the start of a struggle, I believe, that we will never resolve now, a struggle over which of us is going to own up to our life together, to claim us, give us a theme. He was not going to be the one, that was clear.

I wanted to know when he would just get out.

At what seemed to be the end of time, Richard put down the large blue mug I had given him and looked at me. I got a wavy beating-all-over sensation again and then I felt very loose. What did personality have to do with it? We could remake that later, after all, make up, as they say. I went inside his shirt and took it off, kissing his breasts, unhooking his suspenders, which held on to little buttons inside his pants. This aroused him, something honest and forward, and he didn't do anything about it, so I unzipped and then unbuttoned, and he groaned and I kissed him. He was hard and fat and sweet, like a full moon. For a long time, I was dressed and he was naked, so I take responsibility for our becoming lovers.

We did it the first time sitting up, me wrapped around his lap. He took a long time. I had plenty of minutes to wonder. But he kept chasing away anything approaching thought with his tongue in my ear. He was really very good when he got started.

I kept thinking he was showing off.

The last man I had been sleeping with was almost forty. He had been dependable, and sweet enough, and quick to come and never exuberant, and I was trying to think about him when Richard took me by the hand and walked me to the bed where we sat down on our haunches and looked at each other grow more and more naked in the course of the evening. But Jerry would just not come to mind. Richard shimmered, became more handsome. He didn't want to go to sleep. He wanted to do it some more.

We continued on the bed, where it got rough and archaeological. It hurt me, then it stopped hurting. I was dispersed by this time and he sweated so much that coming for me was hardly noticeable, and then there it was, spread out all through us both, like a nacreous bath.

It was okay. Okay.

When I woke up he was no longer tangled on me but lying still beside me with his head flat on the pillow, good as a hot child. I had to get up and think. Nude, I felt a little chill, and lucky, stupid lucky, and felt that the flesh on my bones wore itself well. Sex induces satisfaction with the body. I felt perfect but thirsty. Gulping orange juice, standing in the open refrigerator door, I wondered if he was exactly like the others. I held the principle that it is better to have affairs with men you can take or leave. There in the light cast by the Hotpoint, I could see his hard torso broadening toward his shoulders.

This was not continuous with my past. I slept mostly with men I didn't like, and they ended up leaving or getting me to leave. My generic lover had been about six feet tall, a male always, dark, kind of stringy purple balls, pasty white skin, a hearty eater. Jerry, for example. He is a photographer who shows a lot and lives in Washington, and has two children by his estranged wife. We got along to talk, about galleries and jerks who run them, mostly, but our sex was both rare and strained. I could feel even then, when I tried to think of Jerry, that Richard had displaced him and that Richard was taking over. I gave him very little credit, though. He wasn't grown-up, he took everything on a theoretical level. I figured he was a lightweight, probably still even afraid of going queer, he looked so pretty. So I took on this feeling of unusual control. I wanted to wake him up and bother him.

At breakfast he was weird. Harsh, even. We sat there and we talked about nothing. He said he was going to an Orioles game with his friends. He was in a hurry to leave. He planted his good-bye kiss by remote control. So, that good time would be over, good-bye, good time. So, Alma, go to your studio and stretch a few, apply gesso, or something.

About seven in the evening, long after Richard left, I fell into a sweet needed sleep, and then I woke up at about three in the morning to feel the muscles in my buttocks cramping a little, sore, from exercise. I couldn't sleep; I relished the aches a little. They were the last traces, after all.

Then, maybe Tuesday, I put on baggy shorts and a purple T-shirt and put my long hair in a thick clip to look young and fresh, that. I made coffee and read the *Sun* and at about ten went into the other room in my apartment, the one bedroom, where I painted, all splendid.

The light there came from first-floor windows on the alley, so it is natural only between ten-thirty and maybe two in the afternoon. There are burglar bars on the alley windows, which I opened to get the stripes out. Richard was not on my mind at all. There you are. I was with myself. I had completely forgotten.

Maybe at noon I heard something, jumped out of my skin. He was climbing in the window when I turned around to look. He was wearing his slacks, his suspenders, a *City Paper* T-shirt. He had an open look about him, he was ready for lunch or something. And I was so involved with this mauve color, I was so involved with finding a way that didn't look entirely flat in that corner of the picture—never mind what it was a picture of, it was a joke, that corner, abysmal, if I could make it work I would be a genius, and the last thing in the world I wanted to see was him standing there, I think I growled, if I didn't scream. And in hardly two seconds he was holding me, roughly, starting to undo his pants, saying, "So, do you want to see, you are visually oriented, I know." Then he paused a minute, to say, "Oh Alma, she's painting." And I didn't know how to take it. "It is so pretty. You look so pretty," he told me. He took the clip out of my hair. He pulled my hair, taking out the clip.

And there I was, brush in one hand, like the little interrupted noblewomen you see in the erotica of the Orient, who find big red ones poking out of their male companions' robes at preposterous angles just when they are sitting pristinely on the floor, preparing tea. Et cetera. He had broken in. Then, grabbing again, not my waist, my wrists. And he was holding them too tight, something he would pay for later, even he knew. When he was trying to walk me over to the wall, I heard myself say, "What are you doing here?" so loudly it startled me, and him, and I realized he was panicky, too. I could feel something powerful, gaseous, swirling up from my gut to my heart, in flares, adrenaline.

"All right, all right," he said, letting go of my wrists. "Stop *looking* at me like that," he said after a minute, annoyed. Him annoyed. "It was supposed to be interesting, you know, ambush, surprise, I missed you. And you look like you want to kill me."

Until he said that, I felt ready to apologize for the bloody-murder look on my face—I was even ready to apologize for the pace of my heart. I spook. I spook easy. Sometimes, when half my brain is perfectly interested in something—a turtle, a praying mantis, a penis out of context, I spook, I can't help it. I was the kind of little girl you can spook with her own mother's voice.

But I wasn't going to apologize now, no way. I showed him my wrists, dented, blanched, white. And then you bet he changed, over a few seconds, became contrite. Started to think of something to say about my painting— a still life with refrigerator.

"I'm sorry," he muttered. Then he turned his arm over to show me the ALMA T, in ink, now faintly greenish. "I haven't washed this," he said. "I figured you were not going to get upset about this, you aren't really, are you, come on, are you." He zipped up his pants. We both sat down on the floor. He could read my face. I was really not wanting to be as upset as I still was. And he crumpled, and I felt terrible, but he obviously felt worse, so for fifteen seconds in a row there I had the luxury of loving him without him even guessing it.

"You look so pretty," he repeated. "I did knock," he said. "Then I came around to this window. And I watched you. You look so pretty. You cannot paint bananas, though, it is really hopeless. The refrigerator is beautiful, though. So human, that refrigerator."

"Shut up and talk to me," I said. "Let's get out of this room."

"I wanted actually to take you, once I got here. I wanted to pounce on you."

"Let's have some coffee," I said. "Go somewhere, for sherbet."

"I think I must have thought we were further along than we really are," he said. "Maybe I should get up and go around the corner and phone you up, and if I did what would you say?"

"That I'm busy until four," I said.

"But I really have to see you *now*," he said.

"Why?"

"There's no reason," he said. "But lust."

"Coffee," I said.

"Sure," he said. I meant in the front room, not in my studio. He didn't get what I meant. I was thinking this whole thing was pretty retarded. Me too, not just him. Me because I still had this shock-hole feeling, this pounding, this need to be steadied, him because he was so intent on hanging on to that error, and now to my refusal to see him until my work was over. Infantile, really infantile. And the other error he'd made, pulling me toward the wall, grabbing my wrists. So for half an hour more we tried to let go of the incident. I think I did let go before he did. Not only that he did not stop bringing it up, while we tried to talk of any other thing. Then I started feeling nervous for him—this is why I have to keep my distance from people, because their feelings, if I hang around them too long, become more palpable than my own, they begin to occupy me—and insofar as I felt what Richard did, I had no idea what in the world to do with myself, so I decided to make love to him.

But isn't it always the case with every one of those this-could-be-good situations, this could be good, but. We were on my daybed, him folding forward toward me, the newspapers crinkling underneath him. And you think to yourself, Shoo, shoo, quit thinking, don't think. Breathe, something, but his fingernails are dirty, you aren't familiar with his breath, you are being too critical, too critical, and before you know it he comes crummily and you don't at all, and you figure that in the denouement there may be some marvelous reversal of events, as there is in Maupassant or somebody, there in the last line, you can make it up to each other. And you really think you are trying, but the only thing that will do is to do it all again, and he shoos you away. This is natural, this is how things are, even on National Geographic specials, among lions who are making love, there is this gruffness in the male—but it is critical when it is *me* the gruffness is meant for.

I guess our failure was shared knowledge by early afternoon, our total failure as lovers. We were back where we started, with Richard repeating himself a lot, sitting there in his shorts.

His skin is fair and splotchy, and he has freckles on his shoulders. His arms are more fully formed than his narrow chest. They swell and are rounded at the shoulders, as if his body were developed for reaching, for pulling, for trying. But between those large arms, his chest, his breasts cave in a little, collapse, fail to withstand the pressure of whatever it is he is grappling with— perhaps it is just that it is an unfinished body, his, hardly any wider than mine. At that thought I was consumed with the idea that he would never really do for me, never really *do* for me, I knew it.

And then I tried things men are always supposed to love, no matter who is doing them, I did this because I felt forlorn knowing we would never *do* for one another. I kissed his penis, and after maybe a few minutes of that he said, "Alma, we really don't know what we are doing, do we, baby."

"Baby." So I quit. He was right, and he put his pants on. And I put mine on. And I was relieved that that was over. And then I felt a canyon was opening up inside me, framed on all sides by the fear I'd had to start with, the startle he gave me. But Richard was worse. He told me he'd wait, I could go back and work if I wanted, he'd wait until four. Then he rummaged for my cigarettes, and looked at the messy *Sun,* at my magazines, and went into the bathroom for a while, and came out, and I said I was going to have something, and he just watched me eat, didn't eat. And how could I eat with him standing there, in limbo. He wouldn't be made love to, he wouldn't break bread, he wouldn't go away and call me from the corner, wouldn't kiss and kiss my neck, my ears, wouldn't find out that that was what he was supposed to do, just wouldn't. He was an ass.

After maybe three Marlboros he finally said, "I think I'm going," and I said, "Fine," and then he did, shoo.

I hate to admit this. The rest of the day was terrible because I was alone and I kept hoping that he would come back. The house hours had a desert quality that time takes on when you are involved with a new lover, especially one you want to have a fight with. The hope goes out of food and music and even painting. Everything is arid, desiccated, until you get a call. My life collapsed on me.

He did not call.

Tuesday, Wednesday, Thursday. Long, pasty Jerry phoned and told me there was a John Waters movie opening. I said no thanks, and remembered Richard liked Waters movies. I liked them too, because people I knew were always the extras, and the stars were the celebrities of my quarter. Edith Massey, Divine.

Loretta and Gina had appeared in a crowd scene together. One of the plots was the saga of a sex change, female to male. Loretta called that evening and I decided to go to dent the routine.

There were searchlights outside the theater and most of the cast were in a throng at the base of it, dressed in costumes. A very fat black woman in a tent of transparent fuchsia voile with accordion pleats. I stood behind her, surrounded in her gardenia scent. She had silver sequins on her cheeks. Loretta and Gina had left me there to go and talk to the star, Susan Lowe. Then I saw Jerry with his paparazzo flash, waving meanly at me. He didn't approach.

And I felt childish, like an idiot. I thought it was not being married that kept me so idiotic. If I married Jerry or somebody like him, somebody reasonable, with needs, I wouldn't lead this black-hole life, I thought, the life of a sad college girl, fat or something. And who should be there, like a genie, but the hopeful intruder, looking smaller, flashier, more interesting.

Maybe it was the gardenia that made me suffer for breath. I looked normal, in an atmosphere like a carnival. The teased hair on the heads around me was laced with glitter and rhinestones. Richard looked a little cheap, even.

"Well, hello," one of us said. And we stood there, for about two minutes. We still hadn't bought our tickets, and then we found out we were in the wrong line—the one for people who had appeared in the film. They were getting in for free, once the director, in his tux and ink-line mustache, gave the okay.

There were perhaps three hundred total on the sidewalk now. Richard told me to go to the other line, in a thick crowd. I saw Loretta wave her black and silver lamé glove in my direction, meaning she could get me in. But I had started to get happy at finding Richard, so for twenty seconds I was false with my friends. If I had said, Excuse me, someone's calling me, and followed the silver glove, I could have kept my old life. I have never had that much sense. What was in my mind was below the level of thought.

Richard was saying he was going to call me, but he had been too fatigued. He had been working fixing houses with his friends, like him Hopkins dropouts, mostly from the Classics program. Then, abruptly, he changed the subject. Started delivering a little speech. It occurred to me he was crazy. In no way did he acknowledge Tuesday afternoon, or the first night, for that matter. Anything historic went without saying—our relationship was charged and familiar, right then, right away. I thought that fact meant something.

The subject of Richard's meditation was that I was too old for him, which he called something else; he called it being certain. He used the word so often.

"What I mean is that you are really lovely, and you know what you want. I can tell that, that you know exactly what you want, in general, out of everything," he went on. "I find that really attractive. But . . ."

"Are you breaking up with me?" I asked, thinking this was even tender, that he'd been thinking about us for nearly a week. But I sounded sarcastic.

"No, there's nothing between us, certainly. I would be flattered to be in the position to be breaking up with you," he went on, obsequious, extravagantly polite in a way, his nose five inches from the end of mine. Not at all aware of that, though. Finally, we'd got onto the red carpet leading up to the box office. The crowd was shoving us into one another. "I just want you to know I'm not rejecting you for yourself, or really rejecting you at all. I mean, it is the character of our differences. I admire you, I certainly admire the hell out of you."

This wouldn't do, and I would have to go after him. And there I was, bounding, a regular antelope. I looked up and the wooden block went in front of the arched opening in the ticket booth glass. Two policemen started hacking off the line just ahead of us.

"You know, I've only heard about half what you are saying," I said. "Can we have a drink?"

"I can't see you," he said, his face wagging sideways.

How was I going to get him?

"I know," I said, looking down, fluffing out my bottom lip—I'd try anything. "I'm going across the street for a drink. I came with Gina and Loretta, they're in the movie; they've already gone in. So I'm going to Darling's for a margarita. Then I'm going home. Alone. On the number ten bus. That's all I'm doing," I said, and then I started to appear to rush. This was a risk. I shuffled down to the corner and stepped off the curb and crossed before I turned around to see if he was following me. I was afraid to face his absence.

Midday Sunday, after the false-labor Saturday night, Richard said we should visit the grave for the High Holy Days. We would go after Lucas left. When I finished talking to my mother we tried to get Lucas to eat.

Lucas is overweight, and he smokes during the first half of the day. He has a hardworking life, solving cases for Worldwide Railways and Amalgamated Department Stores, people like that. He is a Washington lawyer, but his ties to me are old ones, and even though he and Richard started out with nothing in common, not age, few interests, they had become very good friends.

Lucas is unusual in my universe as it is constituted now. He wears Oxford shirts and those flat shoes with the laces, half rubber, half canvas, which are meant for the decks of boats. Lucas once did a lot of sailing on Martha's Vineyard, between the time he was a college boy and when he became a member of the invisible nation of corporate law. He sailed and did editing and writing for a little press on the Vineyard that publishes a weekly and books about boats and fishermen, and reproduces woodcuts of Menemsha for calendars. "That life wasn't real," he told me a long time ago. He had spoken of it more wistfully since Carmen left.

When he married my best friend, they lived in Vineyard Haven, over a garage, on food stamps during the off-season. And then he suddenly became seized, as Carmen put it, with the urge to go to Harvard Law.

To hear her tell it, once Lucas got there, he went a little crazy. He'd come home with idiotic ideas, "born of too many categories," Carmen claimed. She had to clean the house, put every cup on a special hook, vacuum daily, "do her part," as he said. Carmen said Lucas was turning into his father.

And Carmen met Mary Ann, who was working as a part-time typist. Mary Ann, as it turned out, didn't have to work—she had a trust fund. She said that she needed a job to order her life at the time. Carmen worked, partly to pay for a housekeeper. Then they both started full-time at the old John Hancock Building, which, inside, is made of gum-pink marble, has escalators of wood and brass. They both got off on the architecture. It was there that Mary Ann started sending Carmen love memos.

Once, three years after Carmen and Lucas were married, Carmen took me to a coffee place on Newbury Street and told me about the notes. Mary Ann wrote that she would wait as long as it took. Carmen said that Mary Ann, although she seemed very plain, was really exotic and extraordinary. She'd gone to school in Switzerland and France. Her father was an economist, had worked for the UN. Her new friend Mary Ann was amazing, she said.

Soon, Lucas graduated and moved to Washington and was hired by one of the best firms, according to the criteria some people use. Carmen never told Lucas, but she kept all the letters and notes from her girl suitor. "... *I've never met anyone like you. Your beauty has always stunned me, since the first time I saw you. ... When I do little things without you, I think how sharing them with you would make them perfect. ...*"

One-minded devotion, really, something nobody will ever get from a man, Carmen said. When Carmen and Lucas moved to Washington, Mary Ann followed soon after.

Carmen left Lucas a little over a month after I got pregnant. She and Mary Ann moved not far away from us, into a place a little too too for me—they had a trash compactor. Lucas described the whole thing as "silly." He didn't use the word "lesbian." But he was hollowed out by it. He hung with us.

Sometimes Lucas thought he might eventually switch to a federal job, which wouldn't be as ass-busting. He kept their terrace apartment near Dupont Circle. Once a week he has a Guatemalan lady come and empty the ashtrays.

I liked Lucas, despite my best loyalties. My sympathies were supposed to be with Carmen, but I liked him even more sometimes. Carmen's complaints about him were pretty mild, the usual husband-wife complaints, until the Mary Ann letters and the seduction. Then her problems with him blew up all out of proportion, and it started to seem she was talking about someone monstrous. Also, I'm a little jealous of Mary Ann, I have to say it. She has Carmen, and Carmen and I aren't as close anymore. We are old girlfriends, pushing thirty, but Mary Ann thinks there must be more to it. I have always had violent feelings about Carmen.

Lucas wanted to stay for the big event. He was excited about it, genuinely, vicariously, dying for me to get the baby out so he could, what? Kiss it? Hold it to his hefty chest?

Richard, good in bed, was up in the air on everything else. To the question "What are you going to become, what are you doing with yourself," he might have said, "Fuck, I know who I am." Lucas made him nervous, but Richard could beat him in chess, so life has its compensations. They probably wouldn't, under normal circumstances, have been friends. In normal times, Carmen would be calling me, asking me what she should wear to company cocktail parties. But Lucas had spent more and more time with us, so we were sympathetic to his loss.

I didn't know any people like Lucas where I grew up. And when I got a scholarship to Bennington, there were some of them around, but so were very rare people, daughters of princes and, at Williams, sons of jazz musicians. Lucas is a boy who went to Exeter, and even though he dallied for many years on Martha's Vineyard, he's a racehorse of a certain race, and he ran true to form, finally. Richard is his opposite, the son of a professor of Russian, some mornings so temporary he could be anything.

Lucas and Richard together made a good amount of male company.

Before he left that morning, Lucas told me, "Saw Carmen."

"How is she?" I asked. It had been maybe months since he'd mentioned her name to me. We talked around and about her a lot, but her name had got very powerful, was not used. "She's getting gray, here in the front, stress," he said, taking a bit of his own hair between his fingers.

"She has beautiful hair," I said.

"Yes, she does." He started to close his eyes and reach for a Merit, to disown the next remark. "I still like her," he said. The pack was finished and he crumpled it. "She said Mary Ann and she are going to buy the place they are living in. She came to see me to tell me. Why did she come over? She could have asked me on the phone to get the money out of money market. It is her money, half of it. Why didn't she just write me a note, ask me to sign the check and send it back?"

"Was it so awful to see her?" I asked.

"No," Lucas said. He said he was not angry, just curious. I knew the most recent cup of coffee wasn't new enough for him. He likes it with that black nut smell. We share a devotion to coffee and cigarettes.

"There's something else," he continued, "that she did." He looked away so I saw the profile. Beautiful, his hair burned off his temples because of so much lawful thought. "Why are you looking at your watch?" he asked.

"Feel the stomach," I said. It was high again, as it had been last night. I could put my mug on it, the mug wouldn't topple.

"It is so hard," Lucas said.

"It's tough," I said.

Lucas went reverent on me. And then, a little later, sadly, he went back to Washington to do some work.

I was out of hand. Look: I met him, asked him to dinner, then he came home. Two days later he came after me again for an ambiguous fuck. Then I heard nothing. A few days after that he went at me in a public place for at least ten minutes in the middle of a crowd while I lost my friends, telling me the reasons he couldn't see me anymore. Why he was worth bothering with at all, I cannot tell you at this time. I had long ago lost the habit of one-night stands. So maybe I felt obliged to mess with him a little more. Richard certainly would not sleep with a lady like me without meaning anything by it. Remember that we paused on my couch before we went ahead. We got some coffee, like good sports. This elevated the lust a little. It was a recognition of territory to be contested, made it somber, certainly. That was the start of a battle over the body. There is usually so much bad sex in early courtship. And women always lose this fight, I'd forgotten. All I really want is to be neuter. I thought I could hunt a little and stay neuter. I was always dumb in some things.

Why were we plowing into each other, anyway? I don't know. It wasn't worth the risk.

I was standing on the corner, half a block down and across the street from the theater throng. I was in front of Darling's pure plush cocktail lounge, which was still a hangout for the same people who went there in the sixties—the people inside were old and lined and lightly alky.

I had crossed the street against the light. When I turned around he was still explaining what it all meant. He was there, that was important. I figured I'd conquered.

"You are really not listening to me, are you," he continued. "You think this is just, I don't know, some kind of ordinary circumstance."

"I don't have any opinion, I just think it is needless for you to go on explaining. It was just one night and one day, and it's okay. Two visits. Forget it. I'm going to have a drink. You don't have to come. You don't."

"I can't," he went on. "You don't see. I'm kind of a wreck, really, I mean it. Don't drink alone. I won't let you. Like what did I do Tuesday?"

We were sitting in a blue vinyl booth. The waiter came. Richard didn't know what to order. He asked to look at the menu. I was thinking, How dear to find a guy beside himself. I recalled Jerry's mean slack wave, and realized as much as he was, as kind, he was nobody to me. The round on the sidewalk with Richard was all wrong. If I hinted at any comprehension, if I gave his doubts credence, then there we'd be, drinking coffee on the couch. The menu was a list of Darling's exotics on a stained manila card with illustrations and silly names, which Darling's offered only to pretend to compete with the once-popular Chinese restaurants in the neighborhood. Soon Richard was sliding fruit pieces off a parasol. He was slipping away from me, not talking.

"What's the real problem?" I asked him.

"You are personally stronger than me," he said. "It isn't that you want it that way, but I feel younger than you, I'd feel, Christ, kept."

I thought about this and knew I had to seem needy. "You aren't weak," I said with incredible presumption.

"I'm not saying I am," he said. "But that time, Tuesday. I felt like this was really a delicious thing to do, you know, bawdy, I guess, how I thought it would be, anyway. But your face, Alma. I was going to take you to a new Caribbean restaurant later, you know, we'd go out like lovers, walk and talk, eat goat. But I felt like crap. You bend me out of shape. I left hornier."

"Oh," I said.

He said, "What did I come over like that for? Ready for battle? What is this? I'm not stable."

"Maybe you were angry at me, wanted to get me." I stopped. What was this problem of his? Had to get that out of the conversation. His guilt enlivened him so, it seemed erotic, got him so excited.

"That's the problem," he said.

"What?" I knew what he would answer with, and then I figured out I'd have to tell him Tuesday was good.

"You are an amazing lover, really," I said. "Every time." I smiled. I felt a little scared smiling.

"You are sick," he said lightly.

"Look," I said. "I agree with you we shouldn't see each other, if you think I'm"—I had to think of something nobody had ever thought I was—"too cold, if that's how you feel."

"I don't think that," he said. "I never said you were cold, just a little terrified, and gentle about it, really gentle. I'm the one who's detached. I told you I've been thinking about us for months. And I wanted it back to that, you know, something I was dreaming up. In life, you're too much."

Richard was getting interesting. I have always been partial to fate.

"I am too fucked up, and that is just it," he said.

"You aren't," I said. "Why else would you feel so guilty?"

"You are a person," he said. "I broke into your house. It was venal. It was wrong."

"Tuesday was, then, all right, but with everything, with everybody, it gets weird now and then. That's the times. It is 1978."

"I broke into your house. That's out of character.

—53—

Totally. You don't see," Richard said. "I'm a good Jewish boy."

"You are a man," I said, lying like crazy. "And it can get to be this abstract assault, sometimes. What do you want it to be, based on mutually agreed-upon principles, like a treaty, grain agreements? It's mystical. You want a contract? What?" I shut up. I wanted to sound truthful.

He drained his glass. I drained mine. He summoned the waiter. Two more sweet drinks. We were getting somewhere. I sat there, telling myself to quit lying.

"You're too much for me, I overreact," he said.

"I'm just a girl," I said, preposterous. I was twenty-seven. I lived by myself. I was past this. "You are normal—"

He looked at me, so I would continue.

"And gentle and nervous," I said. Then I played it. The ace in the hole. "And—"

"What?" he said.

"You gotta be into me," I said. "It is absolutely obvious." I gave him a look. I liked the silliness of this.

"I can't love anybody," he said.

This wasn't worth the trouble, for a few hot nights, but he was so handsome and fun to toy with, his cock would move up and down when it got near me. He was fun. He had red hair. So I said, "I don't want to make you do anything about it."

True to form, I couldn't bring myself to grasp his hand under the table and carry this out. I felt emotional. All that had gone before, although it had moved Richard off center a lot, had been rational, not emotional, for me. Now it changed. I had been planning my every move, my every line, since we had walked into Darling's. Nothing sexy about it, really, but his eyes were wet! Two drinks. A puppy. I lost it.

"I can't get involved with you," he said. "And you are so pretty, really. You looked so nice in the light in your room. I like you so much."

"We don't have to do anything," I said. "We can just slow down."

"You know you scare me?" he said, and with that he went around the blue U-shaped banquette and sat beside me. He came and sat beside me.

"You would not believe how much I want to be with you," he said. "You would not believe how much. It is perverse how much I do."

In a little while we were out on the street, then on our way to my place. We spent the next three days mostly in bed, and in between we had the same conversation several more times and each time he got more emotional and the vein in his forehead showed more often.

I washed his back in the tub once, and he told me about his childhood, and intermittently, miraculously, we would expand and change size and shape, and Richard's face would take on a look of immense surprise, and then we would mix.

On a Tuesday, significant because it followed the first weekend we did not spend together in a month, Richard came to the door with a present wrapped in the funny papers. A used book. Only slightly used. He was hoping I didn't notice it was used, I think. On paintings by Modigliani. If you stretched me out a little I would look like a Modigliani lady. There you are, the prototype. But I wasn't interested in this gift. I didn't want this gift. It was inappropriate. It introduced into the relationship the fact that the giver had no idea who the receiver is or what she wants.

Of course I should have enjoyed the fact that he had brought me a present. I was gracious. I didn't have to say much. He insisted that I looked just like her. She's ugly, I was thinking. Why didn't he get the Georgia O'Keeffe book. I made him some tea. "Read the inscription," he told me, "you ingrate."

For Alma,
Who has given me heart and life,
All my love,
Richard

Well, this sort of sentiment ought to keep us going another few months at least, I thought.

But I didn't think of that prospect as something glorious, because it wasn't: I felt dread, a little. I probably felt dread because he felt a little dread, which he was plastering over with sentiment—sentiment is easier to handle than dread, you can have profound sentiment about people without ever having to do a thing, without ever having to offer yourself to them. What the gift meant was that things had got to a point. What we were engaged in had become so serious we had to start in with the sentiment, pouring a little glaze over it. It was there, the way we asked something whenever we crawled into each other, in the way our bodies kept asking so much of each other and delivering, and delivering, even when it was forced and conscious in the beginning, even when it started out as badly as it did the day he broke into my studio, we always delivered ourselves beyond that now, and so we were attached, to each other and to the room-out-of-time that the other body held. And that room was the dread, that room was really what we dreaded; how much could we lose, falling so often into the other person. It scared Richard more, so he sentimentalized it first, I suppose.

An artifact in plain daylight: Richard declared his love. The inscription shook me a little.

What did he want back?

My life too? I told you, I hate gifts. They are misunderstanding, in material terms. They make it. They cause it.

"How did you know so quickly?" he asked, his feet on my red chair.

"Know what?"

"That I was going to fall in love with you? How could you sense it?"

"I made it up," I said.

"I'm being serious," Richard said.

"I am too," I said.

"You made it up?" He was incredulous.

I'd committed a big mistake. How long before kids like him turn into men, I was thinking. Maybe he won't ever. I'd gone and ruined it. I put my hand around his hard belly, inside his shirt. I started to move in on him quite directly, to be mistress. But here's what he said, proof he was brainwashed.

"Alma darling, you think you always have to be out in front, but just quit it. You live this little simple life, and you can't let anybody in, and I'm here and you don't have to have the pretense that you are running everything. You really don't. I'm not going anywhere. You are afraid that if you let down, something is going to damage you somehow. I love you so much, I love you so much."

I was trying to tug him to bed, to get him to shut up. Now this was brand-new: he was being paternal with me, and I felt tired, so tired. I was too old for this. Richard had range, I'll give him that.

"You act so tough, Alma." He wouldn't stop. "Don't touch me right now," he said, taking my wrists, gently. "Listen to me. I love you. I know you, too."

I hated the gift, I told you. I hated the Modigliani book.

We sat there on the couch for a long time in one hug, and I tried to figure out how to maintain the embrace and the nuzzle-in-his-breast posture and not smother. The first phase of our romance was over. I think Richard started letting his beard grow that day, and I managed to ignore the book.

After we went to bed that afternoon, I got up and

was searching for my eyeglasses, and he started to look, too. He was getting generous. He started messing up the things on my dining table while he searched: piles of mail, *Art News*es, nail files, *New Yorker*s. A box of Grape-Nuts.

"I'll do it," I shouted, from a few feet away, angry.

"You don't want *any* help, see?" he said.

‖ had a curiosity about his parents. It was October and we'd been together several months.

It was interesting, by then, I have to grant that. He had, after all, traded places with me to an extent. I was not sure what had gotten into me. He had potential. Sometimes he was better and better in bed. He came slow, put so much feeling into it. This could last another little while.

He took me to his mother and father's apartment on an avenue in a part of Baltimore I had never been to before. He pointed out the synagogues on both sides of the street. The Conservatives, an offshoot of the Conservatives called Temple Oheb Shalom, the Chasidic commune with a tennis net around it because it was Saturday, he explained. Richard said the net was there so that women could do a little work, like push baby strollers around on the Sabbath, which made no sense to me, what did the men do, anyway. He kept explaining about the synagogues, how one grew out of another and another, and then he told me the joke about the old Jewish man who has been shipwrecked on an island for twenty years, alone. When the rescuers finally come, he shows them his *shul,* and they ask, "What's this other building?" and he says, "That's the synagogue I used to go to."

Mr. Kaplan looked as if an eagle had landed on his forehead and left its wings for the brows. The Kaplans' place was large, open, and more or less bright. The summer slipcovers in the living room were lavender. On one wall were about a dozen paintings, half of which were awful, half of them prints by artists you know—Miró, Chagall, Baskin. Common print-gallery stuff, signed. It was not a simple environment. Everything would be just so, according to a decorator's sense of unity, and then I would notice an awful animal-skin pillow, out of place in any decor, stuck in there, like a mistake.

" 'Alma' means 'soul' in Latin," Mr. Kaplan said as a fact. He motioned to the maid, a woman with a wide sensitive brown face and gray hair. The wine, from Israel, was not sweet. I didn't know there could be Jewish wine that was tart.

"Will you help us in the kitchen?" he asked his son. Richard seemed halting. I sat and finished my glass.

I went out on the porch and looked down the four stories to the street where there were men in yarmulkes, in clumps with their sons, moving toward the main avenue. Only a few wives. Most were back inside the tennis court net, I supposed.

Then Richard's mother, whose presence, like a light beam, I could almost feel without having to turn around. She was wearing a silk hostess gown, hand-painted, that brushed to the floor, and pointed leather slippers.

"How do you do?" she said, and I disliked her instantly. Somewhere in the next few sentences she asked me if I was Jewish, and I told her not at all. Daughter of lapsed Methodists.

"Do you know Richard a long time?" I was dreaming of leaving. These people were weird; I'd take the brief route through the French doors, off the balcony. I felt nine years old. Maybe I could roll down the avenue, disappear.

"Not very long," I said, disowning four months of hot monkey.

"He was very particular about my meeting you," she said, meaning, "You're lying."

"You know he gets very enthusiastic about things," I said, slowing down. "Some things. He wanted me to have the chance to meet you."

"Because I am dying?" she asked, a smile then, some joke.

As if this were an accepted fact, something as consequential as the fact it was Saturday, October. I think it was. I couldn't think at all, just then.

I let her go on, and she did. "I don't know if he's so enthusiastic all the time. He's really rather languid, wouldn't you say, for a Jew?" She smiled and I didn't know how to react. Everything was okay, then, for a second. It was as if she had just put a little plutonium on the table and started playing a game—I was supposed to ignore it, eat a chocolate instead. She was always pulling guns in conversation. Exactly the opposite of Richard's, her manner. A cool, sweet ghostliness punctuated by these insane commercials.

After a few more awful minutes, I saw the skin across her knuckles go white as she pushed up and stood. They were Richard's pale, competent hands. She was Richard in drag, practically—the same red hair, the same face. "You have to excuse me," she said. "I'm not feeling very well." She swayed as she walked out of the room, grasped the doorsill which led to the hall, and disappeared.

"Sorry I took so long," Richard said.

"I was interviewed," I told him.

"What'd you think?" he asked. "How did she seem?"

"Like she wanted to leave it at that."

"What did you think?"

"She said she was dying. I had no idea what to say. Is she dying?"

"No," Richard said; then he said, "Normal reaction.

This has been a test of the emergency marriage fore-casting system."

"What are you thinking?" I said, my heart sinking, a hide growing over me. I was becoming a reptile, sticking still, frozen. Now we were in another doorway, facing the balcony. He shoved me back in and sat at the far end of the couch. He picked up a chocolate from inside a soldered box of bronze and glass, and ate it whole. Without delicacy, without offering me one.

Mrs. Kaplan came back in, on the arm of Richard's father. And both their heads looked wooden, like heads on the bows of gondolas. They seemed to come into the room in waves.

The rest of the afternoon I was only rarely directly addressed. This was okay by me. Cold-blooded now, I was not really there, I was in suspended animation. There was white and brown Jewish food which was too salty, cooked too long.

Later, they had an argument about why Richard and I couldn't take the maid home. All three of them launched into a discussion of how we might fit myself and the maid, Wilma, and Richard into the Triumph. The maid could sit sideways. I could sit sideways. She was slim, she could ride in the back. And the maid said nothing, until I offered to take a taxicab, just so they would stop. But my saying that was an interruption of the game, which I discovered was really something they were enjoying, a riddle. They were being nice to each other. Finally in the car, without the maid, when we crossed a certain place on the expressway, which meant we were in the old red-brick, crowded, good Baltimore, my Baltimore, not the clipped parkland of the suburbs, I felt free again.

"They hate me," I said. "And I'm too old. Look, we'll have a good time, okay. And put a limit on it."

"They thought you were great. An artist who actually makes a living, you. They don't talk to anybody. My mother had ambitions once. You could have asked her.

She had an artistic sensibility, she has one. You could have tried. You could have asked."

"Well, I don't want to know them, at all," I said.

"Hell with you," Richard said. "Alma, frankly, you were catatonic. What did you expect?"

Nine minutes later, we were moving toward the Point. We entered my territory. It was a smoky Saturday afternoon—streets full of people speaking Spanish, girls in braces and hot pants, Polish sausage on a bun with mustard for ninety-nine cents.

"I'm sorry," he said. "They are your basic Icebergs. My mother occupies the upper reaches of the Hopkins faculty-wife class. They changed their name from Iceberg to Kaplan, clever move. I can't do anything about my family. Do you know the joke about the guy Goldberg who is sitting in a restaurant and a Chinese guy beats his face in? And he asks him what the trouble is and the man says, *Titanic.' 'That was an iceberg.' 'Iceberg, Goldberg, what's the difference?' "

I chose to ignore this. "Is she used to you bringing girls home to dinner?" I asked. But who wanted to know? Not me.

"You are the first one for years, since before I graduated," he paused, stripped the gears a little, getting into second. "Look, they are freaked. They told me later. She's had a headache for four weeks. She can hardly walk. She's going for a CAT scan on Wednesday. He just told me this in the kitchen when we were leaving. They never tell me anything until it is already half-over. They don't treat me like a functioning human being."

"I'm sorry," I said. "You don't look like them." He did look like her, exactly like her. I was lying. I was always lying to him.

"You think I'm adopted?" He jerked his head up. "I think so." He paused a few minutes. His toes pointed outward as they slapped down on the sidewalk beside mine. It was an optimistic walk. "I got it wrong," he went on, "in the beginning of the joke, the Jewish guy hits the Chinese guy and says, 'That's for Pearl Harbor.' " Then Richard walked without talking.

"Well, my father has always disliked me," Richard continued later, over a heap of crabs. "He loves Penelope. He came home from the awful war and there was Penelope, his baby girl, his hope." Richard ate with relish, with delight. His fingers slipped out the cloudy, jelly-like pure white meat. He hoisted it to his shapely mouth. We were in a crab house, a place which had been an outdoor garden, now enclosed in plastic mahogany-colored paneling. The picnic tables sat on a nylon floor filthy with cigarette butts, tentacles, thin meatless claws, puddles of beer.

On the enormous TV screen, "It Don't Mean a Thing," a black woman in a disco dress, surrounded by chorus boys in minstrel tuxes, bebebumbebum, bebebumbum.

"He's always hated me," he repeated. "I was hers. I've always been hers. She wanted me to be a doctor, a lawyer would have been okay, or, last choice, a doctor of literature. Anything. She's not proud, at the last, just insistent. Make money, make a living, but don't move out of the house. Classic, really, funny. She has so many ideas. She got me a job through one of her friends who works at Hopkins, in a medical lab. Did I tell you about that?"

The table was stacked high with crab carcasses and under that, newspapers. Soon, a *Rockford Files* rerun began.

"So I had a job for nine months last year. Working for an immunologist. Overseeing the death of thousands of white rabbits. I felt like the fucking SS. He'd have us inject them with an air bubble into a vein; then in a second their ears bled. They looked so angry. He swore they felt nothing."

I made a face.

"She's very ambitious, as mothers of that generation are. She wore out my father with it, tried to turn him into a dean. He was for a while, and got an ulcer, went back to teaching." He waited a minute, then he asked, "What's your mother like?"

The people next to us, all around us, were horribly noisy. These were the last crabs of the season. On the second dozen, dumped by the waitress on the remains of the first, Richard's tapered fingers dove in again. Twenty-one dollars a dozen, huge male underwater insects, scavengers, twenty-four mean, mean eyes. Someone turned the channel from Jim Garner to *Sportscene Magazine*. The recent fate of the Birds against the Royals.

"She sent me to music school for years," he continued. "I never practiced. Twice a week were the lessons. Wednesday and Saturday. The doctor jag started in infancy, lasted the longest. She hasn't given up, although I have given her every reason, every opportunity. I quit school once, for a semester, worked in a bar, lived with some guys on Twenty-seventh Street. 'Richard,' she'd say on the phone three times a week. 'What are you going to do with your life? What?' Now she's a little more subtle, but basically it is the same. Nobody likes her right off. And she is in pain, now, you have to understand that. She said she was dying. I know she believes she is. She had cancer a few years ago. Now they think they didn't get it all—it may have migrated to the brain. I don't know how my father feels. He acts like he doesn't feel anything. He's always acted that way. He's a nit-pick scholar, a real Apollonian, fucking Germanic in the worst way. He likes to do editions, you know the type. He likes to find printer's errors, that's the kind of scholar he is. Working with people literally makes him sick."

All the time, his fingers were stealing through the

seventeenth crab. Eating crustacea has everything to do with talking, with your fingers, and with having sex. I was looking at the red-brown globs of seasoning on the backs of their fluorescent red shells. After a few too many, you notice their expressions, their fine whiskers. They are really a little solemn, wise maybe, like mantises, murdered by steam.

"For my father, I'm some kind of problem, a case. It's impersonal. I overheard him once, talking to a guy, a shrink, at a party, about this deliberately rebellious person, an example, a lost cause. That was me. . . ." Richard went on until the place was closing. Talking about his family possessed him—as a subject it consumed him like nothing else. The air conditioning and the filth and the TV and the ton of dead crabs' shells were so total an environment that I was sure this was the world, and there wasn't any other. We would never get out.

So the outside night came as a surprise. He took me home and laid me. Indian summer—too hot for a blanket. He got up every half hour to pee or to wash his hands. The seasoning seeps into your fingertips. Into the fingerprints, which stay cayenne for days. At four-thirty I awoke and realized he had not yet slept.

"Crabs are *trayf*," he told me.

"What's that?" I asked.

"There's a kosher law against eating things that swarm underwater," he said.

The underwater locusts, an army, thousands with exactly the same pincers, exactly the same half-round eyes, a jillion twins. East Baltimore girls had come out for a French merchant marine ship. Outside, around us, hundreds of small men in navy blue were gathering to meet the American heat.

"Well, don't you love your family?" Richard asked.

ere's the picture. A big pod with one pea. My mother is too old for me to be her first, but I am. I'm a tot. She is five-eleven. She's sitting on the hood of the Nash. The year is 1951. Her bleached hair is piled high on her head, cross-hatched like a pineapple. Me in her lap in a seersucker suit. I am helpless but I have two fang teeth. Her smile is losing its tone. My father is not in the picture because he is still in the Marines.

My mother is someone I do not like to tangle with, I've told you. She's a busybody. She hates to throw things away, and she's the superficially neat kind. She likes cereal boxes, for example ("You never know what they'll ask for, proof-of-purchase seals or net weights. . . ."). She likes to have a drawer for plastic bags left from the groceries. She likes lots of piles of things. She kept a special drawer below the one for potatoes and onions, for string too short to use.

She's allowed me to grow up only in her imagination. For example, she imagined New England to be a place full of small simple stark towns like the one in "The Lottery" by Shirley Jackson, which is her favorite short story, because, she says, the fact is people are mean at heart and will do anything. She loves contests. Even if the winner is stoned to death. She has a hallucination the region is all town greens and crisp churches and houses with large windows of old wavy glass.

Without my request, she sent away for a catalog of each New England college whose name she could find in the library. She spent four hundred dollars on applications for me to the ones she liked the best. She forged the essay to Middlebury in my handwriting. "As a rural girl in the South, life in New England has always fascinated me. . . . My favorite story, 'The Lottery,' gives an excellent picture of the anterural and cooperative spirit of that historical and recreational region. . . ." Farther down . . . "I am a gifted high school senior with a high SAT score who is very interested in your language laboratory programs. I sincerely desire to become a polyglot. . . ."

I did not get into Middlebury. What does "anterural" mean? We compromised. I wrote a basic essay, and she adapted it for twelve schools. Then the letters came in. It was her favorite contest. No one I knew had ever heard of Bennington, and both Mother and I took great delight in announcing its name to people in the trailer park. My father went with me to the bus depot, and I bought a ticket from Durham to Richmond straight away through New York City to Springfield, Massachusetts, and then across the state on the Peter Pan Lines to North Adams, where a limousine drove me into the south-western corner of Vermont. I was surprised to discover, when I got off in North Adams, that so many people there had heard of the place.

Father had moved to downtown Durham years be-fore, where he lived in a boarding house owned by a woman named Marva, but somehow his distance was another kind of presence in our lives, a family issue that lived with us; he was merely quartered elsewhere. He and Mother did not bother to divorce. They have not, even yet.

As soon as he left, Mother filled the yard with stone statuettes. Deer, flamingoes. She made me ride with her to South of the Border once to get the painted iron Mexicans for the back garden. In front of everything was the sign on Highway 751:

TAYLOR'S MOBILE HOME PARK
AND CAMPGROUND

And she planted two scrawny, short Scotch pines on either side of the words. Father left because she wouldn't have him if he drank. He drank, he claimed, because he had so little spiritual and physical room. Mother al-ways wanted him to move out of the way, so she could put down one more thing. "Lead me through," he'd say when he was drunk, "just lead me a path through to the bedroom." She always wanted him to do something. She said once to me that she had more ambition in her big toe than he had in his whole body. He had grand ideas, though, sometimes.

The land came with the house—seventeen and a half acres, next to a white tract-style home built with a three-percent loan in 1951. Then, ten years later, she decided to have it aluminum-sided. There was a huge fight about that. Mother said the house, now at the entrance to the trailer park she'd planned, had to make a decent appearance in the glare of the floodlights she had installed for nighttime. There was an economic reason for everything. This was how I learned to hate money. She added a carport, open on the sides. It was the same year she gave me a box of decent pastels, saying, "I always wanted to draw when I was young, but I could tell I had no talent."

Father said he liked the Marines because, "You always knew what to do. . . . They would tell you." Yet he didn't like the way Mother told him what to do.

He thought the aluminum siding was crummy-looking, and I had to agree. Close up, wood was better. "Why spend good money when we could get Alma a new bicycle or even a pony?"

It looked fine from the road, though, and Mother was often into things for the looks. She would prefer to live about ten feet away from her life, so the cracks and smudges would be invisible to the naked eye. I inherited this from her, I suppose: in my paintings there are no cracks or smudges, as long as you stand five feet, maybe, away. They seem seamless, if you take in the whole.

"Your father had such a good head for figures," she swore to me. "Your father is such a good man. He's refined, and smart. If you knew your grandmother, Almy, you would know what fine blood runs in your veins."

It was 1962. I was almost a teenager, half-listening.

We were in Dr. Brouin's office, on the ninth floor of the Central Carolina Bank Building. My father was not a good man. He drank all the time and he stank. He ran after me and poured ice cubes down my back. Once in a while he'd kiss me too much and I'd lock the door and play the radio. I kept the radio with me at all times. A weapon, surefire, against family life. The black groups were my favorites—The Four Tops, The Temptations, The Impressions, and Ike and Tina Turner.

He'd bang on the door. "Please don't be angry. Almy, Almy, Almy. You are my sweet-pie daughter, Almy. I didn't mean to hurt you. I'm sorry. I'm sorry."

All this mush over ice down my back.

The moccasin on my mother's foot bobbed up and down as we sat in Dr. Brouin's office on chairs of steel tubing with hard cushions. From inside the next room, I could hear my father coughing for the doctor. At Mother's request, Dr. Brouin was delivering the ultimatum—go to the hospital in Asheville and dry out, or get out of your wife's life.

"Whiskey is no good reason to live, Almy," he told me when he emerged. He was being obsequious, the way I hated most to see him. "Do what your mother says while I'm away."

He was in a sanitarium for a few months after that. He dried out, came back, promised me the world, promised me a pony, then he left us. And the land for the pony—Mother started renting off the lots, adding roads, calling in the Lombard Gravel Company, adding electricity, painting half-buried truck tires white.

The following spring, after he took away the last box of his clothes from under the sink, Mother hung four pots of hybrid petunias around the carport. The petals were white, veined with an exotic blue.

"Oh, your father wouldn't like these," she told me with a little glee.

Forgetting he didn't live with us anymore, he would

come home now and then for the next few years. Mother might suffer him on the couch for a day or two, for a week. It continued after I had left for college; indeed, my absence had no effect on the facts of their relationship. Neither, I started to conclude, had my presence.

This made me feel bad.

"I can't stand all these things, sometimes," he told me once, Christmas night, when I arrived after a twenty-two-hour bus ride. It was 1969. I was nineteen. Blue jeans and boots, the Bennington black leotard uniform, some dope in my back pocket. Mother told me at the screen door that my father was home. When you are the only child you think you are the issue of the marriage. You belong to it. I'd provoked their whole lives, I thought.

"Why is *he* here?" I asked my mother.

"For Fred, he's doing good," she chirped.

Daddy had heard me. He looked as if he were about to cry. A person at the county health had been giving him lithium, so he'd become somewhat placid and dull. He lacked ideas. There had been, as I said, some fine ideas over the years. The stable and the horse, then the horses, the thoroughbreds we'd raise to win the Preakness.

"Every table in this room is filled with junk, Jo Ann," he said. This was supposed to be funny. He pointed to a pair of milk-glass poodles. I'd never liked them either. And the clockworks suspended in a glass bell, and the Hummels—two hydrocephalics at a well. She found these at a yard sale—"The lady didn't even know they were authentic," she'd told me in a letter. After blotting his watery eyes, Daddy gave me a dose of his now-rare sharp looks from the old days when he used to have excitements, and he said, "Do you realize how many human lives and minds have been used up on making this stuff?" (He was really smarter than my mother.)

"It is my house and you have no right to complain. I

—70—

like having things. I think you know they give me pleasure. Any harm in that? You think there is harm in that, don't you?"

His old refrain: "You can't even walk around this place anymore, huh, Alma? *You* think there *is* harm in it, don't you?" What did he want, my sympathy or hers? He'd take what he could get.

My father's friend, Dolby Stevens, short and white-haired, worked as a mailman. Dolby took a month's vacation every year and rode his motorcycle to particular addresses from the zip code book. "Star Route, Golden, Colorado," for example. And then he returned, with photographs. He is not a young man, and riding a motorcycle twelve hours a day into the night is not easy. His joints ache and his teeth hurt, in the cold. He doesn't claim to enjoy his vacations. He claims, instead, that they are hero tests of strength and endurance. Because of these vacations, my father thought Dolby was a saint. My father believed in the open road, in *Reader's Digest* man-against-the-elements stories. Once, while a Marine, he supposedly hit the top of a Test Your Strength gong with a mallet at a carnival. Mother didn't like him to mention it because he was on a date with someone else. Since then he's never succeeded in doing that, or in doing anything else, except intermittently he stops drinking, which he says gets easier and easier.

But there was the trouble, the trouble that had bothered me for years—that Mother could never help him and I could never help him, because he was always supposedly getting better, except for the relapses. He was always being helped, going through another treatment. None of them ever really worked, and we knew this— we knew this as well as he knew this—but having a treatment was the way he kept his distance. And Mother had stopped talking about the fact that it was hopeless; she stopped, I suppose, when his dependency switched, when I was twelve, from her to the treatments. So his progress, which was no progress, was what kept us from him, and kept him sick. And this made me so sick, sad, while they both kept denying it, as if they had both decided I could live with the truth, maybe—they would take their substitutes: Mother, her collectibles, and Daddy, his therapies. Let Alma have the truth, she can take it, she's strong, she doesn't care, maybe. The two of them would argue about nothing, about things, about money.

"You two can go to H-E-double-L," she said with a little mirth. "I don't care." Getting meaner, she put in, "You are a pair of dropouts. Two degenerate peas in a pod. She's going to the finest school, and look at her. What kind of outfit is that?" My mother has always kept on top of the largest portion of her rage. Ninety percent of the emotional mass is always underneath the surface.

She was wearing a yellow-and-maroon Hawaiian print robe at that moment. Half Jean Harlow, half Martha Mitchell.

"Jesus," I said. I wanted to see a fight. I wanted to see them go over it again; in a fight at least they might talk about something real, not things. "What does he always want?" I asked, but it wasn't working. Fred was too easy to destroy, an easy mark. He was already a little scared of me, I admit I liked that. "You come home for a little Christmas, Daddy? Sober up so you could get a little Christmas? Some—" I rubbed my thumb across my fingers, his gesture for money.

He gave me a desperate look. How could I say this?

"Leave your father alone, Alma," Mother said. "We've been sitting here since six waiting for you, and you are diving in, don't even eat a rum ball first."

She yanked my arm out of its socket and I was in the kitchen. "Don't you look at me like that. You have to be nice tonight, you hear that? It is Christmas. I did not raise you nineteen hard years for you to sit there like you don't owe me anything, and insult my husband."

"You were insulting him, Momma," I said.

"I was not," she said.

"He's not your husband, Momma. He's not. I know he doesn't love you. He's just trying to get something out of you. You know he isn't any better."

She'd seized on her idea, grabbed it as I'd seen her grab a Victorian lady's-chair at a junk store. "You owe me something," she said, addressing both of us. Daddy could hear. He was sitting by the open door.

She wouldn't say what it was. I knew what it was. I owed it to her to lie about Fred, to "be nice." I wouldn't. I said, "You want money?"

And then I took out some twenties and threw them on the floor and that was the sacrilege that brought Fred running in and threw them both together.

"Take it," I said loudly. I shoved money into his hands. I stuck some in her lap. This was torture to them. But that's what they were doing to me with their "everything's fine." Everything was fine, except their daughter was crazy.

They wouldn't take it. They both could have killed me.

I wanted to stalk out, but as had always been true in that house, there was nowhere to go. I left anyway. My father came running after me. By the buglights of the park, I tried to talk to him. And he kept insisting he was better, he was better. I said that was crap. He said I was so hard on everybody. I was so hard. He told me to go back in and console my mother.

But he wasn't going back in. I'd called him on this.

Maybe if I left their lives completely, they would run out of things to pretend. They'd get together, Mother would quit hating him. And he would quit hating himself, then he would be better. I felt that it was really I who fouled everything—it was on account of me that everything was fouled. Maybe Daddy could stay on the drug, stay the same every day as water from the tap now. And they could get old together.

"You console her," Fred said.

"I won't," I said. "You are supposed to do that."

"Do it," Fred said. He was angry, an emotion he was bound to disown. I was glad he was angry. I could see he had some energy. There was a strain in his jaw. "Your mother is an incredible woman," he began. "But I really don't like her much now."

That tepid word, "like," gave me a pain, as if someone had struck me. He faded. He was dull. "She is kind of mean to me, really. Always has been. She doesn't need a man. She needs a big statue to stick in her living room. Something lightweight she can carry to bed and prop up. A cast of Jim Garner."

When he started to talk like that, I knew he was going to get drunk. And I wished he'd said instead, "I hate her guts," but I have always been one for extreme solutions. I like things one way or the other. Maybe he could have said, "I know you and she both hate me," and I could have stood it. Or if he had changed the subject entirely—"Dolby's gone to Vancouver, Almy"—there would at least have been the attempt at a connection.

I was supposed to say, "I know Momma is hard on you, Poppa. I love you. Get well." I couldn't. After all, it was all on me. I was the creepy adolescent. Daddy's green Chevrolet was parked on a slant in the drive, poised like an alligator. He had never taught me to drive.

I went back to the house and listened to my mother all night. Whenever we were together, the blame went around the room like a hot potato. Who did I think I was, anyway?

She started with a fresh pot of Maxwell House, and we had a visit. As if nothing were wrong. And I were a stranger. If she was hurt, if she was furious at me for driving Fred out of the house on Christmas, she wouldn't tell me. She would just sit there and chant on and on her version of the family history. The years she'd spent trying to save him, the way she'd wasted her life. I knew the words to the song.

"When we were married, he said he wanted to go into sales, after the Marines, so he started at the Chevrolet place, and everybody liked him, you know, when he got going, he'd sell a blue streak. But then he just couldn't go, for almost two weeks he had me calling him in sick. When you were going to start school, I didn't even know how I was going to get you dressed. And then the Lancaster Homes franchise. That was a good idea."

Fred was puttering around outside in the dark, as if he still lived with her. He rolled up the garden hose. He moved tools and ladders around the carport. About every fifteen minutes, another sound. The clang of the garbage can lid, the click of his cigarette lighter, his stomping on a butt.

". . . He quit that in no time, probably because it was going somewhere. Then he went off on that Jumping Jiminy franchise. The trampoline place. I told him it was just a fad. It was. It was just a fad. Who's going to put hard-earned money into bouncing up and down for hours at a time? Rattling all your organs? I mean, miniature golf, that's a challenge. It's fun. But he wanted this outdoor trampoline franchise like it was going out of style, and it did. I don't know if you remember. It was when you were seven, maybe. You got your puppy for Christmas. . . ."

Mother talked, but she was listening to these masculine noises, and every time he made another she looked at me accusingly, and then she'd go on.

"That fat hound ended up having heart disease, remember, and that Negro boy popped his vertebrae one night when the place was closed. New Year's Eve, in the frost, the boy broke into the Jiminy and cracked his back. Poor boy, really. But what an awful thing to go to court. You know your father and I were always open-minded people, but this idea of an attractive nuisance. We couldn't insure after that. Then it was New Year's straight through to his birthday, he drank. I was going to have another baby. Thank the Lord I lost it. And then the pipes froze. . . ."

About midnight, I could hear him open the car door and tune in some carols on the all-night station. He let the car idle for a very long time before he pulled away.

"He'll be back." Momma lifted her chin, hearing his engine.

"He's going to drink," I said, exactly what I should not have said, and my mother started bawling, her face suddenly looking furrowed like a tiny baby's, and I was crying too, seeing my mother like that.

Lucas had left, finally, and Richard and I got to the cemetery around one-thirty. It is an Orthodox cemetery at the end of an older, middle-class, now Polish neighborhood.

Behind the wire fences were single-family brick houses built around 1950. I could see a couple of yellow dogs. Across the street were two white houses with aluminum siding and billiard-table-green lawns.

Hebrew letters on the stones, then the translations. "My darling Herschel." "Our beloved Hannah, from your children."

The graveyard is humble and out of place, a crowd of half-addressed family love letters, slipped end-up in the grass, while the Jews have moved way uptown, miles from here.

We walked in the old part, past Benjamins and Samuels and Sterlings and Gershons, looking for his father's mother. A very solid woman named Ruth, fat, breasts like whole turkeys. I had seen her several times in photographs. She had the solidity of someone who doesn't have to think—she knew the rules, she knew the consequences. She always fit. I named my baby after her.

"Can you walk back?" Richard asked. We were standing at the end of a long line of late-nineteenth-century white marble stones that had lost their Roman lettering.

Then we were on high ground. On all sides behind us were the plain postwar brick houses, with aluminum laundry trees. Past these backyards, more houses with the same skimpy white trim.

Graveyards remind me of New York. I thought, as I was walking with Richard, of moving to New York after the baby was out. Richard sometimes thought of graduate school there. I wanted to live in a loft and to go to good galleries every day. We usually remembered how comfortable it was not to move to New York, especially now, as we were nearly a family. We always fought whenever we went to the City, over which place to go to first, over where to eat, over what was the best thing at that restaurant, over what we'd come for.

I took in a deep breath of East Baltimore small-time and sour air. Richard was standing at the end of another row of old markers. He asked me if anything was wrong.

Now we had to walk to the freshest grave, Rachel's. But it was no longer new—the summer had passed since we buried her, the orange clay had developed a crust and there were scattered needles of new grass.

I tried to hold Richard, but my belly was too big to get very close. I looked down at my watch: three hours since the phone call from Momma and the shooting pains. No contractions. It wasn't going to happen today.

I had to turn away and go up the thin path to the washroom. I felt her there. Rachel. I could not see her. Her essence was benign, and she almost said, in her Goucher accent that I know concealed another one, "Be careful."

Jews wash their hands when they mourn. In every

cemetery there is a place to wash. I had learned, in the last four months, how to mourn like a Jew. I looked at myself in the washroom mirror and she looked in too, it seemed. There was not compassion, but there was fierce interest. What was it about to emerge from between my legs? It occurred to me that she knew no more than I did. She was in the dark, as much as I was. If only she would come out, tell me what she thinks, now.

When I went back outside to rejoin Richard, there was another stale, hot breeze. He was half a block away. I felt a little gush of water, on my thighs.

Richard asked me, "What do you mean you are leaking?"

"I've leaked before," I said.

"I'm taking you back to the hospital," he said.

They would induce me, I was afraid, if I went back. I didn't want to be induced. I wanted to be struck by lightning first.

"Bloody show?" Richard asked, that phrase from the childbirth book.

"No bloody show, maybe water," I said, as he came a little closer. "I'm not even sure about the dripping. If anything real happens, I'll tell you. It is not going to happen today. I swear it isn't." (It was nothing. I wasn't going anyway. I had too much to do. I wouldn't let it.)

I was silent for a few minutes while I tried to climb into the Triumph. My belly was an old globe. I would lift up my dress and there would be the world. "Let's go to Beagles." It was an ice cream parlor in the Point. I wanted a raspberry sherbet.

"Such an exact request," he said. And then we were driving there. We did not talk about Rachel on the way. We didn't need to.

There is a convention among women to relate the progress of their labors in proud, excited terms, as if every one were unique, as if every story were as strange

—78—

and impossible as an origin myth. "I was bending over to play a shot of pool, and my plug popped out. . . ." "I was at a cocktail party standing next to a surgeon, and he kept saying, 'Slow down, drink more rum and Coke. . . .'" "They told me I was a month off, and I was in, cooking tacos for Bill, when suddenly . . ."

Walking around daily, that September, I felt it a revelation that everyone you meet has taken on his mother in this sudden way, has wreaked havoc on her, swelling, nausea, pain worth tears. Every single human being did something like this without even meaning to.

But then it is actually just mitosis on a grander scale, childbirth. Cells go through this kind of thing every second. I tried to get a little perspective, leapt to the universal. I was too uncomfortable to stay for long periods in my body . . . and it was more and more numb by the minute, anyway. Spirits were everywhere. I was susceptible. The top of Richard's car was down—it always was—and I closed my eyes. I careened down the expressway and I felt closer to him than I ever had, and I was expanding. I was closer to Rachel, closer to becoming thin air.

You know the story, you know that she is leaving now. And I shouldn't really bother, because I'm loose from it, from the whole swarm of the earth. I do not have to listen to her shoe boots on the sidewalk, or to the sounds beginning in the house she's left. I don't have to, you don't have to. But you must care for her, in your awkward way, to have followed her out into the street like this. She's on Bond now, and you can see the Chesapeake in front of her, and the gulls, et cetera. And hear the awful industrial whine of a tank truck delivering flour to the bakery. That establishment is enormous. Inside, huge hoses blow unbleached white into vats, men wear masks, they must, and every day a million rolls rise and brown, but outside, the bakery pretends to be part of the Colonial-style street. The bakery is required to pretend to be human, it's a rule the city made that this neighborhood must appear to remain human, in looks at least; but the roar of the siphon in the truck drowns out the baby's cries, and Richard, now, is awake, is upstairs calling for Alma to get her and nurse her, and where is she, three blocks away, cutting over to the electric wall bank on Broadway.

She goes over by way of Aliceanna, and there is a train running down that street, on a track people forget about, a train in the early morning, right down the middle of a normal street, like something in a dream, and Alma thinks for a minute she's never seen a train use those old tracks, which she'd always taken for trolley tracks. And then the locomotive, as if it needed to announce itself again, makes a howling whistle. And Alma thinks for a second how this might be an omen. Of her being wrong.

But here in the wrong, she is comfortable. And she can feel everything so well, the train and its howl are so vivid, so brilliant, and she is grateful for the sensation. The sensation is something she can use, if she can stand it.

So is the money the little machine on the main avenue spits out at her meanly, a little repeating tongue. She is so vulnerable, she thinks. Hundreds of dollars. Everything is coming to her in wholes, now that she has her senses back.

You still follow.

Now she's walking past two bums on the stone steps of the Maritime Union Hall. And her hip sockets cramp a little after walking so many blocks. At the corner she lights a cigarette and rehearses the list of objects in her bag, her portfolio, her purse. On her first drag, her brain floods with the sweet hint of mortality, just a motif though, nothing serious. She isn't going to die.

And now she's watching herself, and you are watching her

walk, past the few open bars and past the stone plaza where she was going to sit with her friend and their two babies, and she notices how hard sidewalks are, she notices she's never felt them as intensely as she feels them now, they hurt her—she can feel the small bones in the sides of her feet hurting her, as if her feet were going to widen till they split.

She thinks of going back and telling Richard to destroy the note she wrote, the note that said she'd left some of her milk in the refrigerator, and that she would not be coming back. She said she loved him, she trusted him, but she didn't trust herself. And good luck with his venture and with their exquisite daughter.

At the corner of Eastern and Broadway—I know geography so much better now than I did when I was alive, and now I'm nearly never lost, it must be my perspective—she hails a cab to the Amtrak station, throws in her bags, plops herself on the sticky seat, a slightly decomposing dark brown seat, and sits there rolling her ankles, popping her toes inside her boots, thinking of when and how in the future she will ever nap.

And you wonder if you could get the train hurtling down Aliceanna perhaps, or get one of the old men on the steps of the Maritime Union Hall to appear suddenly in front of Alma's yellow cab, causing something like a collage—bum juxtaposed to cab, train ramming into the getaway car. Or you wonder why God just doesn't do that, or why don't I.

It appears more possible from here, I must admit, than it does to her, or than it did to me when I was more concentrated, more caught-up, more alive, as it is called, less diffuse.

But she has to go, that's the sad part of it. She has to, and if she's arbitrarily stopped, she'll still have to leave, even if she sees Richard holding that little cabbage, she will still have to leave, and it almost makes me hurt, the sadness of that.

Three years after the money-in-the-kitchen scene that Christmas, I was home for forty-eight hours. Mother started telling me that a Mrs. Locotus, whom she knew, who had a quilt stand on Highway 40, was hired by a lady in the trailer park to do a maroon and lavender bear-claw pattern quilt for her daughter's marriage. Mother was the go-between. The lady at the park went out and bought the yardage. Polished cotton, two simple colors.

Mother then described to me how extraordinary the simple large lavender shapes, like jagged leaves, would look on a field of maroon, "like the Baptist church carpet." I wanted her to go on with the story.

"Well, she was supposed to be finishing the quilt, the sister-in-law, who had less arthritis, was going to come over to help her do it, the quilting part, you know, that takes up the whole living room. Then old Mrs. Locotus died. Her daughter called me the week of the funeral. The daughter lived in a rancher right next to her family's old white farmhouse. And in the living room was the quilt, straight flat out on a frame, supported by two wooden horses. So that you could walk only around the margins of this king-size maroon and lavender pattern. Around the edges, on the sofas, the farm people were weeping," Mother said, raising her finger. "You'd think they would have taken the frame down, but nobody had the heart. Mrs. Locotus said it had to be finished—that was in her will." She took a sip from her coffee. "Well, it was almost beautiful, darling, but there was one big chartreuse bear claw in one corner. Maroon, lavender, chartreuse." Mother paused. I knew it wouldn't be long before she lost her train. Very often with me she didn't finish sentences: basically, always, she talked to herself. "But, there is the thing," she jumped ahead, waited for me to catch up. "So, don't you see?" she asked.

"No," I said, truthfully.

"Oh, you ought to be able to. You are supposed to be so bright."

"Well," I said, "I don't see. The lady dies and she makes a mess of the quilt pattern before that. Had somebody else finished it for her? Did she run out of material?"

"No. She did it that way on purpose. I guess there's a part I didn't tell you. They told me that the week before she died she went out and bought the green. The cotton."

"Yes," I said.

"The same kind as the other, same type. Except this violent green."

"Yes," I said, trying to glean the point of this. "Well, like I said," my mother went on, "there were to be nine bear claws. And the one in the upper left-hand corner was not lavender, but very grassy green. Now, I was dumb. I asked, as dumb as you, 'Was she losing her eyesight in the end?' The girl looked up at me and said, 'No'm, she had to break the pattern. You don't see it as much when something is more complicated, or in a crazy quilt, one that sets its own rules, but she always broke the pattern.'"

"How could you be so tactful, Mother?" I asked, smart aleck.

"Nobody took any offense," Mother said.

"Nobody?" I asked, aware my mother rarely knew how she was being taken, rarely cared.

"The girl said to me, 'She had to get the devil out, Mrs. Taylor. Make something perfect, you tempt God.' Then she buttoned up.

"Well, the family of daughters and daughters-in-law did the hard part, the quilting. They told me the lady in the trailer park had come to get it, but she wouldn't take Mrs. Locotus's last quilt."

"Why not?" I asked.

"It wasn't what she ordered," she said. "She was right. But there, in that living room, I suddenly had this re-markable feeling. That everything was going to be fine, all fine. If I could just get rid of this feeling that things have to be a certain way, I'd feel so good. Oh, I was in a good humor that whole funeral."

"I see," I said.

"I even felt I could forgive your father. After all, if he were perfect, he'd tempt God, wouldn't he? So I went over a little while after, and the Locotus girls gave it to me for half-price since their mother would have received her part on my account, and now there was really no commission to pay, she was dead. It was beautiful. Eight lavender and one green, like a moon in a night scene—outstanding.

"But the green is a little funny," Mother went on, eating corn chips. It was before dinner. I noticed a fly on the new trellis—New Orleans–style wrought iron be-tween the living area and the kitchen. She'd taken out the kitchen door.

"Well, nothing goes with it," she confessed. "So I tried covering it with a pillow."

"Where is it?" I asked her.

"I'd put it in the spare bedroom, don't you listen?" she asked. "But by summer, that green was so electric I just would hate to walk into the room because it would jump out and get me, so I took it off. And put it up in the back closet." She got up and placed her coffee cup in the sink. She wasn't facing me now. "That green bear claw ate away at me like a little devil and I know it was supposed to be there, but I really—" She halted, and walked out of the room. Then she came back, with the folded thin cotton quilt. There was a moon-and-stars stitching pattern, cast by the careful daughters and daughters-in-law, over the bold bear claws. It was beau-tiful work.

"So you can have it," my mother said. "It's not going

to bother *you*. It will be a relief to me to get it out of the house."

I had the quilt in the living room part of my place, on the wall. And then, when we moved, Richard put it in the trunk of the Triumph, where it had been for weeks and weeks. In the three times I had moved since I got it, I had never thought of throwing it out, and now, with it with us whenever we went anywhere, I felt safer having it, but never got any closer to why I had to have it. It was going to the hospital with us, and it did go, and I still didn't know why it had to be with me. It is ugly, the colors are ugly. And it must be painful, whatever it is that it means. Because no matter how long I have it and how worn it becomes, I still have no idea what it has for a secret. I often tell this story, in my own, not my mother's version, but people always think I must have left something out. And I think I have, but I don't know what.

With Richard, Sunday a week ago, that raspberry sherbet was exquisite. Nothing had ever tasted as good as that sherbet.

Carmen called at five. Richard and I were flat on our backs, looking at the ceiling. I tucked two pillows between my legs and lay on my side, my eyes closed. We had promised each other naps. This was the best we could do.

"Can you come to dinner?" she asked, her voice a little squeaky. "Rick's invited too."

I said yes. The phone's rings had started my heart beating.

"We're having fettuccine with pesto sauce."

"Sure." Rick—Mary Ann called him that or Dick—

sat up and made a face. Did he have to go over there?

Carmen paused on the line, something Mary Ann had to tell her. "Are you feeling okay? This part of the pregnancy is really brutal, isn't it?" she asked.

"I'll live," I said, doubting it. "The anticipation keeps me going." That was a lie. It alone was going to kill me. "Lucas was here this morning, spent most of the weekend."

"Oh, didn't he run off to work? It is Sunday, after all, a beautiful Sunday. He must have gone to work."

"Well, yeah, he went eventually. He kept betting I would go into labor."

"Mary Ann says when are we going to have this baby out?" (Giggles in the background.)

"I hate to go over there," Richard said in a chafing whisper. "I hate—"

"Okay," I said. "We will come, that is, me and the unborn."

Now Richard was having a fit. "I can't have you go out by yourself," he announced. "What if something happens? You can have this baby any minute. . . ."

I told him, while I held my hand over the receiver, that I could easily get in touch with him in time. Carmen could take me to the hospital. I couldn't rest, anyway. I couldn't just sit around waiting anymore, pretending to sleep.

"Going over there makes me sick," Richard said; then he paused. "But I'll have to." We went.

At their house it was the same thing. Take off my watch, watch the pair of them make use of fresh basil. If my belly started to rise up between me and the table I would count off the contractions.

Their decor was precious and eclectic. Rice mats, furniture from China, chintz, I told you. Everything was so clean. Mary Ann was in search of order. She had a black-and-white linoleum floor in the kitchen and hall which she waxed once a week, and the next week she used an acid solution to eat the old wax away, so she could then wax it again. The black-and-white mugs with French on them were lined up on the shelves in a particular sequence.

Carmen and Mary Ann were newlyweds. They would have liked us to notice their nightgowns went with their sheets.

You were always surprised at how small Mary Ann was, how delicate. She had a small mouth and a long, unusual neck, which gave her height she wouldn't otherwise have. Her eyes and her head were large, her shoulders incredibly narrow, her hands a child's. Sometimes you would notice she was shapely, like a woman in a painting, someone done in three-quarters life size. She wore loafers and white socks, uninteresting slacks, usually black. She did not smile easily. Her hair was black, cropped short at the neck, and she worshiped Carmen, there was no other word for it. I had noticed how she watched Carmen talking sometimes, when Carmen was saying nothing important, chattering, but Carmen's presence was practically food to Mary Ann, it was something you could see she needed badly.

The black exterior of the dishwasher gleamed like a mirror. Mary Ann and Carmen liked Richard in their own way. They figured if you had to have a man, best he be a consort. He was charming, handsome, too young to do any lasting harm. And a lot of times, over the important matters, he didn't know what to think. They liked that—certainty was what they found so boring in men. Presumption.

The fresh pasta wound in knots around Mary Ann's forks. The two of them had become very precious cooks. And minimalists. There was something upsetting about their food: there was somehow always too little of it, and it tasted awfully good, but no seconds. The desserts were lavish, pies, sliced thin. Richard was being beguiling. No one but me knew he was primarily entertaining himself.

He found Mary Ann rigid and he thought she made Carmen silly, encouraged Carmen to be childish. I suppose I agreed sometimes with that, but Mary Ann encouraged everything about Carmen, and somehow Carmen had become larger, more broad-shouldered, had developed a louder laugh since she'd moved in with her. In college Carmen hadn't been flamboyant like the rest of us. She was the indelible type, almost Phi Beta Kappa, the I-know-just-why-I'm-here Bennington girl.

In my direction, Mary Ann smiled, or tried to smile, often. She was a little jealous, I knew, of my long friendship with Carmen, a fact I took as a compliment. Sometimes I felt as if she hardly tolerated me, and at others I thought she was trying to impress me, show off how normal and broad-minded she was. Broad-minded enough not to say anything disparaging about my being pregnant, knocked up, stuck with this junior on account of my biology. Occasionally she kidded, in a boy-to-boy way, with Richard, which he found a little funny.

Carmen was the first of my friends to marry. The wedding was in Connecticut, and the families were reasonably happy about it. It was on the deep acres behind her house, near Long Island Sound, all appropriateness and practically English dowdiness. Fabric-covered buttons, large sheer hats. I was dressed in The Big Dress, that year's fashion, a mistake. None of Lucas's friends were asking me to dance, and the dance music was amateur. Carmen had added light hippie touches, but few people even noticed. For 1974, stiff. It was a garden wedding to them, not one in the woods. Her dress was an antique, and they spoke their vows aloud to the minister, along with poems, from memory. Well, I was jealous. Carmen was so adjusted. I was downright grumpy.

After the first course (walnut oil on the salad, it was pointed out), Mary Ann asked Richard if he knew the writer Rhea Sanborn. "She lives in Australia. She had a baby at home, with just her friends. Midwives are practically illegal in Australia." She rolled her eyes up. She thought it was unthinkable that Richard and I were so blasé about having our baby in a hospital. "She had a boy. But she knew what she had to do if it was a boy. She gave him up for adoption."

"Who was the father?" Richard asked, perky.

"A coal miner, some rube, she just went out and got him one night. She and her girlfriend wanted to raise a baby, a baby girl."

"What do you think of that?" Richard asked.

Mary Ann gave him a look. "She's interesting," she said. "She has a point."

Richard took her up on it. His feet changed position. He straightened and picked up one of Mary Ann's cigarettes, a diversion. She smokes Gitanes *avec filtre*.

Maybe half an hour later, Carmen and I ended up in the kitchen, the little wives of the evening. She reached over and put the fan on to blow away the smoke.

"Is the pregnancy all right? Rough now, huh?" she asked.

"This part is pretty empty," I said. "You just want it to be over. Except that Richard is so good to me. That will probably end, though."

"He acts like he loves you so much, but how do you know it is *you*?" Carmen always took things so hard. She had taken my being pregnant hard from the beginning. "How can you stand that? I couldn't stand it, not knowing."

I'd known for several months that I was no longer myself. Recently, I cared very little about the person Alma Taylor. She was a nuisance, anyway. I had got worse than she at everything: moving my body, painting. I was a little angry. I couldn't sleep anymore, either. Something had turned out badly.

I could hear Richard delivering a mild harangue about Tiresias to Mary Ann in the living room. When he fought with her, which he swore he didn't enjoy, she would eventually collapse, and then try to rise above the question. "That's ludicrous!" I heard him say. I was so pregnant, I was thinking. I was about to pop. Listening to Richard take a few more jabs, I missed Carmen's beginning. But I caught her last line.

". . . I'm telling you all this," she finished, "because I'm about six weeks pregnant." She hesitated. "You must know already, don't you. Didn't Lucas tell you?"

"No," I said.

"Well, he said if he told anybody it would be you and Richard. He keeps everything in, don't you think?" She was looking into the middle distance at the grass wallpaper over the sink. "Something corny, well, awful really. I attribute it to Mary Ann. She's made me so free. You remember how I used to be. As hard as a little rosebud, say a month before they bloom?" She waited again. "Like I said, the building is going condo. I wanted to know if he thought it was a good idea for me to take the money and put it in here, the money we saved. I guess I was acting like he was the daddy, a little bit, going to him in person for the money. I don't know why I went."

My belly was tightening. I nodded yes. I gritted my teeth for a little stab, down both my legs.

"It was corny," she said, nearly happy. She shook a packet of Sweet 'n Lo. Their machine was making coffee.

I was thinking, It must be happening.

"I went to bed with him. It was nothing like it used to be. It was like it always should have been, so I cried. I mean, it was not bad. It was just an experiment, you know, having sex with my former husband, was that exploitative? That it was an experiment only? Do you think that was wrong? I would never go back to him, now that Mary Ann is my lover. She needs me. I am so important to her. But I came. It was amazingly good. I felt so ambivalent about it, and then I just plain hated him, and then I found out I was knocked up. Why wasn't he a good lover before? He was marvelous, like a dream.

I just couldn't believe it," she said, her wide lovely palm extended for an answer, from me, for that.

"Maybe it was a fluke," I said.

"Oh no, I think it means something," she said.

Everything in Carmen's life meant something, I forgot. She believed in D. H. Lawrence when she was in college, too, so sex always pointed to something. "I just don't know what, in this case," she said. "I think I might really still love him some, can you believe that? There's this connection between us, there really is. It went on for so long, Alma. At some point it was more than that we were just the couple our parents expected, and Greenwich. I mean it was my life. Seven years. Finally, I get pregnant by the right one, I mean, by my husband. Remember when this happened before? Remember the Charles Circle Clinic? I don't want to go through that again."

I hadn't thought about it for a long time. When Lucas was in law school and Carmen was bored, she slept with an Indian guy from MIT she'd met at a meditation retreat in Vermont. I had to be the boy: take her to the clinic, sit in a carpeted room full of nervous or fed-up looking men and tiny, weepy teenagers from South Boston in tight jeans. It made me almost cry to think about it now: Carmen was a wreck for months afterward. Her body had *done this to her*. Neither of us had ever told Lucas. I was almost crying in Carmen's kitchen: remembering that time made me sad. I was full of the hot water of motherhood.

"Fuck, l don't know," Carmen said. "But going back to him seems grisly. I won't think of it. Do you think he'd pay support, while I raised it? I mean, I'm thinking of moving out on Mary Ann, and getting my own place, and raising it." She was rubbing the tile counter now, again and again with a rag. This was the unsteadier Carmen, the one I was more used to, the one who didn't laugh as loudly. She hadn't drunk her coffee. "But on the other hand, having a baby seems really frightening. Alone, I mean. I don't know how you are brave enough to commit to it, even with Richard, I mean."

"I'm not," I said.

"I don't know if I have those feelings, really, I don't know if I care about having a little cuddly, I mean, I don't think that's your reason. But I don't know what your reason is. With me what's making me think of doing this is just the idea of duty, maybe, something my mother planted in me."

"Mary Ann would be devastated," I said. "It would wipe her out."

"I know, I know. But that's what I thought when I left Lucas—that's what he said would happen. And I'd say he's gotten sloppier, he smokes more, but I would not say he's falling apart. Would you say he's falling apart?"

"He's walking wounded, I think sometimes," I said.

"Men are," Carmen said. "I just think all men are. Especially all the men you see now. I mean, they all have these rigid little rules, and if you don't abide by them, well, they collapse, or they walk out, or it turns out you have to walk out. I don't want to be dependent, it's so deathly to be dependent. Or held up, held up as something so special. I can't take that either."

"Isn't that what Mary Ann is like, it looks to me like she worships you."

"Not really. She calls me on a lot of things. You can't get away with as much with a woman. You can't mystify as much. So you just keep getting closer and closer and closer, until you think you might just dissolve, you have gotten so close. So then you do things like take on fetishes, buy hats. You get exaggerated. I feel exaggerated, swollen."

I had to stand up. I told Carmen I was feeling strange. I wanted to come up with an answer for her, but there was this steely pain under my heart. I went into the bathroom and checked. No bloody show. Back, I told Carmen I was fine.

"I'm getting sick already. Could this be psychological? I can't tell Mary Ann, I just can't, and I'm going to have to."

"Don't go back to Lucas, Carmen, unless—"

"Unless I know what I'm doing? Don't you know me better than that, Alma? I'm not going to hurt him. And I couldn't stay with him, so going back for a time would only hurt him. It gets so complicated. It gets fucking complicated. He knows. He said he wanted me to have a baby. He said, and I quote, 'In the abstract, I want the baby.' Can you believe him? He would love for me to have it. I told him I would have the baby, under my own conditions. I didn't want any pressure. I don't want to raise it with him. I can't stand families. I can't stand them."

Her silky hair was hanging down in her face, and she brushed it upward, as if she were coming up for air. "I thought if I talked to you it would help, I mean, you made the choice, I mean, here you are. We could be close again, couldn't we, take our little babies in strollers over to the park, help each other—"

We could hear Mary Ann in the next room, saying to Richard, "*I'm* avoiding the issue, come on, Kaplan." They were still arguing about home birth. "Men have been trying for centuries to get their hands on this labor stuff—knock 'em out, pull it out."

"Let's not get purple," Richard said.

"Don't you admit obstetrics is just this way to get the power of birth away from women? To deny it to them? Show me how it isn't," she said. "One fact. One." Both of them were almost laughing.

"How did you decide to have this baby?" Carmen asked me. It occurred to me to say that Rachel was dying, but there was no way to prove how that had any connection. So I said, "I don't know." I was feeling very strange, not like talking.

"I can't think of a reason, exactly, either, but I have this faith," Carmen said, "that it will turn out well, somehow. Don't you have that faith, that it will turn out well? That somehow you will be happier?"

"I can't say that," I said.

"That this is your fate, then, something like fate?"

"It isn't," I said.

"Then why are you having the baby?" Carmen asked me.

And then I put my head through the doorway, and said to Richard, calmly, like a lady in a movie, "Call Dr. Felt."

"What, Alma?" Carmen said. "Why did you say that?"

"I'm having it," I said. "Right now. It is going to come."

"Lord, Alma, how do you feel?" she asked. "Here I am badgering you with questions. How do you feel?"

It wasn't that I couldn't speak to her, but I felt like saving my voice. Suddenly Mary Ann was there, stretching her long neck toward me, and she opened her small mouth to say, "Heavens, Carmen, let them go. She's in labor."

Three days after I met her, Richard took Rachel to Hopkins for her CAT scan, and he walked from there to my place, about fourteen blocks down a slope to the Point.

"I know she's got a tumor," he said. "It has gone to her brain."

"Nothing's proved," I told him.

"I know," he said. It was four in the afternoon. I was

supposed to be painting. He got up, fixed rum with crushed ice. He fucked me all night. Too many times, too hard, it was rough, rougher than either of us needed. I didn't have the energy left to get him to stop.

They did find a small tumor at the back and bottom of her brain. When they gave her steroids the pain disappeared, and the family waited for the operation. Richard and I went over to his parents' house again and again. Richard's older sister, Penelope, arrived. She was three years older than I, a psychologist in Boston: skinny, nervous, intimidating, twice divorced. What was this woman the cat dragged in doing at Rachel's holy vigil? She showed up about five times before the end, if you included our wedding, and every time she came she chastised Richard and her father for not feeling enough. Every night, there were tense, indigestible dinners with no salt. Rachel had the maid use dill instead of salt, so the brown and yellow dinners were still flavorless but perfumy and green. Penelope was interested in my accomplishments. What degree did I have? Where did I teach? What were my shows like, my reviews? Every time I answered—that I taught at the Institute, that I sold in Washington, and that there had been more than a few shows, in Texas, in a co-op gallery in New York—she seemed unpleasantly surprised. Being a painter was a kind of joke, wasn't it, weren't painters basically just losers, permanent children? (Well, look at her—she's living with my kid brother.) I was a redneck too; somehow Penelope could see it, underneath Bennington and the MFA and the review in *Art News,* deep underneath my best mandarin-collared missing-a-button silk shirt there was a redneck. What did Richard expect from someone like that?

Mrs. Kaplan was more generally cultured than her daughter or her husband (Mr. Kaplan knew music, but not art). She had bought those prints. She had a Stieglitz photograph over the piano. For even minutes at a time,

I would discover that she regarded me as a working artist and a human being, someone whom, in another frame of mind, she might have even admired. But then, quite suddenly, such electricity would short out. She wouldn't hear my answer to her question about the Steerwall Gallery and my reviews. She was looking at my sloppy bun or listening to Penelope carry on about how her car was stolen on Beacon Hill. I wanted to have a family somehow, to know a nice lady like Mrs. Kaplan, but Richard's family wasn't about to have me. Rachel's feelings toward me were always confusing: disappointment knotted, oddly, with faith and largesse. She knew Richard was in love with me. And usually it seemed she took that for a terrible mistake. But occasionally it was clear that she was familiar with us somehow, with me—she wanted to fix us up, repair us, set us right. Occasionally, when Penelope was out of the room and Richard was gone, she would look at me with this wild hope, hold on to my every word, tell me my clothes were pretty, that she liked my hair, that I was so lucky to be an artist, because artists don't owe anything to anyone. And then she might say something else—that a cousin of hers who was an artist committed suicide in her forties, the daughter of a friend of hers was doing fashion illustration because the money, after all, is in commercial art. Had I ever thought of being a buyer, for a department store? Was Richard losing weight?

And then, of course, none of this mattered. What mattered was that she was going to have an operation on her brain. She stalled, saw a second oncologist, but there was really no choice. All this was playacting. The sociability of the dinners was to pretend that we were all gathered for some reason other than to watch her die. The third time I went over to the Kaplans' with Richard, I joined Penelope in the kitchen to get the chocolates and the cream and to pour the coffee into the little gilt demitasses for after dinner. She stood by the sink, the edge of her palm wedged under the last of her ribs.

"I think I'm getting an ulcer," she blurted to me. "How can they keep pretending that nothing's wrong? You can sense that this is crazy, can't you? I just can't stand it. I can't. All this displacement. It is driving me absolutely crazy."

"I think everybody knows," I said.

"*You* don't know them," she spat back.

I couldn't get in this family and Richard wouldn't let me out of it. So I left.

In December, I went to a residence, a little art colony in West Virginia. They gave me a cabin. It was cold, but I thought I could get away from the Kaplans and the tragedy they were bringing me in on. I felt bad about going, though. I did not want to lose Richard. I did not know why it really mattered, but I did not want to lose him. He visited me the weekend before Rachel had the operation. We drove in some purple mountains one night through the next day, with hoods on our heads—he couldn't get his Triumph top up—and he didn't say anything much to me. We made love in the way people who need each other and know each other well will do, and it was good—sweet, hungry. But he was stranger and stranger to me. I was sure it was going to be over, and then I got a letter on the twentieth, which told me that Rachel had survived the surgery and there were two doctors who would swear that they "got the whole tumor."

Christmas at the colony was low-key—coffee, a tree in the director's living room. It was over swiftly, the way I like it. Every Christmas morning I can remember, I've felt, I can't wait for this to be over—gifts cause so much trouble.

I took a bus back to Baltimore on the twenty-sixth, on gray highways heaped with snow singed by car soot.

I could have visited Rachel but I didn't want to go. I went instead to my place. Richard had been living there while his mother was at Hopkins. I expected the place to be a mess. In the cab, I passed the hospital and then we reached the crest of the hill, and the harbor was there, with mean green water and the gulls. Beyond it, the Proctor & Gamble plant and all the iron ships and tugboats. I wanted to take a little stroll, check everything out—it looked strange to me, as if I had been away far longer. I gave the driver a five and stepped out at the Fells Point Goodwill, a few blocks from the Broadway Market. After a couple of steps, though, I felt queasy, very, very tired, as though I had walked much farther. A woman with a white malamute went by me when I sat down on the stoop of a boarded-up church. The dog's cerulean-blue eyes looked glazed: he should have been happy, it was his kind of weather. He was panting. I was panting, too.

My place was worse than I imagined. Empty pizza boxes with red crusts, cigarettes floating in half-melted Styrofoam cups. Three weeks of sports sections spread over the rug. Bottles of National Bohemian beer, an open copy of *On Death and Dying,* my good blue sheets strewn half on the bed and half off. A new brown stain on the mattress. Rinds and pits in the sink. Some of his hair in the toilet, for Christ's sake.

I sat down and cried. I could not overcome this. His dirty sneakers were there underneath the kitchen table, looking vile. I would have to get rid of him. Most of the other men I'd known had had the good sense to leave by this time. But he was too young: he didn't understand what I really wanted. I ate a bowl of puffed wheat with evaporated milk, all the food in the house except for what was standing in the take-out cartons in the refrigerator. I really wanted him to get out, all the way out of my life, and I supposed I would have to tell him that as soon as he got back. He was just stuck on me like a

child. We weren't even personal with each other anymore, or we were too close, and I was feeling afraid. I
was a woman to him, a promise, a way of delivery, not
myself, but some flesh. I put his stuff into boxes as Doris
Day might do. I cleaned everything with zeal, moved
furniture so the couch made a new odd angle, slanting
away from the table. I piled scrawny jade and spider
plants onto a board and stuck them on top of the refrigerator. I organized my paints. I made about sixteen
trips to the garbage bin in the back alley. When I was
done, there were new things hanging. My place was a
little odd. It required a lot of movement of the eyes. I'd
claimed it back; I was going to keep it.

He came in around nine-thirty, a half hour after visiting hours at Hopkins were over. Nothing was wrong,
everything was okay, let's call up and order some pizza.
I just stared at him and a mild tremor crossed his face.
He looked as if he hadn't been outside in a long time.
He looked positively greenish, as if an essence of the
hospital had got into his veins. After maybe twelve minutes, he realized something was wrong.

"What is it?" he asked.

"We are breaking up," I said.

"Yeah," he said, forcing a laugh.

"We are. I can't take responsibility for you. I can't.
You are sweet, but I really want to be left alone."

"I vahnt to be alone," he said.

"I mean it. You're too young for me," I said. "Too
sloppy, too—"

"What do you want? Some fifty-year-old geezer who
fucks once a year?"

"I mean it."

"You don't know what you mean. You don't know
what you want. You are a fucking arrested-development
case." He stood with his hands on the back of the chair.
I could see his teeth more than usual.

"You are the one who doesn't know who he is," I said.

"Who have you been talking to? Penelope the directed? My mother?" He wasn't as angry now. "Look, I got time. My life span is supposed to be about seventy-five years, right? Why have I got to get everything nailed down in the next ten days?"

"I haven't been talking to anybody. I was just happy at the colony, all by myself, you know?"

"Tell me about it," he said. "Tell me about it."

"It has just gone too far, Richard. We are at different places in our lives, we are. I can't do enough for you. I can't be there for you. I'm not. It isn't really me you think you love, it isn't *myself*. This thing is too alien—your sister, your mother hate me, I don't like them. You must be desperate, to have come up with me for a lover. I can't take it, it is getting to my goddamned constitution."

"Listen to me," Richard said. "I don't want to get mad. I don't like to." His voice was rising in pitch. "What exactly is the problem? Is it that your place was a little messed up? What kind of crap is that? Since when have you been so tight-assed?" His voice lowered. He was beginning to walk around the room. "You really think you can get along without anybody. You think you can do without anything. You just think you can do your crappy little paintings and keep your cunt in a jar somewhere." He was pointing at me and what he said went bang, bang. "Your self-contempt is your own business, honey, and leave my family out of it. You are breaking the rules. You think I can get out of my family? You want my mother just to die and get it over with? Well, I don't throw people away. You throw people away. Your family is goddamned trash and you throw them away, okay, but you do not throw me out. You do not throw me out."

Richard sat down in my low burgundy velvet chair, the only chair in the world that I love. I decided to be reasonable.

"Richard, look, I did a lot of work while I was away. Good stuff. Works on paper. New stuff. I was happy. I was happy all over, from morning to night. I am not a painter because I do anything else so well. I don't do anything else so well. I don't have much choice. I do what I do. This is what I do. You and everything you are up to take too much away from me. I am not exactly selfish, I don't have that much to go around."

"Goddamned narcissist," he said, standing. "Don't you get sick of the whole world being you? Doesn't it get a little tainted toward the edges?"

"Okay," I said. "How am I going to change?"

"You." He came to a full stop, pointing his pretty finger at me. It was dramatic, almost a show. "You are going to fucking bust open if you don't," he said in a whisper like a threat.

"Don't intimidate me," I said. "How exactly has this been so good for me and so giving of you? You sponge off me, you trash my house, you trot me over to your family's apartment so your sister can condescend to me."

"So stand up for yourself, why don't you, what?" He was asking a lot of me, almost more of an argument than I could come up with. Why didn't he just leave? I didn't have that much ammunition.

"I don't need it. I don't need it. I don't need any of it," I said. What would he come back with now? I was going to crack.

"Fuck you. You have no idea what you need," he said. And he left.

T en days later, I took a bus up Broadway to Hopkins. I walked up the nineteenth-century brick balustrades into the portico. Under the dome was a colossus of a marble Christ. The floors inside were wet with suds and pine soap. There were custodians and interns with wispy hair. Their coats were open.

It was too early in the morning. There weren't even any Cokes in the machine yet.

On the surgery ward, the patients behind the open doors were gazing in unison at Sunday morning TV on their separate sets. They all faced the same way, with one arm folded across their breasts, their heads listing on the pillow, while in an orange or green upholstered chair in each corner sat some relative trying to be cheerful.

The room was a private one. The bed faced the door, no TV. Her right arm was placed over the sheet, in a manner common to all the patients. I could not tell, from the doorway, if she was asleep, or sedated, or dead.

That part of the hospital is called a pavilion. It is old, and the floors are black and white like the floors in Fred Astaire movies.

She was startling. Her face was swollen. She had a lavender silk scarf on her head, which was cocked slightly to the left on the pillow, just as Richard would do when he wanted to mock me, as if to say, "What now?" She was so still. I got very close to her to see if it was really the person I knew. It could hardly be her. It hardly was.

Over the built-in bureau was a mirror, the frame stuffed with cards. I opened one with daisies on the outside and inside saw the name. "Dearest Rachel . . ." The body was hers, then. There was an open box of chocolate miniatures, a bottle of Madame Rochas, fruity when I took a whiff. The air on the ward was cold and resolute. The scent of a hospital always means to me that some ugly pain is over, now you can have your life. Seeing her asleep, I was going to sneak out and ask the nurse not to tell her I'd come.

"Richard is eating," I didn't expect her to say. "Sit down. He's coming back in an hour. He went to Jack's

Deli." She lifted her hand to say, There's a chair. Green worn-down Naugahyde. When she raised her bluish lids, I felt a little cheer.

"The room is nice," I said, looking at the distant ceiling.

"I got your postcard," she remembered. "Did you come straight here?"

"I've been back awhile," I said. "From West Virginia."

"Was it warm?"

"It snowed," I said. "It's winter."

"Would you like some juice?" she asked, offering me her own. She was a natural hostess. I was sad to see it on such a diminished scale: the cup with a bent straw that the nurse had given her; the chocolate miniatures someone, probably Penelope, had already ravaged. She pointed to the things on the pedestal tray beside her. "Juice, candy."

I took a pink Jordan almond someone had missed.

"Candy doesn't taste good to me," she offered. "I always loved it so."

It had been almost fifteen days since her operation. She was still on steroids. From what Richard had told me in his letter, she was receiving her radiation therapy now. "I didn't expect to live," she said freshly, almost from nowhere, with the slight lifting of the edge of the lips, constituting a smile.

"It is marvelous," I said, "just marvelous that you are doing well."

"I feel terrible," she said too slowly.

"Can I do anything?" I asked. "Would you like some light? Mrs. Kaplan?" Whenever I am nervous, I hear my sluttish high-pitched Southern voice.

"It doesn't matter," she said. "I'd like to talk here, in the blue."

She was right. The light was good and dim and filmy. I saw her through a blurred field. Her head, which had been shaved, was not completely covered. Gray-yellow stubble, not the light red I was used to, came out of her scalp. The drugs to shrink her tumors made her cheeks puffy, caused her head to seem to float above the sheet, angel-like.

"Have you seen Richard since you've been back?" she asked.

"We've broken up," I said.

"Oh. For the best, don't you think?"

I nodded yes.

"He was getting serious. And it isn't good. He's looking for a job right now. He hasn't found himself yet. He's good at so many things. He's a brilliant boy."

"Yes," I said.

"Exasperating, though," she said. Her tongue was slow to leave the top of her mouth. Her hands lifted themselves half an inch from the white cotton covers—what the drugs had left her of her gestures. "I've never known what to encourage. I guess he needs some kind of steady drive. Something to keep his mind on one thing. I think he will never amount to much at the rate he's going. He's a *luftmensch*. There is a word in English." She waited, then looked at me, a little forlorn. "What did I do wrong?"

"I don't know," I said. "He can be practical. He can take care of himself. He's survived this long. He has plenty of friends." I didn't want to have this conversation with her. Richard's future was far away from mine, at the time.

She nodded. "His father and I aren't exactly like that. We have friends, but not the passion he does, exactly." She reached for the cup with a bent straw, the one she'd offered me. I handed it to her. "He was always bringing someone home, someone a little odd, someone we would never have expected. . . ." She stopped. "I'd like to sit up," she said. "The button is here."

I stood and leaned over to change the pillow, put it sideways to support her. She flopped her head forward and I saw the scar: a purple line of stitches across the base of her skull, a sewn smile on a cloth doll. For a minute she was silent, to overcome the pain of movement. The motor that brought the bed upward made a whine. It was a while before we could talk again.

I wanted a cigarette. I couldn't smoke here. I was trying to think of a way to leave the room. Her presence was so strong. It was as if, in the silence, someone were playing low chords on the piano, over and over, something you could not help but hear, something that altered everything you said, made it sound like the wrong words to the song.

"Do you think he wants to marry you?" she said.

"No, no, we broke it off."

She looked at me. "When will you get married?"

"We won't," I said.

"He needs someone who gives him a little push. Do you think he'll find a wife to do that?"

"We had a little joke once," I said. "I said he ought to have a wife in Pikesville who just asks him every Monday morning, 'Where's the pool? Where's the diamonds?' And he'd have to deliver."

I could see that Rachel didn't get the joke. "Wives do that," she said, moving her head downward slightly, in obvious pain. "He needs someone to set the standards."

"Wives don't do that anymore," I said. "It always backfires, don't you think?" I said. "You lose yourself, don't you think?" I asked.

"Well, there are two of you and the husband is the one," she said, "as it has been. A woman finds herself in her family."

"Yes," I said. I opened up my mouth again, but I paused.

"But that doesn't work out too well either, does it?" Rachel asked, and this surprised me. "Think of the last thing you could think of being, the thing you last conceive of as worthwhile, and that is what your children become, it seems to me. Especially if you ask something of them, require that they are good, or perfect, they always become something perfectly awful, I think." She took a drink from the paper straw. "I think Penelope is crazy," she said. "It must have been the psychology, the studying. She spends all her time with crazy people, has married two terrible men."

"She's all right," I said.

"I shouldn't say anything," she said. She meant, Who are you to be listening. But then she turned and looked at me quite intently. "You can be alone, can't you?" she asked.

At first I didn't know what she meant.

"For you, it isn't terrible, is it, to be alone?" she asked.

"I suppose," I said.

"I think I may have wanted that, once, to have some contact with the world that was less confusing than these contacts where you are physically needed. I wanted to make something, be a designer, something with my hands. It's better, you have more control. It is muddled with children, with a husband. What you mean to them is never very clear—you have said so very many different things to them in a lifetime, nothing is very clear. You are fifty years old and you have no idea what you have meant."

"Yes," I said.

"But if you do a piece of work, a painting, a book, then there is no doubt."

"You hope so," I said. I was quite happy she said this.

"But it isn't the same as having love, being in love, exactly," she said. "Love is more mixed than being alone," she said. "It is so much trouble, really. But it is sweeter, isn't it."

Richard, the trouble, was standing there, his pale arm slanting across the heavy yellow door. The dim blue gloom left the room.

I felt a spike, something that made me doubt that I

could stand. Like a feeling in eighth grade, at the peak of a crush. And he set Rachel off as well—she shimmered.

It crossed my mind that Richard's charm was lost on him when he was by himself. It took me and Rachel to wobble at his entrance and then he too took off. How could he be alive without us?

"Lights," he said. The fluorescent bulb over the mirror staggered for several seconds. I stood up and said I was leaving. I kissed Rachel on her cold swollen cheek, said good-bye, and ran out. He couldn't stop me, or he didn't want to.

The Orleans Viaduct is the name, I know, of the thruway. And the cab is yellow, the driver Filipino. And Alma is alone, on the sticky seat. Being alone is one of the solutions.

Dying was very confusing for me. I said all kinds of things in the hospital, to everybody. And then I just gave up. I had said already so much. There was my body, my illness, my face. That was enough, it was fact. The people I knew could assume the rest. That I was hungry, thirsty, that I needed a kiss—they could assume these things. Generally they did, but they wanted me to speak, to sum it all up, give them something to go on. In a way, I wasn't being cruel, but they all thought I was, except Alma, who seemed willing to accept it. Because my dying was abstract to her, perhaps. Or because she was scared half to death of me. Or perhaps she knew what it was—that I was practicing solitude on account of my death. Toward the end, when she and Richard were reconciled, she would come in to sit, and she would not chatter at me. She knew.

Right now her headache is awful. And when she closes her eyes there's a deep sweet darkness that descends from the top of her brain, meaning sleep. But she keeps on thinking, about her baby Ruth, about me, about Richard. Sometimes when she blinks, her baby's face appears. It's comical: it seems as large as a medicine ball—it floats, it hovers. Ruth's eyes are as sharp, as blue, as cloudless as parts of the Caribbean, or perhaps the Atlantic, even, at certain times of day, in one's memory, in one's memory of a youth from which one is far removed.

There are things so sweet and beautiful about the earth, so willing to be loved, so innocent. Scents: azaleas, bought roses, brine, the lullaby of the sea, and the sting of salt air in the nostrils. I am really only the traces of these sensations, their ruins, the debris of these memories. I am a certain ambiguous concentration which arises and subsides: I liked Alma, I really did like her. But life, particularly the end of it, is very mixed, very impure, and language is one of the first things to fail it, to fail you. You come to an inexpressible point—telling of it can ruin it.

The cab is curving around Mount Royal, now, nearing Pennsylvania Station. It is a grayish day, it has rained. The cabbie presses on the brakes. Alma's excited. She has a ten, he gives her change. Inside, the ceilings are very high. She reads the board announcing the New York trains, and the odor comes from foot-long hot dogs. She buys a ticket, and the marble floor hurts her feet, and the wooden bench hurts her buttocks.

When she sits, she thinks and thinks about me, about how I said that love is very mixed, like a soup—the mixing of kinds, neither all good nor all bad. Women are always trying to make something pure, perfect, little dolls, from clay and paste, and wheat and carrots. We all have the dream of a flawless child, the child who will correct the world. And women are the thresholds, the deliverers, the openings. The boundaries between, the places where one world folds into another, the way you can turn socks inside out, or sleeves.

The times for the trains on the schedule board behind the Negro lady with the microphone are wrong—the Metroliner will be late, and the Patriot, Alma's train, will not be. The lady begins to fix things, telling the hour and the minutes, and Alma eats a yogurt, goes to pee, comes back, waits, tries to close her eyes. When she is standing alone in line, her leather portfolio becomes part of a game for two children who belong to a woman in a red Orlon cardigan in front of her. The children keep peeking around behind it—a boy in OshKoshes, a girl with straight bowl-cut blond hair and break-your-heart cheeks, but Alma's steel. Alma picks up her luggage when the line starts to move again down the rusty stairs toward the metal train on track 16. And she stands, eventually, on the concrete platform.

I think Alma is gritting her teeth. She has a very powerful jaw. Oh, she's going to cry. But the adrenaline begins to flare, to force her heart—she steps forward, she's on the train steps. She's inside.

And, end of story.

But the train won't start. The cars are carpeted in purple and red, and it is dark inside, and the lights flicker, then fade.

And now Richard is sitting at the bleached oak table downstairs in Alma's former house, not too far from the back door, and he's just read Alma's tiny note. Her hand is squarish, but slanted. Not too many letters actually connect. He's thinking that her hand is artistic. When he reads "I won't be back," he has tiny Ruth in his left arm, in a gown that touches her curled-up thumbnail-size feet, and his mind is blank. He thinks of screaming. He thinks of phoning someone; I come to his mind, but he can't phone me. And not Carmen, and not Lucas, who's probably gone up to Philadelphia for his law firm. And he needs someone to sit shivah with him, he decides. He needs someone to drape the mirrors, to rend his shirt. He sits this way for hours, it seems, holding his squirmer.

In her train seat, she can feel she's draining. Lochia. The normal residue of birth, the detritus. She feels, she hopes, she might flow all away, go down the drain, in a sense, cease to think. But she cannot. The train is waiting for minutes and minutes and minutes in the unmeaning dark, and she still cannot keep her eyes closed.

After I ran down the hospital pavilion hall and took an elevator with a red door, and came out at the top of the building instead of the bottom, and stood there at a high window next to a Tom's vending machine, I had to stop. In two minutes, I missed Rachel already. I missed our conversation, about what one might hold dear, about the mixedness of love. But I had to stop thinking of her. Something was wrong with me when I thought of her, and I felt simultaneously a hunger, a hard, sort of tugging hunger, as if I were being yanked from within. I took the elevator down.

I am not skinny, but sometimes I forget to eat. But now I felt a tug I couldn't even account for. I had to eat white, bland food in large amounts. I wanted orange juice, white cheese. I took the bus to a restaurant near Memorial Stadium that I knew had an all-you-can-eat brunch. Potato salad, eggs Benedict, milk, coffee, Danish with cinnamon crust. Butter in little curls. The cigarette after tasted like hell. A tidal wave of nausea lasted three minutes.

Then I knew what it was. Carmen had told me how it felt the day she got the results of her test in Boston years ago. "Like you feel when you take two pills, because you missed a day? Or did you ever take three pills? It's like that, but even worse. And everything tastes different. I don't know. You feel like a different person somehow, a different *you*."

Before me was the plate with the ruins of the mountain of food I'd eaten. The kind of food that I don't even like.

There was an episode of *Route 66* with George Maharis in the early sixties. I was eleven, and I wanted to sleep with George Maharis.

He is roaming around America with that sandy-haired sidekick and he drives up to a rickety house in the mountains of West Virginia. A mob of dark-haired men tumble out and begin to beat him up.

The brilliance of the casting! All of those hillbillies looked just exactly like George Maharis. Or just like his brothers. Actually, they beat the daylights out of their long-lost nephew. It turns out their no-good sister gave him up for adoption at birth—she had had a liaison with the rival family's favorite son: George had the bad blood. In the last five minutes he made peace with his roots and his cousins—a bunch of moronic gruffs.

But the herd of them swarming out of the house, like the Hydra's head, all with gaunt cheeks, all with two days' shadow of black beard. That is family and generation, I thought, with dread. George Maharis was never as handsome to me after that episode. I was going to be eleven forever; reproduction and generation and things of the body in general, like blood from a cat or from me, were sources of revulsion. As far as immortality went, I wanted to grow into somebody excellent and hard and odd like Georgia O'Keeffe; I wanted to grow out of time, out of gender.

Photographs for Ivory with mothers and daughters who look alike, and pictures of twins and triplets seated in the sun, of people who look like their dogs—these are all very scary things.

Until Christmas Eve in the eighth grade, when I was thirteen, I hadn't had my period. I was smug about it. I was going to get off, I hoped and prayed. I had only the afterthought of a figure: breasts that slanted slightly, like ranch-house roofs.

Mother asked me once, when she was going to the drugstore, if I needed Kotex yet. That had been years before. When I said no, she said no more about it. She left me a neat fuchsia box and a belt in the bottom of the linen closet waiting—a do-it-yourself kit. She wasn't that interested in the affair of my adolescence. Neither was I. When a boy grabbed my less-than-ample ass during a slow dance at the Presbyterian church hall, he got very little for his trouble, and I was happy about that too. I just thought it was fake, all men were fake: my mother was fake happy, my father made fake efforts to be a daddy, I was a fake in my shirtdress and patent-leather French heels, in the Presbyterian church hall, waiting to be messed with.

That December, I had been riding my bike all over the highway and to a brick subdivision. I was delivering gifts to five girls I'd known in grammar school—I still exchanged with them out of custom, not friendship. It was damp and warmish. When I got home, Father was there, sitting on the edge of the couch with a cup of eggnog, two-thirds whiskey. Next to him was an aluminum tree with blue balls.

Mother was talking about the park, problems with the septic tank. He gave me a kiss and I smelled that sharp sweet odor, and she told me after a hug to change my blouse, "Honey, you sweat."

I went into the bathroom and there it was, soaking through my cotton pants. Chocolate blood. At first I imagined it must be something else: internal hemorrhage, a slow death from having eaten glass, maybe. Poison. My mother, who fed me now and then, wasn't imaginative enough for that. Besides, by that time, I cooked most of my own meals. Her tone changed from businesslike to a haughty one with my father. "You have to pull yourself together, Fred. You have to." My father said, as usual, "Yes, yes."

I heard the pop of a match. I sat in shock. I did not ever want to leave the bathroom. All my liberty was over. I might as well die. That was my strongest feeling: if I were to die now, I wouldn't have to put up with my body's future. The butterflies in the Walt Disney Kotex movie they showed in the cafeteria to the eighth-grade girls were another fake. The napkins were in the hall closet. How could I stand up?

"Honey, what are you doing in there? Plucking your

eyebrows? Come out. It is Christmas! Your daddy is going to the lodge in a little while."

A little later. "Honey! Daddy is leaving! Come out! Say good-bye!" Honey would wad some toilet paper between her legs and honey would come out and say good-bye. I didn't tell my mother for four months.

"Oh my God," I said under my breath, in the restaurant, reluctant to leave the table after the huge brunch. I was pregnant. When Richard and I had that voracious love in West Virginia. Maybe not. Maybe the power of thought got me pregnant. The notion of conception is phenomenal—there must be a supernatural element. I hold this belief somewhere, with others: that men and women beget through processes more mystical and interesting than ordinary intercourse. I have read that the ovaries receive signals when a woman spends a lot of time with a man. I had spent more time with Richard than with almost anyone else. Even women who haven't had periods for a decade suddenly do if they have the man move in. The fact is attributed to "olfactory cues"— read, spirits. Scents that surround us like haunts, bomb us with memories, cause us to swarm and fuck, and cause birds to fly south, infants to know their mothers.

I paid and left the restaurant. I could entertain the idea until I had a test that assured me it wasn't so. I went to the Rexall and bought it. I'd have to take it in the morning. My period was three weeks late. I had been trying to forget that.

Women get pregnant from strong odors and from swimming pools and from decent orgasms and from divine conception. And a woman in New Zealand had a baby after a hysterectomy and another who lived with her mother and never left the house got pregnant in Ohio. . . .

I guess I was a little heady. I ran to the bus stop in

the cold when I left the drugstore, even though I had no breath. In the morning, I saw it there: a brown-yellow circle in the bottom of the glass vial, a little like a cigarette burn. I decided to have a cup of coffee before I called the abortion clinic. I had never had to do this before. They said they'd see me Thursday. This kind of thing happens every day. Women get pregnant over and over and over. Nothing in nature happens just once, as it does in art.

The Wednesday before the appointment, Richard called at about six. He said it was to say hello. I'd known three days and I hadn't told anybody. Instead, I'd gone and had my hair cut short like Joan of Arc's, and had taken to buttoning my shirts to the neck. I was doing a painting called *Boy*. Richard was past tense. The picture was six-by-four and elaborate. It was really a picture of me from the days when I rode a bicycle and tried to get something from my father. My father's head was in the painting. The back of his head.

"Mother's out of the hospital," he told me. "She was even walking around a little today. She's still wobbling, of course."

I said good.

"I'm coming to see you," he said.

"Don't," I said.

"I'm sorry," he said.

"Don't come," I told him. "Don't come."

"Oh, Almy."

"Don't call me that, Richard," I said, hanging up.

It occurred to me to leave the apartment, but Richard wouldn't really come over, I decided, when he didn't call right back. He had more sense.

I had genuinely forgotten about him when he knocked on the door at about ten. I was absorbed in the mood of the sketch of the painting: it was dark, like an illustration for a story by Kafka. Richard yelled my name through the louvered screen door, my whole name.

"Go away," I said.

"No," he said.

"I'm warning you," I said. "I'm ugly now. I cut all my hair off. I'm bald. I look like a boy."

"So what," he said. "You have to see me."

"I don't have to do anything, go away, you are drunk," I said, unlatching the dead bolt on the door, and then remembering and latching it again. It is a habit I have always had. I do exactly what I *do not mean* to do, when I'm addled.

"Don't throw that bolt," he said. "I have to tell you something. Please, I'll stay ten minutes. I promise. Then I'll leave."

"Go away," I said.

"I'm not going to," he said, kicking the outside door. I let him in. There he was, with his red head of curls, the short dark-auburn beard he'd had the last few months.

"You have so much head," he said, seeing my haircut. "So much head, let me see your ears. Oh boy, your ears are so small and clean, like little animals. I didn't know your ears were so tiny."

"Stay away from me," I said.

"How come you are so beautiful?" he asked. "Did you gain weight or something? What happened to you?"

"What did you have to tell me?" I said, standing stiffly in the door, making sure he could not get by me. He did get by me. Somehow he was in the middle of the room, taking the red hassock by my velvet chair.

"Oh," he said, "I have to see you some more. I'm working down here now. I have a CETA gig, at the Hispanic Center."

"Forget it," I said, not sitting down.

"You look so incredible. You don't look the same. What is it?"

"How is Rachel?" I said. "Really?"

"She'll have some time. They always say they got every little bit, you know, of the tumor, and that's impossible for them to say, arrogant, really. You look so beautiful," he said again, sliding back from the hassock into my favorite seat.

"Christ, can't you take a hint?" I asked him.

"It isn't that I'm here of my own free will," Richard said. "Really, I have tried to stay away, with all my might."

"Okay," I said. "Try harder."

"Are you trying to look plain? Your shirt is buttoned up to the neck. It isn't working. You are looking incredible."

"Shut up about how I look," I said.

"You know the story about Thetis, the mother of Achilles? She's in a cave and she's trying to hide from Peleus, this is before she's made pregnant by him. She's a sea nymph. She can change her shape, to keep Peleus away, so she turns into a sea monster, and a snake, and a huge clam, and a giant cuttlefish who squirts black ink—she covers him with awful stinky, stinky ink—vomit— then she turns into Richard Nixon—"

"She doesn't," I said, about to laugh.

"Yes, she does. But Peleus knows, he knows he has to beget Achilles right here in this clammy cave, that's the Fates, the Fates have already told him, so he has the faith. He keeps it. Ultimately, she succumbs to him, after he has braved all the shit." Richard paused, then decided to go on with the story, to take my part. "What makes her do it?" He shrugged his shoulders, answering himself, "Dunno. I think basically she couldn't take all those changes forever. Her limbs were delicate as an eyelid." He reached up and began to stroke my arm.

"Fucking get out of here," I said again.

"Don't you know our fate, Alma?" he asked.

"I know mine," I said, resolving not to tell him.

"What's that?"

"I'm getting along very well without you. And I will live and so forth happily ever after," I said.

"Well, don't you want to hear about my job?"

I nodded my head, not meaning to. I went over and leaned against the window, in front of my shabby plants, took some brushes out of water and started rubbing them clean.

"I teach the South American wives of merchant marines to speak English, down at the center on Aliceanna. I'm a tutor for the city. Mostly Colombians. It's twelve thousand. I can get some new sneakers."

"Good," I said, speaking to him as if he were a little boy.

"Well," he said, "can we make love now?"

"No, Richard." My voice was heightening. "Get out." He reached up again, this time taking my cheeks in his hands. He was invading. His hands felt strange. I felt a little tender.

"Almy, I love you, you love me," he said sweetly.

"Leave me alone," I said.

"Don't you mean exactly the opposite from what you are saying?" he asked. "Don't you know you love me? You love me, you love me, you love me," he said, tugging at me for a kiss.

I backed away and rammed into a plant on the shelf at the window behind me, knocking off its crispy leaves.

"All right, all right," he said. "Just let me go to the bathroom, then I'll go."

I unfolded one of my arms and pointed to the bathroom door.

Three minutes later he was still in there. I went and put my brushes up. I set the kettle on the stove. Then I heard him say, "Ahh, ouch, ouch."

It was a nice time of early night, warm for January. I had jazz on the radio. Being alone was okay. "What are you doing in there?" I asked. It had been seven minutes.

"Your scissors are bad, your razor is worse," he said.

I pushed on the door. "Let me in, what are you doing? What the hell are you doing?" I thought he might be maiming himself.

"Don't you come in here yet," Richard said. "Don't you come in here yet."

"Let me in or I'll call the cops," I said. "I mean it. You have no right to lock yourself in my bathroom."

"All right, all right," he said, flicking the hook latch. "I'm finished. You can come in. You have no patience."

The bathroom was a little crude. The floor was good tile somebody had painted. The little window faced a courtyard where there were generally a lot of cats. In lumps on the floor, like dead grass, were his curls, his beard, and his rusty sideburns.

"I loved your hair," I said. "I really liked it."

His neck and his jaw were fair and nude. He looked younger, very young. "Well?" he said, a thread of blood coming down from above his ear.

Whatever he said seemed more naked and tentative. I didn't know his face this way. He would be a different lover. My heart was floating into my groin.

"You don't look at all the same," I said. "You really don't. I didn't know you were so ugly. Your chin looks a little weak."

"My mother always said I was handsome," he said.

"Uh-huh," I said.

I couldn't let him go. He looked so strange. It fed the memories of the lovers we used to be, to see his head, even his scalp finally, just for a moment or two, so temporary and gorgeous.

When he was there half an hour more, talking about nothing, I let it out. It was the devil in me. I don't keep secrets well. Besides, maybe it would get him to go away eventually. Not quite in a minute, but over the next few weeks. I knew I was going to grieve on Thursday. Maybe it was a test. He could be with me. He could help me grieve. So I told him.

"You aren't telling the truth," he said.

"Yes I am," I said. We were at the table now, with mugs of instant hot chocolate.

"How long?"

"A little over a month."

"Oh my God," he said.

I knew he'd go now. It was working well.

"It is me?" he asked. "Is it me?" he said. "The father is me."

"Yes," I said to him. I thought the shock meant one thing. It was my last card.

"Woooooooooooooooooh," he said.

I sat back in my squeaky oak chair. "Richard, I am not having it, no matter what you say. I'm having an abortion tomorrow. I have an appointment. You can come with me if you want. You don't want to have a kid. Look, you can hardly take care of yourself. What are you thinking of?"

"We will be a family," he said. "Oh, Alma, I'm so happy."

"I hate families," I said.

"Are you sure you aren't making this up?"

I stood up and went to the medicine chest where I kept the little vial that proved I was pregnant. Why did I keep it? It was a little brown stain, something I had to get rid of.

"What does this mean?" he said, pointing to it on the table.

I showed him the little pamphlet with color pictures.

"You aren't making this up," he said. "I can't believe it."

"Don't," I said, exasperated.

For a moment, he was silent. I had forgotten he was wily. He was getting ready for the performance. I couldn't read anything into his quiet face. Then he started again.

"Abortions are boring," he announced. "Everybody has an abortion. Carmen had an abortion in Boston. Penelope had an abortion."

He wasn't going to get me on that. I was a strong believer in abortion in the abstract.

"Oh, I know, you think I'm going to use some kind of anti-abortion bull, don't you. I'm not. You ought to know me better than that. You have every right to have an abortion, every right in the world. It is just boring—it is eliminating an opportunity—"

I was thinking, What crap. We sat there looking like two punks. It seemed his incredibly short hair had started to curl to meet its new length. We were hideous and pale. A phrenologist could have read Richard's skull from feet away. Finally I said, "I can't have a baby."

"No," he said. "But we will anyway."

"Don't be sentimental," I said. "We don't even get along."

"Oh yes we do," Richard said. "And what difference does that make, that level of things? What has compatibility to do with fate?"

"Lord, you are hokey," I said. "I can't stand you."

"So what?" he said. He took a long gulp of his chocolate. "What is the worst thing about you in the world? The thing you never tell anybody?"

I'm damned, he knew that when he met me. My painting is pleasing but shot through with mediocrity. Everything gets me sick: I have a constitution like a pet turtle from Woolworth's. I have redneck weaknesses by the yard. I pick my nose. I don't like men, really. The trouble with me could fill the room. It usually did.

"Elvis Presley," I said. "Elvis Presley was a blood relative of mine."

"You're kidding," he said, fascinated.

"That's right, deep on my momma's momma's side,

among the ugly cousins, there's Elvis. The name is Smith. The eastern Carolina Smiths."

"Well, do you expect me to puke?"

"You want a baby with Elvis Pelvis blood? Did you know they say he lived on fried banana sandwiches? You know he used to get twelve-year-old girls to whack him off at Graceland? He never bathed? Want these white-trash genes dancing with your fresh Jew line?"

"Don't get racial with me," Richard said. "I'll slap you. Now you are going to shut up."

He looked so substantial, I thought of shoving the chair next to me into his crotch. I was absolutely positive I was going to have the abortion tomorrow. All of this was wholly abstract, like chess.

"I know you are a gnostic," he said. "I know you figure you've been imprisoned in the flesh. I know you figure the only way to get free is to stay pure-pure." He waited a minute, lifted his right finger in a rabbi way. He reminded me of a comedian. "You'd like to be a cake of soap," he said. "Ivory, I guess." His tongue was moving around in his cheek. "But that's only ninety-nine percent pure. I don't think you are going to murder tomorrow, or that you are destroying a potential Einstein, a distant relative, I might add—"

"Myth," I interrupted. "Penelope told me that was a myth." He ignored me.

"And entanglements, that's what you think life is, basically. Entanglements, things that get you down, bring you down."

"Well, in your case." I thought I'd dig something up. "Your mother and you are always talking about what she did wrong, why you are such a wreck. I'm sick of thinking about what parents did wrong. Aren't you? Aren't you sick of it by now? You'll get sick of it." I paused. "You are a *shtunk*, I think your mother put it that way—" I was about to go on.

"And you are a goddamned Kali," he said. He knew I didn't know who Kali was. "The goddess of destruction. Ash is pure. Ash is purely pure. White ash. You'd like to level the world to white ash." He flattened both of his hands on the table, then he turned them palms up. I could have drawn the smooth backs of his pretty hands from memory. He started to talk again. "I know goddamned well everybody is suffering. Everything is suffering. Suffering is the universal fact. Always has been. For the last month, I've been in the constant company of people who are suffering incredibly: you've been to that ward. We are all getting ready to die. I mean, we are dying as we sit here, every breath, we die a little bit. Almost half of your life is over already, Alma. You are already half-dead."

I think he'd switched to Buddhism on me. He knew a lot. I knew he knew a lot. He was young and stupid, but he knew a lot.

"So if you are already dead, what difference does the baby make?" he asked himself. He liked to ask himself questions when he was high. He was my petit Jesus sometimes, knocking out the learned in the temple. "I'll tell you—" He paused. Maybe his argument would collapse. Maybe he didn't have an answer, so I could go to the clinic tomorrow. Then he went on. "I'll tell you something you don't know about," he said. "You think you are the only person in America who wants to get pure. You think you are the only person in America who wants to get loose of it all. You think you are the only person in America with this sore you keep trying to daub over with your paintings. You think you are the only person in America who wants to get loose, loose from that. Well, I'll tell you something, we've all got it. We've all got it. Maybe I'm a little less far along than you, but I've got it." He was looking straight at me. He looked wise. I thought he was fake, but I was afraid he looked wise.

"And you want to fight everything off because you don't want anybody else to see that you are covering up this nasty nasty shit you are, so you keep fighting everybody off. Even the baby. Always me. You know making love to you is like pitched battle half the time? I spend half the time beating down the door, Almy—"

"Richard," I said. "Don't say anything else."

"I want to help you," he said. "And we'll get married and have a baby, and we'll get together and split it— It doesn't *matter* if we can't get along, it doesn't. I'm talking about another level of things."

"No!" I said. His hands were on my shoulders, then he hugged me until my boobs hurt. I had collapsed. Here I was going to listen to him in the abstract, and I had collapsed.

"Don't hug me," I said. "My breasts ache."

"Do you feel bad?" he asked. "You ought to feel a little cathartic, maybe. You feel cathartic?"

"Let go of me," I said.

"Do you want any more talk?" he said.

"Booze," I said.

"Wine," he said. "Don't drink any booze."

"I don't believe you," I said. We were standing, still holding one another. I felt as if I would suffocate from his affection. I actually felt a panic. I had to get out of his hold, somehow. He'd beaten me.

"I know this is a shtick," Richard said. "But I have to have you. I don't know anything about you, really. You are a perfect mystery to me. But I got you now, don't I. I love you."

"Why?" I asked him.

He refused to answer.

"Please, don't squeeze me so hard, my boobs hurt. I told you once already."

"I'll fuck your boobs," he said. I realized he had a hard-on poking me in the belly. I had been feeling it for some time, but had not thought of what it was. In a while we were fucking standing up, and then he put me on the bed and he did it again. I was a pushover by this time.

While we were preening afterward, he said, "Elvis was a hideous kid, Almy. I've seen pictures—like a goon."

"You should see the fiend we got now," I said. I got him a drawing from the dictionary under "fetus": a portrait of the American embryo as a gargoyle.

"Ours is gorgeous," he said, unimpressed. I was entering a dream by way of his crazy reasons. This is the argument I lost. I was losing and losing.

We could not sleep. At one, we were walking to Maria's, where Loretta worked. Nobody we knew would be there. It was Loretta's night off. It was quiet for the Point. It was the same pink nighttime, child hookers in halters and fur coats and beaded braids. A window smashed out in the Greek sailor's clothing store. We walked for a very long time, as if the place were miles away, past pitch-dark streets, windows up close to the sidewalk, framing little renovated dens with ceiling fans and prints on the walls, past the mission and the stevedore's union hall, the theater showing generic triple-X-rated movies, a little Elvis Costello from the radio just audible, the huge tall wharf cats, like real animals, who live on fish offal. We were holding each other up. Sometimes he walked so fast he got me off the ground.

But I already told you. I could not live this happy way, I couldn't. Somebody else would have to do it. Neither could Richard. We started to slip. It was already apparent in the way he forced the language out of his mouth, in the way he pushed me forward and held my elbow as if he intended to crush the bones. He was scared to death. I was scared to death. And then there was this third being between us, this third one to whom our fears were inadmissible.

When we left Carmen's that night, we sped down St. Paul to the Viaduct. It was as if I were on another route, a rockier one. In the middle of a sentence I would have to grasp onto something, to hold Richard's thigh or his shoulder. He did not understand the gravity of my grasp, I do not think. He got to the circular side entrance of Hopkins Hospital at about eleven, and I saw a city rat the size of a raccoon in the stiff green junipers banking the walls of the building. There was a guard who pointed me in the direction of the maternity ward and told Richard where he could park. I already knew where to go, but I let the man lead me anyway. Richard and I parted from each other. It would be at least three minutes before I would see my husband again, which was a profound amount of time: time had got very spacious on the way, full of cracks.

"Lord have mercy, it is you again," Mrs. Morgan said at the desk, to be funny.

"It is for real this time," I heard myself tell her.

"I know," she said.

I grabbed the pillar on the side of the nurse's station: yank, yank, yank bang. The pain was steely. As strong as metal. I looked at the high white clock. What a lie, I thought, that the faces of clocks are so even.

"Just wait this one out," Mrs. Morgan said. "Have you had bloody show?" she asked, not expecting an answer. She seemed to know everything that was happening to me. I decided to love her until Richard got back.

"Dr. Felt has already called. You asked for the birthing room. I'm seeing if it's open."

Richard again, out of breath, holding my overnight bag. He got some folded yellow clothes from her, and we went together into the prep room. He helped me undress: my blue denim thrift-shop dress, my dirty white sandals, tangled on the floor. Richard never picks anything up. His digital watch was crap for timing my contractions and now I had to take mine off. I felt desperate to keep track of the time.

Here it came: a roller coaster. Every peak was a new chance to rip me out of my seat. Mrs. Morgan was wrong. The shock of lightning would have been mild by comparison. I had the sense I was moving somewhere, being chased by the pain. Upward, far up, then I swooped down. Richard said I looked scared. "So don't be scared," he said.

Mrs. Morgan came back. "Nobody's got it yet tonight," she said, "lie back." She slipped on the black blood-pressure cuff. I was wearing that and an enormous bra and pants as big as a pillowcase. It was hardly my body, and here I was feeling it so much.

"When did you eat last?" she said.

"Another one," I said. Richard's hand was cold when he took mine. How could it be this bad early on? My back needed pounding, sledgehammers.

"Don't ask her questions," Richard said in a tone that caused Mrs. Morgan to decide to wait.

It was a rattling wooden roller coaster this time, the kind people cherish in the local amusement park, the old classic sort, until it pitches people out, kills them, and makes the papers. I could feel the clack of my bones rattling. Finally the sheer force receded. I had been somewhere else, but here we were, back in this same moment, in life, so to speak.

"Breathe," Richard said. "You are holding your god-damned breath, Almy."

"I'll be back when she's out of this one," Mrs. Morgan said, and she disappointed me. I wanted her there—she could be my momma. "You'll be fine," she said, spanking my hard belly.

"What do they ask shit questions for?" Richard said, diving in the bag for the copy of *Husband-Coached Childbirth.* "You aren't supposed to pant yet," he said. "This is the easiest part of the labor. You aren't in that stage where you pant. When did you start, anyway? Ten? Tell me, what time did you start?"

"Don't ask any shit questions," I said, trying to bite at the pain with my teeth. But it yanked me right on up and that it had pulled me up there before made no difference. Nothing made any difference. I was on top of difference.

"Gut breaths, honey, nice, low gut breaths," Richard said.

"When was onset?" Mrs. Morgan said as she took the black cuff off my arm. Her hand slunk into me. I was nude now, a gargantua, a piece of paper over me like aluminum foil on a turkey. "Oh my," she said. "It is three centimeters already. You were tight as a tick last night."

"Seven to go, honey," Richard said, cheering my cervix. He had more familiarity with it than I did, after all. He'd found the right paragraph. Maybe he could conduct my labor from right out of the book and I could just go home. "This is it." He looked at me, citing reality. "This is it, Jesus."

On no, I was cranking up again. I stoked up to fight it: pressed hard on the handlebars they give you. I tried hitting the bed with a fist just enough to keep my attention away. And then I pressed Richard's hand.

"Now you have to go with it, honey, you can't fight it like that, it will only make you tense, darling. It will only make you—"

When I gasped inward, out of pure shock, he shut up. I held his hand. This one was interesting. I was yanked up on the coaster right up near the top, and then I veered away. I missed the fiercest pain. Others had been worse.

"Those last night were fakers," Richard said to Mrs. Morgan. "She's had nothing like this before."

When she told me to slide back down onto my back, I saw one of her instruments was an enema bag. "This will feel funny, Alma, some people like it. Then it will feel warm."

A too-hot shower in the dark. Richard held up his hand so I could see that it was streaked with white where I'd held it. "Long, deep breaths, Alma, don't fight, honey," he said. "Come on, honey, a long long long deep one."

"I don't want to hyperventilate," I said, inhaling.

"You go take a shower, dear," she said, clipping my pubic hair. "And when you come out, put this on." She held up a buttonless gown like those that Rachel wore. "The enema will speed you up, and well, you are moving right along." Richard was about to follow me to the bath. My right hand was on the edge of the table. I was just between contractions, but I knew another one was chasing me. In a zoom I kicked open the door. This was the worst roller coaster in the world. It went through time, not space. I got the steel handles in the shower stall. The door closed on Richard. Mrs. Morgan told him I'd be all right alone.

He was outside in the main room on the metal stool calling to me. It was the first time I was alone since this had started. And, oh, I want to tell you that I did not want to be alone. I did not want to be here at all, in the tile room with all the stainless-steel bars meant to help cripples to stand. I yearned so much to be back in the same room with Richard and Mrs. Morgan that the yearning hurt more than the pain. Even Rachel's company would have sufficed, in fact it did suffice, for I felt she was there, at least that the idea of Rachel was there. I was isolated, as she had been, by my awful body.

I could hear Richard outside in the main room, on the metal stool, calling to me. I decided I would have to come out and be Alma Taylor again, whoever that was, and find some poise. I would hide the fact that I needed them so much. Then I had another one, but it was going to be weaker, I could tell. Oh Lord, then it went up higher. I sat down and opened my bowels. *"Richard,"* I screamed, "this feels terrible."

As someone else, I came back out; barefoot and white, I slid my arms in the holes of the hospital gown. I thought I was already dead.

"Almy, you aren't breathing," Richard said. "You aren't breathing the right way. You aren't. Calm down."

I wanted to tell him I had felt Rachel in there, but how could I tell him. He would not understand what I understood, I knew. I was quite alone, in a realm where only ghosts could make gestures to me.

I held onto the muscle in his arm. He was wearing a shower cap and a yellow shirt backward. I told him he looked silly. I was hurting his arm, he said.

The birthing room was yellow, too. After some debate I wasn't a part of, he rolled me there in a wheelchair. It was Rachel's hospital room all over again, except the walls were newer. They were hiding the pipes behind Sheetrock and the oxygen behind a stainless-steel plate in the wall. The curtains had a print of balloons and Ferris wheels. A too-large and too-clean version of a motel room at the beach. There was a TV perched on a platform up near the ceiling. Now I was in bed, taking another climb well in front of the pain. I held the two steel bars on the rails of the bed. It kept jabbing me up, up, up, then I got hit on the head and jabbed in the back. Going down, I gasped, and pressed all my fingers into the bones at the bottom of my spine. The moments near the ground seemed almost to sparkle. I was no longer alive in the ordinary way. I seemed to dwell in the splits between seconds.

There were ghosts spliced between the frames of the normal movie. This was the flip side of life, I decided: if the universe was vibrating, I was spending time in the alternations, at the curves of the waves.

Maybe hours passed, I didn't have a watch. Richard

tried to tack up the quilt. In birthing class they had told us to bring a pleasant picture, not a quilt. But it had to be the devil-out quilt. It had to be. If the purpose of the picture was to give your soul a place to settle while your body writhed, well, I had a lot of soul to settle. He got a handful of pushpins from one of the nurses, but they wouldn't hold, so he threw the whole thing over the TV and it hung there strangely, like an ascending shroud. It could have frightened people, had they not had to worry about keeping me alive.

The bear claws, if you followed them, led you right up to the ceiling. Bear claws are short, fat arrows, you must see. And sometime in the middle of the night, I started to bang my head on the ceiling every single time. When I closed my eyes there were little lightning bolts on my retinas, loud neon flashes—green/azalea/pink. When I came down I'd scream for Richard to press my back, and he would until his hands were blanched, before I would notice he was touching my back at all.

There had been some acceleration, ooooh. Down on the ground with the floor and the bed and the husband, a few white people in white clothes were bobbing around in the dim room. They all were beginning to be phosphorescent. Their clothes were Day-Glo.

Then Dr. Felt came in and went on up the canal. "Four centimeters to go, Alma," he told me. "You will be dilated pretty soon. Keep it up," he said, and I felt his palm on my knee. The flash of the stethoscope around his neck seemed to linger when he moved it.

"Check her blood pressure again," he said to a new little nurse.

Richard had talked to all the nurses, all night long, to the whole parade. They had tried to make contact with me, but what kind of night was this to meet strangers? So they talked to Richard, to see if they were doing something wrong. How do you pronounce her name? Is this her first? Does she like massage? Would she like some painkiller? Their presence, it seemed, was meant to fight my climbing and I prayed they would get out of the way, which they did, they did get out of the way eventually, but then another one would enter.

At every grimace of mine Richard leaned forward like a bird dog and stared with his being. "Long, deep breaths," he'd tell me, "through your nose."

The Velcro scratched and chattered as the nurse fastened the cuff on my arm. She pumped it, let out the air in the ball. "Oh," the new little nurse said. "Oh. I'll get Dr. Felt."

She left in a hurry, as if something had actually happened.

"Oh, they like to think birth is a crisis," Richard said, a little too calmly. "It gives them something fucking to do."

Mrs. Morgan was there, and now her presence slowed down the universe for a minute. I remained in a lull for longer than usual. She calmed me.

"What do you call her?" she asked Richard, as if I were mute.

"Almy," he said, which I was glad that he said. Almy was my private name, the one she deserved.

The ceiling was dissolving, and I kept right on going up. Around Mrs. Morgan was a halo, made of tiny sparkles: green/fuchsia/white. "Rub My Back *This is Killing Me*," Alma Taylor said, in a practically normal voice.

"Almy," Mrs. Morgan said. "Do you have a headache?"

"Breathe, honey," Richard said, his fingers forcing themselves into my spine. "Pant, honey, if you have to."

"Almy," she seemed to say with a whisper this time, "do you have a headache?"

Dr. Felt came in, shuffling quickly, his white clogs slapping the floor. He was short and not very sexy, and his white patent leather clogs were funny to me. His moves speeded up. He jerked off the stethoscope and took my hand. Mrs. Morgan shoved the Velcro cuff back on.

By this time whatever they did with metal left a gleaming trail behind it, something practically beautiful. So there were phosphorescent squiggles all around the room, bands of luminescence, shimmers that held still. The air in the cuff went puff, puff, puff.

"Is this contraction over?" Dr. Felt asked.

I couldn't tell. Yes, it was over. In between I was doing something a little more intense than dreaming. I forgot them entirely when they went away, and went back to my deep, busy dream.

"What is going on?" Richard asked.

"Sit up," Felt said.

He yanked down my eyelid and turned on a light.

In my dream, I was at a midway at the beach and I had got stuck on a perpetual roller coaster. I could see the carnival people milling around below. There were people hawking, and people sick from cotton candy. The pink and yellow neon were ribbon bright, surprising.

They sat my body up. Dr. Felt's manicured little hand passed into his pocket. Did he have some candy for me? Over there, down below, not too far away, the place where they have you bang the hammer and the boing goes up, up, up, like a thermometer. The Test Your Strength booth.

Felt took out a rubber mallet.

"Mag sulfate drip," he said to one of the new little nurses.

He hit me on the knee with that mallet.

My foot kicked his glasses off.

"Mag sulfate drip," he said, with Ben Casey authority. Then he said the amount. "And get a fetal monitor on her. She's hypertonic."

"I thought there wasn't going to be any fetal monitor," Richard said, with his toughest, most daddy voice.

I could swear Felt clicked together the little wooden

—132—

heels of his Dutch-boy shoes. And his little blue surgery cap looked like a Dutch-boy bonnet, with the ears turned up, fashionable and so important. He was the best-dressed ob-gyn in Baltimore, Felt was. There, in my incredible state, I fell for his manicure.

"She's in danger," he told Richard. "We have a problem," he said, as if to clarify. He looked straight at my scared husband, in life, as they call it, while I soared.

You want to hear about the wedding? Near the end, a semi-punk band played "Hava Nagilah," according to a reliable source. My being a pregnant bride was not a general subject of conversation until quite late in the evening. Mrs. Kaplan coerced the rabbi into marrying us, using the threat of her impending death. I was sure she was on my side.

I would never have married or had a baby had it not been for the sheer power of Rachel Kaplan, a power which could be found in Richard on occasion, in the form of a kind of bewildering thereness, when he was making love to me, particularly. Rachel and I had the bond natural enemies develop, and something else too.

I hoped she was on my side: that was the subject, really, of the wedding. It mattered that she gave me her blessing. I've already told you I was poised for anything. I was out on an about-to-break limb—feeling old, pregnant, in my third month, too sleepy for belief. Richard's certainty scared me the most. It was Rachel's wedding, you must understand. She was wedding us with her trust, we thought. She got great pleasure even from the planning of it. We took no pleasure in it.

The hotel was in midtown, near the building where Carmen and Mary Ann were living. The room where the service took place was not large. I got the tiniest hall because I didn't expect anybody to come. Richard and I paid part, as my mother said she wouldn't pay any— she had a thing against Richard. He didn't make money. Then she got into it. She sent $750 and a dress. The dress was really an antique ("Honey, it is worth thousands," she wrote, ". . . and it isn't quite white"). Circa 1924, blouson top, pearls like rice in paisley designs, somewhat campy, just about right. I looked like Theda Bara with the eye makeup and the short hair that I curled. "Beautiful," Loretta called it.

But that $750 meant she could hound me four times a day on the phone. "Who are you inviting? Are you expecting Larry and Jeanine?"—cousins from Virginia, he had money. "What do you mean you're not inviting them? Do you want to invite Jerry and Lucille?"—friends from grammar school. I didn't even remember them for a minute. I hated grammar school. What was a wedding supposed to be? A chance for your sorry life to pass before you.

Penelope insisted on having a party too, for the yahoos and the Jews. It was to be a breakfast before what the caterers insisted upon calling "the affair." I remember Penelope's melon balls—little sallow scoops of cantaloupe flesh. I remember thinking, What will I owe her for this?

"How many are really coming?" Mother asked. "How much money do you need?" She didn't send money. She just wanted to hear me beg.

Richard kept telling me, "Don't worry." When I asked could we put it off, he refused because Rachel was dying.

It was she I invested in. Rachel would achieve some actual joy, somehow, from all of this. And I cared that she was proud of me. The Steerwalls said a buyer named Oppenheimer was telling them the other day how proud Rachel was of her daughter-in-law-to-be, the hick painter Alma Taylor. That gave me a lift for a whole day, that was the kind of state I was in—sans confidence, sans self, sans everything. My mood was broken by my mother's telephone call—"What, do you have no friends at all? I'll send out those invitations to people in Durham who owe me something. I know they won't come. At least they will send presents. Your father says Dolby Stevens the mailman will drive him up. I need an invitation for Dolby, too."

It was a very elaborate trap. The whole thing was a trap. Sixteen times worse than an opening. The blouson fitted over my little fishbowl belly, and the red snapper inside kept quiet the whole time.

Rachel finally betrayed me. At the last minute, she delivered an ultimatum: "Invite these four couples or I will not attend, Richard," she said. She spoke straight into his face. Suddenly, I wasn't there. I felt like crying. Out of the Kaplan clan again.

On the phone, Penelope later said, "What do you expect? It is a ritual. Weddings are institutional torture for everybody."

The sisterhood of the synagogue provided a flashbulb in a satin pillow for Richard to slide under his heel and smash at the right moment. Penelope had another custom in mind. The bride and her sisters walk around the groom three times, stepping on his foot at every revolution, so as to show she won't take any shit from him. It was a Jewish woman's addition, and I appreciated the sentiment, but I looked up at Richard and decided that if I kicked him under the canopy, he would probably fall down. At the back of the hall, before the music of my march, I nixed it, told Penelope no. She rolled her eyes up, and her mouth elevated on the left side. It was the only fight I won that day.

I hadn't spoken to Rachel for the six days before the wedding. Mother had come to town and stuck herself in a motel in Towson, sending messages to everybody who would listen. "Tell Richard to come and get me," she'd call. "How many of his family are really coming? If your Uncle Al doesn't show at the last minute, I'm going to shoot."

There were really about forty-five who showed. The Kaplan contingent and the representatives of the Taylors sat on opposite sides of the aisle, not exactly hostile to one another. Most of them didn't know us well enough or care enough for that. The chairs were wooden with oval backs. Their feet sank in the too-deep, too-green carpet. The whole room was fern green, with threatening flocked wallpaper.

There was chaos, a zoo, afterward. The band was the Dull Beasts—friends of Loretta's. She swore they'd behave, but I hoped they wouldn't. Carmen, who had helped hold up the *huppah* with a sad look on her face because Mary Ann had ultimately not made it, told me in the reception line, "Weddings depress me utterly," and I was sure, by then, of exactly why.

I had done this whole thing because of Rachel. I could have had the baby out of wedlock, as they say, for that matter. But Penelope and Richard had urged me. "Come on, Alma, one last party."

The clique of Rachel's friends surrounded her, knowing they'd been invited late because Richard and I were ingrates and knew no social graces. Their presents had already come. Each box was wrapped with an accusation. Richard had kept his incredible multicolored hair shorter than a hairbrush. In his striped suit, he was a pubescent Danny Kaye.

Whom had I married? He had no idea. He followed the script as if it were his bar mitzvah. He said, "I will," loudly. "Cradle robber," I said to myself.

I'm supposed to be happy, happy, happy, I kept telling myself when the band got started. There was Daddy, his face a wizened Robert Mitchum's, his coat sleeves too short by a mile. He hadn't walked me down the aisle.

That was an amendment of Carmen's and Penelope's that I'd accepted.

I could read the pain in his on-the-wagon face when the drinks first came. Then he had a few and talked to Gina and Loretta. Loretta identified with the wedding. So, secondarily, did Gina. Copycats, the two of them. Then Daddy was dancing with Loretta, her orange perm bouncing, also her fat-apple behind.

Gina's thin little legs still had the ball muscle of a boy, but Daddy didn't notice. My mother had put on the dog. Her dress was floating baby-green lace, like a tablecloth. She called the color lime sherbet.

When I saw him dancing his bop, a modified jitterbug, I felt a little guilty about not having let him give me away. What was he doing here anyway, though? I was losing the things that I had been sure of for years: that Daddy was a bastard, for example. That mothers never have your interests in their hearts. I was doing this for so many other people—the one in me, the demi-man by my side, wan Rachel in her flattering wig.

Richard nudged me in the early course of the evening. "Hey, look at the bride in Brueghel's *Wedding Party*." He took my shoulder. "Brides are always miserable. It is part of the program, in every culture. Brides are miserable."

"Brueghel's bride needs some heroin," I told him.

But neatly, the bride died. In the bathroom, a little after the repast and two drinks. I heard Penelope say through her large fuchsia mouth, "Oh, this is wild, Alma. I can't believe this, this is wild. Stand up."

That part of the floor where I lay was carpeted and a little gritty. I was on my back and the world gushed over me. Not people, but things. The brass handles on the vanity cabinets, the sharp patent-leather heels of Mrs. Kaplan's friends, one of whom said through her nose in a singsong voice that could justify murder, "Oh my God, get a doctor." Her name was Mrs. Lys, and she was the bearer of a tale that sent me, eventually, into a long long funk.

The doctor, another friend of Mrs. Kaplan's, was drunk and pretty amused. I thought the band would have driven his kind away, but there he was in the ladies' room, among all the chiffon and the paper towels (from my angle, their jiggly age-spotted arms, their crimson toenails, their pleated slips).

Then one, who I knew was my mother by the clink-clink of her jewelry, engulfed me with her butter-mint—green netting and tablecloth lace.

"My goodness, that beautiful gown," she said, hearing the sleeve tear out as the doctor propped me up.

"I can't believe it," someone else said. "She didn't drink that much."

"She's pregnant," Mrs. Lys said with that voice.

Now I was in a brown room with a beige lattice print on the curtains, flat on the bed. Above me, poor Richard with his general love, waving smelling salts. He was about to cry. Here was his big new lady, already dead.

"Get some ice, get some ice!" Mother had found someone to order around. A small hotel maid from Peru, whom Richard knew from his job. Mother insisted on undressing me.

"She's just overwhelmed," Rachel Kaplan said in tones almost musical. "She's just overwhelmed," she said, entering my field of vision, pressing a towel to my cheeks.

"*Café, café,*" my mother said, all her Spanish.

"Hush," said Mrs. Kaplan, almost kinder than she really was.

She did nurse me, though, for no good reason. She could have gone back out to her last party. She put a cube of ice in my mouth, and I began to apologize to my mother, to Richard, to Rachel, to my mother, to Richard, to Rachel. I am a great apologizer. This whole story is one big apology, you see.

My mother kept repeating more loudly, "Don't apologize anymore, don't apologize, Almy. It is just silly." Outside, down the elevator, in the party in the green room, the guests slowly went away. I was soothed by Rachel's cool towels and the cool beads of water traveling down my arms in little rivers, across my forehead, seeping into my lashes.

My mother said to someone in an alcove a few feet away, "Oh, what an embarrassment. I wish my Alma had more poise. And she's always apologizing. I wish she would just stop apologizing. She is really a lovely girl. If she just had some—"

And then, a tiny miracle. Inside the hotel room, it started to rain. It was a light wavy rain, but indisputable. Everything continued as before: maids in black and ladies in chiffon, the opening and the closing of doors, but the rain softened everything, kept everything moist and floating. The droplets took off and flowed from the ceiling and swirled all around all of them, like a bath of little tears.

"Oh, it is the pressure of all this happiness," Rachel said to me, and I loved her, and thought she'd brought the muffling rain.

Sometime around eleven, Richard propped me up in the elevator and took me into the lobby. I was wearing a suit. I stood, like a traveler, under a brass wall sconce, against a pillar. Richard left me there because he had to take a piss. Mrs. Lys walked by and did not recognize me, since I was so makeupless and dreary. She was carrying a bouquet she had stolen from the center of her table. She delivered her message, then.

"Morris, I was talking to Rachel Kaplan two days ago, Morris," the voice said. "She told me she did not think this marriage would last. She said the girl was just crazy, Morris."

Morris Lys hiked up his blue suit jacket and stuffed

his hand in his tight pants pocket, and walked on in front, out of the building.

Mrs. Lys followed, the bouquet in its plastic bowl and its florist's sponge, balanced on her palm. I could see the line of her girdle. A yellow mum nodded to me, as if it wanted to agree, and then it got caught in the revolving door.

"She's eclamptic," Dr. Felt told Richard, and I swear he stamped his foot when he said it. "But we have it under control. We just can't keep her in labor forever. The sulfate drip won't cross the placenta. It doesn't get to the baby. She'll be okay. Everything will be okay."

The roller coaster ripped out through the trees every time now. I was far, far, far above the midway. My bones stretched and pulled me half-willing up to the plain night, a rough soft surface, a floor of clouds.

I could see Richard was tired. It was morning, someone mentioned. There was a new nurse at 6:30. And two interns were standing at the foot of my bed with slight halos. A man and a woman. They had names, which they announced to me, electricity scattered up and around their long arms: blue/yellow/green.

I grabbed Richard between the legs. He was up on his haunches on the edge of the bed, digging his fists into my lower back. It was awkward, I remember, that I wanted to have sex with him that minute.

The two interns had sweet and musical voices. In unison they said, "We are here to observe." One of them had a tiny slip of paper and she stood to my left, dabbing it into the puddle of urine beneath me.

I called out so Richard would rub harder. The pressure was on my pubic bone now, would he press on that bone, with something harder than his fist. Would he use a rock, a brick, brass knuckles.

"They are here to manage you," Felt said. I was surprised Felt was still here. I was surprised that his feisty presence had not gone away. He usually stayed for only a second—he had other women in beds down the hall, lots of women, after all. "We have to monitor you very carefully," he went on. "Don't excite her," he told Richard and the others. "She's having visual disturbances." He paused. "Dim the lights."

"Now, Alma." He used a seductive voice. "Your waters haven't broken," he said, "and I'm doing that right now . . . your bag of waters," he said, and I spilled like a kettle.

The thumbs in my arms belonged to the male intern, who said, "You won't feel anything. This is the drip. We're putting a tube in your arm. You may feel a burning, flashes of heat on your skin. It is magnesium sulfate. It is to control—"

Yes, yes, little rushes, little brushfires all around the ground, and more people come to watch the burning midway. Back in my seat, I grabbed the handles and the woman intern, at her elbow. Richard wasn't there.

"May I call you Alma," she said, and in a ripple of absolute fear I called out, "Richard, Richard."

"He's out in the hall a minute," she said. "Someone out there has been asking for him, and I think he needed a little rest, some Coke. He's a good coach." She smiled, which brought everything to a dead halt. I felt perfectly fine. When you are in labor, everything is clear: nothing normal clouds your vision. The woman intern was there, as blond and vivid as Cinderella. Dr. Felt was almost gnomish, half her size. Other people did not exist at all. Mrs. Morgan, however, was roomy and warm and regal. I was seeing the world in high bias, I know, but I was positive I could see their souls.

"You are already eight centimeters along—"

"What is your name?" I asked Cinderella, half-drunk.

"Dr. Hart," she said, and I wanted to tell her how well she made me feel, but instead I saw the black monitor they had strapped to my belly, which was hooked to a graph with a needle. The male intern bent down toward me and his finger pressed into my arm: they were putting me back on the coaster, the two angelic interns. Even so, I was all right. They could take me where they wanted to. "You are doing very well, considering," Dr. Hart said. "The fetal heartbeat is great," she said, showing me the line climbing up and down on a blue graph. I heard the crackle of Richard's cellophane-wrapped feet enter the room. "Lucas is outside," he announced to me. "He's been in the waiting room since six. He got up really early, to take the plane to Philadelphia, and for some reason he called us, and since we weren't home at five in the morning, he figured we'd be here."

I was in a lull. Somehow I could respond to conversation. Richard could see I was listening. So he asked me, for a joke, "Is Lucas the father?" His hand grabbed mine. "I love you, Almy, I really do."

"Get my back," I shouted to him. Conversation over. I went up so fast I could hardly trace it, and now I was coming back and it was just as bad returning, but it felt better. But now I was asleep, hiding, curled in a corner behind the Test Your Strength booth.

Just me, closed up like a cat. So many had shuffled through the midway by this time. It was good to be sleeping, hiding out from all the fires. To touch Richard was just a feat of skin, of comfort. I was somewhere else, happy to be here, down in a cozy lull.

"Nine centimeters," Richard said he'd heard.

I told him I was having whole dreams now. I could go to sleep for a long time in between every one. When I was in them, though, they weren't dreams, they were just the underbelly of day life, something you don't usually notice. Below this life was a seedy burning amusement park my daddy dragged me to. I was awakened for another ascent.

I asked Richard what time it was, and he said it had been two minutes since he'd got back in. "It's just eight-oh-four," he told me.

The minutes had such topography.

The two green angels came near me. Behind them I could see the sharp green, lavender, and maroon quilt. They wanted to tug me back to the coaster, but I'd go on my own. There were so many people here I could please by doing it willingly. They were about to tug, but I went willingly, went on up, strapped myself in.

Richard put his hand on my mouth because I was screaming. He told me to stay calm and to take breaths.

But the breaths would just make it normal. It had to go ahead and kill me. Death by burst bones.

It had to be amazing, if nothing else. There were four pairs of hands on me somehow, and I beat them all back, up through the ceiling and then up through the sky.

Now, ahh, ahh, I was skidding on some lightning.

A wooden stick in my mouth. Richard's two hands flew above me like wings and clamped down on my shoulders. He was stronger than I knew he was. Something under his hands as brittle as crockery, my body.

I was going along so well without it and my breath. I skidded along a blade edge, a very perfect edge, with two precise sides.

Then I saw Richard was crying. The color was spilling through his skin. Beneath his face was Rachel's. He was nearly transparent. Milky white. He said to me, "Almy, don't die. You don't. Do you hear me?"

Dr. Hart said, "Get Felt."

In my other dream, there stood my father about to take up the hammer at the Test Your Strength booth.

The top is one thousand. His score is in the eight hundreds. Not even close. He says, "Shit," and he sits me up in the rear of the booth where I want to curl up like a cat and sleep, and slip into the crack of the corner in another minute.

"I'm going to keep trying for you, honey," he says, and I tell him I want to rest, go to sleep, go to sleep forever, and he says, "Forget that. You got to stay awake to see your father beat it." He waits. He is so handsome. "You don't know your daddy is really a winner in disguise, do you, honey; you don't know that, do you, that's cause you don't know that I can change, honey. I'm a lucky man that way. . . . " When he gets the strength to bang it again, no luck. He collapses. I rub his brow and smell his sweet, sick breath. I lift up his heavy, limp arms. I cannot get him to move.

Now there were hotter fires on my skin, I noticed. I would let the roller coaster go on up this time, without me.

"Almy!" Richard's voice.

"Don't shout at her, for Chrissakes." It was Felt. "We'll have it under control."

Richard was kneading my back as always. I didn't have to ask him anymore. I was not conscious. I was meat.

Next to Felt was someone else with warts, and teeth, and a badge with his photograph. He was a wild boar. He said, "Hello-I'm-Doctor-Shapiro." He leaned over me and I knew he was porcine and nasty. He made me hurt worse. There were only monsters, angels, and Richard by this time. The Boar had come to take my labor. Here he'd come to get it.

"Give me an hour," I said, slurred.

"You are completely dilated," Felt said. "She's completely dilated." He turned to Shapiro. "The head's not down."

"Thirty minutes and a C-section," said the Boar, Shapiro, Felt's superior. "She's too ill. Thirty minutes. Get a heart monitor on her."

"It doesn't make any difference," Richard said. "Honey. It is a baby either way."

"I forgot there was a baby," I said.

"So do me a favor, do a miracle, get the head down. It is a big fat baby, pink and all that," Felt said, a little squeaky.

"I don't cut it," I said. "I take after my daddy."

After we got married, I was numb. We drove in silence up the Interstate to New York. I was beyond apology. Richard kept telling me I was an idiot. I did not dispute him. At the Walt Whitman Rest Area, I went in and washed my face and put new makeup on, and came out with a mask. We had reservations for four days at the Biltmore, near Grand Central Station. The breakfasts were good and we read the paper over them.

Later, when we got back to Baltimore early, nobody mentioned anything about the wedding. I think the Kaplans thought, poor thing, no poise, and I didn't want to bring it up. It was a source of soreness all around. I think my mother told my relatives Alma's just a loser—she has no self-control; but the cruder version was, better a knocked-out bride than an unwed mother.

I want you to realize I was a functioning human being before the assaults of love, family, and pregnancy. I guess it is hard for anybody to believe that. It is hard for me, too. After two days of sullenness in a chilly early April in New York, I was ready for a separation. But that would have been superfluous. I wanted a little sympathy. I had an itch of sentimentality about my wedding, something stupid, left over from Barbie dolls. Nothing about it had been fluffy, or a pleasure. But Richard, who was my *husband*—hard to believe—wasn't going to give me a break.

In fact, of all the cool or difficult times in our affair,

which was not really that long-lived at that point, not quite a year, all told, since I'd met him in the gallery, this time in New York, this time termed the honeymoon, was the most cold so far, the most sad. We couldn't agree on anything—whether to have coffee downstairs or in the room, whether to eat now or not eat or eat later, to see a movie or listen to someone play jazz, to make love or not to.

What I took to be his family's attitude was that the wedding was an endurance test of the bride's brute will. And on that score, I'd surely failed. I think he was afraid my collapse represented a weakness he couldn't handle: I had taken the wedding too seriously, too ponderously. He was afraid that if he looked too closely, he might see the weakness. I was shot full of holes, I had always told him that, but he had refused, on principle, to see it, until now.

So we kept at a distance on sidewalks, in city restaurants. In galleries, we pointed to things, rarely talked. I might have said his reaction was disgust, but disgust is an emotion I have only witnessed for sure in my father, in his revulsion at himself. Finally, on the second night in New York, Richard tried to make love to me while keeping his distance, which was the worst sex I can ever remember. My body was tender from early pregnancy, and bloated, and I did not want to be touched. Richard did not really want to touch me, either, only to enter me in an almost celibate, debased way. It was hard to do, remote, not worth doing.

Perhaps it was our being married that made it so awkward. There was the Bic in the Grapefruit phenomenon—I was getting so large, I mean, so sour and lost in myself, so ready with tears. The second time he tried I just started to sob, it was so awful.

"I'm sorry, I'm sorry," he said, pissed. "Do you *want* to be married to me?" he asked.

"Do you want to be married to me?"

"I asked first," he said. "They say where there's a will there's a way. Did you will this?"

"No way," I said.

"You encourage me so," he said. "I think about you. I think about you all the time. And I don't know what to do with us."

I said I didn't either, this was during double coitus interruptus—I'd quit, he'd quit. It seemed that we would never get it right again.

I was pregnant, obviously so—it squirmed, it swam and kicked, Richard could feel it. And our wedding had been such a bust, such a bad omen. True to form, under pressure, I'd cracked. And Richard didn't really know this about me, that I was given to giving way under certain kinds of pressure. He had taken me for rather grand, rather tough in the face of what are called life situations. And there, in a real one, I was worse than he, so I'd come down—I could feel the falling—several notches in his estimation.

And what were we going to *do*, he kept asking, which meant what kind of permanent job would he find, what kind of meeting point. He had obligations now. I was occupied, literally, by the fish he kept finding when he tried to hold my belly. And he had no one to sturdy him up, I could crack with the worst of them, and if we both kept falling where would we land? We were too brittle to make love—we were two Humpty-Dumpties in a pretty blue bedroom in the renovated Biltmore, me crying, him about to, at three in the morning. And we were running out of money. We had no hope, just this terrible revelation that the people we thought we had married were not really who we were.

And with that mutual abuse and disappointment, our career as husband and wife began. All we had left to occupy us was the soreness we'd caused in each other.

It was our new issue, that even sex could hurt us. Then, it seemed, things took a turn, and we started to come near each other again, to try to take care.

On the third morning, we didn't talk about the miserable night before. We were tired, I guess, of looking it in the face. We started to be sweet to each other, conscious we could cause each other wounds. I don't know if Richard thought this kind of kindness was enough, he probably thought it was a put-up job, something he wouldn't settle for, for long. We decided to leave a day early because we were out of bucks. And this newlywed business was a horror, full of expectations we would never meet. On that, we agreed. We were getting closer over breakfast. Each of us had to do something about this hurt other person. And we seemed to be ready to be objectively kinder after that night and that morning. We didn't hold our general failure against each other as much.

The breakfasts at the Biltmore Under the Clock, as I said, were enormous—sausage, Cream of Wheat, cooked red plums, eggs—and I had become such an aficionado of breakfast. Richard repeated, in several contexts, that he was my *husband*. It was an idée fixe with him. And I was hoping for it to pass somehow. All through the meal and the cups and cups of coffee that followed, we talked not about the distance between us but instead about money, which was the substitute, I guess. Over money, or actually over our lack of it, we could come together. We settled upon the enumeration of ways we could get by on nothing, and of ways we could manage the two thousand I'd saved.

It's a terrible burden to establish an economy, but not as hard as trying to be in love. So we kept vowing to owe nothing, to live on rice and vegetables, to purchase all our needs for the baby at the Veterans Warehouse used-anything department store, or from sales in the paper, or we'd go begging among members of his family for swings and Port-A-Cribs.

The next thing I knew we were out in the street—checked out. We were taking a long walk in our sweaters before we went back to the place where we had parked the Chrysler Mr. Kaplan had lent us for the honeymoon. Richard started talking about something new, which didn't seem economical at all to me. He wanted to buy a house. I had just been swearing to him that we could live without buying anything, really, even after the baby came—everybody we knew, just about, lived that way—and then he said we were surely going to buy a house, it was a great idea.

I told him he must be crazy. He said did I know the houses the city had already renovated at the northern limit of Fells Point? There was a kind of lottery to get one of the slightly smaller ones, the two-bedroom mid-nineteenth-century row houses over a few blocks. The floors were to be sanded, the brick pointed, appliances added, the rotting wooden windows replaced with aluminum storm windows. Would I go for it? The lady who ran the library where he worked had applied for one. And the loans were extremely good, less than nine percent. Low down payments. How about it?

I wasn't angry, I was stumped. He sprang this on me only when I asked—the payment was going to be substantially higher than we had to pay now, in my little apartment. And where would I paint in such a little house? The tiny third bedrooms in those places were being converted to bathrooms. And was there any light?

And he said, Details, details, tax advantages, equity, tax advantages, equity. And he said, This whole business was really interesting, what did I think of him becoming a real estate man?

And I said he was a *luftmensch*.

And he said I could paint in the basement—the buildings had dirt basements, and they were going in and pouring floors.

I asked him if he expected me to work in a basement.

He said there was light, he wasn't kidding. Then he admitted to me that he had already put in for a house. He'd already put our names down. We'd know in twenty days or less. The opportunity was incredible, the down payment five hundred dollars.

So I felt crazy by mid-afternoon when we got to the car. Because he had bad judgment, something a little endearing in a lover, and awful in a husband.

"I don't have bad judgment," Richard said to me just outside the Holland Tunnel—high cliffs stacked up to our right, shingled ramshackle New Jersey Victorians— "I have ideas."

"I'm sorry, it's a bad idea. It'll cost."

"We need a home, Alma, we'll have a family."

"I can't work in a basement, baby, I like where we are," I said emphatically.

"Alma," he said, his voice almost desperate—everything had become grave since we were married. "Listen. Let me *do* this."

And I didn't see where I would have any choice.

When we got home it was raining.

I remained, through mid-pregnancy, a sleepyhead, so the miserable days, when I tried to argue and plan and keep faith with Richard, were only half as long as they might have been. On Tuesdays and Thursdays, I could be found, snoring, on a bench of wooden slats outside the life-drawing classes I taught. After a half-hour break, one of the students would have to come and wake me.

Gina applied to model at the Institute. The people who hired her didn't know she was a boy. There was no problem when they found out, though; at the Institute they are liberal.

One day she came in the door a little late and scurried up to the platform. It gave me a shiver to watch her there, to see the sweet little corners of her skinny shoulders, her cheekbones showing, highlighted with blusher, her blue and gray and pink eyeshadow. She waited so long to disrobe and we were all waiting, three times as long as we would have waited for an ordinary model, three times as long as we would have waited for anyone whose gender contained millions of members. She was not a member of either of the common ones. Her penis, when we saw it, as she lowered her blue jean skirt, seemed to be retracting, collapsing, perhaps traveling back into the cavities of her body, and she had a boy's pointiness to her knees, which were hairless, waxed, as was her groin, but she did not seem a child.

High on her hip she had a butterfly tattoo. And blue-red scars on her belly. And I felt as if I were stealing something, I felt the strange freak delight we were all feeling seeing something so forbidden. It took her longer to show us her chest. Under her black voile shirt she was wearing a black padded bra and her bosoms were squarish shapes of flab. The nipples seemed too small, like a little girl's, those of a girl of nine or ten, whose puberty is slightly premature, whose puberty might be misinterpreted.

People were starting to draw, flipping over their newsprint, making the motions at least. And then you could see them make the motions of starting over, as she positioned herself, a nude, her shrinking genitals growing smaller and smaller as we sat there, it seemed.

And when a girl gasped, Gina said, "Hey, this too," and then she repeated herself and said again, "Hey, this too," and it took us a while to understand what she meant—that this is a body too, perhaps, or take this too, take it, take me. A little later she said, "Hey, what are you looking at?" to a boy who leered and didn't draw, so I had to tell them all to get to work, what was the problem.

But they drew pictures of other people, of a short, scrawny jockey type of man, or pictures of a kind of woman with something indefinite pinned between her legs, and nobody really drew Gina, who was an odalisque, a coquette, a seductress.

Later, Loretta told me the whole thing had been Gina's own idea. Gina asked to come to my class especially. Even though she dresses like a gypsy, Loretta is a little prudish and formal. And sometimes, she tried to disown Gina. Occasionally Loretta seemed to want to live in a suburban house with a dog and two kids and a husband who was a lawyer, and to belong to a church, and to have a life like the one Carmen had once and had abandoned, with Lucas. And at other times it seemed Loretta would settle for far far less, as long as Gina was out of her hair—Loretta seemed to want a lot of different kinds of things.

Rachel's headaches started again as soon as we got back from New York. They were more severe than ever this time: nothing, not even the steroids, would make them go away. They put her in the hospital again, and stripped her, and shaved her, and put designs on her scalp with gentian violet. She looked like a watercolor I once saw of the painted-blue Druid priests. The purple lines were for the radiologists who needed to know where to aim.

She was on the oncology floor, in a new tower of the hospital. All the people on this ward with her were made of gray glass. Some of the patients were radioactive.

They had gleaming lead shields on either side of their beds; they couldn't be touched by anyone.

Children with leukemia trekked up and down the halls, walking T-poles on wheels beside them like pets. From the poles swung bottles of liquid, which flowed into their arms through tubes. Two of these children had pedometers, and they kept records of the laps they did around the floor every day. All of them were bald.

Rachel had a little slit of a window and, as usual, many flowers. Penelope came down from Boston again, and then, after an explosion with her father, she left until three weeks before the funeral. They took Rachel home again, and after a week she was back in the hospital. It was May and then it was almost June.

We drove daily, it seemed, either to the hospital or to the remote suburbs to the Kaplan apartment where Rachel would be. Sometimes she looked like an elongated baby—her cheeks swollen so tight by the medicine. Her eyes were constant: fading, the whites blending into the paler and paler irises. The announcement came that there were tumors in her spine and in a short time it went to her liver.

Often, at home, she would be sitting at the metal-and-formica table in the kitchen, next to the toaster, where it was very warm. There was a maid who did everything for her, something the actual Rachel would never have allowed. In the evening, she would rise up to walk into their enormous formal dining room, but most of the day she sat in the kitchen. Her feet were so swollen that she had to wear moccasins Richard cut open for her on the sides. In the gaps in the shoes, fuzz and threads were exposed. She was never warm, no matter if it reached the eighties outside.

Gradually, it seemed, she spoke less and less to Richard and Mr. Kaplan. She refused to talk to Penelope, on the telephone, first. To the maid she spoke, and to casual friends who visited, and to her doctors, and to the rabbi. But she seemed to have nothing to say to her immediate family. Richard would sit for three or four hours every evening, and she would look at him, and he would take hold of her almost bluish hand which was hard from the swelling, and cool, and she would give him looks but not talk.

"I can't take it," he'd tell me.

"It's not that she's holding back," I told him often, "it's that she has such a burden, so many things to tell."

"She's pissed at us," he said to me.

"She isn't pissed," I said, as if I knew why she held back. "She's overwhelmed, maybe. I mean, what can she say to people with whom she's so close?"

"She'll talk to anybody, anybody else," he said.

"People she doesn't know," I said. We were still in my old apartment when this was going on, and I was beginning to really swell. We'd won the lottery—we were among fourteen who would get in line to bid on the houses the city had almost finished renovating, on a street called Dallas. But that wasn't such an issue, because we were undergoing a credit check, an inspection I was sure I'd never pass. "Rachel knows you too well, she doesn't know where to start," I said.

"She blames us for this happening to her," he said.

"Say she loves you too much to speak," I would say back. Invariably it would be at ten-thirty, over tea on my much-loved oak table. Or it would be three A.M., when neither of us could sleep. We had this conversation over and over.

"It's revenge, she thinks we've all been shits," Richard said.

In the evenings when we gathered for dinner, Mr. Kaplan would carry a stiff metal kitchen chair to the dining table. Then he would help her move, in steps so slow it would be hard sometimes to be sure she was moving at all. First she had to summon the resolve, invent the energy.

After a refusal to speak to the family that had lasted several days, she blurted forth at a Sabbath meal. In a child's voice that startled us all, she said, "I want some," and she pointed to the steamy kugel. It was before the meal was supposed to start, really, before Mr. Kaplan had given the *kiddush*. Penelope, who had flown down when her mother wouldn't talk to her on the phone, gasped involuntarily, but the moment was Rachel's. She took an outrageous scoop of noodle pudding, enough for three or four, and then plopped on huge servings of beef and vegetables—this was a violation of everything in the household she kept. The meat dipped over the side of the plate. It was sloppy. Mr. Kaplan practically shook. He hadn't been able to bless the wine. He hadn't sent the bread down. When would she stop?

Richard got the Jell-O salad and carried it over to his mother. He put some on her second plate and said, "This is good, isn't it, Mother." She nodded a yes, brought his neck down, and brushed his jaw with her mouth. He gave his father the nod to go ahead.

About halfway through supper she sat very still, her shoulders rounded over her still overflowing plate. She looked up at us, about to speak, probably to say how so much good food shouldn't be wasted, but she said nothing. She was sad to be leaving. It was wrenching to be leaving. She started to cry.

It was a long mahogany table and she was at the very end of it. And it seemed that every time we ate there she was smaller and farther away.

And I told Richard that the contact of saying good-bye and good-bye and good-bye over and over was too much. She wanted a whole helping from them, she wanted everything still to be abundant and flowing forth, but she couldn't eat and she couldn't think, and she couldn't love them back. So she was failing. He said that was romantic—there was something they had not done that was at the bottom of this. He really wanted to feel rotten.

The second to last time she spoke to anyone, it was to tell Richard how she wanted to be buried. She told him what music to play, and who should come. At the funeral of many Jewish women, they read a poem from Proverbs that goes: "A woman of valour who can find? / Her price is far above the rubies. / The heart of her husband doth safely trust in her, / And he hath no lack of gain. / She doeth him good and not evil. / All the days of her life. / She seeketh wool and flax, / And worketh willingly with her hands. / She is like the merchant ships; / She bringeth her food from afar. / She riseth also while it is not yet light / And giveth good to her household. / And a portion to her maidens. / She considereth a field and buyeth it; / With the fruit of her hands she planteth a vineyard." Rachel instructed Richard that by no means should anyone read that poem. Richard thought at the time that Rachel considered it just too common. But I said no, it was that she knew she was fifty-six and it is very disappointing to die as she was to die, in the middle of things, no longer able to give good to her household. But that was not really what I felt I knew—it was only the surface of Rachel's silence. Rachel's refusal to speak was something Richard and Penelope felt comfortable torturing everyone with—themselves, especially. "Rachel won't speak to us. Rachel resents us for something." Rachel was being selectively cruel, according to them. What had they done to deserve this? This was not overt, overtly they were dutiful and very very kind, even Penelope was kind. I don't know what Mr. Kaplan thought. I think he felt utter panic at being abandoned, so panic-stricken that he was in a kind of shock, and he always mentioned her coming death as if it were a surprise. I gave up trying to talk about Rachel's death with Richard ultimately. Rachel's silence was easier to talk about than her pain and her death. When he spoke about those things—the fact that she needed morphine, the fact that she could hardly move, that she was going through this awful ritual of removal, a cell-by-cell exit from the order of life, he would start to explode and to cry, so we couldn't talk about that either.

It was easier to think of Richard's mother as a personality than as a dying body. And her silence was something the family clung to, so I stopped trying to tell them what I thought. Who was I to think, anyway, that they let me know. Rachel was just someone I knew casually. Someone I had known less than a year. I didn't feel that way about her, though.

I never felt that way about her.

Mirabile dictu, we passed a credit inspection. Then we were sitting at a settlement, and then we were without much furniture in our tiny house, which the City of Baltimore had sold to us with a very low down payment and a cheap loan. It was a bright place, and the new windows were aluminum storms and the wooden floors had been sanded and sealed. And I had no studio. There was a basement, but I hadn't the energy to set up in there. I wanted to sleep all the time. My ankles, like Rachel's, were bags of water.

Every night, I would tell Richard that I wasn't going to see Rachel the next day, and he would say no, he couldn't go either, it was killing him. And then he would meet me after class at the Institute and we would drive directly to the hospital. There we would stand and talk awkwardly to her, offer her something to sip, help her move from the chair to the bed, or crank the bed up and then down, and give her stories about the world she was no longer entirely in.

Because there were so many things we couldn't say to each other, Richard and I were far apart those last few weeks, in the sense that we had no communion, no conversation, no sex. During this time Rachel was also almost completely silent. Everyone wanted to be worthy of her last words, and she held them back.

Then Penelope, very near the end, directed Mr. Kaplan to put Rachel in a hospice. There was only one in Baltimore, Church Home, the place where Edgar Allen Poe died. It was nearer our new house than Hopkins was. There they would give her more morphine and not give her antibiotics, and not force her to pretend she was struggling to live, and not make her still weaker with radiation. And because Richard insisted on going to see her alone toward the end at that place, I also started going alone. Sometimes, when I walked up to visit her there, I would fantasize that the baby was walking next to me when I was in narrow spaces, in alleys between buildings, in the elevator. I could almost take her hand.

On one day when I went to see her at the hospice, I found Rachel alone, which was rare. She still had many friends who visited her, friends for whom she could summon up a few words and make nodding responses. Richard wouldn't be coming until late in the day—he worked until the Hispanic Center library closed on these days.

Rachel's hair had come back and she had little bangs in front—her hair was as white and curly as strands of lamb's wool. She opened her eyes and closed them again, so I knew she was aware of my presence. Perhaps, I half hoped, she would tell me the secret she had been keeping. Or tell me of what she was dreaming. I wanted to know if she cursed Richard and me. But I was also very afraid to be alone with her.

A nurse came in and said she was supposed to have the bed bath now, would I like to do it since I was here? This is actual, true: I didn't have the courage to bathe Rachel. I was frightened of her body, which was swollen now at the belly, like mine was, with fluids it refused to discard. She was not fecund, she was as abstract and tortured as a north European Madonna, and as pale. When the nurse left the bowl and the sponge, I lifted Rachel's thin hurting arm and was frightened of it. She winced for a minute on account of the pain, or perhaps because it was me touching her, I thought, and then she looked at me so hard, with so much clarity I became transparent. Who was I to touch her?

And then her voice—you must realize how rare it was to hear it, I had not heard it since she asked for more food at the table a month before—so hearing her speak came as a shock. It was as strange as if she had been a painting, a sculpture, one of the Grünewald Madonnas she resembled. If one of those had spoken, it would not have seemed any more unusual, or frightening.

I had moistened her arms and her neck, and I had sat her up slightly and was about to slide her white gown down her arm when she said, "Am I swimming?" The way a girl would say such a thing, and I smiled, because I thought she meant it as a comment, because I was lifting one of her arms and then the other, and now her breasts were dampened, and there were drops of tepid water on her chin. So I smiled and said, "No, uh-uh. I'm bathing you."

"I am swimming," she said. "In the sea, swimming." This was another way of speaking, not a child's. In fact it was ferocious. I prayed she wouldn't say any more.

"Will you dress me? Bring me my scarf?" she said a little later, when I was finally calm, when I was done with her calves and feet. Her feet were split in places from swelling. They needed to be healed and closed. Her request startled me. I asked her why, and she didn't say. So I went to the closet, to one of her blouses, and I approached her—she lay on the bed, a sheet draped across the top of her belly, her breasts and knees and ankles and thighs, bony, pitiful, showing. I so dreaded her wretched body. I thought of a bra, went back for it, but she opened her eyes then from a kind of sleep, a momentary sleep, and saw me approaching with a striped green blouse with a bow, and she became enraged, and in the voice of hers I was most familiar with, one I had not heard for months and months, sternly, she said, loudly, *"No."*

And so I ran back to the closet and tried to hang up the blouse, and it fell twice, and then I realized she was there, uncovered, and so I shuffled over to the bed and tried to replace the drape, and I removed the towel I had used to dry her—I have never bathed anyone in a bed before, I had no idea how to do it, and she seemed completely disgusted with me, and I was disgusted with myself. As disgusted as I am right now, indeed, I haven't even thought about this whole scene until now. This whole burdensome scene, Rachel hating me, dumping those last words of hers upon me, words I never told anybody about—I have no idea what they were about. "No" and "dress me" and "swimming." My heart was pounding and I had to get out of there. I abandoned her.

The next day, it was a Wednesday, she went into a coma.

And the same day, Richard lost his job—the city was running out of Carter money, so he had six weeks, then, no more. Unemployment. We thought about rescinding the purchase of the house, but there was no way we could do it—the city wanted us to be homeowners. Homeowners are stable, no matter if they are broke. This was an awful blow.

The next day the doctor had decided I might have twins. He ordered a sonogram. I had swelled so much in one month, doubled in size. He thought he heard a second heartbeat, and then he decided there must be two. Something new for him to do, I suppose. On Monday, when she was still in a coma, I went with Richard to the hospice. He was sweating for no climatic reason, the place was cool. We were drinking milk in the cafeteria. He didn't have to go in to work until eleven—the Hispanic Center opened late on Mondays. We hadn't

really talked in a while, except to make transactions—
transactions concerning moving, and concerning who
would be with Rachel when, and concerning the blow
of his losing his job. He said he wanted to take care of
me, of us, meaning me and the baby, and I said he was
doing that, I had no idea he would not continue to do
that.

"But it's shit if you have to go back to work, in the
fall, I mean."

"I'll do fine," I said. "Lots of people do it. All the
time." I had been planning to take off in the fall, but
when Richard was laid off I had told the Institute I was
available for work, and they'd said they hadn't found a
substitute. Previously I had told them to offer the sections to Loretta, but they said she had said she didn't
think she'd be around, in Baltimore, in the fall, I didn't
know why. "I still have my courses," I said. "I'll be gone,
what, ten hours a week?"

Richard said he didn't know what job he could get if
he had to be home in the middle of the day four days
a week. He said what did I think if he got a real estate
license.

I said fine.

"It's not you, it isn't you," he said. Visibly panicked.
Why were these things so hard for him and me? Most
of the world has solved these problems. Women have
babies, the babies grow, husbands make a living, house-
holds are economically sound. But there was something
obviously wrong with us. We couldn't handle these things.
They were critical, they made us nervous, they made us
sweat, they made me swell, made the veins in my fingers
bulge. I told Richard I had to go see the baby on a screen.
He said, Fine, go, get a Polaroid. His mother was dying.
He didn't want me to stay.

They greased my belly and passed along a microphone and then I saw her—it seemed to be a her, we
could see no penis—on the TV. A female baby who

scratched her nose and swam, sleeping, in the screen. She was floating and gray, like a ghost. There was something indecent, almost, about peeking in on her before her life properly started. How exquisite that she rubbed her nose on the black-and-white TV. She was big and okay, and even though I could hold two, there was only one who spun in all that room. Her face was folded in and her brow was cast downward as if she were miffed at being disturbed. I thought I might burst I was so happy to see her.

Everything would be fine, if Richard could only see her, see how something so perfect as she was could happen to us, was inside me waiting to be part of us. I was ebullient with the news—they didn't give me the photo, they kept it on file, so I would have to report my findings and tell him everything would be fine, indeed, ideal— she had all her fingers and toes, two eyes, a rosebud mouth. And a cast of utter seriousness about her brow. Around two-thirty, when I was just getting home, Richard called. Rachel had cried at the end—but she had said not a word. Mr. Kaplan said he thought it was a cry of relief. But I don't know if that was true. You are relieved when things are finished, complete. I didn't feel she left things complete. She left them unsettled. It was uncharacteristic. I ran up Dallas, crossed over to Broadway, and climbed the hill to Church Home.

I took the elevator to Rachel's floor and went into the room, but Rachel was no longer in it, although there was something still under the sheets. Her face looked the same as it had when I had left in the morning, but in the three hours I had been away, everything that is invisible, what we cannot see in a face but that we know is in it, was gone. She rushed away like that at the end. And her last word must have been, was, the word "no," addressed to me. Penelope hugged me so hard the baby kicked her.

For exactly five days afterward, during the time of the burial and sitting shivah, I talked to Richard only in the morning, before we went to the various rooms filled with demonstrative people. Most of the bereaved in Richard's father's apartment ate profusely, but Richard ate almost nothing. He did not shave, and he did not look at people directly, and circles widened under his eyes, circles of a greenish blue color. In the morning he would say yes to coffee and eggs and then he would not eat them. I think he was unconsciously fasting, because his body acquired a strange metallic scent that approached the nostrils with a sharp cold edge, which then turned hollow, void, and weary.

I was most in love with him then. Of all the days I knew him, I was most in love with him then.

Penelope came to me with some of Rachel's clothes about two weeks after the funeral. Most were stylish, boxy, structured sewn-together knits from the mid-sixties. A few were swishy suits from later. She gave me an odd hat—a pillbox, velveteen with black beads, a sort of "Call for Philip Morris" hat. It didn't exactly fit. My head was a little large. There were several other extraordinary hats, but I kept the Philip Morris hat.

She told me a story about her mother. During the fall of 1945, Rachel had run away to New York, to Brooklyn, exactly, to live with her Aunt Rose. This was her divorced Aunt Rose, who lived in an apartment building near Ocean Parkway. Who worked at B. Altman's, as a buyer. Of hats. This was Rachel's father's sister, who was always a freethinker, someone with a big reddish face, and a few advanced ideas.

Before she went up to New York, Rachel had been living with the Kaplans, Richard's grandparents, two strict people who disliked her—Ruth Kaplan and her husband, Avram. Richard's father was still in the war, cracking codes.

"Mother wasn't really, you know, happy to live with her in-laws. The Kaplans were severe. Just not forthcoming. You know how my father is, his parents were worse."

Rachel wanted, all Rachel wanted, Penelope went on, was to go to New York, and get a job, and be a salesgirl, work her way up into millinery. Become something, a designer. Rachel loved hats.

I told Penelope I never saw her mother in a hat—only in the scarves she wore to cover her baldness when she was being treated, to cover her scars.

"I still find it hard to imagine," Penelope continued. "That my mother ran away from her own obligations, her own family. But maybe she was angry, at the end, I mean, when she didn't talk about this. You have regrets. People do, don't they. They say to themselves, 'If I had had the foresight to know what I should have known,' they say. I mean, after people get to be a certain age, all they really have to deal with is regret, what they might have said, might have done. . . . " She started to cry and heave a little. I had grown used to Penelope's way of crying. First she paused, like a person waiting for a sneeze. But then her weeping came upon her like a stranger, from an unexpected angle. It was always, then, an ambush, no matter how she had prepared herself.

"It's all right," I said, and I touched her. And she took away her shoulder.

"Yes, well, my grandmother told me this. One afternoon, before Shabbos, Grandma Kaplan comes to Aunt Rose's. At Brighton Beach. She has taken the train up from Baltimore. She has come to fetch my mother. Tell her to come back, to greet her son, who is coming back for good from the war, soon enough. Grandma Kaplan thought this was an awful thing, the way my mother ran off, you have to understand. I mean it was *out of her vocabulary,* if you know what I mean. For most of the Kaplans, Mother's running off was a permanent scandal. And Grandma Kaplan comes to Aunt Rose the free-thinker's apartment in Brighton Beach and Aunt Rose lets her in reluctantly. Grandma refuses to leave until Rachel's come home from work. Finally Rachel's home, and she finds her mother-in-law sitting in her room in the dark, and she won't move, she's not going anywhere, night has fallen. Friday night. And she's not going any-where until my mother agrees to come back to Balti-more. Well, my mother didn't sleep all night. And then she snuck out. Went to walk on the beach. She was gone a long time. And Aunt Rose was mum about it when Grandma Kaplan got up. . . . " Penelope waited, as if the story were coming to her in short, separate transmis-sions. She wiped her eyes.

She continued, "Well, you have to *imagine it,* my Aunt Rose, you know, wearing some kind of kimono, and gobs of makeup, red, hennaed hair, and Grandma Kaplan, with these black tie-up shoes, this *frum* woman, that's what my mother always called her, *frum.* The kind of woman who says 'God forbid' all day long, 'God forbid you should breathe,' you know the type." Penelope was almost brightening now.

"And then?" I asked.

"I don't know. The family never talked about it. Grandma and mother fought. Mother ran into the ocean, maybe? Grandma ripped her scarf off. A Liberty silk scarf my mother said she had saved for. Part of a nautical outfit, pleated skirt, that kind of thing. Well, Grandma tore the scarf. Split it. I don't know if this was an accident or not, or was it some shivah kind of gesture. It wasn't a typical thing for her to do, she was a decent woman, really, huge when she was older, fat hanging off her arms, you know, *there*." Penelope took one open hand to show me the truth, what she meant by "there." Something apparent. "Now Father, my father, had been in port in Norfolk three months before. And my mother was, well, Grandma Kaplan knew. But somehow Mother didn't know."

"What?" I asked, though I knew.

"That mother was pregnant with me. Grandma Kaplan said to Mother, 'I've come to bring home my grandchild.' And my mother went. She knew deep down, she agreed. She went back to Baltimore. But before she did she ran into the ocean, I think. And Grandma had to stand and scream for her.

"Now Aunt Rose was the kind of woman who knew doctors, who knew her way around. Nobody ever *said* this to me, understand. But Mother could have stayed in Brooklyn, could have had it taken care of, if you know what I mean. But Mother went back. Maybe she was in shock. Some of the Kaplans never ever forgave her. And she was never a milliner, or a buyer, or anybody with a profession at all. She had us, she had her living room and her husband. It's very sad, really, something very sad about the simplicity of it. That she got to choose only once. When she was not quite twenty."

I found I was holding Penelope's hands, which were trembling out of rhythm with her intermittent sobs. "People like us, doesn't it seem"—this was the only time Penelope had put herself and myself in the same category—"we have to make some essential choice every six weeks or so, doesn't it seem?" she said.

And I wondered what was irrevocable and realized I really wished more things were. I saw my life backward for a moment, and I was grateful for the givens, for my big belly, one far too big, by then, to do anything about.

My labor would never end.

Almy, not much longer. I'll help you. My husband's voice.

The minutes were very dry now for a while and slow. I wasn't moving. I was at a low burn. In the dark everything was glowing. Somebody said they could get me some painkillers and Richard said, *She doesn't get any painkillers, I'll hear about it later if she gets any painkillers.*

I was sleeping near a fire at the Test Your Strength booth. Daddy had passed out too, I told you. I couldn't wake him. And I had so very little strength left, just a little smidgen, a speck, then I would be over and done with. Alma wouldn't do anything heroic, it would hurt too much.

Then they got me to the roller coaster, but the coaster went down into the dark, down into a tunnel. I was so heavy barreling down, forward, down, what a nice and grave feeling. I pulled up my knees so that I could land on my bum. Here I was so heavy, lead in the bed.

Some of the angels were ejaculating. The line on the graph went agggggggggghhhhhhhh agggggggggghhhhhhhh, as the needle scraped up past the blue lines.

There was a hiatus: the line dropped off like a cliff.

Then another tunnel ride. Down, down again, now level, now down, down, centrifugal weight, like the weight you feel on the spinner ride at the midway, the Round-Up, which begins to glow like a neon ring when it spins and you become so heavy you cannot even lift your legs: 20 g's. I could fold my legs but it was my center that was heavy as the iron plates of barbells. The speed made me so heavy.

My knees were starting to bleed where my nails pressed into them. Who was doing that? I conked between the convulsions. Richard was whispering with energy: push-push-push-push, clapping his hands like a baby. It was a party; Richard and the angels were having a party.

Rock down, down. Rock down, down. In between I slept, or died. Even in my dream I was sleeping.

Then Felt came in.

"Time's up," he said.

I stopped. Everybody stopped.

"The head is coming down," he said. "I'll be back in a minute. We're taking her to the delivery room. It will be born in ten minutes."

"Why did he stop everything?" I asked, perfectly well, perfectly alive. The party had taken its own course, somehow.

The interns had something for Richard to sign.

Felt and the Boar were going to take my labor, finally. But I kept barreling on down, so far I was at the ripe core of the earth, hot, red, dark. Four of them came and slid me from the labor bed onto a hard table. The table was rolling across the shining linoleum with my body on it. I was beside myself, literally, somewhere else. This had all become, suddenly, something of theirs. The time I was in was roiling, infinite. Felt explained to Richard that going on any longer, now that the head was crowning, was just unnecessary.

I saw. They were in the place where there was a cause for things, where things had a plot. My time was too roomy for plot. Richard was nodding, holding the clipboard on the male intern's back, and then two nurses pulled him away. The cause for that was the anesthesiologist, who refused to have Richard in the room.

I yelled good-bye to him and my hand flopped over the side of the table.

Now they rolled me into the equipment room in a gymnasium. There were straps on the ceiling, tables, stainless steel boxes on tall wheels. I convulsed downward again into a place where it grew hotter and hotter, and more liquid. It was no longer any trouble to go there. I did it involuntarily and with pleasure. I was near a lodestone, a huge magnet. But the rest of me was beside myself, I told you, and that part thought it best to hide: here came the anesthesiologist, yanking me up into a ball, forcing my knees to touch my chin.

And then for a long, sagging moment, all the concentration of feeling and energy and moment evaporated. I was a bust: two breasts, two hands, a brain. The rest was dead. Two legs, suspended by leather straps in the open air. The table had fallen away.

I had the sense to leave my body—Richard, who had returned, was very near it. Felt, enjoying himself, hung on in my inner thighs.

For a long time I stayed in the realm of presences. Rachel was there, pushing everyone else out of the way. But she didn't seem angry; she seemed curious. As curious as I was to see how this new one coming would fit into the world. I might have merged with her, or changed places: these things were possible.

There was a circular mirror above me and in it I could see a chaotic red and purple storm. It was more than I could be, this storm. Some metal was flashing like a little dotted line. Felt, with zest, was cutting me open with shears. He took up the forceps.

It must be the muck at the beginning of the world. Blackish blood, and then a blue orb emerging, forcing its way out, forming arms and legs and then they had the world in a napkin.

When I saw them carrying her toward my bust, I also felt Rachel take her leave, and two new steel bright eyes looked at me. I had attention again for the first time in a long time; I had consciousness. I asked the world where she had been, and she asked me if I couldn't keep a secret.

Then Felt held up a skirt of blood which he said was healthy and beautiful. There, wide open to the world, I was immaculate.

Her hair had black blood in it, mud of me. She was not crying; she was looking out. It looked as if nothing were wrong, but everything was. We were apart.

Richard was holding her whole doll body and my hand. I was out of the gymnasium and they took her away. The nurse told Dr. Felt that she thought it was a nine, no, the score was ten: the blue was gone from the fingers in less than thirty seconds. When she was good and born and out, she was red. Richard said, "Did you hear that?"

Then I was in another room where I lay on a table and they told me to void. Then they gave me phenobarbital. Maybe the lightning had been a seizure, I saw.

Nevertheless, they kept me there forever, telling me now and then to void, void, void, and then Mrs. Morgan came and felt the top of my belly, and as she pressed it forward I sank down. "I have to find the fundus," she told me. "You have to void."

Richard couldn't come into this room. This was a room where many women lie between suspended curtains and ask for their babies back. I asked if I could please have mine. Could I ever see her again, and they said, She'll be in your room when you get there; you can go there if you will void.

Then one of the interns came in, the lady Dr. Cinderella, and said, "Get her out of here. Dr. Felt said to put her in the dark."

I could move my legs now. Another bedpan.

"Void," Mrs. Morgan said.

Then I was in a hall, falling asleep.

"Okay, you can see her," the nursery nurse said, and they handed her to me there. When I took her hand, she grabbed my finger. She had a red stain on her cheek, had they seen she had a mark?

I named her Ruth.

What would my mother say about the mark?

Richard appeared in street clothes with wet hair. He had already been home, eaten breakfast with Lucas, and called his father and my mother and announced it to several other people who started telling everyone else, so Loretta, and Carmen, and Mary Ann, and the people from Maria's and from the Institute could all come down to Hopkins and see the world in a nursery.

Loretta was already at the hospital, Richard told me, and Gina was here, being prepped this morning. Wednesday when she woke up, she would be a girl, new at twenty-seven, like Sleeping Beauty.

"It's nice outside," Richard said. "It is a beautiful day." I didn't want to hear anything about the outside. I wanted Ruth to sleep with me. Then they came and took her away again. She needed a test on her foot. She was a huge strong baby who weighed more than nine pounds, but they put her in the intensive nursery because her mother was eclamptic.

"The nurse said some systems just get overwhelmed," Richard said, and in her absence I blessed Ruth. I took a vow that she would never be overwhelmed, never have any snags in her strength.

When I dropped off to sleep, all I could see were her two violet eyes. I slept until almost dark.

No longer entirely asleep, I was in my own hospital room. It was a dark double room but I was the only person in it. There were curtains hanging over the windows. Outside, the sky was the color of Ruth's eyes. The nurse was making me draw up my legs and when she stabbed me with a catheter I sucked my thumb like a baby.

Ruth came in, bound up like a country ham, in a waffle-weave blanket. Then a nurse entered and said the doctor said I could eat anything, but the food had to be salt free.

It was six P.M. All day, since before noon, Richard had been outside, having a life. Ruth was sleeping and I wouldn't wake her, and I missed company. I started to cry for Richard.

After a very long time he came in and said, "What do you mean, honey, the nurse said you'd only been awake half an hour." Every minute took so long.

"You are on a lot of dope," Richard told me. "They were scared you could've died, did you know that?"

I told him I had died a little. And it was not so bad. Then Ruth squirmed and sucked in her sleep, and I was alive again. I devoured a white bread sandwich and Richard handed her to me, and I put her to my massive breast, for practice.

Richard was holding my knee and I don't think he knew he was squeezing it. When I looked up, he was repeating to me over and over, "Alma, you won't die, you won't die," saying this with so much force I felt immortal. I don't remember how I responded to him. I think I just talked to be talking. His concern made me grateful I could.

Much later, he said to me, "You aren't making any sense, Alma, you really aren't. You shouldn't bother to talk. You are tough as you can be, Alma."

With rue I'd said they'd got my labor there at last.

"No, no, no, Felt said you did it all by yourself, and in your condition—"

I said, even so, that was Ruth's doing. She votes with her body. She has no snag between her acts and her intentions.

"No, no, no, you are an idiot, sometimes," Richard said. "Why can't you just let go of it?"

What did he mean, it? Body? I tried that. If everything had gone really smoothly I would have gone ahead and died. I knew that. I kept it from him.

Here I was in the bed, all-flawed Alma again, no longer immaculate.

My headache was unspeakable, even through the sleeping drugs. Then I conked out. Ruth snoozed back in her Lucite box-on-a-truck.

Richard hung his clothes in the closet and lay down in the other bed. We would be in the dark another twenty-four hours. People could come tomorrow, one at a time. Lucas would come first, then Loretta, then Mr. Kaplan, then I would take phone calls. Mother would call. Would my daddy call? Would Carmen come, or would that be too much?

I waited out the night while Richard talked to me through my chemical sleep. Twice they brought Ruth back to us, and she opened up little bright holes in the night, and she and I held each other there. Then she would go away and Richard would talk again, and sleep or say he was too excited to sleep.

I didn't have any milk. It would take two days before I would have any milk. While Ruth and I held each other, she got my breast in her mouth, and there was no other real world: she and I drifted along on a little life raft.

Within a few weeks of Rachel's death, Richard had enrolled in a college course to become a realtor. Three weeks of five-nights-a-week training. He got his license in about a month. Since he'd got it, there seemed to be two categories of property that interested him—those he could sell, and those for "investments." He'd actually sold one house, a row house in Waverly, to a pair of single men. That was in the last week of July. He hadn't told me much about the sale at all until the day before the settlement. He was secretive, something which had not bothered me about him before. Secretiveness is another charm in a lover that is an abomination in a husband. His commission was not so great—the other agent and the Colonial Realty Company Richard worked with seemed to have split the bulk of the profits, but he had a check, and we had some champagne. He was also "showing" houses in our neighborhood to the kind of odd people who might choose it. Bored children from suburbia who liked the scale, the sort of Hampstead-Heath-cramped-row-houses-and-tons-of-pubs feel to the place. The windows were so many opportunities for red and white geraniums in boxes. These "buyers" were usually a little unsteady, flaky, maybe. The young women wore espadrilles that were pink enough, but a little frayed. The idea of going *through* with something was a bit vague with these ones, who always wanted space for a darkroom. Mostly, they seemed to enjoy going to Maria's with Richard to chug a few pints. And there were the opposite extremes, the people who habitually bought in the Point, who had no interest at all in sandblasting painted brick or in removing formstone—those were immigrants from the deeper South or from Central America, who worked for Proctor & Gamble or Bethlehem Steel or for gyros places, who didn't want a mortgage at all. They wanted to take a lump of cash and pay the bank off as soon as possible. These buyers were more serious, but they were never very flexible about what they could spend. And none of the people who took up Richard's time had actually bought anything in our area.

Also, Richard had become the agent for a few properties—some from Guatemalans he'd known at the Hispanic Center who were ready to move on to Anne Arundel County, on to cement driveways and juniper bushes. He held the listing for a large bar, Diana's, which three women, two writers and a sometime filmmaker, had tried to turn into a café, into a place for readings. The three were squabbling. Central Americans and independent women were the two types that trusted Richard.

The properties for "investment" were another category—when he had no clients, no listings, no potential sales, which was most of the time, he looked for investments. He never explained exactly what kind of investments, with whose money, he was trying to accomplish. He hinted that he needed to stay abreast of the market, in case he encountered an investor. He didn't mean speculators, exactly—speculators bought houses all by themselves, with no help.

On weekends during the time I was an elephant, he'd get a key from a fellow realtor with an open house, say, and then we'd drive around the city, using the passkey to open locked boxes filled with more keys, and then any given dark red-brick house or warehouse or abandoned factory in Canton or South Baltimore was ours to trample through. Cold brick walls, slits of unplanned light, rotted second floors, unintentionally exposed beams, the smoke of factories coming through broken panes, and the azure Chesapeake—these were the sensations of those Sundays. It was a game, I thought; my feet sloshed when I walked and my hands were entirely numb by that time, but I was still curious enough to get out of the Triumph again and again and walk through the remains of another life, or the detritus of an industry now extinct.

Sometimes there were letters, or mildewed, rotted nightgowns, Buster Brown shoes from twenty years before, old Uneeda Biscuit tins. The people had gone on, but they always left something behind, in a closet, stuck in the wall behind where the stove had once been—notes, initials, rats of hair, tooth powder. One day we went to an old industrial space and found a huge inadvertent sculpture. Thousands of stacked-up Cat's Paw rubber heels, towers of them sorted according to size, in ascending and descending order, like a skyline, or jagged organ pipes.

Part of the game was for Richard to ask me who would we be if we lived here. How would it be if we broke out that wall there? Put in a larger window here? How many people could this place hold? Say it was my loft? Could I paint in it? "Could you paint in *here,* Alma?"—asked in an industrial building, called out to me over three thousand square feet, across an ocean of space. It hardly seemed a question. I could bring in whole houses and paint them in that space. It was an old warehouse near the water that dated back to the 1860s.

This was the fun of the August when I was an elephant. In two months as realtor, Richard had made only something over a thousand dollars. He wanted to make what he called "real money." He wanted that so much. And who buys anything in the summer, especially anything that "needs work"? All the houses Richard peddled and all the places he listed, like everything else in our lives, "needed work."

For him that morning in the hospital was not so radically different from those mornings of the preceding weeks, before Ruth was real. He was nervous, more so than usual, talking up the buyers, describing them to me. To refer to these lookers as buyers may have required a leap of faith, but that was always the case. He was exaggerating to me the features of the flawed houses he was about to show. He was gearing himself up. He was overjoyed about the baby's being out, alive, and so healthy, and he was hot to sell anything.

A nurse came in, whispering, holding a photograph. They said Ruth was a very attractive infant. It was not the Ruth of my imagination, however. My Ruth was enormous and wide-eyed, and this one was only a baby. I said there must be some mistake. The nurse left the whole packet of pictures with me in the half light and said she would come back later.

At four, Richard was there to corroborate. It *was* baby girl Kaplan. He said, "Isn't she beautiful?" I saw no resemblance. Then I thought, "Am I crazy?" and said okay, I would buy the pictures.

Richard went to get the vendor, who came back in

and told me what to write on the check. It was so difficult, to write a check. I perspired profusely. But I had to do it—Richard was broke. Life with a plot was so all-the-time, so full of little pieces to take care of.

Later, I was dozing and Richard was talking to me about a house he'd tried to sell that morning.

"The kitchen floor was mushy! You stepped on this old floral linoleum and your feet literally sank in."

"Was it padded?" I asked him.

"No, don't you listen? I'm talking termites. The floor gave in, it dented, when you stepped into it."

"Oh," I said. "What did you do?"

"You don't lie, you say it is termites. What else can you say? It was a crap day. My daughter is born and the next day is crap. The lady says I lied to her, and I said she asked to see this place, it wasn't my listing. She almost starts to cry, she says, 'Look at it, it's rotted!' Like I am personally responsible. I hate this."

"I love you," I said.

"I have to make a living, Alma, some other way. I don't even want these people from Towson to move down here. There are too many cute parlors down here already, too many miniblinds. I have to do something else."

"What?" I said, a cloud coming over me. Too many things had already changed utterly. I didn't want to hear about how Richard was going to change his life. Our life was too tenuous to go through any more moltings right then.

"Don't act like that," Richard said to me.

"Like what?" I said.

"Like everything I do is a joke."

"I think you are doing fine, really," I said.

"You think I am a schmuck," he said.

"Just don't change anything right now. It's September. School starts. People move, they buy houses. They sell houses."

"I don't want to sell houses," he said.

"Well, what do you want?" I asked him.

"Baby, just be the wife," he said.

"I wouldn't do that to anybody," I said. "Please, I can't fight."

"Okay," he said. "Okay. But what are we going to do?"

It was the end of the second day. Baby girl Kaplan was back in the nursery. Richard had gone to the cafeteria in the hospital. I was in the pure lonely dark, a queen on a catheter, when I heard Lucas's voice. I could make out the nurse saying to him outside, "One at a time, and don't speak above a whisper."

"Alma, honey, I won't stay long," Lucas began. "Loretta's outside, she wants to come in. I just can't believe it. You look great. The baby is unbelievable. You know they had to cut her fingernails already? She's so healthy! You should see some of the other limp little ones in there, with their flimsy little butts, cooking under the ultraviolet. I'm not prejudiced. It's the best-looking kid at Hopkins."

I sat up a little, and Lucas patted me on the shoulder, a healthy congratulatory pat. His green-gray corduroys were low on his ass. He had a bristle beard that caught the faint light. He'd lost weight. I reached toward the little tensor lamp the nurses used.

"No, it's okay, you are supposed to stay in that dark. I can see you. Jesus, Richard told me how tough you were, you wouldn't let them have anything off you. Lord, Alma, you are so tough. So goddamned brave, really." He paused, trying to find some more praise.

So that was the perception. Alma had come through. She'd slid past death, to home. My headaches and my blood pressure were still a little alarming, but here I was, body and soul, and somehow this made joy for everybody. It made Lucas so happy I could see it in his glistening face, and I was happy for him.

"I don't want to stay," Lucas whispered. "I mean, you must want to rest, and Loretta is waiting outside. But I gotta tell you something, Alma. When I was out there Monday morning, and Richard came out and said there were complications, and that you were really sick, I mean, Alma, I said to myself right then and there, if Alma gets through, well. It was breaking my heart. I just resolved, your life has to have a shape. What does securities fraud have to do with fucking beauty?"

Seeing Lucas was a little like seeing someone you know on TV. First, there's this intimacy of recognition, and then you are aware that the invisible millions are seeing him too, seeing things in him you don't see in everyday life. So he glowed as he stood there, took on nuance. At the same time, I couldn't stay for long.

"When you get home, we can really talk. I'm talking about beauty, Alma. I mean, this baby, this is the most beautiful thing you ever did, Alma, have this baby. It is fucking amazing. Carmen's gotta see it. Christ, you must be sleepy. I'm calling Carmen and telling her to come on down. Do you think she'd be chicken-shit? Carmen's gotta see it."

"You've been here for two days?" I asked, looking up a little.

"Had to see if you'd pull through," Lucas said. "I mean, I take a proprietary interest. You and Richard got to land on your feet. I swore to Loretta I'd be here only a minute. I made her promise she'd stay only a few. You got the baby coming in for a six-o'clock feeding, don't you?"

Lucas knew the hospital routine better than I did.

"This rooming-in is the only thing, I swear," Lucas said. "I mean, the babies whose mommas leave them in there, they sit there and suck on the blanket, scratch their faces till they bleed. I know. I've been looking. The ones who can't see their mothers are having nervous breakdowns right there on day one—" Lucas waited a minute. "It's a bitch. What is *wrong* with those women?" He paused, kissed me very quickly on the forehead. "I gotta go. Kick Loretta out if she gets loquacious."

Lucas had meat breath. I wanted him to stay. He shuffled his big legs out the door.

If I painted Loretta I would have to use some of the paints she uses on herself. Maroon, violet, crimson. Her teeth are small and even. Her thighs tend to hike up her skirts. Her hose are often rose-tinted. She is short and chubby; she looks bigger than she is.

"I'm so thrilled," Loretta said when the heavy door closed by itself behind her. "I hear you had a hard time, but I'm sure the worst is over. That's what the nurse said to us, the worst is over."

She took the chair. I was beginning to fade a little.

"And Gina's up there now. She went into surgery at three-thirty. Poor thing, she was scared to death. That was what all that was about the other night when you were pregnant, I mean, down at Maria's, she was scared to death. But what are you going to do? I mean, that is what she really wants, isn't it? Isn't it what she wants? I felt lousy saying good-bye to her penis up there, really. You know she was the first one? The first guy I ever. Oh, I brought you something, look at this, can you believe it?"

There were four rows of ruffles over the built-in rubber panties. The top on the thing was made of candy-striped material. Over that, embroidered strawberries. It seemed too small. It was so Loretta, the present.

She looked strained: her face was puffy and the eyes wilted in the corners, sank lower than her eyeliner. She had a dimple in her chin. It was a Betty Boop face.

I said thank you, I said it was beautiful. Then it occurred to me how many times dear Ruth would have to dress and undress and look into mirrors in her lifetime and flatten wrinkled clothes under an iron and strain in the looking glass for something horrible that went for beauty in 1995, something I couldn't imagine. I vowed I would never put this thing on her.

"Well, Gina was my first, you know. She was my first love. We were about fourteen, and he was sort of a hood. He wore leather jackets. He was short, but the beard made up for that. We were both in the Drama Club in high school. Once we did a scene together and he played Stanley Kowalski, you know, *A Streetcar Named Desire*. And I was Stella. He was a bodybuilder then. My parents lived in Roland Park. I guess you know all this, but I have to go through it, to explain. I have to tell you.

"My parents are sort of Old Maryland. Gino lived in Highlandtown and his parents ran a pizza parlor. We used to make out on his mother's green plastic living room couch. We were so hot back then. We would just come for nothing. You know what I mean?

"We went to see the movie *Romeo and Juliet* over and over, and finally we had to do it, fuck. It was really all right. Then, about the third time we did it, he told me he didn't get off. But then he said that was because he was drunk, and we did it over and over and over. He always swore he loved me. There was never any question about that, that he loved me. He was interested in how it felt for me, and he would do it just so I would narrate. So I would narrate. He could listen to me for hours, really, he would just keep it in for hours so he could listen to me tell him what it felt like. We were a thing.

"My father wanted to break us up, of course. That made it better. When I was seventeen, Gino and I moved out and went to live together in an apartment. It was an outrageous thing to do, to move out of the house before we even graduated from high school, but we did it, and I sort of kissed off my parents. At that point they went to a counselor who told them to dump me. They were very cold and cruel about it all. They had other kids who had 'turned out all right.' What was one black sheep when you've had five kids?"

I felt a twinge at that: how lucky just to get out of your family. I knew Loretta didn't speak to her parents very much, and I envied her being a black sheep. Mutual dismissal: what a relief.

"They thought I was incorrigible. They even thought of putting me away somewhere, and then they found some other parents who had given up on their kids and started a support group and they ganged up on me and decided they had to stick with what they believed in. That was, oh, God knows what they believed in by that time, golf, I suppose, they believed primarily in golf. Oh, it was horrible. I came home on pills, I popped heroin a few times, I was a disaster, I guess, but Gino stuck with me through it all.

"He worked at his father's place, and I entered the lower middle class. No joke: we lived in his neighborhood on the second floor of a yellow-brick row house, and we knew junkies. White kids in the park across the way took angel dust at night. Mostly in the refrigerator were old pizza dough and beer and Pepsis. We went to the high school prom together, Gino and me, except at the last minute he suggested that I wear the tux and he wear the dress. We went that way and they wouldn't let us in. Did I ever tell you that story?

"Still, I got out of high school with good grades. I enrolled at Towson to do a drama degree and Gino went to work at a bar. He was never really into men as men, I mean. He was never gay. He was into me. So much he wanted to be me. He was so into me. If I wanted it, then he would fuck me any time of the day or the night, but we knew by then that he wasn't that crazy about giving it to me. In fact, it was a kind of favor. But he let me go ahead because he liked me to narrate and he liked me so much, he thought I was so beautiful, really, he admired me. I was so goddamned happy at that time in my life.

"I mean, we were in love. He really wasn't very much on the surface, I mean, nobody ever saw what I saw in him, I think you even told me that one night. No, it wasn't you, it was before I went to the Institute. But people were always telling me. And as he got to be nineteen and twenty, well, I had a life and he had me. That was the way it turned out. I would go and see him working at the bar where he'd been for two years and none of the regular customers knew his first name. He really didn't have anybody but me. I had to quit school a couple of times to work, and he helped me along. Then one semester I went back and got a crush on Stark Ruffin, who was the director out at the college, a real lout, it turned out.

"It was just sort of a dumb crush, but I talked about it a lot to Gino, and he listened and fucked me, and fucked me and listened. He didn't say anything about it, really, I mean, he didn't say it hurt him or anything. Then one evening they called from the bar and asked me where was Gino—he hadn't come in. He was fired.

"He came into the apartment about six in the morning and just stood there in the doorway and took off his leather jacket and there was a slice across his belly. He had a tight little belly, with a little arc of muscle. He was crying and he took off his jeans and I saw he was wearing my red underwear.

"It seemed so radical on him and so sexy. Does this make any sense to you, Alma? I never told any of this to you before, did I?"

Loretta was rushing to get it all in. I knew some of what she was saying, but not all. I couldn't get too close to it, though, couldn't see it. I wanted to. It was so important to her.

—183—

"Then he just sat down and cried and cried and said he was really a woman. It hurt him all the time to be a man, it really hurt, I didn't know how much." Loretta paused, put both hands on her cheeks, so that her mouth was shoved up into a rubbery nonsmile. "His cock hurt like a wound—

"Well, I was twenty years old. I thought he meant he was queer. That was something I could live with. But I really didn't know. We were so young. I mean, we just hung out all the next day, and I dressed him up and gave him my old slips and shaved him really close and lent him lipstick and he went out that way. It was like making love all over again for the first time. But now I could be the giver. I was the mother, you see, I could take him to the ladies' room. Do you understand, Almy? Somehow I turned out to be more girly from all of this. I mean, I turned into the drag queen I am today. I was hyperwoman. I had to be. I had been getting very mystical-feminist during this time, under the influence of some people I met, and doing tarot and things, and I thought this was really the most extraordinary thing, that Gino got it: the idea that it is really better, much better, to be a woman. He wanted to express that right out there in his body. I mean, he never talked very much about how he'd come to the conclusion. Maybe in another person, the female would emerge in some mental way, in the art or the poetry or something like that, but with Gino, his only medium was his body. I'm getting philosophical, aren't I. I guess I mean his wanting to be a woman was a little abstract, an ideal, maybe. I don't think it meant he was any closer to needing men, men as lovers, I mean.

"What I mean to say is that I was really flattered that he was turning into me and at the same time, well, I had the balls now. Gino got to be the little woman. We really went through the looking glass, me and Gino."

I was wondering why Loretta was telling me all this right now.

"I don't know what I am exactly to do, now, I mean, Gina will have to have somebody, won't she? She has to leave me after the operation, though; it wouldn't be fair for her to just stay on with me and not have lovers, but I don't know if she is ready for lovers. I don't know if she went through all this for lovers, exactly. It could have been for me. I hate to think that. I've spent my whole youth working on making Gina a girl, and now I don't know if she knows what she wants. Is that part of being a girl, not knowing what you want? What do you think?"

You always start over with Loretta. In that, she reminds me of my mother a little. She leaves out the most important parts of the puzzle, tells you what you really know, and mulls over and over the mystery as well as the other, and you are supposed to guess along. Cause and effect are too mundane. I suppose I knew Loretta was having trouble with Gina's leaving, or with leaving Gina, if, indeed, she had to leave her.

"I love Gina, I really do, and it is love beyond sex, I mean, obviously it is beyond sex. We haven't had sex in, I don't know, six years. We slept in the same bed long after that, we slept in the same bed until two nights ago, even.

"It is perfectly sisterly, now. And Gina wants it to stay that way. Did I do the wrong thing? I mean, she says how could I plan this life for us if I ever thought I would leave? She wants the sort of spinster-sister scene, I think. She wants us to be undying, you know, in our devotion. I mean, I have to have a life, don't I?"

"Sure," I said. Loretta had said these things to me before.

"Say, for example, I have a lover. Who needs me. Gina shouldn't have to need me anymore, maybe. Not as much, at least. Don't you think she should grow out of it?"

"Of what?"

"Her dependence on me. I need some breathing space. I need it. I really do. And I don't need anybody else dependent upon me, not right now. I mean, I don't want to step right out of one into another, exactly. I'd like some air time, you know, equal time. I don't feel like making any commitments right now. Not even to him."

"Who?" I asked.

"The person I came to talk to you about. Somebody you know very well."

"Who?" I said, again.

"Who's in love with me but you have to explain my history to him somehow, can you? This is a terribly tender time."

"Who are you talking about?" I said.

Richard entered the room, and immediately came under my suspicion. Was he going after Loretta in his free time? "Almy—no—Loretta, stay a minute—Alma. Guess who I saw in the hospital cafeteria. Guess who is here right now. You won't believe—"

"I was getting to that," Loretta said, to both of us.

"Your father," they said, exactly together, like a chorus.

"He's totally in love with me," Loretta said, her shoulder hunching upward, her palms facing the ceiling.

I wanted baby Ruth.

"She's a big one," Daddy said Wednesday during visiting hours, and even in the dark I could see his timid look. He was wearing a bluish-white short-sleeve shirt that nearly glowed. The collar was too wide and too pointy. "Richard's been telling me you had a hard time," he said, after clearing his throat.

He wouldn't want me to say anything specific about my condition—that would upset him, I knew. He would not really ask about the lower half of my body. He would be frightened even of my scent and never would find out it was just toilet water. He would stay where he was, four feet off, not come any closer. I knew him well enough to know that. But my arms, my shoulders, my neck, my breasts, my head nearly groaned over toward him, yearned. I wanted him to come closer and to hold me. Then, in a minute, the same wanting became a desire to hold baby Ruth, who would be a better answer. And in a breath I was angry with him at how he stood stiffly aloof, his arms folded. I figured any minute he would call me "gal."

"I'll be all right," I said, keeping it short and brave. "How are you doing?" I wanted him to stay, then I wanted him to get out.

"I would have been up earlier," he went on, "but I didn't know you were in. To tell the truth—"

His "to tell the truth" signaled an alibi.

"I'm in Baltimore to see you and to see someone else, too. Someone important to me, other than you, I mean."

It was the same tone he used when I was a kid and he was sober and he came back from Asheville and stayed awhile, and then said, "Alma, I'm leaving your mother"; he sounded just as committed. I'd been thinking about Loretta and my daddy for about twenty-four hours by then. Even he could convince me. I could be convinced of anything. I was past yes and no, I guess you know that. I wanted my daddy to tell me I looked fine. I thought he looked fine.

"I know this sounds crazy," he said. Then he stopped short. I forgot. My daddy has no guts. I saw him reach for his lighter, then halt, realizing he couldn't, here. I was dreaming we could have one together. "I came to see my grandkid, Alma. You got a name for her? What a big fat red one she is, looks just like you—"

"Ruth," I said. "Richard didn't tell you?"

"That's it? That name in Richard's family?" he asked, without knowing he was being harsh. "Fine people, really, you know I think so."

He wasn't offended, he said, but he was. The baby could be called Mahala, after his grandmother, but the baby was Ruth. I wouldn't fix it now.

"I won't stay long, honey. You don't seem well. We can talk when you are on your feet. How long does the doc say you have to be in the dark?"

"A few more days," I said.

"What is eclampsia?" he asked, but I said they didn't know. I couldn't really think. I felt two ways when he had entered. It seemed my body had already held him and thrown him over to the wall, and I wondered would I go over there and pick him up, and then I wondered would he get out so I could see baby Ruth. He was the obstacle to Ruth, who was my hope. It seemed I'd already done both things. My impressions of the feel of his rough jaw, of his hands pressed onto my shoulders, had at least the reality of memory.

"Well, she sure looks better than the other punies in that nursery. Some of them look like skinned"—he paused, considered it might be tasteless to say something vivid—"I-don't-know-whats." Then he added boyishly, "I swear some of them are yellow as chickens."

"They have jaundice," I said.

"And then there is one colored one in there, I swear, Alma, the little card said the kid weighed thirteen pounds at birth. That head—we're talking a two-dollar cantaloupe. The kid looks a year old. Your friend Lucas told me the mother was a diabetic, said he'd asked a nurse about it. He's a nice fellow. He was sitting out there at the nursery window, telling me about the routine. A baby that big—you know it won't be right. How in the world did it get down?"

If the mother was black, he could approach the subject of the twat. If the mother was me, well, there was no mentioning it. For a few long seconds, he said nothing.

Then, to close the silence, he began. "I've been involved with this person about six months, I guess. I didn't want to tell you about it, until we were ready to make a move, I mean—"

The door opened, my dinner, rolled in by an orderly wearing a pair of deep sky-blue trousers. "Kaplan?" he asked. "Sodium-free?" He slid a ticket out from under the tray. When the orderly raised the insulated cover, the steam that rose had a warm, tasteless body. There were four drinks: tomato juice, tea, water, orange drink.

"You get a lot of food, don't you," Daddy said. "But how does it taste?" He said this last with the most concern that had entered his voice so far. "Why so many things to drink?"

"My milk should be coming in," I said, realizing he might find that another untouchable subject. He said, "Uh-huh. Go ahead and eat, at least it ought to be hot."

I ate, then, and Daddy sat on the chair, watching me eat. The time was the food. The longer I ate, the longer he sank into the chair, seeming to shrink.

"When do you go home?" he asked.

"When they say I can," I said. When was he going to tell me about Loretta?

"I'm thinking I'm gonna be living here for a while. This person is here. Then we'll take it one step at a time. You want to know, What about Jo Ann?" He sighed, then he raised his voice. "Jo Ann will get along just fine. She's taken care of herself fine all these years. She does a good job with the park. She can have everything—she's got it now. I don't want anything. I've got disability to live on. I can live anywhere."

He was expanding a little now. He might even preach at me some. He had been sitting there, forming a fist around the chrome tubing on the chair, but now he let go, began to use his free hand.

"You've got to have your own values, your own values," he said. "You have yours, I've got mine. Jo Ann has hers. You know what hers are. We need not go into that. It's the transcendentals that matter, don't you think? You know, we admire the daylights out of you. You have worked so much through. You are a great gal, Alma."

He didn't preach. I was an eating animal. I nodded. What would he say now?

"We're really interested in the baby and all. I can be a grandpop. When I told Dolby what was going on, that I was coming up here, he nearly spat. But that changed when he met this person." His eyes looked wet. Such cowardice. I could feel it covering him like a fleece. His eyes caught a little light.

"I know now what love really is," he said, with the twang of a country-western singer. "Overlooking faults—"

I had progressed from the flavorless green beans to the cotton potatoes. When he had uttered the above, I felt a phenomenal twang in my armpits. I started to gush sweat.

"We do believe, sometimes, in what we can't see," he said. "It was faith in her, and in you, and in life and in Jesus Christ that got me off the bottle. And that was my prison. Like Jo Ann's house is her prison. This person came down a few months ago. We went to the Blue Ridge there in June, I guess it was. We went up with Dolby, took his van. You know, Dolby likes his beer, and he was being almost mean about it, urging me to have a short. And she wouldn't even let me have a sip. She talked to me all night, you know, talked me through the whole thing. Dolby had to give her credit. Had a god-damned good time, too. Took a walk on the Appalachian Trail in the morning, near Spruce Pine. And we saw a cloud, the two of us. I mean, we were in a cloud. It was the damnedest thing. This cloud just scooted right along with us, kept up with us like a blessing." He smiled like a preacher. "Was I high?" He shook his head back and forth and said, "Mmmmmm. It was a sign, somehow, how that cloud didn't burn off, just stayed there with us. She felt it too, this person. It was something transcendental. That's what this love affair is. Am I coming across to you?" He moved in a little closer, to catch the expression on my face. "She's a helpmeet, a friend, somebody I can talk to, who knows how rough it is to stay in there, to hang on. And yet I feel so free," Daddy said.

He was making me sick. He was at his worst when he was buying the soap. I was holding out. I came to the orange Jell-O, the last plate. I could feel a new set of yearnings toward my father, my gutless father. Why wouldn't he tell me, for Christ's sake. But I didn't want him to leave.

"Yeah, Daddy," I said, almost tearful. It might be so sweet, in a way, I let myself think, that he was in love. I wanted him to hug me, hold me up a little.

"You know, I want you and the baby to be ¡art of our lives." He put his teacup on the tray. Then, when I started to push the tray away, he rolled it down to the foot of the bed. "Richard too," he added.

"Momma will be here this weekend," I said. I meant, did he want me to explain to her that he had fallen in love? How had it got to that?

"Jo Ann," he said, shaking his head, with this awful piety. "She's a tough one," he said.

My poor daddy, the last believer. Somehow, now I was supposed to be on his side, the love side. The cloud convinced me. I don't think he had ever mentioned wanting to be "part of my life" before, either. Was I won over? Then I felt the thought of my mother. A ripple went through me, almost pain. She would tell me Daddy was a horse's ass. An old codger, selfish as the day is long. What a burden to be related to this character. I didn't want to think about it. Then his two dry hands were on my forearm. I wore two bracelets. One had my name, the other Ruth's. He thumbed the second around my wrist bone.

"Your mother will not understand, Alma. We have to show her. We have to let her know how much happier everybody will be now. You have to help her see this is the best. You have to help me, Almy, 'cause I see you understand how happy I am." He looked at me then. He smelled of Zest soap. "I've found my soulmate, darling."

I felt a twang in several pockets of me, a kind of all-over pucker, as your mouth feels when you prepare for a piece of chocolate. Did I want him to kiss me?

All of a sudden, cloudy water flowed down my cotton gown. I was soaking myself. I was a fountain, grinning.

"What in the world?" Daddy asked, alarmed. "What in the world?"

I felt like holding my breasts and pointing them at the ceiling, like dancing. I was potable.

"What in the world?" he asked, actually frightened, as if there had been a supernatural event. "Stop it," he amended himself. I saw a shimmer of spook cross his face. "What a mess," he said, while I continued. He backed into the bathroom and threw a towel at me.

"I need the baby," I said, still thrilled, while I was making little puddles in the white thermal blanket.

Daddy was handing me a wad of Kleenex. Then he zapped across the room and grasped the edge of the door to the hall. "What a hell of a note this is," he said, and I could feel him thinking, "This is just like Alma, to mess me up like this. Right when I'm appealing to her, she has to start in with this *body* stuff." As he was stepping off into the hall, he said, "I'll get the nurse."

"The baby, not the nurse," I said. I was so happy.

"She's soaking her clothes," Daddy said to the first person he saw, "milk." I heard him laugh nervously, and just then I knew exactly what it was I hated about him. But I was flooded with human kindness, swimming in it.

I let my father go. What a relief to let my father go back to himself.

And baby Ruth came in and got it all—she ravished me. She had a bald little head, a few fair wisps of hair, steel-blue eyes. But somehow it wasn't me anymore. It was the boobs. I'd lost out to the boobs. That she did hang onto—they carried her away.

After my father was gone, and Ruth had had her way with me, Carmen showed up at the wide, thick hospital-room door. She had puffy eyes, and her hair was dirty. She looked timid, even scared. I wanted to hold her, as I wanted to do with everybody that week.

She made an almost inaudible "Hi."

Carmen neared the plastic box where Ruth snorted in her sleep. She did not seem to want to touch her, I could tell that. Then she said I looked so well, meaning, I suppose, that she had expected me to look worse. The lights were still out, except for a bulb that gave off a dull orange glow on the bedside table.

Carmen's face had always been legible, from the time when I first met her, when she was seventeen. It was long with very large myopic eyes. She always wore hard contact lenses, so her eyes were often red and murky if she stayed up too late, or if she'd done anything unhealthy, or if she had been crying. When she was happy those eyes looked magical and as if they belonged, they dressed up her face. But other times, like this morning, they were round as two giant marbles, frantic.

"I'm sorry I didn't get up here the other day," Carmen said. "Oh, she's moving," she said, meaning Ruth. "She's so tiny. She's incredible. Look at that little mouth." Then she turned again to me, "Are you still sore? Richard said you were sore on top of everything else, that they let you rip. Lucas finally went back to Washington, huh? Richard told me on the phone that Lucas had been here the whole time. I guess that was sweet, wasn't it. Are you going to make it?" she asked, the hug taking as long as this. Her slowness was evidence of her state of mind.

"Why do I always talk about me?" she asked, after a minute, as she backed away to the chair. "Who do I think I am, anyways?"

The nursery nurse came in. "Now, Mrs. Kaplan," she said, "you know you aren't supposed to have visits when there is rooming-in. It's time to take Ruth back to the nursery."

My baby was out again, conked. She wouldn't know she was being rolled away. I looked at Carmen, who was standing. She was inordinately timid, I'd never seen her this way. "I can come back," she announced to everybody.

"No, stay, Lord," I said. "Tell me what is going on." She sat, which was what she wanted to do.

"Well, it's going to be a battleground," she said. "I told Mary Ann. That I was pregnant, going to have the baby, going to move out, the whole bit. She acted like I was trying to kill her, first, then she got really insulting. I suppose you would expect her to get insulting, I mean, if you think about it—but she is supposed to love me so much. I *told* her I would still be her lover. I just didn't think I could live with her and have the baby. Then she got into the lesbian mothers business. But she wouldn't have Lucas coming over here and dandling the little thing while we do all the work. I said I'm thirty, when am I ever going to have a child. She said I should have thought of that before I moved in with her. And the fact that it's Lucas's. That just—I can't tell you how angry I am. I mean how angry she is. She said go ahead and move, because I've betrayed her anyway, how could we ever expect to get back together. Go back and be Lucas's wife, do that, and she is right. That's what—"

"What?" I said. "You said you'd never go back to him. You said it would hurt him, Carmen, and it would, it would kill him, I mean, if you didn't really love him, it would kill him."

"I don't want to. But I walk around now, you know, and I feel there is this other fate I have to handle, separate from mine, I imagine holding its hand, you know, walking through corridors, when I get into enclosed spaces, I have the feeling that the spirit is really there, in the space with me, I can feel it, it's this tug, this sweet tug, I can't explain it. I know if anything were to happen right now, a miscarriage, anything, I would feel this loss. But you should have seen Mary Ann's face. You should have. She has a perfect way, she's so beautiful, like a bird. I'm going to die. I really am going to die."

I didn't know what to say.

"I mean, when is something ever, ever going to be irreversible? I've been going around cracking up people's lives, now, for a year, first Lucas, I mean, now Mary Ann. I really don't deserve—"

"I think Lucas wants the baby," I said. "I mean I think he would raise it, or share it with you, any arrangement you want."

"Let it be raised by his housekeeper, you mean. He'd *pay* for it," she said. "Pay Mrs. Paloma, from Guatemala. I'm an adult. I'm thirty, for Christ's sake. I make a good living. I have my faculties. You'd think I'd be able to have a baby, wouldn't you think that? Wouldn't that be normal?"

"Carmen, honestly. You're normal."

"I don't think you understand how this really is tearing me up," she said.

"I can see it is, I can see it is," I said.

"Mary Ann could do anything— Do you know she spent some time at a mental hospital, at Riggs? She just told me that six weeks ago. She said it was nothing, girls from families like hers who got sad or inert in college always ended up at Riggs or McLean in Boston. But that's not so. That's a perfect lie. It isn't nothing that she was crazy once. I am her life."

"Carmen," I said, exasperated. "You want the baby, right? People will come around. Make up your own mind, first."

"If I have this baby everything else will just have to fall into place. It will fall into place. It will fall into place," she said, and she kissed my forehead, kissed my hand. "I have to think things will fit somehow, don't I? They will finally fit?"

She wasn't mocking me—she was trying to convince herself.

I said, "Absolutely nothing looks the same afterward. Everything is different. As if this were another world. I feel at sea right now, like I'm in this little boat with her," I said, but it made little difference what I said. Carmen was getting where she needed to be.

"Don't tell anything to Lucas," she said. "Don't give him any ideas, swear this to me. Swear it. He can't intervene right now." She was standing at the foot of my bed. "Swear it," she repeated. Then she paused. "Oh, I almost forgot—"

It was a book called *Boy and Girl.*

"Here's a little propaganda you can read to baby Ruth," she said. "Oh, think, our babies will be only seven and a half months apart. We can get a double baby carriage and roll them down Broadway and sit out in that awful flagstone square they just put up." She faded. "Watch the gulls, just think."

This little fantasy came with such fabricated joy I could hardly take it. Carmen wanted to be so loving, I found myself thinking.

"Lucas wants the kid," I told her. It was the wrong note. "He's mad for you to have this baby, he's crazy about the whole thing. You know he's been hovering around me for days—"

Carmen started to wag her head. "I can't hear this, Alma. Not right now. I am not going to go back to him. I can't be influenced by his obsessions. When he gets obsessive you can't trust him. Don't get into it. I know him. Don't feed it, please."

Then she went to the door. I opened up the book. Inside was an inscription:

For Alma and her daughter, much love,
Carmen and Mary Ann

The book was a series of photographs of nudes—infants, then toddlers. Then there were ten-year-olds, then teenagers. The words to the pictures said things like, "This is Joshua. He has a penis. He is a boy. This is Susan. She has a vagina. She is a girl. Joshua will always be a boy. Susan will always be a girl." The book was endorsed by the Gender Identity Committee in this same hospital, the same people who were working on Gina.

Wednesday night, Richard came in with more woe. He stood at the end of my bed.

"Steva decided to take Diana's off the market. I spent the last two and a half hours trying to prove to her that it wouldn't hold its value. Not with what they are going to do with it. Steva's half brother's going to rehab it, turn it into three stupid storefront apartments. Three apartments instead of a bar. Who the fuck wants to live in a store? Even if he does something about the facades. He won't do anything decent, it'll be something cheap. It's that guy Costello."

Steva was one of the women in the three-way partnership that owned Diana's, the bar/performance space Richard had been listing but hadn't sold.

"They wouldn't listen to me. They just would not—"

"Maybe they'll list it with you later," I said, "when it's been worked on. Plenty of people around here live in houses that used to be shops." My old apartment, even, had a storefront once, in the 1890s.

"That's not it, that's not it." Richard said. "Diana's could have been an institution, if somebody ran it right, put in a regular restaurant kitchen, opened up the upstairs. I don't know, it's a good space— Costello's going in and boxing it up with dry wall. If I could have found somebody with a little capital— Maybe it was too far from the water—"

"Too far from the water for what?" I asked, and Richard changed the subject, slightly, to a more theoretical one: how nice a café with some books and a gallery space for paintings would be. Didn't I think such a place would "round out the Point"?

I wanted to talk about beautiful Ruth in her box-on-a-trolley, not about geography. Her head was so exquisite, so erotic an object. The orb of her head, her smooth, close, folded features. And her padded limbs, her tone, her curling fingers.

But Richard wanted to talk about money and things. He kept saying we had plenty of money, which wasn't so. His father had given him a few hundred dollars that Richard imagined spending several times, on an array of baby tech: backpacks, folding strollers, aluminum contraptions, a device for hanging your infant in the doorway in a parachute seat. We'd been to department stores and looked at hundreds of objects with buckles and straps, devised for every mode of suspension, and collapse.

After we talked about what to buy for a while, Richard asked me when I thought I'd be ready to teach again. I had met my classes at the Institute once, and I had a substitute ready to go in for a few weeks; after that, I'd be returning. But these plans had been before my complications.

"Felt said you'd be okay in ten days, maybe sooner. Pregnancy was the cause. The relief was delivery. You've delivered, honey." He touched my knee.

I was thinking how many aspirin it was going to take to get the nails out of my head. Going to work, ever, seemed impossible to me just then. What a silly idea that I would ever leave Ruth, even for an hour. That I might have any thought in my being about anyone but her.

"What if something happens? If you don't go back. If you can't?" Richard asked.

"I don't know," I said. I was mad. It was obvious, wasn't it, that I wouldn't give way. "I'll go back. I'll go back. Nothing's wrong with me," I said, starting to doubt it.

"Why am I pushing you, for Christ's sake?" he asked himself.

"I don't have any problem with it," I said, which was a lie. I could lie to Richard, now. We were more separate. During the time when I was an elephant, in August when we spent our days climbing stairs and kicking the plywood out of the windows of "investments," and walking through the suburban stores trying to teach ourselves to fold and unfold high chairs, I never lied to Richard.

"I'm supposed to provide—I'm the man, in this situation," he said.

"What difference does it make what sex you are?"

"Oh, shut up, Alma," he said. "You want it all on you, don't you? You want every bit—"

What I had in my mind at that moment was the image

of the two of us, nude, like Adam and Eve holding hands, bumping into each other. This was a grave cartoon, executed by Albrecht Dürer. And then we stepped back, having hit each other good and hard, and we were holding our genitals out of pain or shame or both, and there before us was this helpless egg of a homunculus, screaming, making an unbelievable racket. What had we gone and done? How were we going to make up for it? Toil, I thought.

"You don't have to be a tycoon. I hate money, really, you know that."

"Oh, I don't want to hear that you don't mind starving. Don't tell me that it's okay, you don't mind. You cannot starve. Ruth can't starve." When he pointed to her, she fidgeted.

"Don't be so Jewish, Richard. Nobody's starving."

"Shut up," he said.

"I won't," I said. But I did shut up. I was a terrible Rachel. And Rachel wasn't exactly perfect, either, regarding the Woman of Valour agenda. She could be stingy. She held back. She wasn't an angel. She had run away, once. I wondered how it could be that from all of us losers—me and Richard and Rachel and my father—could have descended somebody perfect like Ruth. "What do you want me to say?" I asked him.

"Just don't poke holes in everything—" he said.

"I don't know, Richard," I said. "I don't know if you want me to need you or not to need you. Half the time if I get involved in what you are doing you get pissed off. Do you want encouragement, really? Well, everything isn't great. And what am I supposed to support? You want threats? What?"

"*Alma,* stop being such a bitch," he said, far too loudly for a hospital. Ruth stuck her tongue out and brought her two fists to her face. She was ready to howl.

I said I didn't know why I was being such a bitch. But Richard would have to solve himself, I felt: I had too much of my own to solve just then—I needed to keep Ruth perfect, and I needed to mend myself, to close up, to heal.

"Look, I love you," Richard said, and I felt terrible, then. Ruth had been making him part of me all these last months, but now she was separate and so now we were all apart. Eventually Richard would see it—with the baby born, our lives together, Richard's and mine, seemed more of a construct now, less of an inevitability. We weren't being carried forward anymore by anything beyond our control. I knew Richard less well. And then I said something quite cruel. "Maybe this is what you want," I said.

"What?"

"To feel out of the garden, miserable. It's comfortable to you. You like it—"

He didn't respond directly. Instead, a few minutes later, quite plaintively, he said my name, and he left the hospital room. When he opened the door it was dark in the corridor. I could see the little bursts of light around the red EXIT signs.

Dr. Felt's clogs awoke me Friday. He turned on the lights in the room.

"And how are you today, Mrs. Kaplan?" he said, or something else right out of the textbook. "Do you want to go home?"

He expected me to say no. And I said no. Wouldn't they let me stay here?

He picked up the chart. "You are healing," he said. "Your blood pressure is closer to normal. Have you been walking around at all?"

"A little," I said.

"Do you hurt?" he asked.

"Everywhere, most of the time," I said. "Headache."

I noticed that his shirt was side-buttoned, doctor-style; it was made out of rough, puckery seersucker and the pants were tight. The arms were hairless.

"I'm prescribing Darvon and taking you off pheno-barbital. You've pulled through. Congratulations. How do you like your baby?"

"She is beautiful," I said.

"So is her mother," he said, which seemed a little off-color to me, for the circumstances. All these months of his sticking his fingers inside little latex gloves, and then into me, and never any mention.

"You can be discharged tomorrow," he said. I looked up and he was gone.

Then Loretta came through the door like a bolt. It wasn't even seven o'clock. None of the hospital staff had started to bother me yet.

"You've got to do something about him," her voice began. "He won't leave us be. I invited him to come up, you know, you were going to have the baby, and Gina, well, he could help me get through Gina's ordeal. But he's not really helping anybody. I thought he was a gentleman, Alma. Does he think I am just going to pick up and leave with him?"

"What does he say?" I asked.

"He loves me. He loves me. I don't know how you take that, I mean. Does it bother you?"

"It's okay," I mouthed.

"Oh, Alma, that's good to know." She patted my hand. "He said I had to make a choice. We're going to live together, or we aren't. I can't decide right now. Talk to him, Alma, please. I mean, I don't know for sure what your relationship to him is exactly—"

It was hardly morning, I already told you. An orderly came in who didn't have the authority to tell Loretta to get out. He went into my bathroom and poured a blue antiseptic down the toilet. I found myself patting a blanket at the foot of the bed, a gesture to get Loretta to sit. Then I told her, "I gave up on him when I was ten."

"How can you be so harsh, Alma, honestly. He can be such a darling."

"Loretta," I said. "Listen to me. I know him. You can do better."

"Are you trying to talk me out of this, Alma? Trying to advise me against this?"

"I don't care, Loretta, really," I said.

"Your father is a good guy. You don't know—" she said. With a half smile on her face.

"I know him, I know him," I said.

"I love him," Loretta said.

"Good for you," I said.

"Are you mad?" Loretta asked.

"He's never done anything I asked him to do, as long as I can remember, except leave," I said. "I can't talk him into anything."

"Alma, you're so bitter. You've only got one father," she said, her head tilted to one side for emphasis. Then for a few minutes she didn't say anything.

Loretta can have a way of momentarily disowning her life, and at the times she does this, you see her face as a mask, and you see she is willing to deny that any of the foregoing was the real Loretta. She can disown her presence, step away from it, just tell you to look at that mess—Isn't it a gas? This can make people feel maybe panic in her presence. She made my heart pump.

"This is so fucking ridiculous, I mean, who do I think I am. Gina's mother? Who is she? Who the hell? Sometimes I really don't care anymore. I want Fred."

"Yes," I said. This made me want to throw up. At the idea of Loretta and my father. At the idea of my father and anyone.

"I mean, Gina's a drag, isn't she? She's a fucking drag.

I am getting so tired of it. That's why they call people like Gina drags, you know. They don't know which way they are going, and I get so tired of trying to pull her through the door." Loretta went on, and I had no idea how to take it. Was I supposed to deny it? I was. She wouldn't let me. It was funny, maybe, but I hadn't any humor. Finally she quit pumping along and said that just babies are real. Just babies. Just babies are unambiguous. And then I did the right thing. A baby was a certainty, a fact. A given. She was holding my foot under the cover as she said this: "If you see Fred, tell him— Never mind."

"What?" I said.

"Oh, that I'm coming. He should just give me a breather. I'm coming along. Gina and I have business to finish up, you know, we were going to take her old penis and put it in a little lace sock and pitch it into the Chesapeake. Does that sound strange to you? And we were going to celebrate, you know, say good-bye to the last twelve years of our lives. Once she heals, that's all we have to do—just little things—"

Loretta kissed me on the forehead, almost sexily, and her breasts pressed on my chin. What now, I thought, and then Loretta said she had to go.

"We're practically related, Alma," she said, and I felt a little dread, and a little more.

The last thing in Baltimore I wanted to do was to leave the hospital. With Loretta gone, all I had was the thought of leaving, and I crimped up, sank. I hated to leave places, really, especially places that are safe. This is the same reason that I did not finish things, the same reason I don't like to drive. If you don't drive, then somebody else, the driver, will always make the decision to leave a place. Also, of course, my mother drives so very well. There was never any reason, when I was younger, for me to go to the highway department and take the test. Momma thought it was Daddy who would teach me, Daddy figured Momma would, and Momma thought maybe the school would. She had me on automatic by an early age, maybe by three or four. The do-it-yourself menstrual kit, I told you. She was a very capable woman, so I must be a very capable daughter, it followed, didn't it? But I was really a crip, a lame-o. Like my daddy, an unstrong lame-o.

I always liked to do pictures, though. In first grade a crayon picture of mine—a brick house with two symmetrical bushes in front and a mother and father and a cute daughter with two fat bushy pigtails (I had only one, and it was limp, I promise you)—won a prize. Even though it was a great lie, that picture. We didn't live in a brick house. I wasn't cute. But pictures executed in crayon do not make you an artist. So I got a box of watercolors. They were fine, the pictures were fine, but I had this internal flaw, this black hole in my being, that kept showing up in the work—brought about by inattention or a change of intention. Too many colors mixed make shit brown, or black, and then I'd try to paint over the muddiness with another color, but then, in the spot of the original mistake, I'd paint over and over and over, until the head of the brush cut a hole in the soggy paper. Lots of pictures I did like that, with a hole in them. It was depressing. My mother threw them out. And then I found out about white paint. White acrylic paint. And gesso, thick white gesso paste, which you could mix with white paint. You could do something two days later and work so well with the mistakes that you could breathe freely and no longer be troubled. This is the reason I became a painter. But you cannot work it over life, can you? You cannot go back and get it right once everything's been ruined.

The sky would fall if I left the hospital. Richard's

nerves would snap. I would have to greet Gina, have to walk again, feed myself and care for my rock breasts, take care of everybody instead of being taken care of. I would get into a car with Richard and we would drive home, and there we would have family life. I was petrified. My mother would come see my life, a mess.

I had smiled when Dr. Felt told me I could go home, because that was the role, for me to smile and be thankful, et cetera.

A little after Loretta's departure I put on the closed-circuit TV shows about taking care of your newborn infant. They were daubing the umbilicus with alcohol. Everybody is born with this ugly piece of mother hanging there, I was thinking, all fine save for that.

I went through the day with a wistfulness, a sense of last things. This is the last set of nurses I'll see—like that—as they trotted baby Ruth in and gave free diapers, and the last bland breakfast and lunch. With all these ladies taking care of me, I really hadn't moved in days, hadn't done more than sit in the hot shower and get back into bed.

If labor brought about anything, I supposed, it was this reappraisal between body and mind, the sense that a body is something that confines you, something that you are caught in, something that holds you here. And your body is so much more powerful than yourself, so much more intelligent. It isn't yours anymore, as much. It is your baby's. You become one who is owned, not one who is her own.

This feeling lasted through much of the chilly, air-conditioned afternoon. Ruth was beside me, her thick cotton blanket kicked down to the front of her bed. I wished she would wake so I could hold her because it is extremely solitary to be with just your alien odd body alone in a room. I began to feel vaporous and large—

as if I would expand, even explode. I was a bag of humors, a sack of gas. I slept like this for a while, and my brain ran on and on, I didn't have to pay attention to it. I slept all over the room. I pressed against the windows. I couldn't go home, it would force me to condense so, to contract.

Richard woke me. There was a forced kindness in his manner that stayed with him for days, like a veneer. He was trying to overlook our argument the other night. He was not picking it up where we had left off. This was a new start—he looked as odd as he had at our wedding. His hair was brushed. It stood up on his head. He was taller, more slender, slightly callow, slightly shocked.

Ruth was away having her discharge exam. We sat and missed her. Richard went to the nurses' station to see about her return, and when he came back he took out a long layette nightgown from a white bag he'd put on the chair. Color: pink.

"I've got her whole wardrobe in here," he said, taking out a pile of doll's clothes and rubber pants.

They were spread over the bed when Ruth arrived, rolling in on her truck, screaming. I sat there struggling a few seconds and Richard crawled closer. The clothes fell to the floor. He breathed on her and she stopped crying. We both held her at the head of the bed, Richard's arm around me, my arm around Ruth, his left arm on her tummy. She nursed. This went on until it got stale.

"There's something I have to tell you," he said. "You aren't going to believe it."

"Yes?" I said.

"Carmen's knocked up."

"I know," I said. This was the first time I had talked and fed Ruth at the same time.

"Lucas told you?" he asked.

"Carmen told me."

"Is it his?" Richard asked. "This I have to know."

"It's his," I said.

"What's Carmen going to do?"

"I don't know," I said, lying.

"I don't believe you," Richard said. "You saw her, didn't you?"

"It is Carmen's business," I said.

"She's having an abortion. That's it. I've got to tell Lucas," Richard said.

"No," I said. "That's *not* it. Where does all this loyalty to Lucas come from?"

"We're working on something," Richard said. "You have to tell me what you know."

"It's Lucas's, it is," I said.

"Will she go back to him?" he asked.

I couldn't tell Richard what Carmen had told me. He didn't seem to get that, though.

"At least tell me if she's going to keep living with Mary Ann."

"I'm not sure. I really am not," I said.

"There are lives at stake, Alma," he said. "Please, honey, don't be stubborn."

"Whose?" I asked.

"Everybody's," he said.

"Richard, you are making me mad," I said.

"So I make you mad," he said.

"I can't tell you any more," I said.

"Forget it," he said, consciously trying to avoid more of a fight. "She's out," he said, meaning our infant was asleep.

Richard talked about his finishing in the nursery, which he had to go home to. The nursery was another surprise. He went away and I took Ruth from her box and held her and slept.

Saturday morning a nurse came in and asked when I was leaving. "Well, here you are," she said. "You should sign these things." She took scissors and went for Ruth, who was propped on the pillows beside me, looking exquisitely blank, never opening her two eyes at once.

"I'm just going to cut the bracelets," she said, and then she did mine and Ruth's and showed me that the two numbers were exactly the same. I signed a paper that said I had no complaint: this baby was my baby. This is the one that *came out of me*. So I wrote the name Alma Taylor Kaplan, and beside my signature was printed in black letters the word MOTHER.

This was the oath, so it was final.

Then I felt quite brave and exalted. I would give it a try. Ruth looked better and better in her second nightgown. I put on my underwear and stepped into my shoes, which were enormous. My feet, which had been swollen as thick as two table telephones, were now just my feet. I could have whatever gear the hospital had supplied, the nurse had told me, so I took it and stuffed it in the shoulder bag we'd brought to the hospital. An inner tube to sit on, a squirt bottle for my tush, two brands of spray novocaine, the plastic shower caps. I even took the samples of cream and soap. It was as if I needed every souvenir. I held everything, including Ruth in her nightgown and blanket, and my sack, and my free infant-care booklets, and sat at the edge of the bed in my underwear. The bed was also stripped.

"You look like a bag lady," my husband told me. "A nudist one." Then he produced a dress from out of my past and old flat jelly shoes and I loved him so much for the time being, for these things. He held Ruth while I dressed, and we walked, with a few vague good-byes to disinterested nurses, to the doors on the very quiet rubber floor. If this story could just end here, as we went outside into the morning, with our very own red baby, it would be delightful, wouldn't it.

When we got to the old Triumph, I saw that Richard had rolled up its ancient, cracked top. Not in all the time I had known him, not in summer thunderstorms nor in the cranky, wet West Virginia snow, had he ever bothered to pull up the top. He'd always said it was stuck for good, and he couldn't get it fixed, but there it was, and I hardly recognized the car for a minute. Ruth would be strapped and clamped into the front, he explained, facing toward us, and I'd squeeze in on the left, and we'd drive.

About halfway home, Richard said he'd got a list of discharge instructions from the nurse. I had heard them too, when she'd brought in the Mother Oath to sign, but I'd paid little attention. I wasn't to climb stairs for a week. I was to take hot baths as needed.

"Don't leave the house," Richard said. "You have to stay mostly in bed. I'll bring food up to you."

I knew this already, but I wanted to forget. I had to avoid the stairs because I'd torn enough, the stitches could fly open. In Ethiopia, a woman doesn't go out of the house after childbirth for six weeks, because evil spirits or odors or probably infections can fly in, I guess in Ethiopia women are regarded as kinds of traps, so they stay in bed a long time. And on the day a woman is allowed to leave the house, the people of the village bring in a goat, and they kill it in the living room, and the new mother eats bleeding liver. Then her period of confinement is over.

"Why can't I go out if I stay on the sidewalk?" I said. "The sidewalk is level."

"Look, Alma, you are still not well, follow the instructions for once, okay? Don't give me a hard time," Richard said jovially, and sternly too.

"Are you going to be with me all the time?" I asked.

"Yeah, but I have to see people one day. About a building. Tomorrow."

That seemed aggressively soon for him to go. "How can you go tomorrow?" I asked.

"Your mother will be here," he said. "She's going to be here. I didn't tell you? She's driving up right now. She called this morning at 6:45, woke me up, to tell me she'd be up today."

This message got me like a lasso and tied me right up. The yellow Pontiac. A million instructions. A reorganization of every room in the house.

We got back to the ritual of all these first things. The first time Ruth entered her house, the first time we went through the door as parents, the first time Ruth heard music. Richard put on music, the Brandenburg Concertos, followed by Elvis Costello.

The house was quite clean—Richard had done his best—and I got a hit of peace, there. Ruth opened one eye and then the other, and for a while I only held her, hot little melon. How hard could this be? Richard didn't want me to go up the stairs to settle in yet, because he wanted to put the lampshade up in the nursery.

What broke her was leaving the hospital, I think. There is so much promise in a hospital. It's a temple if the body is the spirit. And if the healing of one, the body, is a help to the other. Of course, if you are not getting well, the hospital gets tired of you. Or if what is wrong with you is unlocatable in the body, good-bye, they say. So Alma went out the door like any other brave new mother. Richard was being so good, too.

When she thinks of me, when I cross her mind, she thinks of me as solid. As one full of intentions. I can only attribute this to her being by habit a daughter. Or to my failure to reveal myself, to ever speak freely. This is because I was torn, always was, from the time at the end of my childhood—when I was on Brighton Beach, I suppose, and that woman came after me. And I ran into the water with my clothes on.

Alma's passing through Philadelphia now, grim Philadelphia, its heavy-porched row homes are filing by, and it is starting to rain. She's awake for the announcement of Trenton.

I love her now. I really do.

People pull their suitcases down the aisles, to prepare for their exit onto the platform at Trenton. And as soon as the stop's been made, the line forms for Newark and certain men who have seemed all along to regard this train ride as an occupation, as a source of interest, are standing now, to ensure they will be the first out in New York. Alma can't compete with all the men who have been paying attention for hours, so she allows them to line up, like Boy Scouts, prepared. She remembers her portfolio, and she stands, grabs that and her small bag and her purse. The next thing after this passage underground is the City of New York, where her life can start over.

You have to wonder why she's allowed to do this—to hurl herself out of one life and helter-skelter into another. The train should have wrecked. She's so wrong to have left Richard, who was trying so hard there at the end when the baby was born, and to have left Ruth, as if Alma's own body had no say in the matter. Alma's own body, which craves Ruth now like an addict. I think Alma can leave because there are more fissures than seams in the world Alma lives in, more holes than there are places holding together. This is obvious.

Down the stamped metal Amtrak stairs to the track platform, up the concrete steps, to the escalator. Alma hates escalators. Into the main lobby of the station, past the phones and johns and the shops—past a seller of fresh-baked plate-size bagels, under the sign that reads TO STREET TO TAXIS, and into the awful rainy loud New York at Seventh Avenue, in front of Madison Square Garden, where messengers on bicycles are ready to commit mayhem on men or women or cars or each other. New York's shock. And she stands there, getting over it.

She has wet spots on her front and, simultaneously, she's

started to cry for no reason, as they say. And someone, a man in a crumpled black raincoat, sees that she's crying and lets her have the cab he'd hailed. This time the cabbie is a junkie. Who is singing "You Can't Roller Skate in a Buffalo Herd" to himself, intelligibly, and then he follows it with "Vincent" and Alma has to repeat to him four times, "Hotel Salazar, Hotel Salazar, Hotel Salazar, Hotel Salazar," a hotel near Washington Square she's been to once before, where the rooms are twenty dollars a night in 1979, and the man behind the desk in the lobby is in a cage. Of wire and bulletproof glass. The cabbie stops on Eighth Street for no reason he readily explains. It's a pause. It's a double-park. And she's frightened—her sense of geography is poorer than mine, and she panics a minute, because she knows she's not where she belongs—she's stalled, one more time.

And before she's even through trying to decipher the mad taxicab driver's explanation, about one-way streets, about how far he can and can't go, Alma bolts. She's too high-strung for this. She throws a ten-dollar bill at his face and she bolts. She rushes down two streets, and over a block from the town houses facing the park, down to her rotten hotel, where, in the lobby, stand two men—one with an earring, the other with a leather pouch at his belt—and she pays her money to the man in the cage, in advance for the night, and signs her name "A. Taylor."

And everything about her that you already know—everything starting with a year and a half ago up to the birth of her baby— is over, gone through, worn down, wearing away. She's broken with it. She's broken down.

The thing in Room 21 that was once a TV is now used as an ashtray. On the wall near the corner of the bed is a brown stain that looks like dried blood. A large window with insulated curtains of vinyl brocade goes up to the ceiling. A carpet, which is a very unmemorable beige, is on the floor. In spots, things have been spilled—some have been removed, others have not. The Salazar has made a few efforts. The bedspread is maroon crushed velvet, synthetic. And the bathroom is quite clean. Alma thinks this room must be the hooker's room, one usually reserved, and she bolts the door and spreads out on the bed with her legs apart in a V, and her mind goes completely out, zap. It is remarkable how easily a person can actually become no one. In a few hours on a train, erased. It is as if she no longer exists. I have decided this is tragic.

The knock on the door was a kaboom, a disturbance of the shaky order. Richard looked through the lights at the top and said it was my father.

"Where's the new momma?" my daddy asked, slinking in the door, standing to one side.

Our house was quite small. It was easy enough to see me from the door. Richard pointed to the red chair, and my daddy sat on it, and I tried not to feel entirely invaded. He'd never been to my house before, or been anywhere I lived without Mother.

"Want something to drink?" Richard said. Then, remembering, he continued, "Coffee, Seven-Up, orange juice, Perrier. . . . " The fridge was stocked with fluids.

Fred handed me a present wrapped at the Hopkins gift shop. I knew the white paper. A stuffed kangaroo, on the small side. The kangaroo smiled at us both.

"How's everything coming?" He touched Ruth's foot with his thumb. "Just as sweet as she can be," he said, and for the rest of the time he visited, he ignored her completely. We had a dose of silence.

"Jo Ann here?" he asked, and then he gagged a bit. A nervous laugh.

"I think she'll be here tonight," I said.

"Oh yeah," he said. Another silence. He hesitated awhile, trying to find a spot, on the floor, finally, for his mug. He sat, as he had in the hospital, as he did in my mother's overdecorated house, on the tip of his chair, resting more on his knees than on his seat. Why is he so uncomfortable? I was thinking. I could not remember him ever sitting deep in a chair.

Richard went up the stairs with a step stool from the kitchen and a screwdriver.

"Can I give you a hand with that?" Fred asked, but Richard said no, misunderstanding my father was seeking a function.

"Well," Daddy said, finally.

I could think of nothing to start off with. So I said, "How's your life?"

"Oh, fine," his eyes rolled up, meaning not so fine.

"And Loretta?" I said. This sent a wallop right through him.

"You know?" he said. "Well, you know. She must have talked to you."

In the midst of this Ruth made a poop, and I had to open the luggage. The dozen T-shirts and the clinky bottles and potions and aluminum tubes and packets of hospital surplus spilled all over the floor as I felt for the Pampers at the bottom, while I held Ruth in the other hand. My father did not offer to help. It was woman's work, and wasn't I the woman? I noted this but I wasn't angry. Instead I felt sorry that he was so frozen he couldn't help me. It was his limitation. He sat until I was done and Ruth was put back together. He winced at the green-black umbilicus, but said not a word. I read the instructions again. It was to be exposed, outside the diaper. He made some remark about how complicated such tasks seemed to him, and I thought of Richard upstairs, who could build lamps and do carpentry, and get his Triumph top up, and parse out all the straps and buckles on the contraptions for infants, but who couldn't figure out whether to snap the baby's cotton-knit smocks in the front or the back. I wanted to run up the stairs right that minute and teach him the whole code of collars and buttons, of Velcro and snaps. Richard did try, though;

he would learn. He wasn't hopeless like Fred. I sat there and my father and I looked at each other. The cat was out of the bag. Him and my buddy Loretta. Fact.

"How is Gina?" I finally asked him.

"Gina? Gina's coming out of the woods," he said, shaking his head back and forth. "You know what Loretta thinks, I guess, that Gina needs her more than ever now. When's this going to stop?"

"What, exactly?" I asked, knowing full well.

"Christ, Alma," he said, in a confessing tone. And then I understood his earlier reticence. He had been waiting for my entire attention. Had to have it. He was ready to open up. "Every little plan I make, Loretta reminds me of Gina's condition, or her pills, or the surgery. Even if I say we go out and eat somewhere besides the hospital cafeteria, she gives me grief. And she keeps on telling me that 'any commitment right now would be premature.' "

"Daddy, I'm staying out of this," I said.

"I'm looking for a place up here," he said.

"Where are you staying?" I asked, realizing I might even offer a place, I felt that generous. But Jo Ann would be here.

Daddy said he had a motel room with a kitchenette near Pulaski Highway. "I don't need anything elaborate," he said. Then he waited. "You have a problem with me and Loretta?"

"You love who you want," I said. "It is your life."

"She's the one for me, we are going to work it out. We are compatible, you know. Sometimes she reminds me— Never mind."

"Reminds you of what?"

"Of Jo Ann when she was very young."

"Great," I said.

"You really got a hair up your ass about this, don't you?"

"I don't care, I don't," I said to my father, sitting there

with Ruth in my lap, still as a doll. "You like Loretta. Loretta likes you. What have I really got to do with it?"

"I am family," he said, and I saw his bad teeth, the stubble on his weak chin. "We are going to be living right here in Baltimore."

"Great," I said.

"I'm gonna be one of your circle," he said, raising one eyebrow, feeling me out about this.

"Shit, Daddy, look. I've been sick. I just had a baby. I have a new husband who is trying to sell a few houses. It's tough. I've got a headache I've had for a very long time. I have to go back to work in a couple of weeks. And Momma's coming tonight. I'm not dying for Momma to be coming," I said, upset with myself immediately for being harsh.

"I can see where you wouldn't—"

"But it's okay. She'll help. I just don't have any opinions right now about your love life."

"It bothers you, don't it," he said, leaning forward, his elbow on his knee.

"Lord, I think it's great. Fantastic. It is wonderful. I mean it. You need somebody. Loretta needs you. It's great."

He must have needed to hear it badly, because he believed me. "Alma, just tell me what I ought to do—"

"About what?"

"About her being namby-pamby. Putting her he-she Gina in front of us. What do I do?"

"I'll tell you what I think. You promise not to ask anymore."

"Promise?" he said. "Well?"

"I'd go home, Durham. Come back in a couple of weeks. This is tough. They've been together a long time. Longer than you think. Twelve years."

His mouth moved around as if he were searching for something with his lower jaw. He was pissed. "Don't tell me to give up. Alma. You and Jo Ann always expect me to give up. To give up and to give up, I'm not going to this time."

"Daddy," I said. I felt horrible. First he doubted me, then he believed me. Now he doubted me again. Or rather, he figured I had no faith in him. So he doubted himself. Which was my fault, somehow.

"You think I'm chicken-shit, don't you," he said. "I'm not."

I wished he would go. And then he did.

When I stood my head pounded.

I closed the door after my father. And then Richard met me on the landing. He asked me why I was crying.

It wasn't anything in particular, I told him. Just my father's general pitifulness. And the way he always expected—

"Fuck him," Richard said. "Look, are you supposed to jump up and down 'cause he's got a thing for one of your friends?"

"I didn't encourage him," I said.

"Well, what kind of thing is that to encourage? Don't lose it on me, Alma. He's a schmuck. So's my father a schmuck. All fathers are schmucks. I'm the only guy in the universe who isn't a schmuck father. Maybe Lucas isn't. Lucas isn't."

"Lucas?" I said.

"Never mind," Richard said. "The returns are still out on Lucas, huh? Forget I said that."

I did forget he said that. We went directly forward to other things. Richard was planning to unveil the nursery. And establish Ruth in her abode, and to get me to stop moping about my father. He came to an impasse. How could we leave the baby so Richard could help me up the stairs? He wouldn't think of leaving her downstairs alone. Somehow we all went up to the top together, Richard cradling Ruth with one hand and holding me with the other, at the elbow. The smaller of the upstairs bedrooms was painted a faint pink and on the sanded floor was a striped rag rug, a ten-dollar rug, but quite beautiful somehow, in this space. The curtain was an old crocheted tablecloth, a thirties pattern. On the overhead lamp was a cone-shaped parchment shade from the fifties, laced around the edges to the frame. The crib we had found together at the Veterans Warehouse. Richard had stripped it a month ago, but since then he'd sanded it and rubbed it. It was golden oak. There was a rocking chair and a black bureau with a rose-colored cloth on top, where Richard had placed a little tray, with padding, for a changing table. He'd built this. The whole place was a roseate shrine, nestled in our house. Somehow it had the scent of sandalwood. I let down the crib bars and put a sheet on the mattress. It was a dream place. When I had seen the crib the week before, it was in pieces, and the floor of the room was scratched, the walls stripped and ragged. It was a tiny room, ten by seven, but nothing seemed crowded now.

I told him the nursery was beautiful.

"I'll watch her, you go to bed," he said to me.

It was afternoon, later, and I was lying in state when I heard someone opening the downstairs door.

Richard ran up from the back of the house where he'd been on the phone.

"Alma, Alma, I'm here," she said. It was the original yellow lady, my mother. I felt a little odd and sad, upstairs in my old bed. When I went to the landing, Mother was good to see, there in the doorway, in her hairdo and her raincoat. Why is it true that we are always pleased at the first sight of our parents, no matter what?

Richard greeted her with less equanimity than when

he had greeted my father. She'd broken and entered, in order to save us, like a fireman. Our house, our family life, both. Fred hadn't done that—he was a needier visitor. After I had a glimpse of my mother, I wanted to comfort baby Ruth, who was suddenly in great need of something. She didn't want to eat; the breast seemed to make her angrier. She began to scream and turn vermilion. Her red, curled little feet folded up and she nearly convulsed with wails. This seemed to go on longer than it had gone on before, at least longer than my present tolerance. I wanted to be downstairs to see my mother. I wanted to touch her. I could hear her saying to Richard that it didn't matter where she slept.

Then I heard, *"Where's my grandchild?"* And hearing Ruth wail, she clomped up to get her.

"Sit her up, Alma," were her first words to me. "She has to burp. She's got something on her stomach, honey. What a big face on that child," she said, approvingly, actually. "Too bad about the wine stain. She can be bleached."

"It's a hemangioma," I said. "A flame. You can see it gets darker when she cries. It's nothing."

"We call it a wine stain, darling," she said. "That's what we always called it."

Then I wanted my mother to leave.

"I'm your Grammy Jo Ann," she said to my tortured beet-red baby, whom she held in the air like a bouquet of roses, with two hands, a trophy cup. Shortly Richard was in the room too, to ask if he could help. The second time that day Ruth entered his arms and she was, a second time, as if he had a charm, quieted.

Just as Ruth was placid, my mother saw some mustard drip through the diaper. She took the baby from him. Richard was irritated. He made a face to me, as if I could control my mother.

She thrust Ruth down on the pad and changed her

brutally, grasping her ankles and yanking up her feet like two dead fish. Richard ground his teeth during this maneuver.

"Jo Ann," he said, "aren't you being rough?"

My mother looked at him as if he hadn't said anything, as if to say, *Erase that remark.*

"Where's the baby powder?" she asked me.

"I don't know," I said. "Richard put the nursery together."

"We aren't going to use it," Richard said, " 'cause it gets in their lungs. The pediatrician said to use soap and water."

"You set up the nursery here, in this place?" she asked him. Richard nodded.

"Well, it's nice," she said, meaning the opposite. She would have some suggestions soon, I knew, some ruffles, a cushion for the rocking chair. I was still standing there waiting for my baby back, most likely looking at my mother in a kind of panic. I didn't *like* her. Fred was right. She wasn't likable.

I could feel it. I was feeling for Fred for the first time in years. With Jo Ann, nothing was ever wrong, as long as she had control over it. If she did not control it, or have a good reason for it, it *did not exist*. This was true for the following: sex, weakness in herself, indecision in others (she couldn't handle it, wouldn't entertain it, except Fred's indecision, which she paid so much attention to), and any unquenchable desire. No desire is worth noticing if you can't do something about it. My mother was a great editor. Her basic rule for raw experience: there is nothing that she couldn't help, or at least pretty up. She looked dry and crackly standing there, holding my half-grumpy baby. Finally she understood I wanted Ruth back, or rather, she felt like getting on to the next thing. "How long are you going to nurse?" she asked.

I answered in the provocative: "A year, I don't know."

"What?" she asked. "It's a drain. You don't know yet," she said. "I nursed you two months, Lord, couldn't go on. You were so fat. I couldn't go on."

"Why?" I said.

"You smell sour. You walk through the streets smelling like sour cream. Just like sour cream. Like you bathed in it."

Richard was still there with us in the nursery, on guard, so that Mother wouldn't manhandle his princess again. Then he sort of broke into a smile and tried to get us to sit down in the bedroom.

Then he thought he'd bring up some coffee. As long as he was serving and Momma was on the take, maybe everything would be fine. Before she said yes to coffee, she picked up the rocker with one arm in order to drag it into the bedroom, and Richard offered to help her, but she wouldn't be helped.

The evening went the same way. My mother's every move, every gesture, grated on us. The way she held the baby bothered Richard. He whispered to me he'd seen kosher butchers who were more gentle than my mother. It was an exaggeration. She was firm, and she held the little fanny in one palm as she balanced Ruth on her shoulder. But this was not as Richard made it out to be, it was a fireman's carry. She'd come to save us, I said. True, my mother is not the mother of the Ivory soap box.

When Richard was out of the room once, she said, "He's going to spoil that baby, he's too protective. One thing I have to tell you. Just one thing in the way of advice. You have to learn to let them cry."

And instead of being there, in that close, tense minute with my mother, I remembered, vividly, being in my crib. It was as if I could shut my eyes and see it, being in my crib and crying my daylights out. It was not completely dark in this room where I was in my crib. I was in a hall, lit at one end by a purplish twilight. I put my fists in my eyes, finally, for solace, and stared at the fuchsia and yellow and orange lights on my closed lids. It was a strange little liquid movie; I kept pressing and pressing. The lights got brighter and brighter. When I opened up my eyes, it was minutes before I could see. Then I did it again. This, doing this, was my first memory. It was quite available at that moment, as I sat there with my mother. She brought it to me. That was how I learned to put myself to sleep. That was the first time I took care of myself. I was trying to decide if it was a good start. It wasn't.

"You have to let them cry it out, Alma, listen to me," she said. "Are you listening to me?"

"I have a terrible headache," I said, hoping she would stop.

"I'll get you some aspirin," she said, patting me on the knee. Then, without even trying the medicine cabinet, she went to the top of the stairs and yelled for Richard.

"What's he doing down there?" she asked me, as if to accuse him in advance. "Doesn't he go to work?"

"He sells houses, Momma. He doesn't have to go into the office to do that."

"Huh," she said. "He had a job when he married you, didn't he?"

"It was federally funded. The funds were cut. And he has a job now. He is a real estate person."

"He was laid off?" she asked. "From the other, I mean?" She was wearing a shirtwaist dress that might have been quite old, I couldn't tell. The stripes were vertical, a pretty periwinkle blue bordered by lines of orange. It was cotton. The belt was the same material, cut on the bias. She wore tennis shoes, which indicated she intended to do labor in this house. Much of it, as far as I could tell, Richard had already done, but she would think of something soon enough. My mother is a size fourteen because of her breasts, which could have been lower and more shapeless on a woman her age, but they sat up instead, pointing at me. If she had just sat there and said nothing, I would have loved her a little bit.

"No," I said. "The job was eliminated."

"I see," she said. "Well, how many houses has he sold?"

"Some. He's made money," I said. "And I'm working. I'm going back to work."

"Now?" Her legs were straight up and down, like poles, planted in her thick terry footlets. She nodded.

"Why not?" I asked. "Richard's doing fine. He can stay here, clients call him here."

"Yes," she said, as if to say, "I hear you." If she could just sit there and be quiet, I could appreciate her, at least I could like the two lamp-pole legs, which were just like my own now. But she wouldn't shut up. "He's a salesman?" she said. "That's a mistake."

"How do you know?" I asked.

"Because when you have lived as long as I have, excuse me for saying it, you know a few things are predictable: all salesmen are sad sacks in the end. Deadbeats."

"Not a salesman," I said. "He might go into renovating houses, investments."

"Contracting?" she asked. "They will steal."

"Who?"

"The painters, the plumbers. They all drink, you know—" She stopped. "Oh, I'll be quiet."

"Thank God," I said to myself. Then she yelled down to Richard for aspirin for me. He brought up Tylenol. Aspirin would slip into the milk.

"Huh?" my mother contradicted. "I don't mean to say anything, but where did you get that wives' tale?"

"The doctor," Richard said.

"And he said Alma couldn't go up and down the stairs for a week?" she asked.

"She had *eclampsia*," Richard said.

"That's long over," my mother contradicted again.

"Yes, but—" Richard said.

"And everybody tears," Mother said. "A baby tears you open. It happens to everybody. I don't mean to tell you two what to do, but—"

"What?" Richard said, too loudly for the circumstances, even though he was trying to be decent.

"Alma ought to get up and get around," my mother said. "Was that a regular doctor or a young one?" she asked.

"A regular, young doctor. Dr. Ted Felt. The one who delivered Ruth."

"I see," my mother said. She turned to me. "Alma, can you stand spending six days upstairs? Not being able to do anything, not even watch the TV?"

"I'll bring the TV up," Richard said.

"I'm talking to Alma, thank you," my mother said.

"I don't watch TV," I said.

At this point air escaped through Richard's teeth in a gush—as when you let out a bicycle tire. His hands were in his pockets, but his face was getting stiff. He had a forced smile.

"Calm down, Momma," I finally said, my heart beating. My mother seemed so large in this space, in my house. Maybe nine or ten feet tall. Her feet were size tens. She was taller than Richard. When she looked at him, he diminished. They couldn't be in the same place at the same time. I'd have to work out the physics. It seemed insoluble. My heart would not stop beating so I could solve it.

"What's wrong?" my mother asked, actually not knowing, actually having no earthly idea.

"Nothing," I said. "Maybe we could set up the TV," I said to Richard.

"Richard's been working all week, Momma," I said. "He bought everything—the whole layette, the works."

"Uh-huh," she said. After that she was uncommunicative for some time, in the nursery alone, doing something like folding the receiving blankets. While she did this she hummed her own tunes and talked to herself aloud, telling herself things she would do next and in what order. *Straighten out the closet. Ask him to bring up the vacuum, if they have one. Wipes. More Pampers. Paper towels for up here. Cornstarch. And an ear syringe.* "Alma, how are your nipples?" she asked me. "Do you want any of those rubber cups with the pinholes in them?"

I told her no.

"I'll get him to get you some," she said.

"Who?" I said.

"Richard. Will he go out to the K-Mart if I send him?" she asked.

"You could ask," I said. "No, I'll ask him. *Richard,*" I yelled.

"Oh, Alma, get up and go downstairs," she said. "What is wrong with you? You don't have to yell at everybody like a fishwife."

"The doctor told me not to," I said. "I really feel like shit, too."

"Don't say that," she said.

Richard came up, wearing an apron. He had been cooking a soup. Chicken, I could tell. He would not be the first one to address Jo Ann. I'd have to intercede.

"Would you go to the K-Mart?" I asked him.

"I'll give you the money," my mother said. She reached for the small vinyl change purse in her dress pocket, unzipped it and produced a fifty.

"I have cash," Richard said.

"No, no, my gift," Jo Ann said. "Please. I haven't given the baby anything yet."

Richard took it.

"I would go myself—" she said.

"That's okay," Richard said.

"Do you have a vacuum?" she asked. This was all more civil than their previous exchanges. "With an attachment for the windows?" she asked.

"I'll get it," Richard said. "It's in the basement."

"Just tell me where it is," Jo Ann said. "I'll get it myself."

Richard had gone downstairs again, and I thought, He's trying but he's not going to last. Then I looked at the clock.

Like a fist shoving its way up between her breasts, Alma's hunger wakes her. She's in the Hotel Salazar. It is October in New York so it could be light in her room, but it isn't, really, it's a dark whore-and-her-clientele room. The brownish bathroom tiles seem friendly, seem homey, seem clean like a motel. With them, she feels safer. In the main room, the blood and dirt on the walls and on the rug have upset her: she feels that the filth can invade her somehow. She is vulnerable to it.

Alma washes herself. First she soaks her face and neck in the sink, and then she has a shower. She drips the water down her neck, scrubs her cheeks the long time it takes for them to bloom a little. Alma is thinking about her mother's visit. It was wonderful to see her, awful to be with her. And Alma thinks that if she can think about it long enough, perhaps another quarter of an hour while she's preparing to go out, she'll come to a conclusion. She'll find the solution to the problem of how to feel about her mother. Then she puts on a black crinkle-cotton dress, hose, and shoe boots and a long, oversized and overused cream-colored sweater with pockets. And she leaves. For New York, New York, the street.

Chicken with cashew nuts in a red Hunan sauce. Piles of rice. Beef and broccoli with snow peas. Pot stickers. There is paneling on the walls, and Alma's wolfing the stuff down with delight—the more she eats, the happier she gets. Tea. Beer. Tea. Maybe her breasts don't ache so much, she's thinking, sitting at her round table with the single, columnar leg.

After she's been eating for twenty-three minutes, she's through.

And for a while after she strolls through the sweet post-rainstorm evening, bistros open to the street in the West Village. And she sees couples seated at tables with peach and pink cloths, people she would be very happy to be. She would rather be anyone other than herself, and her wish, she realizes, is coming true. Because New York is not another city like Boston or Baltimore; New York is another country, the largest country in the world, if you measure metaphysical space, the density of souls. It's like the Jewish cemetery in Prague, the graves stacked twelve or twenty deep. The city is dense with souls. It is spacious, roomy, vast.

Now I am with her, I wonder if she knows it—and I am holding her hand, almost—I'm as close as that. And I'm in my own eternity, too, where I choose right now to be almost twenty. And where so many people dress so very well, and where the men promenade in the early evening in straw boaters. On early evenings not unlike this evening. Except that where I dwell there is slightly more of a breeze, and a note of the sea. And everything is possible.

Alma felt that earlier today. That everything she sees is something she can use. That she is perfectly independent. And all things are possible. She has her own. She has her own. Which is all she needs. Sometimes, this day, she has felt wild with independence, and she has felt a kind of clarity, a purity, engendered by being untouchable and being untouched. She is entertaining this feeling on her walk. But it is becoming more difficult to sustain.

So she's strolling of an evening in a most dense, most spacious place, like a soul not yet settled upon a body, like a soul that is still looking. Alma floats in her odd waistless black dress and her off-white cardigan with pockets, and I am whisking her, shoving her, back to her ugly little hotel with the whore's clean bath. She has a rendezvous, maybe she does.

And the next thing you know, as if she hadn't existed for the last three blocks of her walk, there she is, seated on her crushed-velvet bedspread in the Salazar. She lifts up her knees and now she's on her back.

It's so remarkably easy to tear away from everything, to rip one's heart out, it's a breeze, she's thinking. To be unbound as she is in her dirty room. It is so easy to be more and more and more detached.

And actually, it is—when I died I felt a remarkable lightening, a delicious feeling beginning in the veins in my limbs. An ebullient feeling, a feeling that something glistening, numinous, something phosphorescent is sifting through your limbs, through a system, perhaps, less definite and specific than veins, something is moving through you and then floating upward, out, not out through a familiar orifice, not through the mouth or the nose or the eyes, but upward to an exit at the top of the head at the exact point where you are perceiving these things, and you are perceiving, too, this pleasure which is not bothered by the way the other senses cease to be as vivid as they were. It is not like falling asleep, which is a descent. Instead the movement is flowing outward, a delirious flowing outward, a shifting outward. She is dissolving. The principle is abandon. And she does not know who she is. And she does not know who she really is now.

Now I took things so gravely it was silly, I thought, sitting there in the rocker, on a ring cushion from the hospital, holding baby Ruth. Suck, suck. Richard was gone. My mother was showering. Downstairs, the same soup was simmering. Richard had made it with a Manischewitz mix. You are taking everything too seriously, I was thinking. Then I got bored. What kind of mother gets bored with nursing in ten minutes, they play it up to be this great pleasure. I was tired, and everything hurt, and then I got a desperate thirst. My mother was right. Nursing gets old. Ruth wouldn't go to sleep. Drip, drip. I was sweating. Jo Ann was such a model, I was

thinking. Am I a mess because she mothered me wrong?
I thought about it. I thought about it not quite so gravely.

"*Alma,*" my mother said. "Where are your towels, hon?"

I just couldn't answer.

"Hon?"

I moved; Ruth lost the breast and wailed.

"Hon?"

"In the hall closet."

"*Freeshow,*" my mother said, as she came into the hall,
holding a small white towel around herself, which covered very little. She was dripping wet, her old body a
little lanky, her fanny flat. Her legs were just the legs
you see on women in their fifties. Her thighs were not
bad, only dimply on the inside. The bottoms were poles,
I told you, sort of cartoons of legs. She said, to the air,
"Where did I put that thing?" and she went back into
the bathroom, emerging a few minutes later in a zip-
pered terry robe, her hair still in a shower cap.

"You coming down for a bite?" she asked.

"I'm not supposed to go," I said.

"Oh, that's right," she said, meaning, "That's ridiculous."

"Okay," I capitulated. "I'll bathe, then I'll be down."

"Richard's taking a long time," she said.

"It hasn't been an hour," I said.

"I'm hungry as a horse," she said.

"We can eat without him," I said. I could feel myself
turning around, turning to her. It was physical. "I'm
really hungry," I said.

"Nursing will knock you right out," she said. "Takes
everything. Sucks you right down so you get a little pea
top. You will lose your bust, but you know that, I guess."
She asked in a minute, "Richard always such a moody
one?" She stood with her arm in the doorway, her face
raw without her hair.

"He's not, is he?" I asked her back.

"Is he always so uncooperative?" she asked.

"What do you mean?" I asked.

"Keeping a job," she said.

"He wasn't fired," I said.

"Okay," she said. "I'll tread lighter."

"Why don't you," I said.

"Honestly," she said, and she came closer to me and said, "Take a bath, you sweat." She took fussy Ruth from me and sent me to the tub. Fussy Ruth in her paper diaper in my mother's yellowish hand.

Hot water and fifteen minutes alone. This would be good, I thought. Sitting in it. The door was closed. I sat there and started to feel a little desolate. I needed water. I took three glasses from the tap. There were approximately seventy-five more minutes to go before I could go to sleep again. My bones still ached, and my groin felt torn open still. I kept running the water until it was steaming, and the tub was hotter than I had intended it to be. The tub was full now, the water geysering steam. In a minute I could stand it. I could see my skin was beet-red. Make it hotter, I kept thinking. I'll never be clean again. In another minute it would cool and I could stand it.

But it was smoking hot. A new wave came up from the ends of my nerves. What the hell was I doing? Scalding myself? I was blue-red as a baby.

"Momma," I said.

"What, Alma?" she asked calmly.

"Help me get out of the tub," I said.

My impulse was to jump out and wait for it to cool, but I wanted my mother. Then out of instinct I scrambled out. This quick movement got me feeling torn all over again. I was hunkered down on the white floor tiles, really miserable. I was going to faint. She came in.

"Alma, what *are* you doing?" she cracked the door open.

"Help me up," I said.

She stood there a minute. "You help yourself," she said.

"I need help," I said.

"I told you to take a bath, not cook yourself, really," she said, bending over to get me.

"Thank you, thank you," I said.

"There isn't anything the matter with you," she said. "Stop thinking there is, and it will go away. I'm telling you the truth. There's nothing the matter with you."

For some time I sat there and cried, in her arms. Everything appeared fluid, it bounced around me, and I was an idiot. It was my dumb heart that hurt me, really. I was disappointing my mother, even. No wonder she gave having a baby only one try. I had no guts, just this painted, made-up heart. I was as bad as Fred. He and I were the same—nothing left of our courage, just little floaters, tidbits of character.

Jo Ann didn't really want to make us feel the way she was making us feel in our own house. She was just still alone, as she lived alone, and she couldn't really see us or hear us for what we were. She moved around in this, a small universe of things she could control and the larger things that she owned. She was nervous in our house, of course. It wasn't hers. She would have to transform it. I thought there that I would have to do this too, learn to live alone, learn to talk to myself, learn to treat myself as a stranger. When she was with me I had no choice other than to turn into her: be solitary, be always on, be a zombie, be dead a little. Richard would be a better mother for Ruth. Not me. My mother was a decent person and I was the best she could do with me. I was going to be terrible at this. When I stood in the bathroom I felt nowhere, nothing. I did go a little blind, standing, and then the world came back to me, the world in the other room, the one I could never make right, and she began to scream and scream.

"Why are you *so* glum?" my mother put to me. "It seems to be coming out of nowhere," she said.

There is nothing the matter with me, I thought. We were entering the nursery. The space in front of me bounced, danced, moved in waves. I was a nutcake, that was the truth. There we saw Ruth squirming, fussing with the blanket, so dumb she could tell me nothing, there were just these processes there—bubbles, swallowing, plumbing, breath. I had no gut-love for her, really. I could only imagine how that felt for normal people. I stood there over the crib and was capable of anything, of any feeling, because I had none.

It was from this wretched moment forward that I started to collect good reasons to leave.

We had finished eating and Ruth was in my mother's lap and I was still more or less gone. My brain had turned into a filing system, like Jo Ann's exactly. All the things I intended to do in the next hour were there enumerated, and I would act upon them in order. Without joy. I took Ruth from Jo Ann, who had her well-dressed and combed and powdered and stuffed down into the blanket like a package, a Christmas stocking maybe, with her head flopped over.

"That mess upstairs," the hour before, when I'd been in the bath and weeping on the floor, would not enter our conversation. I was on my mother's track now, and I was seeing our life the way she saw it: two smart young people moping around in a preventable misery. We'd have to *toil* now, have to grow up, make something out of ourselves, as she called it.

"What's keeping Richard so long?" she asked. "Did he stop somewhere? Is he coming here for dinner? Home, I mean. Did he stop somewhere?"

It was ten. I didn't know. I was worried, too, when she said something. I said nothing. I couldn't get up the energy to worry, or the further energy it would take to suppress the feeling in front of her. She reached over and patted my hand: "You are just blue, Alma, some women get blue—don't take it so hard. I don't believe in postpartum depression. It's just a way of describing how you feel if you pay a lot of attention to how you feel. It's a bad idea to do that, ever. Don't take it—"

"Seriously, yes," I told her, and, since I felt twice as empty as Jo Ann Taylor, this superficial version of a mood was right. There were we: zombie daughter and zombie mother. The debris of my senses rallied.

There is a woman who throws out her own heart and goes hollow, only functions. Pieces of her being stick also to her daughter, but these too are as dead as she, since the woman who is hollow has no heart to bring to her child. Then her child grows up, with only those few pieces, and usually feels hardly alive. If she's alone she can get by—without disturbances, without other beings to disturb her. Then, that one, the hollow child, has a child, a child who doesn't know what she's lost, but she knows she is only a doll, her mother can handle dolls, not beings, and she cries over this, over and over and over. She has only scraps, no heart, because her mother has no heart because her mother lost hers, threw it out—it was too much trouble. I thought this through and sat there holding my bound-up baby, holding her good and tight.

It was after ten, and Richard still wasn't there. My mother felt sorry. Her TV show did not come on. So we sat there and listened to an easy-listening station she had found on the radio. Most of the lights in the house were off.

"Not to change the subject, Alma," she started, but I couldn't remember any subject, so I didn't mind, "but have you heard from Fred? Is he up here somewhere? When I called Marva's place she said he was visiting the Baltimore area."

"That was an odd answer," I said.

"She's like that with me," my mother said. "She's always a little off with me. She doesn't like me."

"Why?" I said.

"Because of Fred," she said, "I suppose."

"What about Fred?" I asked.

"She has a thing for him, you know that. She thinks he's wild. Something different."

"Marva Peacock? And Daddy?" I asked.

"Don't be surprised." She closed her lips together so that her mouth was ringed by multiple creases. Something disturbed her. Whether it was my reticence in answering or the thought of Daddy with another woman, I don't know.

"Well, you didn't answer me," she said.

"He's in Baltimore," I said. "He was here this afternoon. And he came to see me in the hospital."

"I see," she paused. "We aren't speaking, I guess you know," she said. "Since around the time of your wedding he has not said bleep to me." She changed her position in the chair, crossed her legs.

"Why is that?" I asked. There had been a whole year in the past when they didn't speak, so it was not unusual.

"What's the difference?" she asked. "Is he up here with Dolby?"

"No," I said.

"For Christ's sake, Alma, tell me what you know."

I wanted Momma to have sympathy for Fred. I had an idea that we could stand each other for once in our lives, with Ruth to rally around. Momma was waiting. I couldn't come up with a good way to begin. Then she said, "There is nothing your father would or could do that would surprise me," a tough leather voice. "Or even make me mad."

"Okay," I said. (Lord, what will she do? She'll get physically ill. . . .) "Fred's in love," I finally said.

"I knew it." She laughed. "I did know it. You are in on it, too. It's got you involved, doesn't it. That ass," she said. "Who is it?"

"I don't think you know her," I said.

"Is it that porky redhead who was at the wedding? The rouged-up one? With the little friend in pink?"

"Loretta?" I asked.

"That was her name," she said.

I had never exactly seen Loretta as a porky redhead. But now, in the dark with my mother, listening to a thousand strings, I could.

"Loretta," I said.

"Don't you think it was off-color of Fred to go and try to pick up somebody at your reception? Who was he trying to get back at with that?" she said. "That ass. Excuse me, but your father . . ."

"He was successful, more or less," I said.

"There must be something wrong with her," Mother said. "Must be something wrong with her if she wants to get something going with Fred. Must be handicapped or something."

"She's a little tied down. Her friend who wore pink at the wedding is in the hospital. She and Loretta are very close. They live together. Her friend is having an operation Loretta paid for."

"There's something you aren't telling me," my mother said. "What kind of operation?"

"She's a transsexual. Gina, the friend."

"And what exactly is that?" Mother sat there, deep in the futon, rigid. "Could you clue me in?"

"Like that woman tennis player. The woman tennis player who used to be a—"

"That's the ugliest woman I have ever seen," she said, not flinching, just coming up a little closer to me. "Biceps," she said, in an airy whisper of insult. A minute later she asked, "And what does the transsexual operator have to do with Fred? He picks them, doesn't he?"

"Loretta wants Fred to give her some time before they—"

"Get it together? Shack up? He's rushing her? He never has any patience. He never had one lick. That ass—"

My mother had an ease I couldn't quite trust. For a second I was convinced this really didn't bother her. But it had to. So I asked how she felt. She hadn't said anything in a while.

"You think this is supposed to shock me? That he's trying to run off with somebody half his age? He could do nothing in the world that would shock me, darling. Except something selfless, something really noble. He's a deadbeat and a lazybones, and he never would have given either me or you a hair off his head because he's selfish and sorry for himself and an ass. So he has a girl now? A porky redhead? Who's got a two-way friend? So what?" she said.

"Do you mean that?" I said.

"I am fifty-nine, Alma," she said, and she looked rather stony, her let-me-tell-ya, queen-for-a-day gaze. "I've raised you alone, I've nursed and pushed and shoved that husband around, till I finally realized, just last year, that he's a will-o'-the-wisp, he's a lightweight. He's always been smart, Alma, but he can't put one and one together. Neither can you half the time. You have to know a few things if you are going to get along, Alma, in this world. One of them is that there are very few decent men and the rest are just chaff, they are throw-outs and babies. Your daddy is a throw-out, Alma. One pension away from being a—well, a bum. I took care of Momma until I was twenty-six, Alma. She had arthritis so bad you couldn't straighten her out in the morning. She petrified alive. It was hideous. And nobody helped me do it. Nobody. I'm worked out and I'm shocked out. Nothing Fred could do would surprise me. It's occurred to me before that he and Dolby, you know, had a—"

"Momma," I said. "I don't think he goes that way."

"Don't beat your breasts, Alma," she said. "Just about everything is ugly, don't you know that? One way or another."

"It isn't that bad," I said. "Fred could be happy. And you don't need him."

"It's established I don't need him. Well as I've done without him? And he's got no heart to be happy with, Alma. He's—"

"Don't be so down on him," I said.

"These are the facts," she said, lifting to a needless smile, which meant she wanted to mask what she was saying. Her arms were on the wooden frame. Her feet were crossed at the ankles. She was still, in repose. It relaxed her to say awful things. It was cleansing. "I know your father, but you are twenty-nine years old. This month, wasn't it. Can't you face that he's a bum? Look at it," she said. "He's a wreck, not a man. I don't regret anything."

I wanted to go over and hold her around the waist. If I did she would tell me emphatically to go away. I was prepared for a rebuff. She could sit there and tell me my father was an ass all night if she wanted, and she could insult me. And tell me Richard was a bum, too, if she liked. It didn't really matter. If she cried I would sit there and die. There we did sit, me hoping she wouldn't cry, when the phone rang.

And it was Loretta saying Gina had tried to kill herself.

Richard came in with two rattling blue plastic bags while I was still on the phone. Richard could hear Loretta's high, loud, angry whine over the line.

"I'll have to hang up," I told her finally. "I'll talk to him. I'll talk to him if you let me get off the phone. Richard's here. No, you can't talk to him, he's going to bed. I'm sorry, I'm sorry." Then I hung up without her giving me leave to do so. I sat down and saw my mother there in the dark, and motionless.

She startled me. She was sleeping sitting up, like a mannequin.

"Who were you talking to?" Richard asked, after saying hello to Jo Ann.

"Loretta," I said. "Where have you been?"

My mother became animated.

"How come you are downstairs, Alma?" he asked. "Look, you are supposed to stay upstairs."

"I'm going, I'm going," I said. I could smell beer on his breath.

"Alma, don't go up until you nurse this baby," my mother said. "She's not eaten since six."

"Christ, don't wake her to feed her," Richard said. "We'll feed her when she's hungry."

"Feed her now and maybe she'll sleep through, Alma," my mother said.

Automatically, I started to undo my blouse.

"Alma," Richard said, more sternly than loudly.

"Here we are again," I said to myself. And Ruth woke just then, probably alarmed by the tension in the room. *Wah Wah Wah.*

"Oh, go ahead," Richard said. In a minute he said, "I tried to call, but you were on the phone." My mother perked up. She wouldn't ask, but she wanted to know where he had been. "I had to go to the Woolco in Eudowood and then the Hecht Company. Then I went and had a few beers."

"Well, good you got back," my mother said.

"Everything for the postmodern infant, huh," he said, opening the sack and packages. Inside, a little indoor infant seat, in yellow. Sock booties, nipple guards, Nuk pacifiers, a mobile of tiny frogs and bears, a Donald Duck night-light. He hunkered at my mother's feet and reached around to turn on the track lights over the couch. He put a receipt on the table. He said the total price. He gave her four dollars and change, placed the money on top of the receipts. Richard had been trying up to now, but there was an edge to this. My mother loved to be surrounded by objects. She felt safe. I thought of telling him to stop, put the stuff back in the bags, but I was a little shaken. I couldn't persuade anybody to get along. It occurred to me that my protest would make my mother realize Richard was insulting her in a little way. Maybe she wouldn't know.

Much later Richard and I lay in bed. My mother was asleep on the futon downstairs, and you could hear some children or sailors in the street, at a distance, calling to each other. In the nursery Ruth was on her stomach inside a fence, with a new rubber pacifier in her mouth.

"I know she's your mother," Richard said. "I'm trying, I am."

"She's sad," I said. "Think of her as sad."

"I feel sorry for her," he said. "But you are practically a perfect wreck when she's around. Where does she think she is?"

"I'm a wreck on my own, it's not her," I said.

"I don't know about that," Richard said. "So did you tell her about Fred? Does she care?"

"I don't know. I wanted her to understand. I thought she needed to be abreast. She says she doesn't care."

"And?"

"It didn't surprise her. She hates him, she says. He's an ass. He won't talk to her."

"And she's a battleship," Richard said. "How did they turn you out?" he asked. "That was a compliment," he added.

"Gina tried to kill herself tonight," I said. "Loretta said it was my fault."

"What?"

"She pulled out her prosthesis. In the john. She went

into the john and yanked out her vaginal prosthesis. Lots of blood," I said. "A regular period. Worse. This was what the Queen of Swords meant, Loretta said. Remember the cards?"

"When?" Richard said, sitting up, naked to the waist. It occurred to me how young and taut he was.

"Just a few hours ago," I said.

"What did she do that for?" he asked.

"Loretta said it was because Fred went to the hospital and made a scene in front of Gina. Said things that made Gina feel miserable."

"You told him to back off. You didn't tell him to go back there," Richard said.

"It was me. I caused it," I said.

"Come on, Alma, don't be so grandiose," he said. "You think you cause everything. I heard you tell him to go back to Durham. What are you talking about?"

"She thinks I dared him, told him he was pussyfooting around. And so he gave her this ultimatum."

"Why didn't you let me talk to her?" Richard asked.

"She would have bitten your head off, too," I said. "She's right. I said the wrong thing to Fred."

"Look, Alma, I know he's your father. He did the opposite of what you told him to do. It's him. He's an ass."

"No, the whole thing turns my stomach. He *knows* the whole idea makes me sick. Look at my mother down there. She's decided, I mean, she's absolutely positive she will not be happy in this life. She just will not, and that is that. Okay. But Fred, at least he tries. He's tried. I shouldn't have told him to go away. He had to fight back. I should have invited Loretta over, talked to the two of them."

"Listen," Richard said. "Your father is a jerk. An ass. *A-s-s.*"

"No, no, he's not," I said.

"Okay, he behaves like one. Will you grant me that?"

He had his Airedale look. "Now what happens to Gina?"

"They pry her apart tomorrow. They put the thing back in. Even overnight she'll start to close up. Loretta kept telling me Nature abhors a vacuum. Nature abhors a vacuum."

"You are crazy to blame yourself. I can't believe you'd blame yourself—"

"Okay, okay," I said. "Don't make me feel worse. I can't be for others. I'm just not very good at it. Fred or you either. I'm rotten at this. I don't have a heart."

"You are getting a little crazy, Alma," Richard said. "Baby, don't be crazy."

Now, near morning, I woke up again and heard the monkey cry, the sawing razor cry, of my baby. At first it sounded alien. I heard a whelp, felt myself rise in bed, and then I rememberd where my feelings were—I had left them in a dream where I hated my father so much I wanted to explode. I was a murderer, actually, I woke from a dream where I was trying to explain why I'd done him in. The fact was I was Lizzie Borden, except that I used scissors.

I moved into the nursery and she was standing there again. This time I would nurse. I sat in a rocking chair and thought over and over. Fred is hopeless, a jerk, and my mother is right. And Richard is right. I felt okay with this emotion. It was familiar.

"Take her into bed with you," my mother said, and I walked right back into my own bed, still full of the meanness of the dream, feeling nothing of the milk coming down or the sucking. I did not go back to bed. When I went back over Fred's visit in the hospital, the day the milk came down, I wondered why I hadn't taken out a gun and shot him. Hating him was a reasonable feeling, it was the emotion at the base of my life, and I'd been putting it aside, denying it. The sadness of my mother's life was something I could actually touch. She was solid sorrow. Female sorrow. She *was* the cold Queen of Swords. Abandonment. I could go back into the nursery and be with my mother and my baby, and that was actual life, that was the center of it. I felt odd that Richard thought I was crazy. He meant it. He'd said it as he rolled over to his side of the bed, with an aura of disappointment, of rue. If I took everything so hard, *how would I last?* I felt this sinking, as if I could never resurrect us. Instead I would always be crazy and he would always have doubts.

Very early in the morning, she's awake. She can't sleep. Who is forcing her to stay awake? She walks around the room, trying to find whatever it is that keeps her, keeps her awake. And she hopes an idea will come to her. And something resembling one does come. She thinks of going out. For coffee. For a head start on the first day of the rest of her life, as some people put it.

In the restaurant, which is down on the far corner to the west of Washington Square, she eats the advertised $1.99 special, which is served to her by a man who looks Turkish, whose belly fills a white T-shirt, who looks as if he has never been asleep. The tables, the counters, are plastic butcher-block ribbed with metal. Two eggs, any style. Coffee, one refill.

The other two people at the counter look as if they have been dancing somewhere below Canal. Alma envies their youth. Their black clothes, the fact that they seem never to have had any past. She envies their several silver earrings.

And then something happens. And she thinks she sees someone she does not entirely expect to see, someone who startles her, although within a few seconds she is not so surprised that this one has startled her. It is someone she has to follow. And so she follows her.

And certain things ensue: going underground, coming up

for air, for fresh air, the air of Brooklyn, perhaps. And certain things are recalled and are seen. And are felt. And are even known.

And then it is morning, morning all the way. And somehow Alma has returned. The telephone in her Hotel Salazar room is chocolate. It matches nothing else. She dials an "0," gets advice from a Puerto Rican man, the one in the cage at the desk, and she dials a "9" then, gets a new tone, and dials a number in Maryland. And she stands by the window, sliding back the vinyl curtains which cover the airshaft, and she expects there to be sunlight. The end of The Winter's Tale, where the statue, the cadaver, the lady-with-the-very-bad-headache, turns into a living being again. Sunlight would have been nice, but this is the Hotel Salazar, and nothing is perfect.

And in Baltimore, in the tiny house on the treeless marble-stoop street called Dallas, Richard and Ruth are finding a rapport. He's propped her up in the infant seat in something, in one of the insulated blankets from the hospital. Her yellow gown is closed at the bottom with a drawstring. So she's a bit of a sack of potatoes this morning. She is a potato, he has decided, a russet—round and dimpled, awkwardly shaped, with pink, pink tender skin. He feeds her his former wife's thawed milk in a four-ounce bottle with a fancy Nuk nipple, as she sits on the table in front of him, and he devours her with his love, like a meal.

He is wondering what Alma will do when she wants the paintings, not just the slides she's already taken. When she wants the canvases in the basement, the ones off the frames. And there are others at the Steerwall Gallery that she'll have to send for should she find someone new to represent her, wherever she went. Would she write to the Steerwalls or would she leave all that work behind, the way she left Ruth and Richard?

Richard is thinking these practical things, these logistics, when he can no longer bear the anger, when he can no longer stomach it. Just when he had started to put together a life, when he'd erected a deal, a plan that would make so many people happy, just when all the struggling he'd kept her out of not to

*bother her, so she wouldn't have to worry about all the details,
was over—just when he'd finished and happily-ever-after was
around the corner—*

*Poof, she disappears. She didn't deserve, she didn't succeed,
she failed, she was failing, it was all her fault, she couldn't,
she can't. And so she left. And he thinks that if he ever sees her
again he will kill her, he thinks, after he tells her all the ways
she did fail him, off with her head. After she hears his whole
story. And then the phone rings. At nine fifty-eight in the morning. Richard is absolutely sure who it is before he answers it.*

Richard, Richard was nothing like my father. My father
was whatever they said—jerk, bum, selfish. "Alma's
very tired," I heard Richard on the phone. "My mother-
in-law took her and gave the baby a bottle in the middle
of the night. I think we all need some rest. She's sleeping
like an angel now." Then he said, "I'll be there about
ten-forty." And he hung up. In the upstairs hall I could
see he was dressed to go out.

"I'm going to Washington," he said. "I have to talk to
an investor."

"On Sunday?" I asked and he said yes. And I said,
"Okay," and he was abandoning me. There you were.

"If you need to reach me I'll be at Lucas's place," he
said.

"What is this about?" I said.

"I don't want to thread you through the whole thing,
Alma. You've got enough on your mind right now. I'll
tell you soon. We will talk about it when what we are
doing is more coalesced."

"Who is 'we'?" I asked.

"Never mind, baby," he said. "I'll be back either tonight or noon Monday. I'll call around seven."

My mother had made pancakes with corn in them. She asked several questions and Richard was evasive with her too. He looked at me. I was supposed to tell my mother that he didn't feel like talking about it, but I thought that it was all stupid—he'd surrounded himself this morning with a little citadel of nerves and mystery and sweat. He was wearing his only sports jacket. I wanted no part of it. I was angry with him, belatedly, for having stacked up the baby garbage around my mother, like a little boy tying up a baby-sitter in a chair, a regular Red Chief. I wanted him to go with his self-importance and the rest of it. Men don't really belong around women in childbed anyway. They can't take the serious heat of women. Richard left. Immediately my mother started asking me why we'd decided to marry, to go ahead and have a baby, when so little about our lives was settled, before anything was really under way. She loved this subject.

I couldn't think of a single good answer to her questions.

At around eleven, she started to watch an effeminate evangelist on TV who stood on a midnight-blue linoleum platform in front of a stage set of a pavilion in the clouds, where the sky-blue-clad choir sang. This was a Wayne Newton type, only shorter. I asked her how she could look at that crap and she said, "Oh, Alma, you know I have awful taste," and I said, "Oh, yes, you do," and I watched the castrato with her. He had a good tenor.

At lunch we were back on to Richard, because she started asking me when he'd be back. I told her what he'd told me: I was in no mood to defend him, and she asked me if he was mean to me.

"No," I said.

"Does he always resent it when you ask him to do things?" she asked.

"No, he's very helpful," I said.

"Helpful, how?" she asked incredulously.

"He's good to me. When I was in the hospital, during labor, after, he's good to me."

"Why do women want their husbands to see them like that?" my mother asked. "I don't really think men have the stomachs for childbirth, if you want to know the truth. Your father"—she used the past tense; he was dead, after all—"never had the stomach for anything. Could never sit through a horror movie, even."

"Labor isn't exactly a horror movie, Mother," I said.

"Same elements," she said. "I don't know. I never watched one. But don't you think men are really prissier than women?" she asked me. "Be honest."

I could agree or disagree, it didn't matter. On the subject of Richard I would become a bit sad, because I did see him today as she saw him—as abrasive, as sullen, as no one to lean on, as exploitative, even, of me. She implied he was using me, well, wasn't he? I carried the mortgage on the house, I had a job, he did and he didn't. Except for the parts about Richard that stuck with me, her chatter rolled on like water, and it mattered not at all to me what she said. It was a fountain. It was the sound of her loud voice. It was sweet to me. I felt kept and well, while she eroded my faith in my husband.

The whole day would be a little holiday from life. Around noon we got out the plastic bathtub Richard had bought at Woolco and I felt his resentment attached to it. It smelled like new dolls at Christmas, and then my mother took it into the bathtub and filled it with hot, hot water. Then she took Lysol. It is my mother's way to scrub things when they are brand-new, so they are then really yours, wiped blank, prepared for possession. Her ritual gave me pleasure. I undressed Ruth completely and my arms collapsed around her. There is nothing you can do with a naked baby that small but surround it. My mother waddled in, carrying the heavy tub, half-filled with water. I put my hand in. It was too cold.

"Add some warm," I told her.

"She'll live, she'll live," my mother said, and I didn't stop her from lowering my raw new red baby. First there were a few seconds of sheer silence, then a wail that came directly into my chest. I was being cut with a razor.

"Mother!" I screamed at her.

"All right," she said. "It's too cold. All right."

Ruth was purple.

"Wait," she said.

Why was my mother so bad at this stuff, I was thinking. Better not to think that—I was the product of the rough handling. At the same time I was acting at the beckoning of an extraordinary sawing in-and-out cry. It was a zoo cry, it wasn't human. It made my arms move, find velour towels, stuff the source into them, cuddle the source until the source's face was less violet, more cerise, and the zoo cry was fading.

"It wasn't so cold," my mother said. She was standing there, lifting her arms when the saw began to ascend and descend, not knowing exactly what to do, tracing my motions back and forth like a mime. I didn't feel like yelling at her. Suddenly Ruth stopped. Ruth was asleep. Her own cry, after twenty minutes, exhausted her.

"Do this later," my mother said, and she carried the tub out. "They all hate their baths, Alma," she said. "You will have to put her into one sooner or later."

"Yes," I said, as if the simple thing she had said had another meaning. She was still right.

As long as I wasn't myself, we could carry out the hours even with a little aplomb. Everything Momma did was fine. She was treating me rather decently. This was unusual. I'd been through it—there you are, there, I'd got a baby pulled out of me, and this, so peculiar because it is a loss, not a gain, to deliver a baby, had delivered me to my mother. Here I was. I could understand her, we had an understanding. I felt as if I knew everything, there for a second. Finally, a good daughter.

We ate supper together, her kind of food, yellow and white. Breast of chicken, egg salad, cold bread. While we ate this, Ruth sat propped up in the plastic infant seat, and she stared at the light fixture. She could not keep both eyes open for long periods of time. Mother had put her into the idiotic fancy dress with ruffles and lace that Loretta had bought her. In this dress her skin looked raw. The creases in her arms were pronounced, and her tiny legs came out at the bottom, still curled from the womb. She was a dolled-up chunk of misery.

"How are you feeling?" my mother asked, which surprised me. But not to dwell on pains, because either they go away or they don't, in which case you are dying, and there were no immediate signs I was dying, so.

"I'm okay," I said. "Maybe I'll go out tomorrow."

"No," my mother said. "You shouldn't, that's all," she said. "It's your confinement. Enjoy it. I'll grocery-shop," she said, "if Richard stays away."

"He'll be back," I said.

"Yes," she answered. "You'll catch a cold if you go out," she said. "Rain is coming. It's equinox rains."

"We don't have them here," I said.

"Maybe you call them something else," she said. "You'll catch cold in your womb," she said. "The doctor said you shouldn't go out."

"You said keeping me upstairs was dumb," I said.

"Not climbing stairs was silly," she said. "You have to be able to get up and go downstairs and open the refrigerator, drink some juice," she said. "You've got to take care of your baby," she said. "Drink so you can nurse. But you don't have to go out all over Baltimore in the pouring rain. It's your confinement. Go out when you are decent."

"Okay," I said. "Okay." It didn't matter, anyway. I was afraid to leave the house.

Not much later there was a nighttime thunderstorm and the pressure dropped very quickly, as it does just before a hurricane. Jo Ann was right. The rain came in the upstairs window, and when I went to close it I could see Ruth curled in the corner of her crib, uncovered. How could I have taken so long to come up? She could catch cold, she could get pneumonia, she could die. The receiving blankets were too light. The only heavy blanket in the room was the bear-claw quilt Richard had put in the bottom drawer of the chest. I tucked it around her, being very careful, giving her plenty of room to breathe. She seemed grateful. I listened to her breathe. She breathed so quickly, as if she were so eager to live that she couldn't wait to catch the next breath. I wound up the music box on the mobile. *Twinkle, twinkle, little star.*

"What have you got that filthy thing on the baby for, Alma?" my mother asked from the doorway. She came in and took it off. "I swear, Alma, do you want to smother her or what? That's not fit to wrap a piano with."

I was angry with myself, not with her. I would have to learn. I would have to throw it out. "She needs a change," my mother said. "Don't sit around all the time, Alma. Actually, I'm surprised you're so dopey these days. Don't go into a slump, for heaven's sake, just because you had a baby."

I got up and changed her. I handed her to my mother and performed the domestic chore of spreading out the quilt in the hall and folding it five times, and I put it on the floor of the nursery closet. My mother watched how deliberately and neatly I did this, and she seemed pleased. It was the way she would have done it. What will I do when she leaves in six days, I thought. How will I know what to do then?

The phone call from Richard came a little later. "Alma," he said. "How's our baby?"

"Asleep," I said.

"I'll be back Monday afternoon," he said.

"Why?"

"You're okay, aren't you?" he asked.

"Come home," I said. I wanted to see him again, check him out, see if he was who we thought.

"I'm with Lucas. And some investors. Friends of his. It's exciting."

"Oh no," I said. "I was afraid Lucas was being dragged into this."

"Your mother getting to you?" he asked.

"Come back," I said.

"I'll be back, I'll be back."

"What are you doing?" I asked.

"It's with Lucas. It's business. I'm superstitious. If I tell you it won't work out. I love you so much. You don't know. Don't be crappy with me. I have to talk to a bank."

"Richard—"

"I'll tell you when I get back. I can't take your mother," he said, and this was too strong. I told him so.

"I take it back," he said. "But she's not exactly crazy about me, that's obvious. I didn't marry her," he said.

"Maybe," I said.

"Are you on something, Alma?" he asked, half seriously. "I mean, last night, when I came back, when you hung up on Loretta—it was spooky, you know that? You two were sitting there, it could have been a wake, the way you were sitting. And you know, you didn't react. Your face was perfectly flat. I said hello to you. I could have been talking to the TV. You and she get on this circuit, it is weird, Alma. I don't really belong there. It's my own house, but I don't feel comfortable in it with her there."

"Leave her out of it," I said.

"I'll be back. I'll talk to you tomorrow. Obviously I can't talk to you now."

"Don't hang up," I said.

And he hung up.

The baby was screaming so I went upstairs. Where was the enthusiasm? *Wah Wah Wah.* Animal cries. The ten-o'clock feeding. Then my automatic thirst. "Don't sit there by the open window like a cow, Alma," my mother said as she went downstairs. "Cover yourself." I uncovered myself.

There was a hell of a lot of rain. I stood up with the baby in my arms and opened the window with my free hand and opened up my mouth to drink in the raindrops. This seemed perfectly appropriate, numinous, like that. Something to think of doing, drink the equinox rainwater. Something poetic to think of doing. I thought of baby Ruth's head hitting the concrete, and I yanked us both in. The hood of her blanket was utterly soaked. This was proof I was coming undone.

It was late Sunday night.

"Alma," he said. "Jo Ann there, honey?" he asked.

"Daddy?" I asked. "It's one in the morning."

"Jo Ann, Alma, honey," he said.

"Is that for me?" my mother asked, not in the voice of a drowsy woman, even though she'd been in bed three hours. "I'll take it, Alma," she said. "I'm awake."

"Fred wants to talk to you," I said.

"I'll take it, Alma," she repeated. "I'm awake."

"Fred wants to talk to you," I said.

"Jo Ann," he said. I was still on the line. "How's the grandbaby?"

"Just fine, Fred, and how are you?" my mother asked.

"I'm here," he said. "I'm in a place where the waitresses are half-naked. Called the Box Office. It says Box Office on the matches. It also says 'Earn while you learn in tractor-trailer school.' Should I do that, Momma?"

"Where are you, Fred?" she asked. "I'll come and get you."

"Don't do that, Jo Ann, don't come dry me out. And go through *all that* again." He was yelling.

"Isn't that what you want me to do?" my mother said, her voice all softness, a voice that sounded forged. It was the exact complement to the whine in his, somehow. For a minute this was romantic. My mother would go out and find him in a filthy bar, in the middle of the night, in the driving rain. It was still raining. How romantic.

"Jo Ann," he said. "You are the one," he said.

"I'll get you, Fred," she said. "Where are you? On the Block? The strip-joint street? I'll be there, don't move."

"I can't," he said. "I'm too gone. It's those bitch friends of Alma's. One of them tried to tear herself up and they both blame me. She hangs out with the wrong kind of people, Jo Ann."

"She's learning," my mother said. "She had a baby. She's got plenty of troubles of her own."

"Maybe she's a bitch just like her friends," he said. "She keeps herself terrible. In the hospital, you know what happened?"

"Shut up, Fred," my mother said. "You're drunk. You don't know what you are saying."

"Loretta is the purest bitch I ever saw," he said. "How could I have been taken *in*?"

"Shut up and hang up, Fred."

After she hung up, I did. In the loudest voice I have,

I said at the top of the stairs, "Mother, don't go out. *Don't.*"

"Oh, don't be so dramatic, Alma," she said. "Don't run down here, for heaven's sake."

When I reached the bottom of the stairs, I saw that she already had the lamp on and the yellow pages were opened. She was looking for the address of the bar.

"I'm going, Alma," she said.

"It's sick," I said. "He's crazy."

"Don't you tell me what to do," she said. "I thought you cared about your father."

"I hate him," I said.

"What kind of thing is that for you to do?"

"You said you couldn't stand him. You said that last night."

"I said it," she said. "So I don't mean it. Everybody knows people don't mean what they say."

She was standing there in her slip and her hose. She hadn't taken them off.

"Did you know he would call?" I asked.

"Honestly, Alma, I think you are a little paranoid. You are practically thirty years old. Grow up, for Christ's sake. I'm going out to find your father. Your father is an ill man. He needs me. He's sitting down on the Block, on Baltimore Street, in some joint, drowning. I'm going. Why be so overdramatic? I can't take two of you," she said.

"Two what?" I asked.

"Two babies. Two infantile— Never mind. Go back to bed. I'll take him to a motel. You are a mother now. Grow up."

"Don't do it," I said.

"You look," she said. "It was your trash— No. I won't say that either. I shouldn't talk about people I don't know. I don't know how you got through life this far without the slightest idea how to judge people. Here you are married and supporting a pouty little boy, and upstairs you have this newborn, and your friends, as far as I can see, are all perverts or maniacs. All the fringe, Alma, honestly. I won't say any more. Except that I don't see how you are anyone to tell me what to do. Besides—" she said. I was standing directly in front of her. She couldn't reach her purse or get her suitcase. I wouldn't move.

"I didn't want Fred and Loretta to get involved. I didn't," I said. "I had nothing to do with it. I didn't even know—"

"Oh, let me pass—"

"You didn't finish. Besides, what?" I asked.

"You can, I don't know. I always thought you were like me. You'll see, you'll have a hard time ever seeing your children to be different people. Different from yourself," she said. I let her pass. I sat on the futon. She had never turned down her covers. She'd been lying there awake, in her slip and stockings.

"I always thought you could take care of yourself. I thought you would just osmose, you know, what you needed to know. When you were born you seemed to me so self-possessed. People used to comment that you practically raised yourself. I used to brag that you raised yourself." In another minute, her hands were pointing through the armholes of a clean striped dress. "I had to think that, I suppose," she said. "You were a girl," she said. "Men are the babies." She stepped into her shoes. "But I guess it wasn't really like that, was it? You didn't catch on, did you?"

"To what?" I asked, but I knew.

"I have to go," she said. "Take care of that little thing. Here, let me kiss you."

"To what?"

"Why do we have to talk about this now? They will probably have thrown him into jail by the time I get there."

"To what?" I asked again.

"To my mistakes," she said. "I didn't want your life to be ugly," she paused. "I have to get your father," she said. "I'll be back."

"Why are you going?"

"He has nobody else," she said. "Now let me get out of here."

"Okay, good-bye," I said.

"Good-bye," she said. "I'll be back. I'll put him in a motel. I'll be back sometime tomorrow."

"Okay," I said.

"Why did you even come?" I said, feeling desperate.

"Well, if you are going to be like that," she said.

"You've only been here one day," I said.

"Well, I said I'd be back," she said.

"No, you won't," I said. "How can you go off like this and sop him up? You can't stand him. You said yourself that he's an ass and a bum. He's a shit. You ought to hate him."

"I didn't say that," she said.

"Yes, you did," I said.

"Honestly, Alma, you remember every blessed thing, and it doesn't matter at all. It really doesn't. And you don't give an inch. You've never given anybody an inch."

"You've never given one," I said. "I've always been this little problem you have. He doesn't need you. He drinks because of you," I said. "You don't help. You don't."

"Don't you say anything more," she said. Silence now. A kind of pure, sad silence. She was only an old, blond, weary woman. She looked at me. For a moment she seemed just there, perfectly alone, cut out of the background. What was I hounding her for? How could she help any of this at two in the morning?

"I really couldn't give a damn what you say," she said, like a girl, stiffly, like an insulted girl. "He's my husband and I am going and get out of my way." She picked up her suitcase. "I know where I'm wanted," she said.

"Mother," I said.

"Don't 'Mother' me," she said. "You are the one with the problems," she said. "I pity that baby of yours. It is the gospel truth, I pity her," she said.

I just stood there. Neither one of us could be right.

"Alma," she said at the door, taking her car keys out, gripping the wooden mushroom they hung from, "don't be so angry. You love Richard, don't you?"

This seemed a horrible thing to say. Since she'd stripped me of Richard, I couldn't think of him, and then here she was, dumping him back on me. So I said nothing. I wanted to slap her down.

"Don't take it so seriously," she said. "You take everything so seriously." She gave me the fight-back smile, a Margaret Thatcher smile, and I swung my arm back to hit her. She did not flinch. I stopped short of hitting her.

"There is something wrong with you, Alma," she said. "I don't know what it is."

I thought I'd feel a sheer loss when the door closed, but it was more complicated than that.

*A*nd there was Alma with no mother, no father, and no husband. She'd have to raise herself, except she had no time for that. There was the one to raise. Upstairs. Zoo cries, fists in the eyes. All the rain her mother had predicted. The rain that moved up the coast. Every drop. I can't blame her now, when I recall this. Her mother zooming off in a yellow Pontiac for a sleazy bar, for her sodden husband.

At the Salazar, she finally hangs up the chocolate telephone for the last time. And it's almost an hour later. After many long communally held pauses, after many gasps, several hundred tears, after she dropped the phone and momentarily dazed it, and after she made promises, and accusations, and after she was dared, and damned, and almost apologized to and told she is needed by certain people, Alma is packing. And then she's paying the man behind the bulletproof glass, primarily for the phone. All the other charges were paid for in advance.

She's dressed oddly. In ankle-strap shoes and black gloves with parts cut out—holes for the knuckles, what used to be called Italian-style gloves. And a black velveteen pillbox hat that looks a little small. That must have been mine. Overall, she could be a girl in the sixties on her way to mass. Her jacket has a peplum. She's lovely really, lovely. Not Jewish, but sturdy. And the rule is that she makes our ways her ways. It's a simple rule. Not the same one I had to follow with the Kaplans, but it comes from the book of Ruth, which she ought to read, I wonder if she has.

Alma could be Della Street, she could be Sophia Loren, but with straighter hips (her hair is short and curling beneath the hat). She's lovely. A cab. Her portfolio. Her uneasy entry (her bones still ache, the bending bones especially, her hip joints) is accompanied by the two thousand things she wants to say. And the thousand she wants to take back. She used to believe that you couldn't go back and do it over in life, as you can in paint, but you do go back.

So I can leave you here. But I don't want to leave you here. And her reasons for leaving aren't finished and I'm not finished, and I don't want it to stop, exactly.

On Monday morning I had an idea for a painting— my mother and my father fused together into one person. She in her dress, with Robert Mitchum hair, like his. The face kept being hers and then it was his and then it was that of neither of them—a composite. I thought of all the time that she'd been lying downstairs in her girlish garter belts, slip, and hose, and I was too sad to be angry.

I was stiff in the hips and in the backbone. Outside, it was raining and chilly. Ruth was next to me in bed. We were bound up so tightly in the covers I felt pregnant again. It was a pleasant feeling. When Ruth slept her face was completely closed, hardly a face at all, a group of creases on a pink orb. She was back in a womb sleep.

Somehow being alone was okay, as long as she slept. Except for the phenobarbital hours in the hospital—the at-sea hours the week before—I had not been alone for months, it seemed.

I wanted to fix everything, make it so Ruth wouldn't have to depend on me, because I really had so little certainty, so little belief, so little presence. I wasn't as false as my mother, but then again I probably was. I didn't love anyone, and I pretended to love everybody.

The truth was that my father was the story of my mother's life. He would die someday from the deterioration of his pancreas or his liver, and I'd have to sit with her somewhere and listen to her invent him— exciting, intelligent, wild, needy. I hated them both that morning. As long as I was alone, not pressed by the presence of others, I could know things and still breathe. It was when I had to act that I felt shaky.

When she got a good suck she let out a wail. The milk tasted bad. I suppose I'd tainted it. It dripped all over her face and then she went on wailing. Holding her with one arm, I went into the nursery to find a bottle of sugar water. The set of four from the hospital was all used up. That was a surprise. My mother must have been awake all night her first night here, if she'd gone through that many. I tried to nurse again, but the result was the same. The sound was unearthly, wild. When your own baby cries, your body is a sounding chamber. I tried to rock her, I tried a pacifier. Each would last a few seconds, and then the battering sound again. I walked her downstairs, holding her on my shoulder, and she spat up the little milk she'd taken, on my hair. My bathrobe had a stench now, the one my mother had mentioned. There were puddles where the milk had flowed down. She cheesed some more, in my hair.

Why can't I handle this, I was thinking. It had been forty minutes of continuous wailing. Wait it out, I thought. She'd have to tire. Then there was a series of fierce unbelievable wails and she doubled up where I had laid her beside me on the downstairs bed. I started talking to myself, "Drink some milk, Alma, calm down. Put her into the seat, and drink some milk, make some more."

She had been crying for an hour now, and I had drunk three glasses. Most of the hour she'd been in my arms, but now she was strapped in a chair, propped up, screaming at me from about four feet away. I reached down to try to nurse again, and wails that had just passed evaporated, and for a few minutes it worked and the cries of a while ago dissolved completely, and my nerves subsided a little, went back into my skin. My mouth went slack like a smile, and that was all I could take. Good. She would be calm now.

But she wouldn't be. The next bout was wilder than the first. She was practically blue with screaming and I could hardly hold her—it was as if she were fighting her way out of my arms. "Stand up and walk her," I said to myself. "Get up." I got up and the cry lost a little of its force, as it fell behind me, from the Doppler effect, I supposed, as I rushed into the dining room and back into the living room, and back to the living room window, pacing, almost running. I walked like this for more than half an hour and it just kept coming and coming, so with my right hand I covered her mouth and heard nothing for a minute.

The only thing I thought of was that if I got somebody to come over everything would be better. Obviously not

Loretta. And no more of my mother. Lucas and Richard were gone. Carmen.

Calling Carmen is what you call a fatal mistake.

I got her at work. It was lunch in that world. She could talk.

"How *are* you, Alma?" she asked cheerfully.

"I'm alone," I said.

"Where's Richard?" she asked.

I told her what I knew, that he was staying with Lucas in Washington.

"With Lucas?" she asked. "What could they be doing?"

"Probably just hiding out," I said. "My mother is gone too."

"That was quick," she said.

"Well, we fought," I said. Then I went on with the rest, told it to her quickly.

"Slow down," Carmen said. "What happened?"

"It doesn't matter," I said. "I told my father the wrong thing, Gina pulled out her plumbing. Loretta and he are kaput, I think."

"What happened?" Carmen said. From the start she had been having trouble computing Fred and Loretta.

"I'll tell you about it," I said. "Can you come over?"

"How is she?" Carmen asked.

"She's a holy terror," I said. "Then she sleeps."

"Oh, I want to see her," she said. "Can you wait until tomorrow morning, though? I can stay all day tomorrow. I've had a personal leave day scheduled for tomorrow. I can be over early, if you need me to bring things, I can bring them."

"Bring some wine," I said.

"Is that all right?" she asked.

"Yeah," I said. "And maybe a gallon of orange juice."

"Do you need anything now?"

"I'll be fine," I said. "As long as you promise you will come."

"I will, Alma, oh, you sound so forlorn," she said. "I'd come tonight, but there's this fucking budget presentation, and then dinner afterward, with the board. And I have to go home and talk to Mary Ann, I haven't seen her in four days, you know. She's been at a convention. Can you make it? If you can't, I'll make up some excuse."

"Oh, I'm all right," I said.

"You don't sound it," she said. "Eight-thirty, I promise. Take care of yourself."

As I hung up I could see Carmen kind of rising up before me, with her little shampooed helmet of hair, and her enormous eyes, an archetype, moon and stars behind her.

I realized then that I could sleep for eighteen hours, and if I did, I would only have to be awake for an hour and a half and Carmen would come with wine and orange juice. Why was she so kind to me—I couldn't think of a reason.

I looked outside. The sky was a weak, almost unseeable blue. The air was damp, still. It could rain anytime, or it might clear. I had the impulse to dress and take a little walk—just to the corner, or another block down.

Then I thought: I have a baby. Upstairs, asleep. What did I want to do, abandon her, I thought to myself, and then I knew that that was exactly what I wanted to do, and the desire to do that wasn't alien at all, it had been with me from the beginning. It seemed so palpable, entire.

I ate some peanut butter, and then the phone calls started.

In the middle of the afternoon, having survived another bout with Ruth's cries and her indigestion, a fit that was shorter than the previous one if you looked at the clock, but which was really harder, I was sitting on the edge of my chair, trying to think of reasons not to trust my impulse to go. I was drinking tea with milk. What Carmen might have served me. Ruth, crumpled in her yellow prop-up seat, twice reached out to grab hold of something, with both tiny hands, with her toes. This was in the baby books: the Moro reflex, left over from monkeys, meant to save babies from falling through the trees. It happens whenever they are dropped in space or startled. They grab the thin air when they fall into sleep, too. It is the same as the dream in which you begin to fall down stairs just as you are going to sleep, and you stiffen and waken; it is an animal dream, a universal dream. The bough breaks and the cradle falls. Ruth sat in her double plastic straps, her yellow molded cradle, stationary as you please, and startled three times from dream-falling; then rest; deep somewhere—I had no idea where she went when she dreamed—and I felt remorse that I couldn't go there and catch her fall. But wasn't that a desire to go too far, to invade her. It was raining again.

The phone rang, mean as a rattler.

It was a husky, a studied, almost male voice, groggy.

"Alma, you have to get it. You don't get it—"

"Who is this?" I asked.

"This is Loretta," another voice said. One I knew. "Gina, get off the phone."

"I have to tell Alma, she's in the dark."

"Gina, you are fucked up, honey, now get off the phone," Loretta said. "She's on all sorts of tranqs, Alma. Hang up, Alma."

I didn't hang up. Gina and Loretta continued to talk, pulling the phone back and forth between them.

"You've got to get off, Gina. Lie back down," I heard Loretta yell, from somewhere else in the room.

"Alma," Gina said.

"Alma's off," Loretta said, struggling with Gina. "Don't bother her. Alma's not worth it."

"Why?" I could hear Gina yell.

"She's not a friend," Loretta said. "Hang up or I'll take the phone out. Alma's an asshole."

Click. That was it.

I went into the kitchen to get more tea. Four minutes later, the phone rang again.

"Alma, I want—" Gina said. "I want to save it—"

Loretta broke in again. "Gina shouldn't be on the phone," she said.

Click.

Gina's words were running together, thick as mousse. Being an asshole was the least of my problems. I must have started to dream—I was stumbling on steps. Then I was awakened again, opened up again, by another bell. Loretta this time.

"What did you tell your father?" she asked.

"To go back to Durham."

"Well, he started giving me, us, these ultimatums. He's sixty. Alma, why has everything got to be this minute? What's his problem?"

"He wants to prove something."

"Like what?" Loretta said. "He just blew up at us. I hold you responsible," Loretta continued, "for Gina's mental and physical setback. Absolutely. Did you tell him I was putting up a front? That I really wanted to leave her? I always thought you were another way, that you were loving and giving, but you are really incredibly mean and I don't think you care about anybody. You don't give a fuck."

"Okay," I said.

"You don't have a heart, Alma," Loretta said.

"Okay, okay," I said.

"And I mean anybody," she said. "Good-bye. I'm not your friend anymore."

I said nothing.

"I can't hate you," Loretta said. "It would take too

much energy. But you are goddammned poison, Alma, and I pity—"

"Who?" I said.

"You," she said.

"My baby's crying, and I have to go," I said. "Don't call anymore. You are waking her up."

"Don't worry," Loretta said, and she hung up.

Ruth really wasn't crying. But I was in a lying mode. I didn't want to mean anything.

I still had this furious feeling for Ruth, though. Passion. It was nothing I could easily take or leave, when I dressed her, when I put her hot ball body in the strapped seat: I couldn't handle it or sentimentalize it, degrade into combing her hair or fixing the sheets or fluffing her up with artificial love; I didn't do many of those things and I didn't talk to her. We were alone and I was her mother and my feeling for her came from where it was dormant and it was messy, outrageous. It couldn't be good for her. It terrified me even when I was alone.

Ruth and I went on the way we were through the late afternoon and the evening. She had needs and I was capable with them. They were hers but I was the vessel for them, the conductor toward their satisfaction. That was who I was. I also knew, though, that I couldn't live this thorough way, where the whole truth is your baby. It would have to subside, but it kept swelling up. I was gone. I was a goner.

Richard finally called after nine. I had been waiting for him to show up so long. My hope of seeing him come through the door had deteriorated into a generalized expectation and sharpened hearing. "Baby, I'm not there," he said.

"No lie. Momma left. Daddy summoned her. Loretta dumped him."

"Shit, you're alone," he said. "Ruth. How's Ruth?"

"She's fine. And with Momma gone, I don't have to think of myself the same way. I'm all right."

"These friends of Lucas's are here. We just got back from dinner. I didn't believe the time."

"It's all right," I said.

"How's the baby?" he asked again.

"She's the truth, the perfect truth," I said. And then I told him to finish whatever it was he was doing. I promised him I'd get through the night.

"I want money," Gina said on the phone. It was three-thirty in the morning, but it really didn't matter.

"Or I want to be changed back the other way. Loretta said it can't be done. I should be happy now. Are you happy? Alma? I think being a girl is dangerous. It was better when there was this art and style to it, but it is basically dangerous. It was better when they didn't have a name for me. You never called me anything. You just looked straight through me, couldn't even find a pronoun. Couldn't even find a fucking pronoun. You never called me anything. But it was interesting, neutral, lively, as if I were outside of everything. Nothing was holding me down. Do you get it? Now your daddy and everybody want to turn me into a lady and be done with me. Loretta knows it is over, even though she holds on, our friendship is over. Girls don't get along. They are always bitchy to each other. Loretta will find somebody else. She will. You should have told her it was crap. I wasn't afraid of your daddy leaving with her. I couldn't give a fuck about Loretta. I want a brick house with a lawn somewhere that is nowhere, I want that cul-de-sac feeling, that suburbia-primeval feeling, and I want two white Volvos, and Levolors, and HBO. I want to be on a street that they just named two weeks ago. I want money. People will have to forget about me. I will not be fucked over anymore. I want to go where people won't talk about me anymore. I want to make raw vegetable platters somewhere, give barbecues. I want to be lost and be safe. I want to be tucked away, with a husband who does everything for me. I want to be a woman. That's what I wanted," Gina said.

"Loretta's in love with you," she continued. "That's what all this is: she wants to be a woman just like you, don't you know that, independent, in touch with her art, that crap. Art is crap. I want to have the right shoes. You were the goddamned model, Alma, which is why she's so upset. She sees now you are just not wonderful. She didn't see before that you are scared to death and that everything you do and say is a lie. She spent fifty-six dollars on that pink thing with ruffles and she told me you just said almost nothing, I mean she shopped for four hours. She shopped. She wanted to be the step-grandmother. And I was going to be the fucking aunt. Do you care? What do you care about? Nobody is there for you, anyway. You are a goddamned zombie. You aren't wonderful. Even Fred thinks there is something wrong with you."

"Leave me alone," I said. But I didn't hang up.

"You and your agenda are shot full of holes, Alma, that's all I have to say. You have the wrong idea. And one more thing: if you are the model, I would rather be where I'm going to be, at the end of the world, where I don't have to work, somewhere I can shop every day. You're full of holes, honey. I thought when I became a woman I could just go to sleep, find me a guy with a job and go to sleep. I want to just go to sleep. In Anne Arundel County someplace. . . . It should be so easy to play dead. Why isn't it? I figured if I was a girl it would be easier to play dead."

"Shut up, Gina," Loretta broke into the line. Again she said Gina was on something. So Gina did not get to finish.

Carmen was standing in the living room. She undid the tiny button beneath her mint-green raincoat collar—Carmen is the only person I have ever known to fasten that button. She stepped over the baby goods on the floor—blue rubber rhinoceroses, rattles, the stuffed kangaroo from Fred, the pillows, my other shoes, the Nuks. When she got to the coat tree, in a corner of the living room, she hung her coat on it, although it was difficult to find a space. I saw my mother had left her sweater there. She'd be back, someday.

Carmen was aware of her role. I could see her taking on size and weight as she stepped toward Ruth and me; I could see her rising to the occasion. "Ruthie is so cute, look at that sweetie, Alma," she said. "She's a darling." She came over toward us, her hands forming the shape of Ruth's little head.

I think I knew, by that morning, what I was going to do. It was underneath my thoughts, waiting for me to notice it. I didn't want to tell Carmen that I was afraid I might leave. I assumed that certain resources would rise up, from some place where I never knew they really were. That blind love or the total dependence of a little baby would buoy me up. That the baby, as a given, supported her own new logic. That was what Carmen had decided to believe. She told me in the hospital. So I would, now. But the two of us were suffering from a seepage of nerve, it turned out. In a while, Ruth dropped off the breast. She had all the beauty of someone you have to say good-bye to.

"How are you doing?" Carmen asked, too gently.

"Fine, really," I said.

"You don't look fine," she said. "I mean, you look tired."

"Could you bring me the cushion?" I asked. It was a little damp from spat-up milk. Carmen covered it with a receiving blanket from the coffee table. I had already told her that my mother was off drying out my father, and that Richard was wherever he was. That Gina and Loretta had been harassing me for their reasons. My baby started to fuss, then she fell asleep on her stomach.

Carmen had her hand on my shoulder. "Mary Ann is getting better. She's even beginning to accept the situation, I think. In her own way. She and I talked all night. I didn't get any sleep either. I brought you orange juice and coffee instead of wine. Smell these beans—they're Hawaiian. I'll boil some water."

She opened the brown bag from a specialty store, and the sweet sting hit my nostrils.

The kitchen was as my mother had left it. Carmen could find her way around it. I didn't get up. ". . . So I'm going to move to a place in Mount Vernon and set it all up. It's on the fourth floor of an old town house: there's a room that's gorgeous, a little alcove, actually. The ceilings aren't quite high enough for big people—it's the ideal child's bedroom. So cozy. This is fate, isn't it. . . ." She was talking over the sound of water from the spigot.

She said she'd tell Lucas when she had the guts to. She was building up to that. She repeated that Mary Ann was coming around. To what, exactly, well, that changed as she spoke. When I told her how Lucas was, she said she couldn't think about him right now.

"So you think he will leave you alone?" I asked.

She sat down with the coffee and handed me a brown mug. "He just will, that's all," she said. "I say he will and he will. He wouldn't do anything to me. He has boundaries. I just have to have faith. So does Mary Ann. I still love her, don't get me wrong. I'm still bound to her. She's coming around, she is."

"You keep saying that," I said.

"What?" Carmen said.

"That Mary Ann must be coming around," I said.

Carmen took a sip and put her cup on the floor. "Well, she's not entirely. She was so mad she couldn't see straight.

I thought she would strike me last night," Carmen said. "This morning, she'd cooled."

"Then why have you been telling me the opposite?" I asked.

"Well, you don't need horror stories." Carmen looked lovely, rosy. You could see her pregnancy in a fullness around her face. Her eyes didn't betray that she'd been up late. "I have a confession to make," she went on, "I made an appointment for, you know, an abortion. Weeks before I told you about the baby, a long, long time ago, the day the test came out positive. That's why I have this leave day today. But I'm here, see, I'm not going."

"Are you sure now?" I asked her. It was sweet of Carmen to think of me as someone who deserved the complete truth. "It's a lot to take on," I said. "Alone, I mean. It's incredible."

"It's not terrible," Carmen said. "Look at you, Alma, I mean, you are tired, but you have this aura, this softness, you are a different person. You are doing fine, fine. It's as if you are a different sex, more beautiful, somehow. It's wonderful."

"I don't know," I said.

"I'm prepared for those things," Carmen said. "I am."

"Which things?" I asked. Then Ruth was crying in her pillow, cramming her miniature fingers into her mouth, waking, sucking, waking, sucking. She looked desperate to me. I picked her up, held her head in my palm.

"For starters, for my mother's reaction. For Lucas badgering me."

"It's just interest, Carmen. It isn't exactly badgering. With Lucas, I mean."

"Oh, with him it's proprietary. It's ownership. It isn't love, it's something else."

"You are going to need other people," I said. "When you start looking like an elephant. When it's hard to move. Later, when it's born, and you get confused."

"You and Ruth and Richard will be here," she said.

"Yes," I said. And then I became aware that no, I wasn't going to be there.

"And our babies will be friends, huh?" she said.

"I suppose so," I said, feebly.

"What is it, Alma?" she said.

My face was beginning to collapse into a grimace. "I feel perfectly worthless. Hopeless at this," I said. "Richard's gone, my mother was horrible. I can't. I don't know what's wrong with me."

"What are you talking about? Nothing is wrong with you." She reached out and put her arms around me, kissed me on the cheek. "Oh, Alma," she said. "Darling. I can't stand to see you like this. You are fine. You are fine."

Ruth squirmed, but stayed calm and trusting, in my lap.

"It can't be that bad. You are just depressed. Postpartum. That kind of thing," Carmen went on.

"I feel like I'm shot full of holes," I said. "Listen, Carmen, don't have a baby unless you know what you are doing. Unless you know who you are. I mean it," I said, and that was something very wrong to say. Murderous.

"Alma," she said. Carmen put her hands on my shoulders again. I calmed down. She left the room and was busy in the kitchen. I realized when Ruth and I joined her there that I hadn't eaten since the day before. That was why the counters were the way my mother had left them. Carmen grilled little croque-monsieurs on sourdough rolls. Which we ate. And then I nursed Ruth, and it hurt. My baby was pink as a balloon, her legs pathetic, sticking out of the oversized diaper. For the first time I could see her for what she was, not a god, not the whole world. My daughter. I was her mother. She was a very tiny red helpless being. Sad, squirmy, completely dependent. Devoted to me.

"I love her," Carmen said at the table, opening her large eyes larger still, and facing us. "I'm going to clean her up a little," she said to me.

And then I started to cry again. Carmen shooed me into the living room. And I stretched out on the futon, with one forearm drawn across my brow, a regular Sarah Bernhardt pose. Prostration. Collapse.

After she rinsed the dishes with one hand while holding Ruth in the other arm, Carmen came back into the living room. She was exasperated with me. It was really not our style for me to be abject. Carmen was usually the one undergoing overwhelming emotional duress. But she was tough. For me, that day, she was being tough. I don't think she knew I was grateful. I *know* she didn't know I was grateful. She placed Ruth very carefully back on the pillow. "You know you need something low to the ground, a bassinet, a cradle," she said. "And you know what you really need? Richard," she said. "Where the hell *is* he?"

"I think he's at Lucas's," I said, knowing that she would never call Lucas.

"Well, I'll call Lucas. For you." She actually went to the phone and called him. "Hello. This is Carmen. Can I talk to Richard? . . . How come you are home, anyway? . . ." She went on in an agitated whisper. I heard her say, "You never give up, do you?" and a little later, forcefully, "Put Richard on or I'm hanging up." Finally, Carmen did hang up, and she turned to tell me she hated her husband. She sat there and didn't speak. She opened her mouth, then something held her back. Then she went on.

"I really think he intends to devour me at this point. Eat me alive. Sometimes he's so angry. He scares me. I really wonder, Alma," she said.

"What?"

She was reluctant to tell me. "If I can resist him, that is all, I mean. Things have to make some sense. My having this baby can't mean I'm surrendering to him. You can't be entirely sentimental. You have to have one decent reason to have a baby."

"You have some," I said.

"Yeah, dyke's last chance. That's about it. Mary Ann thinks I don't want to accept my sexuality. She has theories. I shouldn't tell you what we fought about last night. I shouldn't."

"It's okay," I said. "Richard's coming. I'm okay. I come out of these things, they come in waves."

"I'm still freaked out about, about who I am sexually. I prefer to be a celibate single mother. Mary Ann says it will complicate my life just enough that I won't have the opportunity to be involved, I'll always have the excuse . . . with a baby, I mean."

"You don't have to listen to her, Carmen," I said.

"Well," Carmen said. Then she was silent. She lost focus, for a second. As if she were looking into some remote room, one not apparent to others, not exactly contiguous with this one. She stared, then she spoke again. "Richard will call you as soon as he walks in the door. Lucas said they were both going to drive straight here. If Lucas is driving, that's fifty-five minutes. I've got to go. I really have to go. I'll call you later on this evening. I promise. Ruth's going to stay asleep for a while, isn't she? Don't they sleep for long stretches after they are born? I'll call you later." She was putting on her raincoat. "Can you think of one good reason? One natural reason?"

"I thought the logic started with the baby. The baby was the given. Something unambiguous about a baby," I said. "Carmen—"

"Yes," Carmen said. "I love you, Alma; take care of yourself," she said ambiguously. "Good-bye, Alma," she said, with remorse. And then she was out the door. It was two hours or more before I was certain where she was going.

Richard strode in, in the same sports coat. And the endless interval between the last time I had seen him and this seemed to disappear, to be eradicated. He still had that skinny-man-with-a-pompadour look. The hour since Carmen left, I had listened to the radio—Vivaldi—and so had Ruth, but the entrance of her father and his best friend set off those odd monkey wails, so I was up again, I was a floorwalker.

"Let me see that baby," Lucas said.

I jiggled her. I said, "Shoo, shoo, shh, shh."

"Can you go out, Alma?" Lucas said. "Carmen still here?"

I said no, and found a pacifier, offered it, and Ruth was calm. On her feet were pink booties Lucas's wife had placed there, pink booties decorated with white pompoms. One fell off her tiny foot and Richard picked it up.

"She can't go out," Richard said, meaning I couldn't leave the house. My confinement. I forgot.

"Let me hold her," Lucas said. "Where'd Carmen go?"

I told him she'd spent the day with me, then, at quarter to three, she'd left. Right after she'd talked to him, he said.

"Did she say what was going on with her and Mary Ann? She's told Mary Ann she's knocked up, I gather? Are the two of them going to try to adopt the baby or what? What has she got in mind, exactly?" Lucas asked.

I didn't know which question to answer first.

Richard said, "Alma'll get to it, Lucas, calm down. Maybe she ought to hear what we've got to say first."

And then they filled me in on what it was they had to say.

The main investor in Washington Richard had been talking to was Lucas. And there were also a couple of Lucas's friends at the firm he worked for. Gerald something; David something else. But mostly Lucas. And Richard would be a full partner. With sweat equity. They were buying a building. This purchase had already been started in motion. The huge warehouse on the waterfront Richard had taken me to once, during the time, long, long ago, when I was an elephant. There were several thousand square feet on three floors. (Richard beamed as he recounted this. And Lucas seemed to calm, to enjoy imagining it. Lucas made broad gestures. He kept his hands out of his pockets for long periods. Richard lit a cigarette. I begged him for a puff. He wouldn't let me have one.) The plans were for a complex—an art gallery on the main floor; downstairs, a café and bar; and upstairs, on the second level, with the cleansing-blue Chesapeake light, would be loft space, studio space, for rent. For artists. For not a whole lot. Sometimes, during openings, maybe, people could go up and look at the studios, talk to the painters. And I, Alma Taylor, the painter, would have to show in this gallery, instead of at the Steerwalls. Would I say okay? (I got no time to answer. Richard put out his cigarette.) Lighting, high ceilings, a place for people. For the painters who were having to flee the Point. Because the rent was becoming too pricey. (Didn't I think this was great? Didn't I think this was a great idea?) Richard and Lucas. Co-managers. For a while, during the renovations, Lucas would be in Washington, and then he would be moving and coming to Baltimore to live. About the time Carmen had her—their—baby. And he would be in the same town, and they could work out a custody arrangement. He was even prepared to raise the baby himself. How did I think Carmen would adjust to that? (Champagne, wasn't there any champagne?)

I said Lucas ought to call her. I was not behaving in an enthusiastic manner. After forty-five minutes of this amazing scheme.

Richard would be supervising the renovation job. For the next few months. He'd be getting a salary for that. What would go, otherwise, to a contractor, how could they trust a contractor as much as they could trust Richard? It would be a hassle, something for a person who could handle a lot of details. The other three, Lucas and his friends who needed something to do with their money, had already borrowed the amount. They were ready to go on this. There were enormous tax advantages—tax credits, because the building was historic, a place where ship's chandlers used to store their goods, with offices upstairs, circa 1861. Which meant research, and smarts, and time, on Richard's part. But it would become such a center—better that than the place becoming a condo-marina complex, or some crap like that. With the credits and the shelters, doing it over would cost practically nothing. And you, Alma, you could get your studio back. Your studio. And the bar would bring in the cash flow. And the real people of the quarter, not to mention—

"There's no risk?" I asked.

Richard put his feet on the coffee table. "It's a way to keep people here. Keep painters here. Keep them working here."

"Plus, plus," Lucas said, kneading my shoulder a little. "Plus, I'll move here. Whatever Carmen has said to you, she's never expected I'd move here, has she? That I would quit being a lawyer? She didn't expect I would do that, did she? We'll have a shared thing, split custody. But not between Washington and here. But between here and here. Hell, I'm willing. I'll take Carmen and Mary Ann to Lamaze classes. Carmen will have two coaches. What do you say? Huh, Alma? Did you figure I could stretch like that?"

Their delight was catching. It even seemed Ruth was giggling. But I wasn't getting it. I had as much faith in them as I would have had in two little boys who plan to dig to China or to make thousands on a lemonade stand.

"I'm going to raise my baby," Lucas said tenderly, like someone drunk, almost.

"You had better talk to Carmen," I told him. "Before—"

"What?" he said.

"Call her, see if she's home. I'd better tell you," I stopped.

"What?" Lucas asked, curious, now.

"She supposed to be moving out on Mary Ann, and going to live alone, to an apartment in Mount Vernon, fourth floor, with a little eave."

"So, good, I hate Mary Ann," Lucas said.

"She was going to have the baby, but she didn't intend to share any custody rights. At least that was what she was telling me. But I don't know that that's what she was really planning to do when she left here this afternoon," I said. "She was here, taking care of me, she wanted to encourage me. I wanted to encourage her. But we didn't get too far, exactly."

"I know, I talked to her this afternoon, remember? What do you mean, she *was* going to have the baby? She's been telling me all along, you know, that under her own conditions she would have this baby. There has never really been any question, I mean, fundamentally. Just the arrangements. The conditions."

Both of them amazed me. It seemed very simple. They seemed to be lovers, back from a two-day date. I thought they looked so handsome and easy that it must be impossible. Their scheme was complicated, crazy, not easy. Artists don't have any money. The galleries were downtown, not here. And then I knew why Carmen had rushed out the way she had. "Please, please, Lucas, call her. Make sure she knows what you plan to do. Don't scare her. Don't threaten her. Talk to her. What time is it? Call her now. I mean it."

Lucas said, "Alma, you talked her out of it. You did. That's what you did. You are the only person who could have. You—"

The rest of this won't take long to relate. Events went inward, came together in quick, flat pictures. It started the minute that Lucas called me a cunt. That's what he thought, really, that I was a cunt. The same man speaking who'd held my hand when I was numb as a lump of heaven last week, full of baby, the same one who still loved Carmen so much he scared her, the same Lucas who was changing his life to get his wife and her baby, or at least the baby, back, the same decent man as all that called me a cunt. So I was a cunt.

I don't even remember where I was in the house. The two of them, the Boys Club, Lucas and Richard, sat on the couch and yakked, but I wasn't exactly there anymore. Richard thought it was not so terrible that I was called a cunt. They hadn't got the word yet, anyway, about Carmen. Richard told Lucas he was sorry, terribly sorry, and told me Lucas was just really wildly upset, not to listen to him. This was the Lucas Carmen had warned me about.

Lucas had called and called Carmen's number, and by six it was clear she was out, then Mary Ann answered and said she didn't know where. At seven she was still out, and at eight-thirty Carmen answered. But then we all feared, from my elaboration and my intimation, that Carmen may have decided not to be a single mother, or any mother at all.

I thought the bar-gallery wouldn't work. Richard had never managed anything before. And it would be awkward having Lucas as a boss. Who thought I was a cunt. But I held all my opinions too and listened to Lucas, who thought I was a cunt.

"Carmen," Lucas said, finally with her on the line. "How are you? Listen, I'm moving to Baltimore. Going in on a joint venture with—

"Richard, that's right." (Cough, clearing of the throat, the evocation of his lawyerly voice.) "I'm at their house now. I'm calling from Richard's. Yes, of course she's here. Alma can't go out. No, listen . . . I'm coming here so we can have some kind of custody plan. I am ready to talk conditions. The baby." (The baby. Long silence. His lips went slack. His countenance, at total rest, was uglier, older.) "Alma said you were going to move to an apartment in Mount Vernon." (Another long wait and he lowered his eyelids, didn't close them, but it was a tougher look.) "Listen, Carmen . . ." (He had to stop again, and I knew and Richard knew, we were sitting there, the three of us together, a family on the couch, listening to everything he said.)

And Carmen was filling up the phone line with a ton of feeling, for a very long time, and then Lucas said in a tone you would have to call chilly, icy, distant, this:

"Just tell me why you did it. Just tell me why you did it. Just tell me why it was your decision. Just tell me that." (He was aware of us, newly, the two of us on the couch, me with Ruth, and Richard; then he stood and went into the hall, halfway to the kitchen, both of us frozen, listening, and as his awareness of us there gained, the colder he became on the phone, the farther away from all of us.)

"Just tell me . . . I don't want to hear what Alma said to you. I don't give a shit about Mary Ann. I'm sorry, but I don't. Just tell me why, you are an adult."

A little after this, something in the household collapsed, and Lucas continued listening and talking, but he did not want us to hear.

Richard felt it first and went into the kitchen, and I got up and walked up the stairs to the second floor with the baby, and found a place in the house, in my bedroom under a comforter, where I could almost not hear Lucas anymore. At about the same moment the wrath that had been in his voice turned.

I felt it too, his grief, and I blamed myself, as it was I who'd been with Carmen. We all went our own ways and waited what seemed an interminable time, while

Lucas saddened and saddened, and it felt as if none of us was related to each other as we had been earlier that same day, or even a week ago. We were breaking up, and none of us was as close as we had been for so long, and I felt equidistant from my male friend and my husband. I always act as if words were made just to die out, the way my mother acts, but instead they can turn into other things, instead they make your life. I had said things you don't say, murderous things. I really ought to just shut up.

Carmen wanted to talk to me. Lucas yelled this up the stairs, with contempt in his voice. Pausing half a second, then saying I was asleep, he put down the receiver. He had decided Carmen and I would talk later, not now.

Richard came in from the kitchen and I heard him say, "She had the abortion?" which was what he already knew. I did too, upstairs.

Lucas didn't answer. Then he said, "Why was she talking only to Alma, for Christ's sake? Whose baby is it, anyway, was it?"

"She wasn't going to have it," Richard said, "Face it."

"That's what she said, she'd been carried away, you know, with the life of it. It wasn't really 'her' to have it. She kept saying it would crap up her relationship with Mary Ann. What's a goddamned librarian with a dildo next to this, so help me."

Richard said, "I don't know. It's the times, the times are fucked. Nobody has nerve." Then he yelled up to me, "Alma, what did you say to her this afternoon? What went on? Alma, get down here."

Alma, me, I did not answer. I lay on our bed and nursed Ruth, and hoped they wouldn't come up after me, and I pretended to be asleep.

Richard came upstairs and I felt him looking at me, but I continued to be asleep. I thought if they did leave, I could call Carmen.

I could feel Richard moving away from Lucas and me, me and my guilt, Lucas and his grief. He felt blameworthy, too, as he hadn't told Lucas everything, as he, too, had assumed Carmen would see the light since Ruth was dynamite.

Richard kept telling Lucas that it had to be the way it was, and there was no real changing it now, but he didn't defend what I did do or didn't do—I had moved away from both of them and sunk into the nursing couple, and as it was mysterious, what had passed between Carmen and me that afternoon, they attributed all kinds of things to our day together. What happens between women, anyway? Who could Alma be? What did Alma say? Lucas considered these matters downstairs, and came up with answers no better than I ever had.

Carmen had drawn a little picture, one day in the hospital, of the two of us with prams, on the ugly flat sunny plaza the renovators had put up at the Fells Point Dock. There we were with our little kids propped up in our laps, pliant as dummies, under the seagulls, two pair. I liked it. But now Carmen and I had broken up, too.

I thought of coming back down to tell them I felt awful, to give them the whole thing, including my mother and my father and the phone calls from Loretta and Gina, but none of this could be a cause. Events were never causes, except in a few rare cases. I wanted to tell them what I felt like when Lucas called me a cunt and Richard nearly let it pass. But in essence, because men are simply better concentrated, their opinion of me was stronger than my opinion of either of them. And anyway, my Ruth was my own business, and so was everything that passed between Carmen and me, so I stayed upstairs in a mammalian rest. And Ruth's time and mine were somewhere else, beyond explanation.

I could feel that Richard, who had a wife and a kid, something that Lucas didn't have, was starting to gain on him, and that difference between them was waxing as the evening got older, and Richard was siding more and more with me, and closing off his friend. First he tried mentioning the future, then the concrete future, the plan, the warehouse, the gallery, and then Richard was almost condescending about Carmen, called her less complete, less finished, and Lucas picked up my husband's tone and didn't like it—after all, it upset the order of their relationship. Their conversation got competitive and then less so, just colder. They were drinking something stronger than beer by then. When it got later still, I heard Lucas crying, growing sloppier as he got drunker, and Richard said, "I don't know. I just don't know." While Lucas ejaculated, "What do they fucking need? What do they want?"

"They" were women, me included, though Richard was increasingly taking exception about me; "they" was clarified to mean all women who are out there, except Alma, who, Richard insisted, was basically good, unlike all the other women in the universe.

His taking exception for me was kindhearted, but it was wrong, as it cut me off from my sex and from Lucas, and I felt mightily alone already. I had the creepy feeling Richard was forming a defense around us—creating a belief, forming a family faith—*Alma is goodhearted, Alma is not entirely blameworthy,* and it felt cloying, even inbred. The same kind of defense that sent my mother off after Fred. Family feeling, it is called.

When it was very, very late Lucas said several times he wasn't drunk, he wasn't drunk, and he could drive to Washington fine because he wasn't drunk, and Richard did not fight this very much. Richard didn't because baby Ruth would be demanding time and attention, too, quite soon, and he had to reserve some; he couldn't talk all night or play chess and drink and drink and drink, and Lucas was sloppy with grief by this time, regretting everything he'd done since he was twenty-one, grief which would be a cloud over our household in the morning,

I think Richard was thinking, and so he let Lucas leave. I don't know where they left their joint venture. Maybe I would find out someday where they left the lofts and gallery and café, I thought. When Richard let Lucas out, the two of them were less close friends. I had not wanted this to happen.

Richard didn't have me either, so he had nobody. He had a family.

As I lay upstairs, not capable of sleeping, Richard's defending me turned in upon itself, and I felt less and less and less attached to him, and this great distance began to spread into miles, practically. He was protesting too much, defending me too much. We were in neither the same space nor the same time together, and I realized if I stayed I would have to acknowledge the distance between us, the true severance, which was painful, which had already started to hurt.

Wake up." Richard shook me. The skin around his eyes was very white, I noticed, and made them look small, like holes in his face. He looked strange and insubstantial. His hands, another being's.

"Carmen was having an abortion," he said, factually. "You knew. I don't know what we are going to do about the warehouse deal. Lucas could crack up. I shouldn't have let him go. He insisted. He said he had to go to Philadelphia tomorrow. He's been putting it off for a week."

There was liquor on Richard's breath. He was crisp and alive, even though. I could feel the hot tiny heart of our baby beating between us on the bed.

"I'll take her," he said, seeing I wasn't conscious enough for conversation. He went out the narrow doorway into the hall, and placed baby Ruth in her crib. He was going to go downstairs, then, but he stopped, he halted.

I was thinking, Please, Richard, please, Richard, don't come after me. Don't hit me. Richard would never do those things. My father would do those things. He smelled exactly like my father.

"What is it, Alma?" he said loudly, in case I was really asleep.

We knew each other so well we didn't need to talk to fight. We could fight by remote control, in separate parts of the house—send out charges to do injury.

"What do you want? Huh?" he asked me.

If he had laid a hand on me I would have startled, jumped. I was terrified. Because he had to hold me there. I was on my way out. I was leaving. He did not touch me. "You'd think," he said, "after all this time—"

It had been hardly any time at all. June to June, now it was October. In fifteen months, married, with a baby. It was normal we wouldn't last. Statistical.

"Alma, baby, you look like you think I want to kill you. I don't, I don't. I just don't understand. Can I touch you?"

He had to touch me. And I shrank away.

"Lord, Alma, I can't take you like this."

He was waiting for me to say something. I didn't say anything. "You turn into a crocodile, this hide grows over you. I can't get near you. I'm in love with you. I'm the father of your child. I tell you about this whole thing we are going to do. I mean, I thought I'd solved a lot of our problems. But we can both tell what you think. You think we are, or at least that I am, idiotic."

"I don't. I just thought it would be risky. Borrowing money from friends. And artists don't have any money. And these people we don't know. You've never done anything like this—"

"I'm making money for Lucas. And he doesn't want to be a lawyer anymore. Since Carmen left him he can

—284—

hardly get to work. They already let him know he wasn't going to make partner. And he's miserable in Washington. What difference do Lucas's problems make to you?"

"I know it's my fault," I said. "I was supposed to keep Carmen here. She told me as much when she came in."

"You knew, okay. They would have to have cut the baby in half, anyway. Don't you think? It would have been a judgment-of-Solomon baby. Just another baby. Would have fucked up Mary Ann's self-realization, I guess. Carmen's too."

I said, "Carmen was open to anything. She *wants* to love somebody."

"Well, do you want to love somebody?" Richard said. He was in one of his swing moods. He tolerated me, then he hated me. "Besides yourself, I mean. Besides the constant landfill job you are doing on yourself, I mean. Filling in the fissures, I mean."

I was beginning to cry, to sound like an idiot, the kind of crying where you gasp and there are no tears.

"Is it that difficult?" Richard asked. "To be there for somebody else?" He stopped. He started to touch me. "Is it that you feel responsible for everything? So you can't do anything?"

Then he took my lower cheeks, near my chin. He was going to hit me across the face. He was.

"Carmen is another person. I am another person. Ruth is even another person. Is this so difficult?" The places on his forehead that color and splotch were darkening. He wasn't going to hit me because that would be too emphatic a thing to do. It would draw too much attention to itself. His feeling was too large, almost too large for his body. "Do you understand?"

I said nothing. I was terrified. I was silent, white. For a long time, I tried to think of something to say. "I don't know, I'm not even—"

"I don't want to hear about what you aren't," he said. "I've got the whole catalogue of what you aren't." He let go of me. His presence, his clarity, started to fall away, entirely, as if a window had been opened, as if there were a terrible relief, a breeze, coming forward, and then he said, "I never wanted to think this. But this is what I think now. That you can't."

In the morning, I awoke and I looked down at myself. My belly was a rubber joke. I knew what I was doing, finally. I went downstairs and pumped my milk into plastic bottles. I put them in the freezer. And I slid my bottom into a tight green skirt with an elastic waist.

Finally, I wasn't going to be contradictory. I was going to complete an action. Finish something. I was doing something pure for once, something clean, unambiguous. Something I could do.

I had to go because of what Richard said.

I finished dressing in street clothes: my old low boots and my pinky-beige Romanian-made raincoat. After I kissed Ruth good-bye, I would flee. With my flight bag and my slides in a portfolio, I'd go first to the twenty-four-hour teller on Broadway, and get four or five hundred dollars.

I had to leave because I was terrible at being for others. I almost hit my own mother. What I said to Carmen was murderous. What kind of mother could I be? I had to go because of what Loretta and Gina were saying. I can only be myself when I am out of the range of others. I am too susceptible and can do so little. Richard was right: the truth was, I just am not able.

I had to go because I didn't know what kept Richard so attentive and alive. He was, after all these months, still a stranger to me. I did not know what occupied him, what kept him. I couldn't teach Ruth about loving men, about what that happiness is supposed to be like.

I had to go because I was too much like my own mother. And she has no truck with her own heart. I had to have less truck with mine. And I didn't want Ruth to have any distance from herself as my mother and I do. I wanted her to be like her namesake: a woman who fit in easily, who was part of the ensemble. I wanted Ruth to live in a world where thought and feeling and material have merged together, into a fabric, a medium. I didn't want Ruth to have to think.

I gathered together most of my slides. And then I went into Ruth's nursery—it was a beautiful nursery, it still smelled of sandalwood—and I kissed her good-bye once, and it felt sweet to leave.

And so, after fighting with Richard, and talking Carmen out of her baby, and losing Lucas's faith in me, and putting Ruth out the window to get her to stop crying, and having caused Gina to seize up, and after hearing my mother tell me that in my infancy I never needed anyone or anybody, and after having them take my labor away from me, and after learning that Rachel was always sure I was just too crazy, I decided that must be so, and so, down the stairs, out the door, and things began to be only in the present tense. I couldn't take the further risks of thinking about the future or the past, consequences or causes. Just the moment, the delicious, fugitive moment.

In my quarter I pass the familiar streets, see a train go right down the middle of the street on Aliceanna, an ordinary train, on what I'd always thought were trolley tracks. It seems an omen, somehow, a train on a narrow residential street, as odd as an automobile in a living room, and I am thinking, Maybe someday I will paint that, it is something I can use. In fact, everything is something I can use, even my own fatigue, my own voluptuous sadness, my own face, arms, legs, life. And then I am out of the neighborhood in a Filipino's cab headed for Pennsylvania Station, which he speeds me to with no idea, no idea, how I am running away, from home. So what; a woman going to New York. I give him a ten and then I'm getting a ticket and I'm on the train, and I'm thinking, about the last twelve days, and the last fifteen months, and the whole general problem of being myself and how I might get rid of this problem, and keep enough of this person to stay a painter. I want to use everything. I said that. Everything should be something I can use.

And by the time I reach New York I am outside the station, in front of Madison Square Garden, crying like a little baby, and a man gives me the cab he's hailed for himself, such a pitiful sight I must be. It is raining, and I am drenched. My feet are wet in my boots. It is raining, I'm drenched, and then I'm on Eighth Street in front of an odd-lot store, and the insane cab driver is trying to tell me why he can't make it to the Hotel Salazar, and that this is the farthest he can go, it's here or nowhere, and I'm out of the cab, with all of my possessions, and into the hotel, near Washington Square, not far from anything, a hotel once referred to romantically by Joan Baez, and they give me the whore's room, he does, the man behind the cage in the lobby with a sign that says NO LOITERING. The room has a crushed-velvet spread and some bloody dirt on the walls, and a high window on an airshaft. But the bathroom is clean. The phone is brown, and there are cigarette butts in the broken television set. And I sit down and fight thinking of Richard and Ruth and Rachel. I think about how I'll spend tomorrow, walking through the galleries on Spring Street, and the other streets, Great Jones, Greene, and how I will casually look on their little laminated printed sheets that explain the gallery policies for viewing portfolios. And that night I eat Chinese food, gobble it up, and try not to think about anything but comfort and sleep. I have not had any sleep since Richard said what he said, and since Lucas said what he said too, not quite twenty-four hours ago, in another life, when I was connected to other people.

My bones ache, I am very sore, but after dinner I actually enjoy myself, as I walk through the fresh wet streets. Things have that after-a-rain sheen, and people are lovely to look at, yes, they are watching me walk past them from their café tables, from behind the boxes of bistro greenery, and I am there like a ghost, present and absent, outside of everything. And by nine I am too sleepy for words, and I go to my Hotel Salazar room, and express the milk that has built up in my body into the sink, and rinse it away, and then I'm ready to crash, abruptly, on the velvet spread. Out. Like a light, as they say.

And finally I find some sleep. And for a while I feel like a dead noggin, a piece of wood, and if I try to imagine that I have a name or that there is a time of day, that there is any orientation possible at all, my imagination and my present fail me, and it is so gratifying to be this way, so restful that one is no one, so restful that one is nowhere. And then later on this long night I have the intimation that even the feeling of a lack of sense is slipping away, and I am fading entirely, or being erased.

It is as if someone has shaken me. At five.

I take my key, and I'm on the street. I'm walking at a clip, in the same black dress, the same large off-white sweater I was wearing yesterday. I go to a coffee shop and order a pair of eggs. Across from me are a fellow with a black studded jacket and a woman with an expanse of lavender eye shadow beneath her brow. They seem to have been out all night.

And now a girl walks in, in an odd, out-of-style, almost nautical dress. It's antique, and the girl is awfully young.

She looks a little like Penelope Kaplan—the pointed nose. But when I look at her twice I know that's not it, and she's more delicate than Penelope, less solid. And so much younger. She's sweet. There's a sweetness to her.

Underneath her wide collar is a floppy bow, like the bow of an artist's smock in a cartoon. She removes it, rubs her neck, and puts one finger of her right hand on the first package deal on the breakfast menu—Danish and coffee—and shows this to the man behind the counter. A man with the kind of mustache you could joke about if you wanted to.

The coffee's served.

I bet she takes it black. Coffee is still something sophisticated for her, like Scotch, you take it straight.

She takes it straight. And the Danish sits there. It's awful, it has little ribbons of icing. She's rubbing her fingers over her napkin now, as if she's getting up the nerve to take a bite.

She takes a bite.

Her eyelashes are blond and matted with sand. Under her powder are freckles, I think. I think she would keep her change in a little beaded purse.

She reaches into her bag, and out comes a little beaded purse.

Her hair, her hair is in what you call a bob. Waves around the face, little honey-blond wisps that refuse to be straightened, but I bet that she tries, with a wand or an iron. She's trying now, to smooth her hair, to put it behind her ears. It's five-thirty in the morning. She might look at the clock and she might not look at the clock. I think if she looks at the clock she'll decide she has to go. It seems to me there are these kinds of clouds behind her, around her. She is surrounded by this aura, this spirit, I don't know whose. But it has its own design. It is tugging her out the door.

I find the correct change. $2.15, with tax. And I follow

her. She's scooting out. I could paint her. Perhaps that is what I want to do. But for right now I most want to follow her.

In the street the air has almost a chill, I notice now. And there's a crevice in the blue darkness where the light is coming through. And in this place the sun is yellow and pink and purple.

Now she's rushing down some subway stairs. First I watch her race while I stand on the grid at street level, then I'm following her down. Her turned-under hair flies up behind her as she descends. It goes whoosh. She is almost so familiar.

She buys her tokens, and then I do. And I follow her onto the train, and we are riding underground through the city. Through black rattling places where the stations we pass leave their names like an after-echo.

We are on the IND D train, and I think we are headed out. Out where, I don't know. But I'm worried about her. She is nodding a little bit and her face tilts to one side and then to the other. She's actually starting to doze. I wonder if she's on drugs. No, there's something too innocent about her for that. For her, coffee is a risk. Coffee is dangerous. She has some hope about her, almost. That's the sweetness, I think. I'd like to go up to her, say something. But I don't know if she would be able to talk back, exactly.

I think she could be from another time.

If this train goes to Brooklyn, then she is from another time.

This is Brooklyn. De Kalb Avenue. We stop. Atlantic. Church. Beverley. Cortelyou. We are above ground now. We stop at every station now.

She's slumped over to one side. Then the jogging of the train wakes her and she catches herself, as if from falling.

We are at Kings Highway now. I'm standing, holding onto a strap, moving closer, to see if she's all right.

It means everything, whether or not she's all right.

I do a little two-step. And the swaying of the train makes me stagger toward her. I am going to make sure. My hand is holding a pole. Our subway car has been twice emptied of almost everyone, twice—at Atlantic, at Newkirk, bodies have gotten on, bodies holding newspapers, arms in olive-drab jackets. But she's not conscious of me. She isn't. She's conscious of no one.

But I only see her. For now she is the only soul in New York City.

We are coming to the end of Brooklyn.

I'd like to tell her she can become a milliner if that's what she wants. If she wants to make dressy hats, she can make dressy hats, with coated cherries if she likes, with chiffon, grosgrain, silk flowers, floppy brims. She can make hats and do whatever else she likes—break rules, drive on Saturday, take walks without telling anyone where she's going.

She's almost twenty. And now we are at Sheepshead Bay. We are above ground, and more of the darkness of the sky is peeling away. And the purple-pink-yellow color is fading to white. This is called dawn. She'll be getting off at Brighton Beach, I think. She'll stand right now. And step off here. And walk to the end of the platform, and take the stairs down.

Finally the subway makes a squeaky stop.

I think she's broken and she's sad. Broken in half, almost. Or torn, perhaps that's the word for it, torn, rent. She's standing. I'm almost surprised she's standing. She doesn't see me or know of me. I'm really not here, hardly here. Her presence is so much more vivid than mine, so much more entire, somehow. The moons in her fingernails, the tiny rip in her scarf. Her green eyes. Her kind of huffy, girlish remorse.

She's going to get off at Brighton Beach. And so do others—a man in dirty, crumpled, gray seersucker. Two women in denim service-station jumpsuits. The sky is lighter, more open, now. It is a yellow day, and like no other day.

And she's going to go down those stairs to the street and across the avenue I see below.

She does those things.

She is Rachel.

I'm following her.

She can take me to meet Aunt Rose. And Aunt Rose and I can talk about the childless life. And we'll leave Aunt Rose and go to the beach, and she'll talk to me. Tell me how she's so glad she came. How she's never going back to Baltimore. She hates her mother-in-law— who wouldn't? The woman is so severe, and she has breasts like whole turkeys.

It is still possible she could be an ordinary girl. In an old dress from a shop in the East Village, perhaps, with a pleated skirt, an ordinary girl in 1979, just going about her odd day. It is possible, but it isn't true.

If she goes to the beach, I'll talk to her. We'll go sit under a striped umbrella, take off our shoes and stockings, and she'll tell me what she wants to be, and I'll smooth the way for her, make it possible for her. Make everything possible for her. Tell her she can go home to Baltimore and still come back, she can go back and be a mother to Penelope and Richard, and still come back and dress hats, buy hats, collect scarves, closets full of them, trunks full of stiff linen and velvet hats. And I'll tell her not to be so hard on herself. Not to listen to her husband's mother. Not to feel as if her life can be only one way or the other. Tell her her life can be graceful. It can be. She shouldn't resist it.

She's crossed the avenue called Surf, now. And she's going over to the gray wooden boardwalk, and I think from there she'll find the stairs and descend to the beach. The big silver sea is rocking up and down in one motion, heaving, sighing. There is a briny wind.

I'm on the boardwalk too. Hoping I can avoid startling her. It's a delicate thing, a shattering thing, isn't it, I mean her mother-in-law could be following her, to tell her to come home and have those babies. Once you have them, you are never the same, Mrs. Kaplan will explain. Just the scent of them is like a drug—it can create an addiction. The freshness of them can change your life, turn you inside out. Shatter you and make you feel whole almost at once, almost at the same time.

The original Ruth Kaplan will say that. But I'll say something else. That a choice that is made can be changed. You should never lop off parts of the whole, if you do—

At the top of the boardwalk stairs, at a certain distance, I see her slipping off her black canvas shoes, the Chinese type, with brick-red soles.

She starts to look up.

I can't tell if she is frightened or angry. It could be she's neither.

I don't think she sees me yet. I'm maybe seventy-five feet away, but I'm nearing her. There are a few scattered joggers, people in sneakers and green sweatshirts. She's gone down the stairs now to the strand. From the railing where I am standing I can see the top of her honey-colored head.

And I can see where they had to shave her head. And where they had to cut into her neck. And how her feet were so swollen they had to split her shoes, and her swollen belly. I can see all these things. Especially when I close my eyes. When I close my eyes she does not go away. Her face is as big as my baby Ruth's face, right in the middle of my brain, that face, when I close my eyes.

So I open them, and I see she's way down on the beach. Marching practically like a soldier. Almost two-thirds of a block away. On the part of the beach where the ocean's splashing now and then. And the scarf tied around her neck is flying outward, like a flag, so I can still follow.

I've gone down the stairs now, and I have to catch my breath almost, but she's walking so fast. Fast enough, I think, to get away from her future, for now. And I have to catch up with her and make it whole for her.

She's two blocks up the beach now, rushing past trash and old Styrofoam cups, the skeletons of gulls, hot-dog papers. I keep moving.

It is harder to see her now. Just little flashes of the burgundy dress, fish flashes, flickers. Then they aren't there anymore.

And I see her again. Then I lose her again.

Do I see her beginning to wade into the water? No, it is someone else.

I've started, I've noticed, to run. I'm holding my shoes. But she's so far ahead of me now that she is about to disappear. If I lose her I'll die.

I've lost her.

Now I begin to sink inward, downward, and I'm sitting on the sand. When I close my eyes her face is there, and my baby's face, one face. Then the other face. The water touches my feet but it doesn't soothe, it doesn't help. Not at all. In fact it hurts, and the salt air hurts. And everything about this life stings and causes pain. This must be the end of the world. A beach, a few sad people. Coney Island in the distance. I'm falling off this edge now, this one here, and there will be no catching me, unless I can hold her again. Unless I can make completely sure she stays in one piece.

This will kill me; it won't make me stronger.

There is a hole here, a pool, not exactly the sea, fed by the sea, and even though it is almost day, a darkness is puddling around me. I'm sitting hunched forward, armpits hooked on my knees. I don't know when I sat down or when I lost her. It is getting later and later, and this will kill me, it won't make me stronger.

Somehow I go back upstairs to the boardwalk, and from the boardwalk to the avenue, and from the avenue to the station to the train, and past every stop to the one that's mine. And minutes or years later I am sitting on the edge of the bed. And I know what I most want to do. And that it contradicts me. I want to go back, and erase having left, and heal. And mend. Or try to. Here, in the Hotel Salazar. As I sit on the bed, on this hideous purple spread, I am turning inside out. In this stained and fouled, blood and brown room, this place where one world folds into another.

The solutions were not ornate they were simple.
And I call Richard after wanting to for so long. And he is there, of course, he is there the second day. I have been gone one whole day, and now it is another. He's with Ruth, it is almost ten, and he's watching the absorption she has, the way she is utterly abandoned in the act of sucking, the purity of her.

And I say hello. That it is me.

"Shit," Richard says. "You left. You," then he waits.

"I couldn't stay. That's not an excuse. I have no excuse."

"The milk is gone, Alma. I've got one more jar. Two ounces. Then I have to take Ruth out with me to the drugstore for some formula. It's cold. It's a chilly day. Your baby is ten days old."

"I want to come home," I say. "I'm so sorry."

"What am I supposed to do? Tell you 'fine'? You fucking abandoned us, Alma."

I say, "I don't want to be here. I want to be with you. Please, please."

"It was because of Carmen, wasn't it. Lucas blamed

you. He shouldn't have blamed you. He talked to her too. When he talks to her he sounds like a drill sergeant. She spooked. I don't think it was your fault entirely. You aren't responsible for Carmen. She had a choice. That was the problem, maybe, that she had a choice. I don't know. And I gave up on you. You tire me out. I can't stand the chorus, Alma. Something is wrong with you. Something's always fucking happening *to you*. I'd say, right now, that something is happening to me. That this crisis isn't yours entirely."

I say, "I know."

"I'm feeding this completely helpless daughter of mine and yours. And the only allies I've got are my asshole sister and a borderline lawyer from Washington. My daughter is ten days old. And her mother ran away. I should hang up on you. I really should. The only reason I'm not is that essentially I'm generous."

I am stretching over to the laminated bureau to get a Merit cigarette, and I drop the phone. And for a second, on the other end, I hear nothing. "Richard, Richard?" The phone seems numb, stunned. And that will be it. I won't have the strength to call back. Essentially, he is generous.

"I'm here," he says.

I tell him I dropped the phone. I say I'm coming back.

"I don't know if that's what I want. Who's to say you wouldn't give up again. I figure it is likely you would," he says.

"You gave up on me," I say.

"Well, long before that you gave up on me," he said. "About the day we got married, you said to yourself, Lord, this loser, better protect myself. Everything I've done—buying the house, getting a real estate license, working, putting together this project with Lucas—you never—"

"I know I never did," I say. "But not because there's anything wrong with you and Lucas opening a gallery. It's fine. It's fine. It's me. I'm an idiot."

"Shut up," he says.

"I think you are doing fine, I really do. I mean it."

"You don't even know *how* to believe in anybody, Alma."

"I'm scared," I say.

"Of what?" he says.

"Of being your wife, I suppose. Of being usurped, used up. Swallowed. Being a zombie. I'm scared."

"I have to go," he says. "She's got herself tangled up in the straps on this infant seat. Give me your number one time. Her arm is caught."

I give him my number.

He says, "New York, Jesus, you don't mess around."

I tell him to please call back, and when I hang up I'm trembling, and I go blow my nose. Then it is ten-ten. Ten-eleven. Ten-twelve.

"Hello," he says in the brown telephone, not quite neutrally, there's something else there.

"Hello," I say. "I don't know why I'm afraid. I could maybe stop being afraid," I say. (I want to go back.)

"Why?" he says.

"I'm her mother. I'm her mother. I'm not a daughter, a fuck-up daughter. That's what I used to be. I'm your wife."

"All of a sudden," he says.

"I'm slow," I say. "I want to fix things. That is what I really want, what I've wanted all along, to mend."

"Not everything can be fixed," he says. "I don't want to usurp you or use you up. I don't know how much you have to work with. I don't know."

"I know," I say. "I know now. And you want to be with me. You do."

"But that doesn't mean everything can be fixed. You left us, Alma. Walked out. It's a crime, what you did. I can't ever trust you."

"Please let me come back," I say. "To try."

"I need your tits," he says. This is the kindest thing he has said so far. "Without your tits this is very rough."

"I've started to turn inside out," I say. "I am starting to."

"I still can't believe that you left, Alma, that you actually left. I can't let go of that. I won't be able to—"

"Please don't hang up," I say.

"I'm just telling you," he says. "You ought to know."

"Well, listen, shut up," I say kindly, having found my first opening. "I'm coming back. At four o'clock. It gets to Baltimore at four o'clock."

In the background Ruth is wailing. "I have to hang up again," he says. "She's— Call me," he says.

And I sit there on the bed. It is almost ten-thirty. I wait. Ten minutes. I start to pack the little I have unpacked. My loofah sponge, my bottle of shampoo. I think I might go out. I'm afraid. I dial. It rings four times. Finally he answers.

"Train, bus, what?" he says.

"You don't have to come to the station. It's too hard, with her. She's so tiny. Didn't the pediatrician say not to take her out? Until she's two weeks old?"

"Well, she's hungry. We're going out, anyway. You have to swear you'll get this train, though. Swear it."

"I swear," I say. "I don't want to be here. I swear, okay," I say.

"Okay, he says. "She's fine, she's huge. She's nine pounds of bulk. She'll do fine. She's tough."

"Don't assume that," I say. "That she's tough. Wrap her up and put a hat on her."

"Okay," he says. "Don't hang up," he says. "If you hang up your voice will go away."

"Richard," I say. "I love you so much."

And there is a long passage on the phone. Until ten forty-five o'clock, we breathe. And I say, "If things don't have something wrong with them, they aren't beautiful, they are banal."

"This isn't banal," Richard says. "I'm thinking too much for this to be banal. I want to fix you," he says.

And I say, "You do, you do."

"Of course I do," he says. "Hang up. Be there."

And now we are hung up. I can come home.

I'm riding on a train through Newark. And it stops in Trenton. There are signs out the window for Marlboros and *A Chorus Line*. And I'm wearing my odd gloves with holes at the knuckles. And a pillbox hat. Altogether, a sexy-widow Sophia Loren way to look. Richard likes me this way. It's art. Lord, I need to nurse that baby.

Now they say, as they always say, "The only stop in Philadelphia."

I swallow hard. I involute. Because Lucas is getting on the train. And walking into this car. His coffee is in a Servomation cup. A pillow. I'm looking for a pillow. Or a way to hide my mascara eyes, behind my peplum jacket, maybe.

For October it is a cool day. It is a 58-degree day. And I have a jacket. To hide my face in. But he sees me. Smells me out.

And when he is about to address me, I think of saying, "Alma who?" but I love his jowly face and the thought of his thick hand makes me crimp and sweat. And he sits. And then I tell him, because he asks what in the world I am doing going south on this train. I tell him the trip up and I tell him the trip back. But nothing of the other venture, the one to Brooklyn. I pretend I've never been to Brooklyn. And after a minute, a kind of I-hurt-you-terribly-the-last-time-I-saw-you lightning has flashed between us, and it has seemed it was bright enough to cause us both to blink. Lucas's eyes are khaki green, like Army surplus pants, I notice. His suit is wrinkled, doesn't fit too well. And his shoes are heavy wing tips.

I'm not used to him in his lawyer gear. He holds his Styrofoam cup while I take a sip. The huge fields of squat cylinders of oil and gas and chemicals and solutions that make up Delaware glide past us.

Even though we've been talking half an hour, it still doesn't matter—when his hand comes close to me, the breach between us begins to arise again, and I feel a kind of fire, or maybe just some smoke, in my gut, and I take two fingers, to touch around the lip of the cup, and then I draw back and he says, "Alma, I'm not angry with you." And I say, my armor relaxing, my shoulders falling, "Okay, okay, I'm not angry either."

And I let his thick hand cover mine.

He says he'll get off in Baltimore, not Washington, because he has to see that dynamite baby. The one he practically saw born. And I look tired, he says, but I look different. There's this dark softness around my features, he says. Maternity, he says.

And I say, Lord, it's makeup. Don't be a gentleman.

Lucas says he's a wreck too. Then Wilmington. Then Baltimore.

And through the window I see them. Just about directly underneath the sign that says TRACK TWO. Stand Richard and Ruth. Ruth is wrapped in the quilt of the Locotus ladies. Ruth wrapped in that whole messy thing. Her head right smack in the off bear claw, the place where the devil is let out. Richard is pale and greenish-gray around the eyes. He's waving. The finger of his right hand is encircled by her tiny hand.

I want to hold them so much I don't think I can stand. My knees almost give in the aisle of the train. Lucas reaches for my luggage. We walk, Lucas holding me up. Coming down the steps to the track platform, I stumble again. I stand. And Lucas is there behind me. Flight bag, shoe boots, my purse, my breasts, are all giving way. I am beginning to squirt.

Now I'm holding Richard and Ruth and they are holding me. My arms are under his, and then his arms are under mine, and Richard asks me if I am having a problem. That I am stumbling so much. "Is something wrong?"

"I feel naked," I say. "I'm scared," I say.

And Richard says that I am beautiful. And then he touches me on the cheek and says to me, so no one can hear but me, not Lucas, not Ruth, not anyone. "Alma, we can start here. Right now. I am willing," he says.

And then I shudder, and then I don't.